LOVE IN
STORE

Published under licence by Brown Dog Books and
The Self-Publishing Partnership, 7 Green Park Station, Bath BA1 1JB

www.selfpublishingpartnership.co.uk

ISBN printed book: 978-1-83952-150-8
ISBN e-book: 978-1-83952-151-5

Cover design by Kevin Rylands
Internal design by Andrew Easton

Printed and bound in the UK

This book is printed on FSC certified paper

LOVE IN STORE

STORE

The barrow boy and the heiress

BILL CARMEN

BROWN
DOG
BOOKS

I need to thank some people for their input into the writing of this book. To my wife Clare, thank you for your patience and support when it all got a little difficult . To my daughters, Sarah and Sue, my son-in-law Rob for the website and IT stuff, and Janney Hewitt and Carol Preston, my creative writing class tutors. The kind folk who read my book and gave me feedback. Last but no means least, Douglas and Frances from SPP publishing who worked hard to teach an old dog new tricks. I am delighted with the outcome.

Thanks to you all
Bill Carmen

CHAPTER 1

LONDON 1958

Tim's mother awoke and smiled at her thirteen-year-old son who was sitting beside her hospital bed. Using her thumbs, she wiped the tears from his cheeks. Then she sank back on to her pillow and closed her eyes. He heard her take a short breath in followed by a long, long, breath out. Then… nothing.

Tim spoke to her enquiringly, then more loudly, now he was shouting, 'Wake up, wake up, Mum, please wake up.'

A nurse appeared at his side and stopped him shaking his mother's shoulder. After checking for a pulse, she said, 'I'm so sorry, lad, she's gone. She's passed away.'

Tim looked up at the nurse, unable to take in what she was saying, his mother could not be dead. The nurse could see the disbelief, the shock and the fear his face displayed.

Fifteen days earlier his mother had come down with the flu. She had been to the doctor's, who said she would be better soon, but he would keep an eye on it. His mother had informed Tim it was nothing to worry about.

The nurse tried to move Tim away from the bed. He locked his fingers around the bars of the bed so firmly no one could move them. Seconds later there were doctors and nurses surrounding him all talking at once. Their mouths were moving but he could make no sense of what they were saying.

All he knew was that his mother was dead. His whole body was shaking. The tears were cascading down his face, he was uttering a high keening sound, a product of the terrible pain he was in. The terrified voice in his head was calling out, 'Mum come back, please, please come back.'

At home that night Tim lay in his bed shivering and crying. His whole world had fallen apart.

Tim could hear the roar of his father's grief being torn from him as his loss overcame him. During that never-ending night Tim wandered through his nightmare crying out for his mother, sometimes he imagined her calling to him. He found himself running down endless corridors, hearing her footsteps but never able to catch her. Sometimes it was just a hint of her perfume that made him turn left or right down yet another blind turning. Once again, the tears and the pain engulfed him.

Tim slept badly for months afterwards. His mind kept replaying all the details of her death in the same terrifying nightmare. When awake he would often find himself involuntarily returning to the night his mother had been taken into hospital. The memory of it was so painful, like scratching an open wound.

He remembered being woken at 3 am by strange voices in the hall outside his downstairs bedroom. He had heard his father's voice and had recognised his fear.

He recalled rising from his bed and opening his bedroom door, there had been voices emanating from his parents' bedroom. Then he had seen two ambulance men backing out through the doorway, each carrying one end of a stretcher with his mother strapped to it. She had lain unmoving; was deathly pale, her eyes tight shut. He had not been able to see any sign of her breathing. Tim had been sure she was dead.

He relived the fear every time. He recollected taking two trembling paces back into his unlit room so as not to be seen. He had been a shadow amongst shadows, invisible.

No one had been aware of his growing fear and panic, nor of the silent tears that shook his small body as he stood in the dark, shivering, his arms clasped around his chest.

Tim had watched his father in disbelief as he followed the stretcher and the ambulance men out of the front door, closing it very quietly behind him as they left.

Tim had stood perfectly still for some time expecting his father to remember him.

Time slid by. He recalled he was crying and very cold when he went to return to his own bed then changed his mind, leaving all the lights on; he'd walked cautiously upstairs turning other lights on as he went. His parents' bed had been roughly pulled together and there was still some warmth trapped by the blankets.

He remembered deciding to stay awake until his father came back, but eventually sleep overcame him.

His father had returned in the early morning, waking Tim as he closed the front door. Not finding him in his bedroom he had called out, 'Where are you, lad?'

Tim, woken by his father's homecoming had been standing at the top of the stairs. His father had looked up, seen him and said, 'Sorry I left you, lad.'

Tim, terrified, had whispered, 'Is she dead, Dad?'

'For God sake, don't say that, you daft little bugger,' his father had shouted at him. 'She is very poorly but she will get better now she is in hospital.'

Tim, shocked and in tears had run down the stairs into his bedroom and shut the door.

His father rarely shouted at him and he had never heard him swear. He knew his mother would not have allowed it.

✳

It was his great aunt who came to stay with him and his father for some time afterwards. She was his grandmother's sister. Tim always thought of her as very regal but very kind. She was an example of another age. Her diction, her manners, were impeccable. Her apparel harkened back to another far more grandiose age. Her husband, Edwin, had died in the same year as Tim was born. Old photos of him showed him to be a tall thin upright man in a three-piece suit and trilby hat with a stern demeanour. He was standing with one hand on the door of a large old black Bentley. He had inherited his father's publishing business after his return at the end of the First World War and had become very wealthy.

It was his aunt who made all the arrangements for the funeral, notified Tim's school, found a cleaner etc. She would cuddle Tim when his sorrow overcame him. It was she who insisted he carried on with his attendance at Scouts.

'It will provide a break,' she explained. She meant it was a chance to get away from the bleak environment that was now his home life, but she did not say it.

His relationship with his father became ever more difficult. The death of Tim's mother had rendered his father incapable. As the months went by his father had slowly become more and more reclusive, occasionally Tim would find him still in bed when he arrived home from school. Often, he did not shave for days at a time.

Money became a problem; his father went to work less and less frequently. On one occasion Tim asked for money to pay the suppliers and the stall rental.

'They will have to wait,' shouted his father.

'We are a week late already,' remonstrated Tim. 'They'll throw us off the pitch and if the suppliers get fed up, we will have nothing to sell.'

'Don't you criticise me boy,' the last word said with unpleasant emphasis. 'Keeping you in food and clothing is a major expense.'

His father continued, 'I will open the stall tomorrow, now get out of my sight.'

Tim left the house and wandered the streets, hands in pockets and shoulders hunched, muttering to himself, 'How can he have changed so much? I don't recognise him now.' He couldn't think of any way of altering anything. He was so desperately unhappy. His future looked pointless.

In the middle of his fifteenth year, on the days when his father got up for work Tim went with him, playing truant while he learnt the business. He often manned the stall on a Saturday on his own. The Italian stall holder next door, Harry Trentino, helped him a lot. Tim, out of necessity learnt quickly.

On his fifteenth birthday he started work full time, leaving his father in bed, who by now, often didn't even answer him. In truth he had not been to school for some months. He decided his birthday would be recognised as the start of his working life.

His great aunt Victoria called in frequently to cook for them both. She offered him a place at her house, but Tim knew his mother would have expected him to assist his father.

CHAPTER 2

TIM'S FATHER

1962

Shortly after Tim's seventeenth birthday he received an enormous surprise. His father told him the house was sold and he was downsizing to a one bed terrace house a little way away. Tim would have to find some digs in the next two weeks. He was dumbstruck, he was being thrown out. There was a vigorous conversation between him and his father which ended with his father shouting at him again. This was by now a regular occurrence.

'I have no money, and this is the only way I can see of getting out of debt.'

Tim now hurt and angry said, 'If you went to work instead of lying in bed all day there would not be a problem.'

'Get out, just get out,' shouted his father really losing his temper, 'and don't come back.'

'Do you mean that?'

'Yes! I damn well do,' replied his father, walking into the kitchen and slamming the door behind him.

Tim stared at the kitchen door. He felt as though he had just been slapped. The closed door stared back at him. The sound of the door slamming kept replaying over and over in his head. He realised his father meant what he said. He was being thrown out. He was going to walk out, then he realised he would need some clothes. Mounting the stairs at the run and reaching his bedroom he plonked himself on his bed. He was completely confused. His life had just changed out of all recognition. Now he was homeless. Starting to stuff clothes into his Scout rucksack, he only chose what was necessary.

Arriving back downstairs, the kitchen door was still firmly shut. Tim picked up his wallet, shrugged on his coat, and slung his rucksack on his back. He began to lose his temper. Debating whether he should say goodbye he decided not to. As he left the house his temper finally overcame him, he banged the front door shut behind him so hard an ornamental vase jumped off the hall shelf, hit the floor and shattered into a thousand sharp pieces.

At the end of the road he stopped and looked back, hoping his father would change his mind. He stood for a long time. He experienced a riot of emotions, as his anger cooled, the loss of his mother had plunged him into sorrow, this would never have happened if she had still been alive. Finally, head down, his clenched fists rammed into his trouser pockets, he walked on. For the first time in his life he felt totally alone and very frightened.

He made his way to his great aunt's house. She was, as always, glad to see him, then noticing the look of misery on his face she took his arm and guided him indoors.

'Whatever is wrong, Timothy?'

'My father has thrown me out.'

'That cannot be true, he would not do that.'

'Well he has,' he was not sure himself how he felt about it: he was too stunned. He explained what had happened.

'I will ring your father now and we will get this sorted out.' She rang three times over the next twenty minutes, the phone remained unanswered.

She was aware that Tim was pacing up and down, a clear indicator that he was becoming ever more distressed. Replacing the phone she turned and hugged him.

Holding him away from her and looking him in the eye she reassured him by saying, 'Tim, you are not homeless if that is what you are thinking, you can live here for the rest of your life if you want, although I do realise it is a long way from the market.'

'I think everything might be easier if we gave up the stall and I just got an ordinary job.'

'I believe you would regret that, Tim.'

Later that evening after shutting him in the lounge so he would not be a party to her conversation, she managed to get through to Tim's father.

After a lengthy conversation she re-joined Tim, 'Your father is in a bad way, he is very depressed, he was close to tears throughout our conversation. He has not ignored his problem. He went to the doctor's and was given pills that made him feel worse, but he has not been back since. He has agreed to see us tomorrow evening.'

He rode the tube to work the following morning already dreading the evening meeting with his father, it was on his mind all day. After work he stood by the river looking down, the comings and goings in front of him did not register, he was only aware of the river's powerful endless flow; its constancy was in direct contrast to his present precarious position.

Scrolling back through the pictures in his mind he recognised his childhood had, until his mother's death, been a happy one; his mother was a lively vibrant person, she had a beautiful singing voice, there was always love, warm laughter and music while she was alive.

It felt as though someone had pressed the mute button after she died. Home had become like an old, sad, silent black and white film, and it was cold, so bitterly cold. His mother's passing had somehow sucked all the comfort and warmth from his life replacing it with this constant dreadful chill wind.

Looking from his new perspective he was aware that his father had always been a quiet figure in the background. His parents' house was the only home he had ever known; it would never be home again.

Later, walking to his father's, a range of scenarios were going through his head. Would his father want to sell the business? Would he stop Tim working for him? Where would he live? It was kind of his great aunt to offer him accommodation, but it was too far from the market and it was not fair on her. His future appeared uncertain; he could see no way forward.

Arriving he saw a large black Bentley, his great aunt's car, was already parked outside the house, her driver, Mr Graham, was in the vehicle but he could see she was not. Approaching the vehicle, he said, 'Hallo, Mr Graham, how are you?'

'I am very well, Timothy, thank you, your aunt is inside.'

Thanking him he turned, walked down the path and rang the doorbell. Tim recognised how symbolic it was. He no longer felt comfortable walking into what had been his own home just a day ago, unannounced.

His father answered the door washed, dressed and shaved. Tim said nothing. His father nodded at him and then shook his head sideways to indicate that Tim should enter.

Although he retained a key to the house, in the future he would always ring the doorbell.

With his aunt's sympathetic encouragement, a lot was achieved that evening.

Monosyllabic at first his father eventually opened up. He explained that there were three main reasons for moving; the first was financial, the second was that he needed a fresh start. He could see his wife everywhere in the house and it was driving him crazy. The third thing was the paperwork associated with running the stall. He admitted that he did not understand a lot of it. It was overwhelming him, he needed to simplify his life.

'Your mum always dealt with all that. I don't feel I can move on while I am living here. Financially I will not have to worry, there will be a decent lump sum left over from this house and my pension starts soon. I have been up all night thinking about this. I am going to retire.'

Tim's heart fell, no home and now no job. He could see how easy it was for people to end up on the street.

His father noticed his distress. 'I am not going to cut you off, Tim. I am handing the stall on to you if you want it. I would like to see it continue. You will have to find some digs, the new house is one bedroom, but you will have a job. I am happy to help with the products, where the stuff comes from and who to talk to, but I won't help with the paperwork, you will have to deal with that. I am no good at it. I know you think I am throwing you out, but you'll manage. You take after your mum, you're clever. You'll do fine.'

On the way back to his aunt's house in the back of the Bentley, initially Tim was silent and withdrawn, his aunt sat close to him and held his hand offering comfort without speaking, allowing him to gather his thoughts.

Tim was staring out the side window seeing nothing. 'This would never have happened if Mum was still alive,' he observed. The catch in his voice was very audible.

'I cannot argue with that, Tim, your mother was a very different person to your father, but he has skills as well. Look at the way he has built that business up from nothing over the years, he is an excellent salesman, a skill you have inherited. I know you are hurting Tim,' she said squeezing his hand, 'but if we look at it in a positive light you now have the opportunity to build the business back up again. It will be hard work and long hours, but I believe you can make it better than ever; you are young and strong. I have great faith in you.'

'Thank you, Aunty, but I am not sure I can do it all on my own.'

'You have been doing it all on your own for the last two years at least, and you are not on your own. Harry has always watched over you, that will not change. What he does not know about running a stall is not worth knowing.

Should you need a second opinion Mr Woodman, your godfather, will be happy to advise I am sure, and your father has indicated he will help with suppliers, et cetera. Not much will change really, Tim. The big difference is that you can do it your way from now on.'

*

The following evening Tim shared his problems with Mr Woodman. He owned the hardware shop opposite Tim and Harry's stalls. Tim's mother and father had known Mr and Mrs Woodman ever since they were teenagers and had grown up together. The two women had been very close. Before the wives had died Christmas would be spent at one or other of their homes.

Mr Woodman was tall, and still had a good posture and he appeared younger than his years. His greying hair was the only real clue as to his age. He always dressed in his usual working attire; a clean newly pressed navy work coat, blue shirt and tie and highly polished brown brogues. He had never told Tim, but he had always wished that he was his son.

Although Tim and Mr Woodman were separated in age by many years, they had a lot in common. Tim recognised that he was a thoroughly good man. He always thought of him as family. Although he never knew his real grandfather, he always felt that the older man fulfilled that role. They had grown closer still since Tim had begun running the stall.

Mr Woodman sat in silence in his flat above the shop while Tim related what had happened between him and his father. Occasionally, he shook his head.

When Tim finally stopped speaking, and after a long pause, he said, 'It's a long way from your aunt's isn't it, Tim? I can put you up on the couch here for a short while, but it is not a long-term solution. We need to find you some digs, lad.'

'Thank you very much, Mr Woodman, I don't want to be under your feet. I think I will stay at my aunt's for now, if you don't mind, she has been very kind to me and there is more room. Thank you anyway. I will have to find somewhere more permanent in the very near future though.'

They went on to discuss the Cuban missile crisis. It filled the newspapers. They agreed that they were both scared.

Mr Woodman said, 'I hope the first missile lands right next to me. I don't want to survive a nuclear strike.'

Tim noticed when out that if there were a loud bang people were checking the horizon for the mushroom cloud and that everyone was concerned. He knew he would never forget the fear.

Tim told Harry the stall holder next door that he needed some digs. It was he a few days later who came up with a possible solution.

He handed Tim a scrap of paper with a phone number on it. 'That was from an advert in a shop window near me. It's a lady with a room to let, bed, breakfast and evening meal. It didn't say how much though. It must be worth a call, lad. Why not use the phone box on the corner and give her a ring? I'll look after things here for a bit.' Sensing Tim's hesitation he said, 'Go on lad, you've got to sort something out.'

Three days later found Tim ensconced in a good-sized room on the second floor of a large Victorian terrace down a cul-de-sac. He was to become very fond of his room with its funny shaped sloping ceiling. Situated at the top of the house it was more private than the floor below where he could often hear people coming and going.

Mrs Clarke, his landlady, had welcomed Tim and offered the room saying, 'You're young, I don't suppose you will mind the stairs.'

Tim smiled and replied enthusiastically, 'No, I love it, thank you for taking me in.'

Mrs Clarke replied, 'You're welcome, just remember the rules and you will be fine.'

He was fascinated by the view from his window. The juxtaposition and different angles of rooftops and chimneys caught and held his interest.

The following evening found Tim sitting around the table in Mrs Clarke's house with four other men having dinner. Tim was the youngest, there were two elderly men who were very quiet and a young man who had just left the army.

A few days later walking home from the shop he passed the paper boy plying his trade. His usual cry of, 'Standard, Standard, read all about it,' was today followed by, 'great train robbery, read all about it. Standard, Standard.'

Tim bought a copy and read the horrid details of how the criminals had been so cruel to the driver who had sustained serious injuries. He stuffed the paper into the next rubbish bin. If he lived to be a hundred, he would never understand the mentality of those who could behave in that fashion.

*

Over time Tim and his father managed to put the ill feeling and angry words behind them; Tim called in regularly for a meal or a cup of tea; he was not sure though if they would ever be really close again.

It was clear that his mother had been the driving force in his parents' marriage. She was very determined and clever with a strong sense of right and wrong. She was a staunch republican when it was unfashionable to be so. She was always angered by the disparity between the pay for men and women when both genders were doing the same job. As a young woman she had volunteered to distribute leaflets arguing for equal pay for women, often ending up in fierce arguments with chauvinistic men.

She also abhorred the apparent disparity in the law, one law for the rich and another for the poor. Tim could still hear her saying, 'Don't let them snobs put you down; remember you are just as good as them; their money or their accident of birth doesn't make them special, lad.'

Tim was still worried about his father; he appeared to be in the grip of a terrible lethargy, everything was just too difficult; there was a range of excuses why he could not do whatever was suggested. He was either too tired, or it was too cold, or he would do it tomorrow.

Tim's life settled down to a regular routine, rising at six, breakfasting at seven, walking to the stall to open at eight. He was now working seven days a week trying to undo the damage his father's malaise had wreaked on the business and clear the debts at the bank. His Sundays were taken up with paperwork and orders.

He remembered a story of the ploughmen who were expected to be ready in the lee of the hedge at dawn, with the horses harnessed to the plough, waiting until it was light enough to see. They then ploughed until dusk. This gave birth to the expression, 'working from can see to can't see'. His existence was not dissimilar. Long hours on the stall and then paperwork in the evenings. He often woke in the small hours having fallen asleep fully dressed, lying on his arms at the table.

The years sped by. Slowly, so very slowly he started to claw his way back into profit. He was still living hand to mouth, no new clothes, no smoking and little drinking.

With the passing of the years he was personally unaware that he had grown from a callow youth to a very good-looking young man. Too busy to notice, he did not see the second glance that girls sometimes afforded him.

Tim was walking back from visiting a friend when he was drawn across the road to join a small crowd of people watching the television through a shop window. Finding a space where he could see he realised everyone was watching Churchill's funeral. Two of the men had removed their hats, a woman, holding a hanky to her nose was crying gently.

Tim was very aware this was the end of an era. He and his family had a huge respect for the man. Churchill's death in 1965 had Tim and his father talking at greater length than they had for years. They were sharing a Friday night meal of fish and chips at his father's house.

'He is the last of the great men. I can't think of any modern politician that comes anywhere near him. Were it not for "Winnie", we would all be speaking German,' stated his father.

Tim had to agree with him.

'I tell you what, son,' continued his father, 'can you remember your mother used to say that he was the only man who didn't think we were beaten in 1940?'

In a strange way Tim recognised the evening's discussion had brought the two of them a little closer together. It was an advance that his father could discuss his mother without becoming maudlin.

The work continued remorselessly over the next year, but things were improving by dint of hard work and total dedication to the task in hand. There was a small surplus at the end of each month.

One weekday at lunch time he walked into town and for the first time in years he bought a new pair of pale blue chinos at Marks and Spencer's. Over time he made carefully considered purchases for his wardrobe.

There was a drunken night in July 1966 when England won the World Cup. He woke up on a floor under a kitchen table. He had no idea where he was. It transpired he was at a friend of a friend's. The conversations as people gathered themselves and departed were quiet and stilted. Arriving at his digs he went back to bed.

In the autumn of 1966 he became twenty-one. He spent the evening alone; he had not arrived back until late. Mrs Clarke had left a meal for him on the top of a hot saucepan on the stove. He had a card from Mr Woodman. Nothing from his father who never remembered birthdays.

Standing by the river in the gathering dusk one evening enjoying a pint at the Boat with his father as the decade was drawing to a close, they were discussing how much had happened in the sixties.

'The pill must be one of the most important,' said his father, 'for the first time, women are able to decide when they would fall pregnant, if at all.'

'The Beatles,' offered Tim.

'No, Tim lad, ballroom dancing is the thing, you get to cuddle your partner, all this throwing the girl around, that's not dancing, and while I'm at it, why do The Beatles have such funny haircuts?'

Tim loved to jive, for him it allowed his youth full rein. He smiled, and moving the conversation on said, 'Sputnik and Yuri Gagarin.'

'Yes, do you remember how upset the Americans were because Russia got there first?' laughed his Dad.

'Yes, Dad, but the Americans got to the moon first.'

'Aye they did, but apparently it was all touch and go.'

'What about the mini skirt? That was important,' threw in Tim, smiling, knowing it would wind his father up.

His father took the bait as he suspected he would, 'Good God, lad, sometimes you can see their knickers, heaven knows what my mother would have said.'

'The Cuban missile crisis, I thought I was going to die, Dad, I was so frightened, if there was a loud bang, I was looking for the mushroom cloud.'

'I think we were all the same, son. Thank God those in power saw sense.'

'Dad, I had the same conversation with Mr Woodman some time back. He thought he was going to die, too.'

They both fell silent, immersed in their own memories.

Tim felt privileged to have been alive during the transformation of the dull, grey Britain of the '50s to the technicolour vibrant country it had become. He recognised, looking back, how much had happened in the Swinging Sixties. The new colourful clothing produced for the young, and the young at heart by some clever newcomers on the fashion scene like Mary Quant.

The excitement of the sixties would be the main memory he would carry with him into the future.

Tim was lonely occasionally. He envied the young couples walking hand in hand in the sunshine. The two attempts he had with girlfriends ended when they discovered he was married to the job and that they came a very poor second.

He received no prior warning of the changes that were about to alter his life for ever.

CHAPTER 3

THE MEETING 1969

Tim tightened his grip on the handrail and braced his legs as the tube train began to brake for the next station. He was almost unaware of the noise of the train clattering over the points; the squeal of the wheels protesting as they rounded the curve; the bounce and jostle of the train's movement as it tried to unbalance him.

His thoughts were with his great aunt Victoria whom he had visited that afternoon. Over the last few of his regular visits he began noticing she was ageing. Her appearance now reminded him of a piece of fine porcelain, beautiful but fragile. She was the epitome of a grand old lady from another age. He could never repay her for the love, help and affection she had afforded him ever since the loss of his mother eleven years ago.

She had complimented him on his appearance earlier with his dark hair and slim figure dressed as he was in his crisply ironed pale blue shirt, navy chinos and brown brogues.

'You have grown into a fine-looking young man, Tim.'

'Thank you, Aunty,' he replied laughing dismissively. He did realise he had his faults, his temper occasionally got him into trouble, especially if he perceived an injustice to himself or others.

Nowadays her mind was still as sharp but her growing frailty, poor sight and her continuing insistence on living alone was causing him real concern. She did have a housekeeper and a handyman driver; they had worked for his aunt as long as he could remember.

Tim became aware of the warm feminine perfume of the young woman who had just boarded the train at the last station and was now standing beside him. A glance showed him she was dressed for the office; a formal, expensive looking black pinstripe suit with trousers, a cream silk blouse, a small string of pearls and black patent leather shoes with a low heel. Her black leather handbag was on a long strap hung on her left side. Her blonde hair fell to her shoulders. She was, he realised, a very beautiful young woman.

Suddenly the train lurched as the brakes were applied a little too hard and she was thrown against him. She grabbed his hand to stop herself falling over. A strange sensation ran through his body, a kind of internal shiver. It was not something he had experienced before. It had left him bemused and very surprised. Shaking his head, still mystified, still trying to understand it, he wondered if she had felt the same thing.

At first, he was unaware that she had spoken to him. Then he was unsure of what she had said, turning to her he asked, 'Sorry, did you say something?'

She had looked away but then turned to face him. Tim was presented with a pair of cornflower blue eyes and a very beautiful face. He noticed that she was a little pink with embarrassment.

'I am sorry I grabbed hold of you, did I hurt you? I would have fallen had you not been there.'

One thing he was sure of was the fact that her mode of speech was as beautiful as her appearance.

He smiled, and said, 'No.'

Tim, keen to continue the conversation asked, 'Do you use this train a lot?' He knew his question was banal but could think of nothing better.

'No,' she said, 'I work for my father who owns a shop, I have just had lunch with a very good friend. What do you do?'

Tim explained he owned a stall on the banks of the river. A mini delicatessen selling food that was difficult to find elsewhere. He described his trips abroad to source his products and his travels through Italy and France and the friendships he had formed with his suppliers. He suddenly worried that his enthusiasm for his business may be boring her. He apologised.

'No,' she replied, 'it sounds really interesting.'

On an impulse he asked, 'Would you like to see it?'

'When?'

'Now, and I can supply a cup of real Italian coffee; we have it shipped in from our suppliers and you can try the very best confectionery in the world made right here in London, then I will see you back on the train when you want to go.'

She was surprised that this stranger had asked her to visit his stall. All her father's warnings were ringing in her ears. She realised she did not want this conversation to end. To her surprise she found him very attractive. This was not something she had experienced in a man before. She also found herself drawn to him because of his infectious enthusiasm for his business. This echoed her own enjoyment of hard work and achievement.

In some ways he reminded her of her father. He exhibited the same drive, energy and determination. Unlike the men her parents had lined up; a long list of chinless wonders who came from the 'right' families and were very wealthy.

She recognised that her upbringing often separated her from other people: her Westminster Nursery Service-trained nanny; her schooling in an expensive private college for girls; the finishing school in Switzerland; always travelling first class and of course the long summers spent in the family villa in Puglia, Italy and her good degree from Oxford.

It did not help that she had been painfully shy as a young girl, but she felt she was growing out of it. She knew she still gave in too easily to her father who was Italian and domineering. Also, as a result of his very successful business he was now very dictatorial.

She was aware that she had been blessed with a good mind and therefore grasped things far faster than most of her friends and acquaintances. She shone at university both academically and on the sports field, playing hockey for the university first team.

On occasion she had met men who appeared interesting but who had left after a while. Her very good friend at university, Jessica, explained it was that they felt threatened by her intellect. It was pleasant to find someone who appeared straightforward and attractive.

Tim had realised he had been foolish to ask her. He was now deeply embarrassed.

I expect I've bored her stiff, he thought. Why would she do it? There was going to be a long, embarrassed silence until the next stop when he could pretend that it was his station.

After a short discussion and, much to her surprise, she found herself agreeing to do as he asked. After all, he seemed nice enough and it was broad daylight and very busy.

They left the train and rode the elevator up to the street. Neither of them talking. As they were nearing the top Sophie began to have serious doubts about what she was doing but could think of no polite way of changing her mind.

As they left the station, he indicated that she should walk ahead of him through a narrow gap in the crowd. He noted that she walked beautifully. Each step appeared considered, her toe was pointed, and the stride length was perfect. Later that evening she would reveal that she had attended ballet classes for some years until she had grown too tall.

A short walk in the bright sunshine brought them to the banks of the river, a row of plane trees with their strange mottled bark were set back a little from the black railings that guarded the drop to the river. Between each tree a black wrought iron bench faced the water, afforded shade by the foliage above. Many of the seats were occupied; the elderly sat in silence watching the river; a mother sat with a baby on her knee making the child laugh by pulling funny faces; a man in a suit, his tie loosened, his head between his shoulders, his forearms on his knees stared at the ground between his feet. He occasionally took a long draw on his cigarette, then, blowing the smoke out between pursed lips in a long thin stream still without raising his head. He was clearly lost in thought, temporarily completely unaware of his surroundings.

The pigeons pecked around looking for scraps, lifting off in a flurry of wings when disturbed.

Sophie looking ahead noticing a line of stalls that were situated on a wide pavement bathed in sunlight that curved away to the left following the river. They were all of a type, a tubular steel frame covered on three sides and the top by a blue canvas cover. There was a row of small shops on the opposite side of the road. The couple walked past the first few stalls with Sophie fascinated by the activity and the occasional call of a stall holder advertising his wares.

Sophie, drawn to the river's railings and leaning over, noticed that the lower section of the fifteen-foot high river wall had a band of dark green moss, kept moist by the rise and fall of the water. Looking up and seeing Tim was waiting for her some distance ahead, she ran a little to catch him up. Walking on, her attention was caught by a child blowing bubbles that the breeze lifted into the air. Still watching the child, she did not realise Tim had stopped at his stall until she noticed he was not beside her anymore. She turned back.

Looking around she said, 'It is amazing. I have never been here before. I love these small markets.'

In the stall next door a short but strong and stern looking man with a wonderful Italian accent and a thick white beard welcomed them and asked, 'Who is the beautiful woman, Tim?'

Tim was mortified, dreadfully embarrassed and bright red in the face he began to apologise.

'Please do not apologise, my name is Sophie and anyway I did not know your name until just then.'

'My name is Tim, Tim Cooper,' he replied. Apologising again he introduced her to Harry, properly, who immediately began to flirt with her complimenting her on her beauty.

Looking embarrassed but smiling and going a little bit pink again she thanked Harry. Now it was Harry's turn to apologise but laughter behind his eyes gave away the lie.

Tim said, 'Oy! Harry, back off, or I will have a word with your wife.'

Sophie was admiring the wide range of confectionery on Harry's counter. He explained that it was the work of his wife and her artistry and it was all made in the back kitchen at home.

'Please, try some.'

She chose a chocolate liqueur, bit into it and then licked the outside of the chocolate where a little of the filling had escaped. She popped the sweet in her mouth, chewed for a minute, swallowed and then said, 'Harry, that is amazing.' Her wide eyes and open smile further endorsed her appreciation of the taste and his wife's skill. When she had finished the second one, she put the tips of her forefinger and thumb in her mouth in turn to avoid any waste of the delicacy. She would have been surprised had she been able to read Tim's mind; he had found the whole process very attractive and extremely feminine.

'One well-known international confectioner regularly offers my wife a lot of money for her recipes, but she always refuses. Many of them are her mother's recipes. She had to promise her mother she would always keep the secret. All the sweets have names, some are still in Italian.'

'Harry, they are incredible. I have never tasted anything like it. Tim they are so special.'

'Harry's wife Sara is a genius. People come from some distance to buy them. This is my stall,' Tim continued pointing next door.

A pair of trestle tables sat across the front of his stall covered in white plastic. There were jars of stuffed olives. Dried pasta in a range of shapes and sizes in large Kilner jars. Sausage and smoked meats in clear plastic topped boxes. Bottles of sun-dried tomatoes, promising the taste of an Italian summer. A range of various cheeses ready to be cut into portions. Bottles of olive oil and balsamic vinegar were lined up side by side with a row of jars of foreign mustard.

A set of black iron scales stood on the right. A shiny bowl for the produce on one side, with a black flat plate on the other, this to receive the appropriate small, polished brass weights of various sizes.

A naked light bulb hung from a central pole and swung in the breeze off the river. At night its light danced across his display.

Harry made them all a cup of coffee on his small gas stove and encouraged them to sit at the back and drink it.

The coffee's wonderful aroma took Tim back to his last visit to Italy. He described to Sophie his memory of sitting in a small open-air café on the edge of a mountain, under a pergola with bougainvillea growing over it.

'I was glad of the shade; I love that amazing quality of light that only seems to exist in Italy. I'd taken the coach up to the café, looking down I could see how steep and narrow the road was.'

Just for a moment, he had a clear mental picture of the winding, sand coloured road as it meandered through the olive groves down to the plain many hundreds of feet below.

'I decided not to look out of the window as we went up the climb. The sheer drops on the edge of the road were really scary.'

She laughed and said, 'I would have had my eyes shut.'

Wondering whether she should share information about her parents' villa in Puglia and the frequent visits to this, their second home, Sophie decided against it. Information about her family's wealth and lifestyle had frightened others off in the past.

When Tim asked her what she did she explained that her father owned a large store and that she was the company accountant.

'That is very impressive, how long have you worked for him?'

'Since I left university.'

'Which university?'

'Oxford, and you?'

He laughed and smiling broadly revealed how different his life had been, 'I started work at fifteen and was working Saturdays and some weekdays before that,' he went on to explain very briefly the loss of his mother and that his dad was unable to work.

'Oh, poor you, that must have been awful?'

He raised his eyebrows and nodded in agreement, but then added, 'Harry has always been here to help me. I could not have done it without him.' Tim returned to the present when Harry called him to help serve. Afterwards going back to Sophie, he lowered the corner of the rear canvas so that they could see the river.

The two young people sat talking. He occasionally left her to help serve. Sophie watched Tim as he laughed and joked with his customers. She realised that he was very attractive with his dark curly hair and finely drawn features. His choice of clothes suited him.

Her attention was drawn to the river as a line of ducklings swam by, bobbing up and down on the waves like corks. Sophie laughed softly. Tim turned from serving and smiled as she pointed out the small procession.

Sophie was beguiled by the different sounds of the craft engines and the occasional horns of the tugs. She listened to the rhythmic sound of the wash from the boats slapping against the moss green stonework at the foot of the river wall. All the different lights on the river looked like sliding shards of coloured glass. A deep booming horn on a much larger ship broke her reverie. Sophie shivered, the light had faded without her noticing and a cool wind was blowing off the river.

Tim was busy tidying up under the table.

Sophie walked forward and said, 'I should be going.' Tim offered to walk her back to the station.

Initially she refused but Harry, overhearing the discussion, apologised to his customer and said quietly to Tim, 'You must see her to the station, I will clear up.'

They both waved goodbye to Harry and then set off. The slow journey back to the station was filled with an exchange of information and funny stories. The one that made her laugh the most was when he explained that an old friend of his, who was short in stature, played rugby at the weekend. His mother always said the same thing as she saw him off, 'Don't get muddy, if the big boys want the ball let them have it.'

She did not move away when their shoulders touched occasionally. They stood close together as they waited for her train.

CHAPTER 4

LOVE LOST

Tim explained that he was going abroad the following day to look at a new range of Italian food. He realised that he had no way of contacting her; hearing the singing in the rails growing louder, announcing the imminent arrival of her train he asked very quietly, 'Can I have your phone number, please?' his tone of voice betraying his uncertainty of her response.

'Of course,' she replied, making eye contact and smiling, then, searching in her handbag and jotting the number down on the back of an old receipt.

With the paper still in his hand he waved her off. As the train gathered speed the wind snatched the paper from his hand and blew it away. In blind panic Tim broke in to a run and raced alongside the train on the very edge of the platform dodging other passengers, trying to catch up with her compartment but failing whilst shouting her name in the vain hope that she may hear him. He was oblivious to the growing roar of the train as it accelerated faster and faster, carrying her further and further away from him. His panic had blotted out any awareness of danger.

A very angry railway official tackled Tim and slammed him to the hard-concrete platform just short of the tunnel mouth. The man was shouting at him, his face was so close and angry, Tim felt his spittle. He was unable to hear what he was saying but he recognised that he had badly frightened the official.

Tim kept repeating, 'I'm sorry, I'm sorry.'

The man held Tim down whilst he radioed for assistance. Tim put up no resistance, it would not have achieved anything; the man was twice his size. He recognised that his actions had been entirely irrational and out of character. A transport policeman escorted him from the station.

The policeman said in a very gruff voice, 'You need to be more careful, lad.' He could think of no way of explaining so he simply apologised.

On his way home, he knew through his anguish that for the first time in his life he was truly in love and had just met the woman who was supposed to be his wife. He was experiencing an unfamiliar pull on his heart; it was more than a sense of loss; it was much larger; deeper than anything he had felt since his mother died.

His father always said that he had seen the girl who was to become his wife across a dance floor and after a brief introduction had fallen in love. Tim had always taken the story with a pinch of salt but now realised his father had been telling the truth. He recalled his mother's gentle smile when his father recounted the story.

The following morning before leaving for the airport he had told Harry what had happened and that he could not contact Sophie and that if she came to the stall would he explain?

Tim went off as planned.

Sophie was surprised when Tim had not rung a week later. He had said he would be away four days. Whilst she would not admit it to anybody else, she realised that her feelings for him were not just a mild attraction. His energy and enthusiasm were very compelling. On more than one occasion at work she found herself daydreaming, recalling something he had said or the way he laughed. When he was close, she had loved the way he smelt. To her very great surprise she realised she wanted to see him again. As the days went by, he was often on her mind. Towards the end of the week she was becoming angry with herself. She was moping about like a lovesick teenager. It was time to deal with this problem head on. She decided she would go to the stall on the following evening.

Walking down to the riverside on the next day after work Sophie was very nervous, she was slightly short of breath and was dry mouthed, experiencing the same fear that a trip to the dentist generated. This could all turn out very badly and be dreadfully embarrassing.

Twice stopped by indecision, the last time she had turned and taken three paces back towards the station. Eventually moving on she thought, I will do this, otherwise I will spend the rest of my life wondering, what if? Walking on, looking at her reflection in the shop windows as she passed a new worry took hold; perhaps the dress, so carefully chosen, was over the top. Should it have been more subdued? Did it look as though she was trying too hard? Becoming cross with herself and thrusting all this negativity aside she quickened her pace and strode on with the determination to see it through. The beginnings of a possible dialogue began to form in her mind. One thing was certain if it became too difficult, she would leave.

She could see the marketplace in the distance. Reaching the beginning of the line of stalls she crossed the road and walked down the opposite pavement in the shadow of the shops, hoping not to draw attention to herself. Arriving opposite Tim's stall she could see that neither he nor Harry were there. Expressing her disappointment by pulling a face. An attractive woman that Sophie did not recognise was running both stalls. As Sophie got nearer, another trader walking past called out, 'Hi Kate,' and the woman waved in acknowledgement.

Crossing the road and waiting until the woman had finished serving a customer Sophie asked, 'Is Tim around?'

'Who's asking luv?' Kate enquired looking Sophie up and down.

I am overdressed, thought Sophie, as an aside.

'My name is Sophie. Tim was going to contact me,' she continued. She felt the other woman's attitude become cold and defensive. 'I know he has gone abroad on business, I wondered if he had returned.'

Turning to serve another customer she said over her shoulder, 'He hasn't said anything to me love, and he always confides in me. I know him very well if you gets my meaning. Sorry I can't help, now I must get on,' her harsh tone indicating the conversation was over.

What Sophie could not know was that Kate was one of Tim's old flames and still carried a torch for him. Sophie left believing that Tim and Kate were a couple. As she walked away, she felt a strong sense of loss.

Tim returned from what had been a very successful trip with a lot of new produce to sell and the promise of more to come. He was very upset that Sophie had apparently not returned to the stall. Questioning Harry and Kate they were both adamant they had not seen her. He made numerous visits to the station but never saw her. On two occasions, he stopped women in the street and had to apologise when it was not her. His friends became ever more concerned for him.

She often came to mind; he always felt a strange pull on his heart.

Finally, Harry, some months later said, 'You have got to get a grip, lad. You are pining for a girl you spent two hours with and are never going to see again.' Tim recognised Harry was right although he knew that the woman who would have been his soul mate had gone.

CHAPTER 5

THE PROPOSITION

Mr Woodman came across the road to talk to Tim and Harry one Monday morning. He explained that he wanted to retire and that he had a business proposition for them. He had noticed how busy they had become and how very short of space they were. He would not discuss it now but if they would come to his flat above the shop that evening, he would let them know what he had in mind.

It was now high summer. The sun blazed down pushing the temperatures into the high twenties. Coincidentally both stalls were very busy. The two men were on their feet all day and were very pleased when they could seek the sanctuary of Mr Woodman's hardware store.

Tim loved the shop, the dark familiar interior with its hundreds of different things for sale, from brooms to bed knobs. The wonderful medley of smells; the scent of a range of oils; paraffin and soap; rows of small wooden drawers containing every size of nut and bolt, screw and nail. The shop seemed to contain at least one of everything.

All the woodwork had aged to a warm honey colour.

The flat above Mr Woodman's shop was scrupulously clean as always. In all the years Tim had been here he could not remember it being untidy. The faint smell of lavender furniture polish was ever present. The small dark-wood table and four chairs, shining like all the furniture in the room, stood on a navy-blue carpet in one corner. There was a capacious, buttoned, mid brown leather armchair where Tim, as a very young child, often sat on Mr Woodman's lap listening to the elderly man recounting tales of his own childhood all those years ago.

Tim's favourite story was the one about Mr Woodman's grandpa, the pipe and the war. Mr Woodman told Tim that he used to help his grandpa in the shop when he was very young.

'My grandpa,' he explained, 'was a big man with a beard and moustache and a headful of white hair. He had piercing blue eyes that shone out from under his bushy eyebrows.' He recalled that when the shop was not busy, he and Grandpa would sit on stools in the corner and Grandpa would light his pipe.

'I was always fascinated by the ritual,' said Mr Woodman. 'First, he would dig out the old stale tobacco with a special spike that sat with other implements in his penknife. Then he would knock the dottle out into the waste bin.' Mr Woodman went on to explain that his grandpa's old leather tobacco pouch was kept in a pocket in his work coat. He described how it had acquired a high shine and a deep glowing patina, like a new conker. Then he recalled, 'The tobacco was teased apart, loaded into the bowl of the pipe and using exactly the right amount of pressure it was tamped down.

'My grandpa had a trick when lighting a match; he would hold the match upright in his fist and flick the Swan Vesta with his thumb nail. The match flared into life, then it was held over the bowl of the pipe and with much puffing the pipe was lit.'

He and his grandpa were enveloped in a cloud of aromatic smoke. Once the pipe was properly lit Mr Woodman remembered that his grandfather would recount stories of his war, the First World War. It was supposed to be the war to end all wars his grandfather told him, but it was not to be.

His mother would sometimes cough from her position by the till and Grandpa would reduce the vivid descriptions of death and disaster.

*

There were two things about Mr Woodman's room that had always been there, recalled Tim, his mind returning to the present. A large very attractive antique brass oil lamp with an ornamental red glass shade had pride of place on a wooden dresser, a small faded photograph of an attractive woman sat beside it. Many years ago, Tim had asked who the woman was.

Mr Woodman explained it was his wife taken just after they were married, picking it up as he spoke. He was silent for a while stroking the face in the photograph with the ball of his thumb. 'Ah well,' he'd sighed, returning it to its place.

Mr Woodman had the kettle on, and all three men were soon seated around the table with a very welcome cup of tea in front of them.

Mr Woodman said, 'I want to retire or certainly do a lot less. I have just had my seventieth birthday.'

Tim and Harry wished him a happy birthday and said that he didn't look seventy. Mr Woodman replied that they were very kind but that some mornings he felt a lot older.

Tim felt a pang of remorse that he did not know when Mr Woodman's birthday was. Tim said, 'I don't understand why you want to retire? You still look very well.'

'Thank you, I am well, but as you both know once you shut the shop your day is not over, there are a dozen different tasks to be done; balance the till, call the suppliers, tidy up and so on, I have had enough of it, Tim. I want to put my feet up in the evening. You never know I might even go down the pub.'

He said, 'Let's get down to what I am offering. Your stall, Tim, is not big enough now for all your merchandise and Harry is being extremely generous in letting you overflow on to his.' Tim went to say something, Mr Woodman, raising his hand, asked him not to interrupt.

'My proposal is as follows,' he continued, 'I know that neither of you could afford to buy my shop and I don't want to sell it; this has been my home for many years, and I am too old to move, and I don't want strangers taking over downstairs. My grandfather started this shop before the First World War. My proposal entails you two going into partnership and running your business from here. I have no one else I want to leave it to and Tim you are as close as family.'

'Crikey,' said Tim.

Harry had rocked back in his chair, apparently rendered speechless.

Mr Woodman went to continue.

'That would take a lot of thinking about,' said Harry, interrupting. 'Your offer is incredibly generous, but I have been my own man for many years, it will be difficult for me to have to get agreement to do things I want to do, and I need to talk to Sara; without her on board it will not even get off the start line, she is the business really.'

'I would not expect anything less,' responded Mr Woodman.

Tim sensed Harry's reluctance. He was not too sure himself. It would change everything, and it would be a major leap in the dark for all of them but, he did recognise Mr Woodman's amazing generosity.

'Mr Woodman, this is an incredible offer, but I think you could find some nice people to rent the shop. The income would help with your retirement.'

'Tim, as you are aware, I have been on my own for many years and the business has been very profitable. What I am about to say is not for public consumption, but I am very comfortably off. I will not have any money worries.' After a short pause he continued, 'I know you two are separate businesses, but I am certain your customers see you as one shop. I would suggest you develop Tim's delicatessen ideas whilst retaining the confectionery. As Tim will tell you, he believes the country is ready for new things; new music, new clothes and why not new foods,' Mr Woodman concluded by saying, 'and Tim, I agree with you.'

Tim Broke in and said, 'Mr Woodman, there is no way I could find even half the money you would want to rent this shop.'

'Tim, you don't need to,' he replied. 'As I have just said, I do not want to sell, and I do not want to rent it. I expect to retain a life interest in the property so that I will always have somewhere to live. The crux of my idea is that between us we work out what you can afford, and you pay me that every week as a pension.' Holding up his hand once again to silence the two men he continued, 'I will still live upstairs; you allow me to work part time in the shop as long as I am able and when I die, my will shall make you both beneficiaries in my estate. The shop will pass to you free and clear, Tim.' Mr Woodman continued, 'I intend to have a doctor declare that I am sane and in my right mind and my solicitor will draw up the requisite paperwork.'

Harry said, 'I don't know what to say, Mr Woodman, it is an amazing offer, but I need to think about this long and hard, I have no idea what Sara will say.'

'I will have to talk to Dad,' added Tim, 'the deli was his idea after all.'

Moments later thanking Mr Woodman again, Harry stood, and apologising for his rapid departure said he needed to get home, calling a goodbye to both, he made his way down the stairs and left the shop.

'That was abrupt,' said Tim not understanding what had just occurred, very surprised at Harry's rush to leave.

'We are asking him to change everything he has been doing for years and he is of an age where change comes harder. I must admit that I did worry that this may be his reaction,' responded Mr Woodman.

Stopping at the foot of the stairs, Tim turned to Mr Woodman and said, 'Your offer is very generous, people will think we are taking advantage of an old man and I would never do that to you, but, if Harry says no, I won't do it without him. I owe him too much to do that.'

'I know you would never be anything but considerate towards my welfare, Tim, and Harry's. l meant what I said to you before, all down the years I have thought of you as family and that is why I am making my offer;

we will pay no attention to what other people will think.'

Tim offered his hand and Mr Woodman grasped it in both of his, the handshake lasted a few seconds.

Tim, emotion evident in his voice said, 'Thank you very much, Mr Woodman, that means a lot to me.'

With his arm round Tim's shoulders he turned and walked him towards the door and said, with a laugh in his voice, 'And not so much of the old man.'

Holding the door open for him he watched as Tim walked away down the street. He thought to himself, 'You'll do alright, lad, but it is a shame you are so unhappy over the loss of this girl.'

Walking home Tim was surprised by Harry's reticence, he began to wonder if he would agree to do it. For himself he felt a growing thrill tempered by a note of fear. It was so much bigger than anything he had ever dreamed of. He realised it might just work.

Harry was at the stall earlier than Tim the following day. He sensed a change in him, he was quiet, polite enough, but avoided conversation about the shop when Tim questioned him.

'Sara would like you to come to tea, we can talk about it then,' was his only response. There was no loud Italian laughter, no banter, no barely veiled inuendo making the women blush and smile and look at him under their eyelashes. At close of day the two men walked home to Harry's house in near silence. Sara answered the door and stood aside to let the two men in. Harry kissed her in a rather perfunctory manner, Tim got his usual hug and a smile, but he could sense the latter was rather strained. They followed Harry into the lounge.

'Would anybody like a drink?' he called out as he approached the drinks cabinet. They both declined. Sara raised her eyebrows when he filled a large glass to the brim with a good red wine, swallowed half and topped it up to the brim and drank from it again.

'Dinner is ready,' called Sara, 'if you would like to come through.' Harry brought the bottle with him. They were halfway through the first course that had proceeded with occasional stilted conversation when Harry banged down his knife and fork and said, 'Sara has asked me to wait until we have finished eating but I have things I must say.'

Sara jumped in saying, 'Harry, please wait.'

'No, I won't wait,' he said firmly, his Italian accent getting stronger. 'Tim needs to know how I feel. I must get this off my chest, it's burning me.' He paused and then said, 'During the war we followed a false prophet in Mussolini. We were fed promises and lies. At the end of the war we were a defeated nation. We are by nature a proud people so after the war a terrible depression settled over both the people and the country. I had married Sara and we were penniless. All my family were advising we come to England.'

Sara added, 'I saw grown men cry, Tim.'

'We had little more than what we stood up in. My family and Sara's scraped the fare together, so we could come to England. When we first arrived in London it was hard, I worked in a factory during the day. Sara worked as a cleaner all day and I had a second job in the evenings washing up in a restaurant. The stall and the sweets were Sara's idea, at first it was just weekends, it soon took off. Finally I was working on the stall full time, twelve-hour days, it was better than the factory. We bought our own little house.'

Leaning forward to add emphasis he explained, 'I don't think I want to start all over again, I don't have the energy, Tim.' He was almost pleading for Tim's recognition of how he felt about the whole thing. 'We are doing ok now, I will not put Sara's welfare, and mine come to that on the line again.'

'Harry, I need you to know I will not do this without you, I need your common sense, your experience and your retail skills. I am not arrogant enough to believe I have the ability to do this on my own.'

'Tim, that is very kind of you to say so, but I don't want to become some big businessman making all sorts of tough decisions affecting people's jobs and so on. I would hate to do that. Sara says I am an old softy, very emotional, and that I wear my heart on my sleeve. We would have loved children, but it was not to be. So you see we have no one to leave the business to, therefore I am quite happy to just toddle along.

'I like a glass of wine from our home country, sometimes more than a glass.' Tim could see Sara nodding.

'I enjoy working with my customers, laughing with the men and women. And of course,' he paused, the depth of his emotions in plain view, 'I have my wonderful Sara who makes my life worth living.' The two exchanged a look. There was another long pause...

Sara spoke first, 'Harry, you have not asked me what I think!' Her usual soft Italian voice was now edged with steel. 'People now come from all over London to buy our confectionery. We have a growing reputation. So, what if the shop fails, I will sell my recipes to the very large company that keeps offering me more and more money, with the understanding that I can continue to make them myself, and perhaps promise to give them the new products I come up with as an added incentive. And we go back to a stall.'

Neither man had heard her speak so forcibly before.

They were both silent for a long time while they considered what Sara had just said. Tim stayed quiet recognising this was a crucial moment in the dream that was growing in his mind. The silence grew louder as the two of them focused their entire attention on Harry.

Harry settled back in his chair while stroking his beard, his eyes fixed on Sara. Still he was silent. On and on it went, Harry's attention to his beard was the only movement.

Eventually he declared, 'You are a very brave and clever woman, Mrs Trentino.'

Sara replied, 'Thank you, Harry. I believe with Tim's help we can take this to a level we never dreamed of,' glancing at Tim as she spoke, who nodded agreement.

'Harry, I promise this will be done properly. We will look at every angle and get professional help where required to make sure this is done right, and everybody is protected as far as possible. But just think what it could become?' enthused Tim.

Later that night when Harry had left the room for a few minutes, Sara said, 'He will come around ,Tim, I think it is very exciting.'

Hoping to change the subject Tim asked, 'How did you two meet?'

'We lived in the same village at home in Italy, we were aware of each other at school, but we didn't speak much, we were both painfully shy. My family were staunch Catholics, we children were to be seen but not heard. He and I would find we were standing on the side lines watching others do things.'

Harry returned and asked, 'What are you talking about?'

'I asked how you two met?'

'Sara was a mouse, a little shy mouse, but a very beautiful one.'

'Harry you were as bad as me, but remember, I spoke first, otherwise you would still be looking at me when you thought I couldn't see you.'

'I don't remember that, what did you say?'

'"Hallo!" You were very shy.'

'Why was that, Harry?' asked Tim.

There was a long pause, then Sara said, 'You had an older twin brother, didn't you?'

'Yes, he died as I was starting school, he was one hour older than me. He was the dominant one. I didn't speak properly for ages; he would translate my gibberish for other people.'

'Your mother told me that it took a long time for you to get over his death,' said Sara reaching across the couch to hold his hand. 'You never really made any advances towards me, Harry, but I would find that suddenly you were standing beside me. You were always there. I quite liked that. Later on when we were older the other students were pairing up, with boyfriends and girlfriends. You didn't even hold my hand.'

Harry nodded and paused again, then he said, 'Because of the death of my brother I really believed that if I should become fond of someone, they would die, so I had to pretend to myself that Sara was just a friend.'

'Harry, you have never told me that before,' said Sara sliding closer to him so she could wind her arm through his, reaching for her hanky as she did so.

Tim asked, 'So what changed?'

Sara said, 'There was an explosion in the factory where I had started work, we were all girls, apart from the managers. One of our team was killed, she was very young.'

'I heard the bang from about two miles away,' said Harry, 'We were all trying to work out what it was then someone said it was Sara's factory. I started to run,' turning to Sara he said, 'all the way I was praying to God that you were alright. I knew I could not go on without you. As I got closer, I could see this pillar of smoke shooting into the sky. When I arrived, I was exhausted, I had to stand for a moment with my hands on my knees to recover, I could hardly speak.

'The flames were ferocious and very hot; the police were keeping everyone back so that the firemen could do their job. I was asking people, all the people if they had seen you, finally you were pointed out to me. It nearly broke my heart.

'Tim, she had her arms wrapped around herself, she was covered in soot and she was crying.'

'Harry, I remember you were crying and kissing me and trying to wipe the soot out of my face and brushing my hair into place with your hand and saying, "Thank you, God," over and over. I couldn't work out how you had got there. Then you held me close. What did you say next?'

'I told you I loved you, I didn't know I was going to say it, and then what did you say?'

'I told you I loved you as well.'

'The rest is history as they say,' said Harry.

Their story of how they fell in love once again caused Tim pain as he remembered Sophie and how much he missed her.

*

None of them could have anticipated the welter of things there were to be investigated and decided upon. Harry insisted that everything was crystal clear, and nothing overlooked. The weeks went by. Finally, he agreed to give it a go.

Late one evening, sitting above the shop the three men decided that they had done as much planning as they could to cover all eventualities.

'We think your offer is very generous and we would like to accept,' said Harry. 'We did wonder if you would like to be more than a part time employee?'

Mr Woodman broke in and with a small smile said, 'Thank you very much for your kindness but the worry of running a business is one of the major reasons I am retiring, but if you ever want another opinion, I am quite happy to put my tuppence worth in. Also, I need to say that if ever you think I am interfering please say so. I shall sulk for a week, but I will get over it.' They all laughed.

Tim said, 'I think you might be called upon for your opinion more often than you realise.'

Mr Woodman walked over to the beautiful old dresser and brought a cut-glass ship's decanter and three heavy whiskey glasses to the table.

'I think we should have a drink and shake hands on the deal, providing we all want to go ahead.' The three men stood, raised a glass to the new deal and shook hands. Tim and Harry left soon after.

Walking home Tim surprised a couple kissing in a doorway, for one heart wrenching second, he thought it was Sophie. When she turned to face him, he saw that although similar in appearance she was too tall. Walking on, his grief overcame him. The loss of his mother and Sophie was so painful, when he remembered them, it tore at him.

A hundred yards down the street he stopped outside a darkened house, grasped the railing and with head down the tears flowed unheeded. When he finally gathered himself, he looked around grateful that no one had seen him. It was a poorly lit street anyway.

CHAPTER 6

THE SHOP 1970

Tim did not sleep much that night. His mind full of the new partnership. He so wished Sophie could have been by his side to share his excitement. At 4.30 he gave up trying to sleep, got up, found his slippers and dressing gown and made a cup of coffee. He had managed to accumulate a small nest egg. He realised that the shop would require some work although he did not want to change it too much. Its antiquity was a great part of its appeal. An estimate had been secured for the work the shop required. Tim recognised Mr Woodman's enormous generosity and vowed to ensure he was always comfortable.

The next morning the sun shone, the birds sang in the line of plane trees that lined the embankment, dogs barked for fun, and the girls were out in their pretty clothes. The world felt a bright and happy place. As always there was a shadow. The memory of Sophie was always with him. He had tried every method he could think of to find her. He did not know her surname or where she lived or worked.

He recognised that he had never really got over his mother's loss, he felt sure that he would carry the memory of Sophie and his mother for the rest of his life.

Mr Woodman came out of his shop and hung a 'half-price sale' notice across the top of the window. When he had done, he walked across the road to the men's stalls.

Tim said, 'You don't hang around.'

Mr Woodman replied, 'At my age, Tim, there is no time to hang around.'

It was a few days later the three men stood in the empty shop. It was quite a large space, deeper than it was wide. There were wooden varnished counters running each side of the shop. The stairs up to the flat above the shop were set against the back wall, rising from right to left. Under the stairs on the left was the till; a monstrous device made of brass and steel. It had huge square numbers that popped up inside a clear plastic box on top of the machine. Next to it a small door led out to the back yard. The ceiling and the beams were varnished wood that had grown ever darker with the passing of the years.

Tim recognised that the décor would need brightening, a coat of lime wash was suggested to make it look clean. For a few minutes they tiptoed around the appearance of the counters.

Mr Woodman said nothing but scratched his head. He was suddenly aware that his shop that had supported three generations of his family and had always looked the same was about to change completely.

There was a knock on the door. Mr Woodman walked swiftly to it, opened it, saying, 'Hallo, Charlie, thank you for coming.'

Their visitors, Charlie's son Tommy had come with him, followed Mr Woodman back to the centre of the shop. He then introduced them to Harry and Tim.

Charlie walked around the shop listening while Mr Woodman described their thoughts so far. When Mr Woodman stopped talking Charlie looked around, crossed his arms and said, 'Sounds ok but them counters 'ave gotta go. You can't serve food off 'em. You need ones what are easily cleaned. Those wooden tops 'ave goodness knows what soaked into 'em. You'd be lucky if you didn't poison some poor blighter. I realise you wanna keep the feel of the place but they 'ave gotta go. They gotta be glass aren't they?'

Mr Woodman raised his eyes and pulled a face but said nothing.

'What about the flooring?' asked Harry.

'I visualised pale blue and white tiles, again something hard-wearing and easy to clean,' said Tim.

'What you gonna call the shop?' asked Tommy, who up to now had been silent.

Tim remained quiet while the others swapped ideas without coming to any real conclusion.

'Can we call it "Sophie's" he asked?' No one answered.

After everyone had gone Mr Woodman walked around the shop on his own, running his hands over the counters that had become satin smooth with use over decades. He looked up at the small drawers that rose to the ceiling on the left, each furnished with a small brass handle that housed the paper labels that were now brown edged with age. He never needed to read them. He could still see in his mind's eye the former contents of every drawer. He paused at the till. He had a clear image of his wife sitting on the same stool that was behind it now. Looking round he no longer recognised the shop that had supported them for so many years. It had changed irrevocably. Now it was just an empty shell, it had always been his touchstone, his intimate knowledge of every tiny part of it grounded him. Now he felt cut adrift, terribly alone. A tsunami of loneliness and sorrow broke over him.

Overcome, he bent double, one hand on the counter, fighting to hold back the tears without success. A bout of deep sobs shook him to his core. Slowly he regained control of himself. Blowing his nose on a large bright white handkerchief he went slowly upstairs to bed.

He moved the photo of his wife to his bedside table. He had not cried for years. One of the reasons for his distress was his growing awareness of his own mortality, this was generating a strong sense of urgency in him. His sense of time was altering. The hours between waking and sleeping were shrinking, the days themselves fled by ever more quickly. His memory took him back to his childhood when the span of a day was endless. Now the flow of the sand in the hourglass of his life was inexorably gathering speed. He lay awake for some time before he finally fell asleep with the radio still playing quietly in the background.

The counters were the first to go. They left pale oblongs on the floor where the flooring had been protected from the years of wear. All the surfaces had been washed down with sugar soap and had been given a light sand and then one coat of lime wash. Charlie had treated the old black rafters on the ceiling in the same manner; the spaces between them were now white; it looked smart and modern but still nodded towards another age. Finally, the painting was finished. The change in the appearance of the shop was remarkable. The exterior was now glistening white gloss with a thin pale blue surround.

Tim was very aware that his most recent appraisal of their financial situation meant they very likely could not afford the new glass counters.

The next Sunday he explained the problem of the counters and the lack of money to his father.

His father apparently disinterested said, 'Well I hope you manage to find some, lad.'

'Will you come and look at the shop please, Dad?'

'I've seen it from the outside, can't see much of the inside because the windows have got that whitewash on them, I will look in one day.'

'Why not today, it's not too cold out and it's only all possible because of you. Please come and look, I think you will be surprised?'

His father hesitated but Tim's enthusiasm and obvious desire for him to see it persuaded him. They both donned their overcoats and set off in the light of the thin winter sun. His father had donned his old cap that Tim remembered he had always worn, and he was still wearing his old mid brown suit with the baggy knees and the shiny cuffs. Tim noticed his walk had slowed and he was becoming stooped, his father had never been very tall but now he seemed to have shrunk.

Ten minutes later they reached the river's sparkling water and then turned left towards the shop. Tim had always had a deep emotional tie with the river. This river. His river. The River Thames. He had seen lots of other rivers and he was always drawn to them, but they weren't this river.

He loved the bustle of the river traffic. The smell. The vast assortment of boats. The tugboats with their tail of barges, some deeply laden with very little freeboard, others empty and showing a tall rusty side. The ferry boats threading their way across the river between all the other boats. The ferrymen rowing them with an easy skill polished by years of practice. Some of the ferry boats had been owned and crewed by the same families for generations.

A pretty yacht, white hulled with a blue plimsoll line just above the water was motoring upriver with its mast lowered to fit under the bridges, home from the sea, seeking its rest at its regular mooring.

Besides all this Tim was aware of the power of the river, every year it took its toll of human life. The careless, the unlucky and those poor souls whose lives were so desperate that their future seemed hopeless. The river was beautiful, but it demanded respect.

When they reached the shop, Tim noticed Mr Woodman leaning against the black wrought iron railings opposite the shop watching the river. As they approached, Tim called out to him. Mr Woodman turned, saw Tim and called, 'Hallo,' and began to walk towards them.

As he came closer shading his eyes with one hand the better to see them, he said in an enquiring tone, 'Is that your father?'

'It is,' Tim's father replied.

Well, well, well,' said Mr Woodman. 'Who would have thought it?' 'We haven't seen you down this way in a long time Mr Cooper.'

'Well I am here now,' he answered a little brusquely, sensing criticism where there was none. 'Tim has asked me to look at the shop if that is ok?'

'Of course it is, I think you will be surprised,' said Mr Woodman as they stepped through the door and put the new lights on.

'What do you think?' asked Mr Woodman.

'Oh my, it all looks very exciting. I must admit I was taking what Tim told me about your ideas with a pinch of salt, he has in the past sometimes been prone to exaggeration but not this time.'

Tim was very surprised, his father seemed to have shrugged off his malaise and appeared genuinely excited by the new venture.

'We still need new counters and a new blind,' said Mr Woodman.

'And the solicitors bill has to be paid,' added Tim.

'Tim has mentioned the counters; I may be able to help with that. There's a chap I know down in the East End who does shop and house clearance, he may have what you want.' He paused, and then said, 'I hope you don't think I am butting in here, but I would like to help, this is just what I've been missing, something to interest me. I can't help financially but I would like to help even if it's just as the tea boy.' They all laughed.

'Speaking of tea,' said Mr Woodman smiling, 'how about a cup?'

On the journey back to his father's house Tim hardly recognised the man walking beside him. His posture had changed; he was more upright, and his gait was more urgent now rather than the near shuffle he had used on the way to the shop. His conversation clearly indicated his enthusiasm for the new venture.

'I won't come in; I have a mountain of paperwork,' said Tim.

'I understand,' said his father. He reached for Tim's hand and holding it in both of his said, 'Son, you've no idea what you've done for me today, I feel ten years younger.'

Tim strode back to his digs with a smile on his face.

After Tim had left, his father found himself humming while he filled the kettle.

Tim was reading his mail a few days later and opened a letter from their solicitor. The invoice enclosed was very much more than the estimate. The solicitor insisted that Mr Woodman had to be a partner because of his very large stake in the business, i.e. the shop. Reluctantly he had agreed.

Tim had considered going to see his bank manager, he was terrified of him, but he realised that the time had come. The following morning Tim advised his partners of the worrying financial situation. He then disclosed his plan to help solve it. Both men immediately objected and offered to help pay. Tim refused saying this was what he wanted to do.

He made an appointment with Mr Murdoch, the local branch manager. Three days later Tim was shown into his office. The manager was a tall Scotsman in a very smart three-piece dark pinstripe suit and a navy-blue tie. A gold watch chain was suspended between the twin pockets of his waistcoat. Mr Murdoch had a very deep voice with a heavy Scottish accent. The manager did not rise as Tim entered the office.

'What can we do for you, Mr Cooper?' he asked as he waved Tim to a chair.

Tim started to explain his requirement for a bank loan. Mr Murdoch interrupted him by asking if he had any details he could see. Tim handed him a folder with all the information about the shop and his partners. The manager flipped the folder open and started to read. At the same time, he picked up his phone and asked someone to bring in Tim's file. The office was very quiet, the only sound the loud ticking of the grandfather clock that stood in the corner. Tim looked around the room, the walls were covered in dark wood, the floor was highly polished parquet and a picture of the Queen hung on the wall behind Mr Murdoch's desk. The silence was broken by a soft respectful tap on the office door and a very smart young lady in a black frock and black patent high heels came in and made her way to the manager's desk.

As she placed the folder in front of him, she asked, 'Will there be anything else, sir?'

'No thank you,' he replied.

After she had left there was another short silence while the manager read the bank's file and then closing it, he said, 'What can I do for you Mr Cooper?'

Tim, summoning his courage said, 'I would like to borrow five hundred pounds please.'

Mr Murdoch roared with laughter. When he had regained control of himself, he asked, 'How do you think you will repay it?'

Tim, taken aback by the manager's response replied in a firm voice, 'I assumed there would be a monthly repayment plan.'

The manager laughed again. 'Son, there is nothing here that shows me that you could afford to repay that much money.'

Tim had grown quite cross because of the ridicule. Looking the man in the eye he said, 'Mr Murdoch, I am working fourteen hours a day to make this a reality and if necessary, I will work longer. I will succeed, sir.'

Mr Murdoch returned and held Tim's gaze. Both men stared hard at each other for a few moments. Finally, the manager asked Tim, 'How much do you need right now?'

'One hundred pounds will see me through the next month until the shop opens,' he replied.'

'I will tell you what I will do, Mr Cooper, you have convinced me that you intend to give this a proper go. I cannot see myself how you will find enough people that like this foreign food. My wife would not have it in the house. However,' he paused, 'I won't give you a loan. I will grant you a £100 overdraft, you will only pay the interest until you can pay off the capital.'

Tim jumped from his chair and shook Mr Murdoch's hand. 'Thank you very much, you have no idea how important this is to me.'

I think I do, thought the manager.

After all the paperwork had been done Mr Murdoch said, 'Mr Cooper, I admire your work ethic and determination. Please stay in touch and come and see me when you need to.'

✳

Tim frequently found himself searching for a sight of Sophie in a crowd in the street. Much of the time he was unaware that he was doing it. It had been the same with his mother after her death. For months he did the same thing. Sometimes he believed he had recognised the back of Sophie's head or the side of her face: for a brief moment his heart leapt, his pace quickened, he went to call out. Then he recognised his mistake, his heart fell, and emotion washed over him. On one occasion he had tapped a woman on the shoulder and at the same time calling her Sophie. She was very frightened and had shied away from him. He apologised profusely, she hastened away watching him out of the corner of her eye.

Late one afternoon the shop was quiet when Sara approached Tim and said, 'We are all worried about you, Tim. You are still missing this girl so badly. We do not know what to do to help.'

'Thank everybody for their concern but this is something I have to deal with myself.'

His partners finally agreed to call the shop 'Sophie's'; they were unable to come up with a viable alternative and they recognised how important it was to Tim.

Tim's father called around to the stall two days later to say that he may have found some counters for the shop.

'The old guy I know in the East End that I had mentioned has some. He does shop and house clearance. They look alright to me, I admit they need some work, but he wouldn't discuss money with me. We could look at them on Sunday if you wanted?'

The following Sunday was grey and dripping and quite cold. Mr Cooper drove them in his old green van that was, despite its age, very reliable. Tim's father always said it was like an Irishman's shovel where the blade had been replaced twice and the handle four times. The windscreen wipers worked intermittently, and his father had to regularly wipe the inside of the screen with a grubby old piece of chamois leather to remove the condensation.

Tim sat on a crate in the back. Mr Woodman was having dinner with some friends and was therefore unable to come.

'It's just around the corner here,' said Tim's father and with that turned left down a narrow alleyway paved with cobbles and deep puddles. The alleyway was flanked on the left by a railway viaduct and on the other by an area of wasteland bounded by a dilapidated wire fence. The railway viaduct had doors set into the arches that hid a mixed array of businesses. The old van lurched and swayed, finally coming to a stop outside a peeling blue wooden door that had 'Joseph Gold and Co' written on it in fading gold paint. Exiting the van and stepping nimbly across one particularly large puddle, Mr Cooper knocked on the door. Tim was surprised and pleased to see this sign of the recent improvement in him.

The owner appeared; Joseph Gold was short and round, his face and his body the same shape but he gave off a feeling of being very strong. His eyes were sharp and quick indicating a bright and agile intelligence. He was dressed in old wellington boots with black trousers that only just met in the middle and were held up by a wide leather belt. The sleeves of his white shirt were rolled up to the elbows exposing the obvious strength in his arms and a tattoo on his forearm, an apron tied around his waist completed his ensemble.

'Good morning, Joseph, how are you?' asked his father.

'I'm well thank you, Tom.' The two men shook hands and Joseph gripped Tom's upper arm for a few moments. Later Joseph nodded at Tom and finally let go; nothing was said but a lot was implied. Tim was aware that there was important history between the two men; he had been told years ago that they had served together in the war.

'Come in, come in all of you,' said Joseph, waving at Tim and Harry who were just climbing from the van. 'My wife has the coffee pot on,' he continued.

'Oh, Tom, how lovely to see you,' said Mrs Gold kissing him on the cheek. 'I missed you the other day when you called. You must not be a stranger. The coffee is on, but I expect you want to look at the counters?'

Mrs Gold, though now in her later years, was still an attractive woman and Tim surmised that in her youth she had clearly been a real beauty with her wonderful complexion and features. Tim's father introduced Tim and Harry.

Joseph led them to the back of the store. They had to weave their way around stacks of chairs and other furniture, boxes of household items and, strangest of all, a full-size stuffed brown bear standing up on its back legs looking very dangerous. It was a little moth-eaten. A fine layer of dust covered most of the items and there were signs of the work of spiders.

In a nearby dark musty corner were three glass counters with wooden frames. The glass top on the nearest one was cracked right across and they were all filthy dirty. The varnish on the frames was peeling, scratched and generally in very poor condition. One of the wooden corners was split.

'I have only got the three not the four you wanted,' Joseph said.

Tim started to speak, 'I don't think they are what—'

His father jumped in, interrupting him, 'Beggars can't be choosers son. What's your best price, Joseph?'

The store owner stroked his beard and after a moment named a price. Tom Cooper said, 'That price obviously includes renewal of the broken panel.' Joseph smiled and knocked a couple of pounds off.

At that moment there was a growing thunder from overhead that grew to be a rhythmic cacophony. Joseph Gold mouthed, 'Train,' at them. The vibration generated a fall of fine dust.

When they could hear themselves speak again, 'Dad they are too old,' Tim observed.

'They are grim,' agreed Harry.

'Now hold on fellas. I tell you what, I will do them up and if they are not satisfactory, I will pay you for them, and I should point out that Joseph is being very generous.' His father's voice indicating his annoyance at their response.

They loaded the counters into the van after Mrs Gold had brushed off a lot of the dirt. They were very cramped all sitting in the front seats on the way back, the coffee had been very welcome.

Tim was distracted and quiet on the way home, certain that they had wasted their money. His father noticed Tim's mood and urged him not to worry.

A week later Tim had still not seen the counters his father was supposed to be restoring. One evening Tim went across the road to check on progress. He was surprised when he found the door locked and the lights out. He knocked on the door and waited. Nobody came so he knocked again. He heard some movement and then the door was opened. As he stepped inside the bright new lights came on and Tim saw the counters in position. His father had done a splendid job; the broken top had been replaced and all the glass shone in the light. As he walked towards the nearest counter, he became aware of his father standing beside the gleaming newly varnished woodwork.

Tim, speaking to his father said, 'I owe you an apology, they are superb.'

His father smiled and Mr Woodman, having followed Tim's father downstairs patted Tom Cooper on the back saying, 'Well done Mr Cooper.'

'Tim, shall I see if Harry and his wife can come around this evening, so they can see it?' asked his father.

Tim, nodded.

The couple arrived some twenty minutes later. Harry apologised and said that it had been hard to convince Sara to come. Her look of rebuke aimed at her husband clearly indicated there had been words spoken before they arrived. She took no part in the discussion unless asked a direct question and then she replied in a soft quiet voice with her gentle Italian accent.

Harry marched about the shop looking at the counters and the new lighting and then, throwing his arms wide, said loudly, 'Lady and gentleman, I think this business might fly.'

The date of the opening had just been placed in the local papers so now they were committed.

*

As they were leaving the shop his father turned to him and said, 'Have you eaten, Tim? I need to talk to you, how about I treat you to fish and chips?'

Later, sitting in the fish restaurant his father said, 'Tim, lad, I have things I need to say, please do not interrupt me until I have finished. I need to get this off my chest. I owe you an enormous apology, lad. I shall never forgive myself for how I treated you after your mum died.' Sensing Tim was about to interrupt he held his hand up to silence him. 'I need to explain some things. Your mum was very much like my mum. Both very strong women. Your mum regimented my life in the same way as my mother had, go there, sit here, do this, do that. She did all the paperwork for the business and the house. Sometimes I complained, but in fact it made my life easier. When I lost her, I was cast adrift, rudderless. All the decisions I was asked to make just overwhelmed me. Everything seemed pointless. I know you tried to help me, Tim lad, but I just couldn't do it. I wanted to go away and hide. All the paperwork that flooded in, I didn't understand most of it.' Thrusting both hands out in front of him this time palms up he said, 'These are the clever parts of me, Tim, I can build almost anything with these, I am not an academic or a pen pusher, lad.'

In the ensuing silence he admitted to himself that for a long time he had blamed Tim for his wife's death having put a jinx on her by asking if she had died, this upset him whenever he thought of it, it was a terrible thing to have done. This was one fact he would never share with anyone. Continuing he said, 'Tim, I also realise that on occasion I took my loss out on you, I shall always feel terrible about that. I am very sorry, lad. I hope that given time you can forgive me. I wish I had been stronger, better able to cope but I couldn't.'

While his father was speaking, Tim had a memory of his dad sitting at the kitchen table opening the post, having read it he would pass it to his wife asking, 'What do you make of that?'

Scanning it quickly, explaining it briefly, she would then say, 'Leave it with me,' and place it on the dresser.

Tim could also remember neighbours tapping on the back door carrying something that had fallen apart or was broken and his mother telling them to leave it, 'Tom will fix it.'

Tim reached out and took his father's hand. For the first time he had some small idea of the loss his father had suffered. Whenever he thought of Sophie he was filled by a strange longing, a kind of ever-present ache that was always there just under the surface.

The next morning Tim was opening his post when he recognised his great aunt's handwriting. As he pulled the letter out of the envelope a cheque fell onto the floor. He bent down to retrieve it, then unfolded it and was struck dumb. He read the attached letter.

Dear Timothy

Your father has written to me and told me about your new venture. He is obviously very enthusiastic about it; indeed, it would appear to have given him a new interest in life generally. I have been worried about him for years. You are to be commended for having wrought this change in him. I would very much like to come and see what you have done when it is finished. Your partners in this enterprise would appear to be very experienced and sound people. I believe the mixture of experience and youth can be a very powerful combination. I know that any new business consumes money at a frightening rate, so I have included a cheque for £500. It is a gift, so you do not have to repay me. When you open the shop can you let me know the date and the name of the shop so that I may tell my friends? I wish you every success.

With much love.

Victoria

Tim was dumfounded. He reread the letter, looked at the cheque again. He knew that his great aunt was not poor. She was a strong-minded lady and Tim realised that she would not have done this on a whim, but only after considerable thought. He recognised that she was from a different age, he could imagine her working with other members of the privileged classes building the British Empire. People would be wrong to underestimate this short Victorian-looking lady.

Her strength of will, her intellect and her determination made her a formidable adversary.

She had always promised Tim that he was her sole beneficiary and had shown him where to find her will after her death. Unlike many people she was very clear about what she wanted for her funeral and the manner of the disposition of her estate.

Tim sat down at his small table and wrote a reply, he explained how much he appreciated what she had done and how opportune it was. He informed her of the date of the grand opening and the address and name of the shop. He would explain why the shop was called Sophie's when he saw her. He signed off his letter thanking her for her enormous generosity with very many thanks and much love.

Harry and Mr Woodman were stunned when he told them.

Charlie wrote 'Sophie's' above the shop window. Tim was very moved when he saw it. He walked a little way up the street and stood looking out at the river, not really seeing it.

Harry spotted him and walked over, put his hand on his shoulder and gently shook it. 'I can't think of anything to say, lad, but if ever you want to talk just say so.'

Tim thanking Harry cleared his throat a couple of times blew his nose and together they walked back to the shop.

One of the last jobs Harry and Tim did before the big day was to close down the stalls and end the rental.

When all was cleared away, Harry, looking at the floor space where his stall once stood, mused, 'I wonder how many thousands of hours I have stood there over the years?'

'Think on, Harry, now you get to stand indoors.'

CHAPTER 7

THE GRAND OPENING

The days before the opening kept all three men very busy, there seemed to always be one more thing to do. Harry's wife brought a nice feminine touch to the shop dressing it with flowers and advising on the displays of food.

She had suggested strings of garlic hanging from the ceiling above the counters, smoked hams hanging on hooks from the shelves. There was a range of continental sausage on white trays on the glass shelves on display. A large machine in bright chrome with a wicked looking circular blade to slice ham stood on one counter, prosciutto and other meats stood on a shelf behind. Next, in a similar fashion to his old stall there was a display of different cheeses both English and imported, there was a choice of pasta and rice. There were jars of pesto, sun-dried tomatoes in olive oil and a range of pickles. The different varieties of foreign food continued over the next two counters.

'Harry,' said Sara almost whispering in her soft, attractive Italian accent, with eyes closed, a smile on her face and drawing a long breath in, she said, 'I am back home in Italy in the shop on the corner of our street; it smells the same; I can see our neighbours' faces and Roberto the shop keeper. It is wonderful.'

Sara had furnished their counter with a beautiful array of confectionery including two new examples of her remarkable skills. One shaped like a seashell the other a chocolate horse chestnut, half shelled, in two colours.

It was decided that each person who visited the shop on opening day would be offered a free glass of wine and a taster of the different foods.

The night before the opening they all stood in the shop looking at the displays and checking to see if anything else needed doing. Tim was so pleased with the way the shop looked. The food looked terrific, the flowers were beautiful, the glass counters and the white paint bounced the light around and made the whole shop sparkle. Mr Woodman had fitted a thick navy removable rope with polished brass ends with hooks across the bottom of the stairs that looked very smart but barred entry to his flat.

Tim remained after the others had gone home to bed.

Mr Woodman noticed him lost in thought. Resting his hand on Tim's shoulder he said, 'A penny for them, lad.'

'Oh sorry,' he said coming to, 'I was just wishing I could show Sophie this.'

'You are still missing her aren't you, Tim?'

'She is always there,' he replied, 'I hear her voice, I see her face, I search for her in the street, it hurts, Mr Woodman.'

'Tim, it never goes away, but it does get easier with time.'

Tim slept little that night. At first light he got up, dressed, and not up to facing breakfast set off for a walk. The weather gave promise of a nice day. As always when he wanted to think he walked by the river. It was already busy, commercial craft ploughing their way through the water. A rowing eight sliding along with their coach pedalling hard on his old bike trying to keep up. Tim was always struck by the precision of the oarsmen as they pulled and then feathered their blades on the backstroke. He suddenly realised he had walked a long way during his musings, he turned around and started back.

9 am arrived, the advertised time of the opening, there were a few people

waiting. By ten o'clock the shop was heaving. Tim could hardly hear himself think.

Tim's great aunt arrived mid-afternoon by taxi with a small group of friends. Tim introduced them to his partners and Sara.

His great aunt spotted Tim's father and said, 'I am amazed at how much better you look, Tom.'

He just smiled and thanked her and then found chairs for the elderly ladies. Soon, after a short rest and a glass of wine the unknown fare on offer drew them from their chairs and they soon became busy tasting small samples of the various delicacies.

Tim's great aunt Victoria took him aside and said how impressed she was, 'Please don't think me rude, Timothy, but it far exceeds all my expectations. I think you will have to do quite a bit of advertising, but it deserves to succeed.'

Tim thanked her for her kind words and promised to take on board what she had said. Hugging her he thanked her again for her generosity.

In the late afternoon after his great aunt had left, Tim was talking to his father when he had a real shock. Mr Murdoch the bank manager walked in. Tim told his father who he was and said, 'Please come and meet him.'

After the introductions Tim explained that the stall that had been across the road was originally his father's, but he had handed it on to him. He momentarily left the two of them talking while he rounded up his partners to come and talk to the bank manager. Mr Murdoch asked some very penetrating questions whilst drinking his glass of wine then he said, 'If you would like to come and have a chat, we can look at how the bank may be of service to you.' Shaking hands all round he left.

At six o'clock they started to tidy away the chairs prior to closing when a group of very well dressed rather loud young people walked in. The women were clothed in bright coloured dresses and skirts with expensive shoes, the men in sharp suits and striped shirts with cufflinks. They made straight for the free wine but then the wives began buying in good quantities. It soon became apparent that the group were well travelled and already knew about foreign food.

Tim recognised one of the couples as former customers. He went and said hallo and as he stepped forward to shake the woman's hand, he recognised her perfume. He experienced a brutally sharp emotional shock, he felt as though he had been punched. A deep sense of loss overtook him. It was the scent Sophie had been wearing on the day they had met. In his mind's eye he could see Sophie sitting watching the river. He excused himself and stepped away tidying some boxes while he recovered. Surely, he thought, he would not have to experience this awful emotional pain for the rest of his life.

For the next two hours the shop was busy with this much younger age group. At eight thirty it began to go quiet again. They finally closed the doors just before nine. This late-night surge had given Tim an idea, but he was not going to discuss it until they had all had some sleep. They all said goodnight and Mr Woodman shut the door behind them.

Tim walked home, stripped his clothes off and pulled the blankets up and fell asleep almost instantly. His last thoughts were of the girl and her wearing Sophie's perfume and an image of Sophie laughing at something he had said.

The following morning Tim woke with a start. He had slept through the alarm. Scrambling from his bed he had a quick wash and a shave and without breakfast left for the shop. The weather was trying to make up for the previous long period of sunshine: a large cardboard box flew past him; someone's side gate was banging backwards and forwards; a swirl of leaves was blown high into the air. When Tim reached the river, he could see the waves on the surface being hurried along by the strengthening wind; when he was just a few paces from his destination down came the rain. He began to run, but by the time he got there he was soaked.

Harry met him at the door and said, 'Morning.'

Tim apologised for being late.

'Don't worry, the only person who has been in was the owner of that restaurant in Dollis Hill. He wished us luck.'

'I hope we don't need it,' replied Tim.

The two men stood watching as the force of the rain intensified. You could no longer see across the river and the rain was now bouncing back off the pavement. Unheard over the noise of the storm Mr Woodman had come downstairs to join them. The sky grew darker and the wind stronger. A great spear of lightning struck something across the river and was immediately followed by a heart stopping clap of thunder. All three men jumped.

Few people came into the shop during the afternoon.

'While it's quiet,' said Tim, 'I would like to talk to you both about an idea I have had. I noticed last night that there was a good number of late-night customers that spent a fair bit of cash. I think it may be worthwhile staying open later. I would like to try it tonight, what do think?'

'How often would you do it?' asked Harry.

'How late would you stay open?' enquired Mr Woodman.

Tim thought for a moment, 'Um, every night until about eight or eight thirty.

What do you think?'

Harry made a face and pulled on his ear lobe, 'Sara has already asked can we spend more time together now the shop is up and running. I don't think she will agree to me working evenings as well.'

'Sorry Tim,' said Mr Woodman, 'I don't want to work evenings.'

'No, no, no, I didn't expect you two to do it, I meant me. I might as well be here as anywhere. Do you mind if I try it?'

Both men shook their heads.

Mr Woodman came downstairs at 8 o'clock and said, 'Was it just the one customer, Tim?'

'Yes, it needs some advertising, I will call into the newspaper offices tomorrow.' Tim came away from the newspaper's office quite pleased with himself. The proprietor Mr Jobson was a jolly round little man with a red waistcoat stretched across a very rotund stomach. He had peered at Tim across the top of a pair of round lensed glasses perched on the end of his nose. He was bald on top with bushy wild hair either side of his head and rosy cheeks.

Tim explained what he required. After some discussion it was agreed that Tim would pay for the smallest advert, but the paper would enter it the next size up for one year. Tim hoped the advert would make a difference.

When he arrived back at the shop, he was very surprised by all the activity. Sara and Harry were positioning a table outside the shop window. As Tim crossed the road Sara threw a pale blue and white check tablecloth across the table. Mr Woodman came out of the shop carrying a range of glass jars and small trays.

Tim, wondering what was happening said, 'Good morning everyone.'

Sara turned towards him and said, 'I hope you don't mind, Tim, but last night I could not sleep, and I suddenly had an idea.'

'She woke me at 4 am,' grumbled Harry.

Sara put a restraining hand on Harry's arm.

'Let me tell him please. I think people look at the empty space where the stalls were and think you two have closed or gone away. I thought we could replace the stall outside the shop. People are more likely to see it.'

Tim stepped close to her and hugged her. 'What a brilliant idea,' he said and kissed her cheek. Sara blushed bright red and smiled. For the first time Tim recognised that although she was in her middle years, she was still a very attractive woman.

'Harry,' said Tim, 'you're a very lucky man, beauty and brains all in one package.'

Sara's blush deepened.

She had arranged her confectionery on one side of the table and some jars and bottles from the delicatessen counter on the other. Whilst she was putting the final touches to the display a small group of women gathered around the table and started discussing the various items.

One of the women, completely oblivious of Sara's presence said, 'My husband wouldn't eat that, he says it's foreign muck.'

Her companion nudged her in the ribs and nodded at Sara.

Another lady said to Sara, 'What do olives taste like?'

Without thinking Sara whipped the lid from a bottle of green olives stuffed with pimento and said, 'Try one.' All but one of the women did.

One lady covered her mouth and spat the half-chewed olive in the kerb. Quick as a flash Sara offered one of her sweets to take the taste away. At the same time out of the corner of her eye she saw the rude woman take another olive. Three of the women went into the shop and came out later with small bags of goods. They called goodbye to Sara and went off commenting on the contents of the shop. For most of the afternoon there was a small group of people around the table which generated a trickle of customers entering the shop.

'Can I go home now?' asked Sara at five o'clock. The men were suddenly aware that she had been on her feet all day.

Tim apologised saying, 'That was a very clever idea, Sara, and giving people tasters is clearly the right way to go. Especially as the foods are new to them.'

Later Tim and Harry had a discussion over Sara's hours. 'She won't complain,' explained Harry, 'but, she is not getting any younger and I worry about her.'

'Would she do a couple of hours at lunch time Harry?' asked Tim. 'That will give us time to take it in turns for lunch and have a brief rest.'

'I will ask her,' he replied.

The following week improved weather-wise day by day and the custom with it. The following Saturday dawned bright and clear. Tim, woken very early by the sunlight was standing watching the early morning traffic on the river. His attention was taken by movement at the foot of the wall. It was a mother duck followed by a line of ducklings bobbing up and down on the waves. His mind went back to a year earlier when last year's brood had been pointed out to him. Taking a long breath he strode away to work.

CHAPTER 8

SOPHIE FINDS THE SHOP

Sophie had spent the day with an old school friend. Her camel hair coat was open, the day had turned warmer than she expected. The fur collar on her coat was a mixture of golds that complimented her shoulder length blonde hair. The round necked angora wool top flattered her figure. It matched the colour of her coat as did the tailored calf-length skirt. Her stockings were a very pale sand, her shoes were light tan patent leather with a dark Cuban heel. The only jewellery she wore was a tiny set of pearl earrings and a small pearl necklace.

As she walked back to the station, she realised that she was close to the river and Tim's stall. Thinking back, she was surprised when she worked it out that their meeting was almost a year ago. Sophie once again experienced the same sense of loss when he came to mind. She was sure that on that evening she had spent with him there had been a mutual attraction. Her disappointment that it had not developed into anything was still with her. She was puzzled as to why this had not happened.

She stopped walking for a moment, undecided, then curious to know if he was still there, she set off. I can make sure he doesn't see me, she thought. Arriving at the river she turned into the street with the stalls, she saw that Tim's stall was missing. Harry's stall was there but it had changed, there was a stranger selling crockery. Not quite sure what her emotions were, she turned and crossed the street.

Then she saw the name, her name, 'Sophie's', on the shop opposite. She was completely confused, her mind was in turmoil, she was incapable of logical thought.

Curiosity drew her across the road and into the shop doorway. It took a moment for her eyes to adjust, then she saw Tim at the back of the shop.

Tim looked up and saw Sophie, bathed in a golden glow. It looked as though she had captured the sun itself. Tim was deaf and blind, for him the world was silent, he could not hear the customers or the cars passing in the road outside. His whole being was focused on the image in the doorway that was giving off light.

Their eyes met and she panicked. Turning around she started to hurry away down the street. She felt such a fool. Memories of her meeting with Kate whilst he was away came flooding back. Kate had clearly indicated that she and Tim were an item. It was months since they had seen each other, he had almost certainly forgotten about her. With her face flaming with embarrassment she hurried away.

Tim was shocked into immobility for a few seconds, then, gathering himself, and apologising to his customer ran from the shop and sped after her calling her name.

Sophie, hearing his voice broke into a run, then realising she could not outrun him stopped and turned to face him. Both were out of breath.

Sophie started to apologise for calling into the shop and embarrassing him. 'I did not intend that you should see me,' she said, 'I saw my name and, and, I was drawn in. I will walk away now, and you can forget this ever happened.'

Tim struggling to get his breath back waved her apology away. 'Can we talk,' he panted, 'would you like to find a café, or shall we walk?'

'Walk please,' she replied.

Tim explained to Sophie that he had lost the piece of paper in the railway station and that after he had come back from his buying trip, he had visited the station a few times in the hope of seeing her.

'When you did not ring me, I went to the stall and met Kate,' explained Sophie.

'She made it sound as though you were a couple. I was rather confused. You had asked me for my phone number, and she was telling me you were in a relationship. I did not know what to think.'

Clearly annoyed, he pulled a face and said, 'I went out with her a few times three years ago, nothing since, she works for me occasionally.'

Tim related how he had chased after the train trying to get her attention and had been tackled by a huge railway guard who threw him to the ground and called him a mouthful of very rude names. 'I realised later I'd scared him.'

'I visited the railway station at the same time I met you to see if I could find you. I began to believe I would never see you again. I was very upset; I have stopped some women in the street that I thought were you.'

Now he was so scared, so frightened of saying the wrong thing and driving her away. Then he continued, 'I saw you in the shop doorway, I couldn't believe it, and then you ran away.'

'I saw my name on the shop front; I was really shocked; I did not know what to think. Was it a coincidence? Whose shop was it? Was it named after me? Suddenly I was standing in the shop doorway staring at you; I was terribly confused. Then when you saw me, I was so embarrassed I panicked.'

Turning to him and looking up into his face she asked, 'Did you name the shop after me?'

'Yes.'

'Why?'

'Can't you guess?' he asked.

Sophie shook her head looking very young.

'I have missed you every day since the night we met.'

Sophie stopped and looked into his eyes seeking confirmation of what he had just said. They walked on in silence for a while in the golden evening light.

Sophie slipped her hand into his. Tim was overjoyed. He looked down and saw that Sophie had tears in the corner of her eyes. He hugged her and apologised for upsetting her. They wandered on exchanging information about themselves, especially the phone numbers, and friends and family.

CHAPTER 9

THE RESTAURANT

'Shall we eat somewhere?' she asked. 'I have had nothing since lunch.'

'Oh heck,' he said coming to a standstill.

'Whatever is wrong?' Sophie asked.

'We will have to go back to the shop,' said Tim. My wallet is in my work coat.

She burst out laughing. Tim was frantically checking his pockets for the third time very disturbed and very red in the face.

'I will buy dinner,' she said, through her laughter.

'It must only be a loan,' said Tim.

'Do not worry,' smiled Sophie, 'although perhaps we should not tell my parents.'

'I will repay you,' he promised.

Passing a phone box, he remembered he had raced out of the shop without so much as a by your leave.

'I had better ring the shop,' he said.

Sophie followed him into the box and stood watching the river through the glass, obviously deep in thought while he dialled the number. Mr Woodman answered the phone. Sophie slipped her arms through his and stood close to him.

Looking down at her he whispered, 'This is nice,' she smiled up at him. 'What's nice?' asked Mr Woodman.

'Sorry you were not supposed to hear that. I am sorry I left you in the lurch. I am with Sophie now and we are going for a meal, is that ok? Can you manage without me or should I come back?'

'We are fine, Tim, is Sophie alright?'

'They want to know if you are alright?' he asked, looking into her upturned face for confirmation.

Sophie smiling nodded vigorously.

'She's fine, thank you.'

Replacing the phone he went to leave, Sophie had not moved away, she still had her face tilted up to him. Tim moved in very slowly. The kiss started off as a tender touch of their lips but then it deepened. His arms went around her waist, her hands found his neck and her fingers were in his hair as she leant into him.

Suddenly there was a rude knocking on the glass of the phone box. Breaking apart they found an angry old man wearing a long black overcoat and a brown trilby rapping on the phone box with his black walking stick.

As they were sidling out the box the old boy said in a loud stern voice, 'This is not the place for that malarkey.' Tim apologised; Sophie was giggling.

Sophie led Tim to a small French restaurant by the river. It was down some old stone steps with ornate black wrought iron railings. Each step had a red geranium in the left corner. There were dark wood tables and chairs outside with deep maroon canopies over them.

The maître de recognised Sophie and showed them to a table inside overlooking the water.

The sun flooded the floor with light, casting interesting shadows under the chairs and tables.

White china sat upon a dark maroon tablecloth, he noticed the china and the cutlery all carried a tiny image of the house name.

The low ceiling crossed by dark oak beams gave a clue to the age of the restaurant.

Tim was very uncomfortable, 'Sophie,' he whispered, 'I can't afford somewhere like this. You need to know before we go any further, I am just keeping my head above water with the shop.'

Sophie realised how genuine was his discomfort and embarrassment. She leant across the table, took his hand and said very quietly, 'We will split the bill. It is a celebration of our reunion.'

What Sophie could not know was that Tim was always first to the bar to buy the drinks or pay for the food. He despised those who hung back waiting for others to pay or queried every penny on a food bill.

The waiter arrived to take their drinks order. Sophie settled for a glass of rosé and Tim a glass of house red. The food was excellent, and the conversation flowed easily with lots of laughter; there were no uncomfortable moments as there had been on dates with other women.

Tim looked at his watch and said, 'Goodness me, we had better get you home, it will be dark soon.

'I suppose so,' agreed Sophie. He hailed a taxi and as it pulled up to the kerb Sophie wound her arms around his neck, pulled him close and kissed him hard. After a few moments the taxi driver pipped his horn and Sophie reluctantly broke the embrace.

'Crickey,' said Tim his senses reeling.

'I will ring you tomorrow,' said Sophie as she swung her pretty legs into the taxi.

As the vehicle pulled away, he stood waving until it went from sight. Tim walked home unaware of the distance or the detail of the walk, his head full of the way Sophie felt in his arms and the wonderful warm smell of her. A mixture of her perfume and her womanhood. He was the happiest he had been for many years.

Walking down one quiet street Tim suddenly shouted, 'Hey, hey, hey,' out loud, his joy needing an outlet.

An old man walking his dog down the dark street crossed the road and hurried past on the other side, watching Tim out of the corner of his eye. The rapid tap, tap, tap, of his walking stick indicating the speed of his passage. Tim ran the rest of the way home. He lay awake a long time that night eventually falling asleep with a smile on his face.

✳

The next morning, a Saturday, a fine rain was falling as Tim walked to work, he hardly noticed. He was whistling as he walked in through the shop door.

Mr Woodman was up early and busy as usual sweeping the shop. He stopped and leaning on the broom with his hands cupped under his chin looked at Tim and said, 'You're in good form.'

'I certainly am, Mr Woodman,' he replied. 'I certainly am.'

The shop was slowly growing busier and much to the three men's relief they were kept gently occupied all day. Sophie had rung in the morning and said she would come around after work. Tim warned her he would be staying until late. 'Not to worry,' she replied, 'it will give us a chance to talk.'

Sara turned up at lunch time. At the end of her two-hour stint she approached Tim.

'May I have a word please, Mr Tim, if you are not too busy?'

'Of course Sara, what is it?'

'I have had an idea,' she replied. 'Most English people know nothing about continental cooking. I wondered if you would mind if I put some recipes together on how to prepare meals using your goods. Please tell me if you think it is a silly idea.'

'It's a very clever idea, but it is our goods,' responded Tim. 'You are a major contributor.' Sara's blush was back. 'How would you do that?' he asked.

'I thought maybe there could be cards pinned on the wall, just two or three at a time.'

'That's a very clever idea, Sara, can I suggest some small printed paper versions for the customers to take away with them. Let me know how much you spend, and I will reimburse you.'

'Thank you, Tim, I will show them to you before I put them up.'

CHAPTER 10

SOPHIE AT THE SHOP

Sophie arrived as promised at five-forty-five clutching a bag of food. Walking into the shop she was met by Mr Woodman saying, 'Good evening, how can I help you?'

'I am here to see Tim.'

Mr Woodman, his intuition working overtime, said, 'You must be Sophie.'

'Yes, she is,' exclaimed Harry as he walked across the shop towards her. He engulfed her outstretched hand in his two large ones and shook it vigorously. His Italian accent growing stronger than ever, Harry said, 'This is a surprise, how wonderful to see you.' Releasing her hand, he turned and called excitedly, 'Tim, Tim, look who's here.'

In the meantime Mr Woodman shook Sophie's hand saying, 'Welcome, I feel I know a lot about you from what Tim has told me. What's this, coals to Newcastle?' he asked noticing the bag of food and peering inside.

Sophie laughed, 'I was not sure if I was allowed to eat the profits.'

'You couldn't do that anyway,' laughed Tim from the back, 'there aren't any.'

Sophie walked down the shop and gave Tim a quick kiss.

Mr Woodman said, 'Well I never did,' pretending to be shocked.

'Don't look, Mr Woodman,' called Harry laughing.

Sophie, bright red in the face again said, 'I am sorry if I embarrassed you.'

Harry said, 'You are Italian, we Italians kiss people anywhere and everywhere.'

'Would you like a cup of tea, Sophie?' asked a still smiling Mr Woodman.

'Yes please,' called Tim.

'I will make us all one,' Mr Woodman replied.

Later that evening the young couple, with the place to themselves, sat at the back of the shop on two hard wooden stools, their knees touching, sharing the picnic Sophie had brought.

'This is very nice,' she said.

'Not quite as grand as last night,' responded Tim. 'I had better start paying for some food before you begin to believe I'm only after your money.'

'I know you are not,' said Sophie, with a frown on her face and a serious tone to her voice.

Tim noticed the change in her but was unable to question her further as a customer arrived asking if the shop was open.

'Please, come in,' said Tim, 'what would you like?' Soon more customers arrived, and Tim became quite busy.

'Tim, can I help?' asked Sophie.

'No, I will be fine, you have a rest.'

'Tim, I have worked in a shop since I was young, honestly, I would like to help.'

'Well if you are sure you don't mind,' he replied. 'There is Sara's apron hanging on the back door. Use that so you don't spoil your suit.'

Moments later she was standing behind the counter and saying to the customer,

'You are my very first customer, I do not know where anything is but let us see what I can do for you.'

For the next hour with Tim's guidance she quickly began to find her way around the shop. The male customers were clearly awestruck by her looks and charisma, the ladies liked her general demeanour and desire to please.

Just before closing one well-spoken young man asked Sophie if she would go out with him?

She replied by saying, 'Thank you for the invitation but I have a boyfriend and he is standing over there,' pointing at Tim.

The young man whom Tim suspected had perhaps had a drink too many, turned to him and said, 'I hope you realise how very lucky you are, sir.' With that he picked up his purchases and left the shop.

As the door closed Tim said, 'I certainly do, sir.'

Sophie gave him a little curtsey. A short while later Mr Woodman came downstairs as he heard Tim tidying up the shop.

Sophie asked, 'Where is the loo, please?'

Mr Woodman said, 'There is one out the back, but it's cold out there, come upstairs and use mine.'

When she came back out of the toilet Mr Woodman said to her, 'I was very worried about Tim when he thought he had lost you. He lost a lot of weight and had no interest in anything except work.'

'I had noticed he looked thinner,' she replied.

'He loves you very much.'

'I know he does,' she replied.

When they got downstairs Tim asked what were they talking about? 'Oh, this and that,' responded Mr Woodman.

Tim smiled and nodded.

'I have had a wonderful evening,' Sophie said.

'Really? I was wondering if I should cancel the late-night opening because you would find it boring.'

'No, please do not do that, I never get to work on the shop floor anymore and I miss the interaction with the customers. I have had a great time, but now I am going to have to go, I have a really early start in the morning.'

Mr Woodman said, 'I will finish up, Tim, you can walk Sophie to her taxi.' They exchanged goodnights and the couple walked to the taxi rank.

As they strolled along, Sophie with her arm through his explained that she would not be able to see him tomorrow as there was a big do at work in the evening and her father would expect her to be there.

There was quite a crowd at the taxi rank. Standing in silence, very close together, he felt her shiver, pulling her inside his overcoat she reciprocated by putting her arms around him and drew him close. Tim buried his head in her hair breathing in the essence of her, it filled all of his being, indeed it affected him so deeply he felt a little giddy.

Shortly afterwards she looked up at him with her chin on his chest saying, 'You smell very nice.'

'I was just thinking the same about you, you smell wonderful.'

A tall man behind them tapped Tim on the shoulder saying, 'Do you want this taxi or not mate?' The goodnight kiss was perfunctory and hurried, they had not realised the next taxi to arrive, would be theirs. As the cab eased away from the kerb, she leaned out of the window and waved goodbye.

The following morning Tim woke early. Drawing the curtains, he saw the day promised to be fine. After breakfast because he was early, he took a slightly longer route than normal that enabled him to walk further along the river. The early morning sun was bouncing off the water in a thousand different reflections. A flock of seagulls were performing wonderful intricate stunts above the river.

Arrowing down towards the wave tops they pulled out of the dive inches above the surface. Flying upwards again. Reaching the apex of their climb they tipped themselves on to their sides and with their wings closed repeated the previous manoeuvre. A perfect illustration of their innate skill. He could never understand how they could miss each other or why their wings did not fall off because of the G-force. He decided they did it because it was exhilarating.

After a while Tim stopped by a set of stone steps and gazed down at the water. On the downstream side of the steps a small eddy formed a relatively calm area out of the main current. The stones under the water wore a fringe of bright green weed. Looking carefully, he became aware of a small shoal of tiny fry just below the surface.

Tim was always amazed at how the shoal moved as one, keeping perfect station one with another whether they were moving or not. Glancing at his watch he suddenly realised the time had slipped by. At a brisk walk he set off for the shop. When he arrived, he found Mr Woodman up an old wooden ladder cleaning the windows.

'You shouldn't be up there doing that, Mr Woodman,' said Tim smiling as he walked past.

'Tim,' Mr Woodman replied in a firm voice, 'I have been doing this for over fifty years, I see no reason to stop now... there is tea in the pot,' he called to Tim's retreating back.

'Thank you,' responded Tim.

He was always struck by how good the inside of the shop looked on sunny days with the light streaming in through the front windows. The white paint and glass seemed to magnify the sun's intensity.

A customer came in just as Tim was finishing his tea. It was a little earlier than the usual opening time, but business was business. When he had served the customer, he found his father waiting for him.

'Hallo, Dad,' said Tim, 'it's nice to see you. Are you here for a reason or is this a social call?'

'I have an idea to discuss with you, well with all three of you but I think it needs to be after work if that's ok?'

All three men nodded; Harry reminded him that the shop was open later in the evening now.

'That's not a problem,' said Mr Cooper, 'I'll see you later,' he called as he made his way to the door. 'Will I get to meet the lovely Sophie tonight?' he asked Tim.

'It didn't take them long to let that cat out of the bag,' said Tim in a loud voice. Mr Woodman and Harry laughed.

'No, Dad, she is working for her father this evening.'

Tim and his dad stood for a while outside the shop. Tim promised to bring Sophie round as soon as he could.

'I will look forward to that, see you later, lad.'

He reappeared just after seven-thirty accompanied by Harry who had been home for his dinner. Tim was busy with a couple of customers when the phone rang.

'Shall I get that, Tim?' called his father.

'Yes, please,' replied Tim. He realised a couple of minutes later that his father was still on the phone. 'Who is it, Dad?' Tim asked.

'It's Sophie for you,' he replied. 'I'll take over, you come and talk to her.' As he passed his son in the middle of the shop he whispered. 'She sounds lovely.'

'She is,' confirmed Tim, slightly put out, worried that his father may have interrogated her.

'Hallo, Sophie, how are you?' Tim could hear the noise of a crowd, the occasional loud laugh and the clink of glasses.

'It is chaos here,' she said. 'I am sorry, but this conversation may be cut short. I just wanted to hear your voice.'

As if to endorse what she had said Tim heard a man's voice calling her name. 'That's my father,' she told him. 'Oh, he has spotted me. I am going to have to ring off. See you tomorrow,' she said, replacing the phone.

'Bye then,' said Tim into the dead phone; he felt very upset at the brevity of the phone call. He paused with the phone in his hand by his side then lifted the phone and looked at it and listened again hoping she might still be there. Replacing the handset in its cradle he realised that the shop was empty. He flipped the open sign over to closed and locked the shop door. He walked slowly upstairs surprised at how emotional he felt. He admitted to himself that when she was not with him, he missed her like hell.

Mr Woodman placed a cup of tea in front of him as he sat down.

'Are you alright, Tim?' he asked, noticing that Tim seemed preoccupied.

'I think so,' he replied.

CHAPTER 11

BREAD

'Can we talk about my idea now?' asked his father.

'Carry on,' said Harry encouragingly.

Tim's father explained how the son of a good friend of his had just returned from France and had been working in a boulangerie learning how to make a range of continental bread. His father had been a baker for many years and would be adding the new bread to their range. 'They would be very keen to supply us if we were interested,' he said.

'How would it work, Tom?' asked Harry, 'It would be a very early start I expect,' he added.

Tim suddenly realised how deep his love for Sophie was and that he was prepared to do anything to have her become his wife.

His father was explaining that he awoke early these days and he would be happy to come in at say, seven, and open the shop to sell the bread.

Tim was struck by the realisation that he had nowhere to live with Sophie. His landlady was a lovely person, but he couldn't see Sophie living there. He became aware that his father was talking to him.

'What do you think, Tim?' asked his father realising that Tim seemed distracted.

'Think about what?' queried Tim.

'Have you heard anything I have said?' asked his father growing angry.

'I apologise, so you want us to sell bread. What does a loaf cost?'

His father took a slip of paper from his pocket and gave them some prices.

Harry whistled, 'I don't know how we can afford it. If it doesn't sell on the day, we have to throw it away or eat it ourselves. How come it's so expensive? If you multiply those prices by say fifty loaves that is a significant amount of money.'

'Because it's all handmade,' said Tim's father, taken aback that his good idea was being challenged. 'I have thought this through. As I have said, I am happy to come in every day at seven to open the shop and receive the delivery. I expect the bread will be all gone by say 10 am and then I will go home. 'And,' said his father raising one hand, seeing that Tim was about to interrupt, 'I will work for free until the shop goes into profit. I think it's better for me to be in here helping rather than staring at the walls at home.'

'How much bread do we have to order at one time?' asked Harry, still clearly unsure.

'I don't know,' replied Tom Cooper, 'but I will find out. They have said they will deliver,' he added.

'We obviously need to know a bit more yet, Tom,' said Harry. 'Why don't we work on it together?'

'That would be good,' he agreed.

'Mr Woodman,' said Tim. 'How do you feel about the shop opening earlier?'

'That's not a problem,' he replied, 'I am always up at six myself. I will have breakfasted by seven. I can take the bread in if it's early.'

'Ok,' said Tim, 'sounds as though we have a plan.'

He apologised again to his father on the way downstairs.

'Don't worry, lad, I know you have a lot on your plate.' Outside the shop they all exchanged goodnights and went their separate ways.

*

The weeks flew by, with Tim and Sophie spending time together as often as possible. Walking in the park hand in hand on a sunny Sunday afternoon they stopped and sat on a bench.

Sophie, dressed beautifully as usual, wore a pale delphinium blue dress with a fitted bodice and a full skirt, the hem of which played around her knees as she walked. Her navy shoes, clutch bag and string of small pearls completed the ensemble.

When Sophie met Tim that morning in his white shirt, blue jeans and a mid-blue thin jumper draped across his shoulders, she commented on how well it suited him. Tim responded by saying how, as always, she looked stunning.

There were a lot of families with small children sitting on rugs and playing in the sunshine.

In minutes they were in stiches laughing at a very young child trying to play football with his brothers. It was apparent he had not long conquered the intricacies of walking as frequent tumbles bore witness. However, he refused to give up, climbing once more to his feet he tried again. A few minutes later the ball rolled towards their bench, Sophie stopped it with her foot. The little man toddled over to them and became transfixed by Tim putting one hand on his knee. The child's mother rose from the family rug and came over apologising as she did so.

Sophie reassured her saying, 'Really it is not a problem, he is lovely, what is his name?'

'Jeb,' the mother replied. 'His grandfather's name, he was American.'

'It is unusual but nice,' added Sophie. With that the mother hoisted Jeb to her hip and re-joined her family

They were both quiet, both watching the children. Tim, to his complete surprise became aware how much he wanted a family of his own. To be a dad, for Sophie to have his babies, lots of babies. On occasion he had been very lonely as an only child. Then even that was made worse by his mother's death. He visualised a home of his own, safe, warm and loving, with children to dandle on his knee and take for walks in the park. Not any children, his and Sophie's children, and her to go home to. He wanted it so badly he became frightened, he and Sophie had no agreement, had made no commitment to each other, she could leave at any time.

Interrupting his thoughts Sophie rose from the bench saying, 'Can we move on, please?'

Tim walked on a few paces, then stopping and taking her hands in his said, with a very serious expression on his face, 'I have something I must ask you.'

Sophie's brain was racing; Why does he sound so nervous? she thought. He is never nervous. Her brain stopped racing, she became sure, He is going to ask me to marry him. Wait though, he has never even hinted at anything like this yet. Oh please, please let me be right.

CHAPTER 12

THE PROPOSAL

After a long pause, looking deep into her eyes and taking a deep breath, he said, 'Will you marry me?' Hurrying on, he announced, 'I have loved you ever since we met on the train, I have no ring today, but I promise you I have never been more serious. I love you more than anything; I am terrified of losing you again; please, please say yes.' His words were tumbling over each other. His fear of refusal almost rendering him inarticulate. Much to his surprise he saw that she was laughing and crying at the same time. But she had still not answered him.

Sophie was so excited, speechless, her hands covering her nose and mouth and her feet shuffling back and forwards, she was so excited she wanted to jump in the air and shout out yes, yes, yes. With both sun and rain still showing on her face she threw her arms around his waist and cried into his chest. Her head was a maelstrom of emotions and pictures. The man she loved with all her heart and soul loved her. She experienced a kaleidoscope of pictures, white cars and roses and beautiful dresses. Babies! Babies?

Tim was starting to become alarmed, 'Is that a yes?' he whispered.

Sophie, struggling to speak, looked up, nodded vigorously then said, 'Oh yes, please,' and kissed him. They walked a few paces then she stopped again, and she kissed him very softly and said, 'I love you too.' Tim picked her up and swung her round and round and round until he gave into her pleas to stop.

'You are mad,' she said laughing as she held onto him to stop herself falling over. They walked on slowly, arms around each other, turning to him she said, 'Mrs Sophie Cooper sounds nice.' She suddenly blushed and asked, 'Am I being too forward?'

Tim laughed, 'No, you silly thing, I am the happiest man in the world.'

Thinking out loud he said, 'I would love children; I always wanted a brother, but it was not to be. I was very jealous of the boys at school that had brothers and sisters; would you like children?'

Tim was still chatting away when he realised Sophie had suddenly gone quiet.

He looked at her sideways and asked, 'Are you alright?'

She turned to face him and took his hands. 'What about my parents?' she murmured going pale as she spoke.

'What about them?'

'I think my father will be very angry,' she replied.

'I can understand that,' said Tim. 'If our daughter comes to tell me that she is going to marry a man she has just met I would blow my top.'

Sophie managed a little smile. 'I really am worried. I love my parents and I do not want to hurt them.'

'Whatever happens I can't give you up,' he reassured her, 'I have been in a black hole ever since I thought I had lost you but now I'm the happiest I have ever been. As far as I am concerned you are my life and my future.'

Looking into his eyes she witnessed the depth of feeling behind his words. 'Thank you, Tim.'

'We will give it a lot of thought but,' said Tim, 'I am not prepared to deceive anyone, especially your parents. Please don't worry, I'll do whatever it takes.'

She squeezed his hands, released them and they walked on.

The young couple spent the rest of the afternoon walking and talking, planning their future. This was interspersed with hugging and kissing.

A few days later Sophie rang Tim early in the morning. She was very distraught. He could hear the tears in her voice.

'Tim, my mother and father know about us and they are very angry. Someone recognised me in the shop and asked my father if he was paying me so little that I had to do a second job working in a shop in the evenings. I tried to explain how exciting I was finding it and how much I loved you and that we wanted to get married. He said I was a damn fool to throw my life away married to a barrow boy and sent me to my room.'

'Sophie darling, nothing on God's earth will stop me marrying you. Ask your father when I can come and talk to them both. Can you do that today, please?'

'Tim, are you sure you want to do this? My father can be really horrid.'

'Sophie, do you still want to marry me?'

'Of course I do, but Tim, you have no idea how bad this is going to be.'

As Tim got ready for work, he realised how the death of his mother had hardened him.

Things that would have caused him real distress in the past now only caused him mild concern. Whatever happened tonight would not affect his decision to marry Sophie.

Sophie rang back an hour later. 'My father will see us at eight o'clock tonight. I have never seen him so angry. I am really frightened.'

'Sophie we are meant to be together. It will all work out. See you later.'

She gave him instructions to find the house.

CHAPTER 13

THE ROW

At ten to eight that evening the taxi dropped Tim outside a huge double fronted detached house in a very expensive part of town. He realised he was a little nervous but not frightened. The street was tree lined and all the lawns and hedges were immaculately trimmed. A black cat ran across his path as he checked the name of the house on the front wall. He wondered, momentarily, whether the black cat was a good omen or not.

Confirming that it was his destination he started up the long driveway. He rang the bell and heard it chime somewhere deep in the house. The large heavy, varnished front door was opened by Sophie.

'Hallo, Sophie,' said Tim.

Before she could reply a woman's loud and authoritative voice, said, 'Sophia, her name is Sophia.'

Tim guessed that the middle-aged very attractive person striding down the hall towards them was Sophie's mother. It was obvious where Sophie got her looks from.

She stopped just in front of Tim and said, 'You must be Timothy?'

Tim replied, 'Please call me Tim, everybody does.'

'Young man, I am not everybody,' she replied in a very firm voice.

A tall angry-looking man emerged from an adjacent room at the same time as Sophie had offered Tim a cup of tea.

He growled at Sophie, 'He will not be staying that long.' Turning to Tim he said, 'Come into my office,' holding the door open for Tim to enter. Mr Vieri was clearly used to everybody doing as they were told. He followed Tim into the office; closing the door firmly behind him he said, 'Sit.' Mr Vieri could not see that Tim's face had changed. Sophie's father moved behind his desk, sat down hard in his large leather chair and asked, 'How long have you known my daughter?'

Tim said, 'I met her a year ago on a train but then we lost touch, she found me some months back.'

'And then you fell in love and decided to get married. That is absolute rubbish. I suspect that in the interim you found out how much she is worth and decided that if you got back in touch you would pursue her. How on hell's name will you be able to keep her in the style she is used to?'

'I can't, sir,' Tim responded.

With that Sophie's father opened his desk draw, pulled out a cheque book, slammed the drawer shut and said, 'How much do you want to go away? How about a thousand pounds?'

Tim, with his voice betraying his own anger and before he had given it any thought said, 'I don't want your money, sir. In fact, it might be a good idea if you disinherit her because as sure as there is a God in heaven, I will marry her.'

Leaping from his chair Mr Vieri stood opposite Tim and shouted in his face whilst pointing at the door.

'Get out of my house you arrogant little—'

Sophie's father was stopped from using whatever expletive he was going to choose because Sophie entered the room in hysterics. Her mother unable to restrain her.

'Please, please, stop,' Sophie cried. 'I cannot stand it, Father. I love him. I have never been surer of anything in my life and if you throw him out, I will go with him.'

Tim said, 'Sophie you must stay, this must be done properly.'

'But Tim I want to be with you.'

'We will be together, Sophie, I promise, but not like this,' his own anger was very apparent.

Mrs Vieri was going to correct him again over Sophie's name but, when their eyes met, and she saw the terrible rage that he was struggling to contain, it silenced her.

Her father ordered Sophie to her room. She turned on him like a wild cat saying, 'I hate you, and by the way you can stick your job, I resign.' She kissed Tim on the cheek and left the lounge.

Tim, his anger a fire roaring within him, left the room, strode down the hall and out of the front door, calling, 'Goodnight, Mrs Vieri,' over his shoulder and, using great restraint closed the front door quietly behind him, overcoming the desire to slam it.

He strode away down the drive. Tim said aloud to himself, 'I'm arrogant, what the bloody hell does that make him?'

A little later he found himself standing in the middle of a bridge over the river. With his elbows on the parapet and his head sunk between his shoulders he stood watching the water rush by underneath. The pavements were wet and cold. The icy rain running down his neck chilled him. The night was very dark. The yellow streetlamps hardly made any difference. He could see no way forward, no way of undoing what had happened a little earlier.

His train of thought was interrupted by a scruffy little old man reeking of drink who asked, 'You alright, son? I hope you aren't gonna do nuffink silly. Go home to bed, lad, it'll all look better in the mornin.'

Tim gave him half a crown. The old man promptly dropped it because his hands were shaking so badly. While he was retrieving it, Tim walked away.

'Thank you, lad. It'll turn out awright you'll see.' The old man called after him.

Without turning around Tim waved a high goodbye above his head and made for his digs.

CHAPTER 14

SOPHIE'S JOB

Tim had little sleep that night. He finally drifted off as the early dawn light slipped in through a gap in the curtains. His alarm clock woke him two hours later. Tim staggered from his bed and into the bathroom. He saw himself in the mirror, his red eyes and sallow complexion were indicators of the night just gone. He washed and shaved and not wanting breakfast set off for work. The phone rang as he let himself in through the shop door. It was Sophie.

'I am so sorry about last night. I am dreadfully embarrassed that he behaved so badly. I knew it was going to be difficult, but I did not expect it to be like that. Did you get any sleep?'

'Not much, you?'

'No, I lay wondering how we are going to sort it out.'

'How was it this morning?' asked Tim.

'Huh, he tapped on my door this morning and said I needed to hurry up or I would be late for work. I reminded him that I had resigned, and I would not therefore be going to work with him this or any other morning.'

'What did he say?' asked Tim.

'He told me not to be so ridiculous and that he would be leaving for work in half an hour and I needed to get a move on.'

'And did you?'

'No, he came back upstairs banged on the door and said, "Are you ready?"' I opened my bedroom door still in my night clothes.'

Tim gave a short half laugh and asked, 'So what then?'

'He told me I was a damn fool and went to work. Mother has asked if she and I can discuss this whole ghastly situation, my words not hers. She referred to it as a "little difficulty" and then went on to say she felt sure that if she and I talked it through I would see sense. You can guess what she meant by seeing sense. I am going to get up and make some phone calls, see what I am worth and find out if anyone will employ me.'

'Sophie, please don't do anything rash. I am sure your father will come around.'

'No, Tim, the amount of responsibility he heaps on me at work and then he still treats me like a ten-year-old. I am a twenty-four-year-old woman and I am damn good at what I do. I am pretty sure I am not paid what I should be. One of our biggest competitors has said more than once if ever I wanted a change, I was to ring him. I am going to call him this morning.'

Sophie rang again in the late afternoon.

'Tim, I have been offered a superb job.' He could hear her bubbling with excitement. 'I rang that chap who owns the other store and he said he would very much like to chat. As I was not at work, why not today. Apparently, he was going to give me another ring in the very near future.'

'What will you be doing for him?' enquired Tim.

'Tim, you will not believe it,' replied Sophie, growing ever more excited. 'His present financial director is retiring. Apparently, he has a cottage in the South of France and he and his wife are going to retire there.'

'So, you will take over from him?'

'Well the plan is for me to shadow this chap until he retires and if I shape up, I will be offered the directorship.'

Tim went to say something, but she continued, 'And, and,' she said, 'the money will be about two thousand a year more than I am earning now and if I get offered the directorship the money is negotiable. I told you my father was paying me peanuts.'

He thought to himself, I wish I was earning the two thousand let alone the rest. 'Sophie, what does your father say?'

'I have not told him yet. Obviously, that is going to be difficult. Mr Wells, the owner of the store has suggested that I offer to work a month's notice starting tomorrow rather than just walking away.'

'Have you decided to take the job?'

'I have, I talked it through with Mother and she said I must take it. Working for Father I would never really know what I was capable of. This way if I succeed it will all be down to me. The only negative for us, Tim, is as Mother said, this chap, meaning you, might not want to put up with only seeing me now and then.'

Sophie continued, 'The hours will be long whilst I get a grip of the job. But I am so excited. Will you be alright with that?'

'Of course, my darling, if this is what you want, I am very happy for you.'

'I think Mother was very impressed that you stood up to Father. You are numbered among the very few that have ever done that. Oh, by the way I am going to my aunt's tonight so I am sorry I will not see you.'

'Sophie, I am very pleased things are going so well for you, but I must get on, Harry is waiting to go home.'

'Please apologise to him for me, I love you,' she added as she hung up.

'And you,' said Tim into a dead phone. When he and Sophie were not together, he missed her dreadfully. Also, he was desperately worried what the effect would be on their relationship given her father's reaction. He realised how lonely he had been prior to meeting Sophie, now it would be made far worse by the brief glimpse of happiness he had experienced with her.

Tim's father was waiting to speak to him when he turned from the phone, 'Hallo, Dad, to what do we owe the pleasure?'

Harry, on his way out of the shop called, 'Goodnight everyone, see you tomorrow.'

Father and son both waved.

'You ok?' asked his dad noticing Tim's demeanour.

Giving a big sigh he replied with a drawn out, 'Yes… it's all a bit difficult now.'

'I am sure it will come out alright, that girl loves you and she is not about to let you go.'

'Oh God, I do hope not,' Tim said, clearly very worried.

'Changing the subject, Tim, with your agreement I would like to start the special bread on Saturday. Harry and Mr Woodman are ok with it and it's all arranged at the baker's end; we just need you to give it the nod.'

A pair of customers walked in and Tim had to break off to serve them. He became busy during the next half hour with a steady flow of people. The late-night opening was starting to pay off.

Finally, his dad said, 'Why not come around the house after closing? I will get fish and chips in and we can talk properly.'

Late that night the two men pushed their chairs back from the table having dined well on an excellent fish supper, all washed down with a cold beer. Mr Cooper had explained what he had learned about the different types of bread from the son of the baker.

'They recommend we start with three types of bread; baguettes are the most popular, then the French sandwich rolls and the third either the *pain complet* as a brown loaf or the sourdough loaf.'

Tim was impressed with the variety although he knew they could not afford to carry the whole range immediately. He was very surprised at how expensive it was going to be for them to stock it. He was even more surprised at what the bread was being sold for.

'The only thing we must agree with the suppliers is that we won't undercut their prices,' said his dad.

'We need to trial it,' decided Tim. 'We can't afford to lay that much money out every day.'

'No, I didn't think you could,' said his father. 'The baker suggests we stock it just on a Saturday to start with,' he added.

'Dad, have you spoken to Mr Woodman?'

'What, about the signs you mean? It's all in hand. Mr Woodman may be doing them as we speak.'

'Ok,' said Tim, 'let's give it a go. One month and we'll look at it again. Are you alright with that?'

'Yes...' said his dad sounding very unsure and slowly rocking his head from side to side. 'I suggest we put the table out the front. I am happiest out there. It's what I am used to.'

The conversation then moved on to Sophie. 'Tim, I am very concerned about the huge discrepancy between your and Sophie's lifestyle, income and social position. They are going to say she has married beneath herself.'

'Dad, I have a vision. In a few years' time there won't be one Sophie's. I intend to have delicatessens across London and maybe further afield. Thanks to you, your groundwork and ideas we are now able to reap the rewards. The world is changing. The world has been black and white all through the war. Now look around, it's really buzzing all in glorious technicolour. As I have said before there is new music, bright fashion. Why not new food? We are perfectly placed to profit from it, if we don't others will.'

'You certainly seem to know where you are going, lad. Good luck, you deserve it.'

After Tim had left, his father mulled over their conversation and realised how determined his son was to succeed. Later that night, as he turned over to sleep, he said under his breath, 'Good on you, lad.'

The couple's relationship descended into infrequent phone calls. In one call she informed him that her father had rejected her offer of working her notice and growling at her said, he could manage perfectly well without her, thank you. Sophie had told him that she was working horrendous hours at the new job but thoroughly enjoying it.

Tim could not remember feeling so miserable or so scared. He immersed himself in the job. Opening early, closing very late, staggering home and falling into bed. One morning he awoke still fully dressed sprawled across his bed. His dinner cold and untouched on the table. Whilst he was washing up, he found himself fighting to control his emotions. He cuffed his eyes with a sleeve. He had begun to believe he was going to lose her. On his walk that morning he was completely unaware of the sunshine, the swirl of the pigeons and the quiet streets.

When he got to work, Mr Woodman was waiting for him with a fresh cup of tea. 'Don't open up yet Tim,' he said firmly. 'This has got to stop. You left here after ten last night and it's not seven o'clock yet.'

'I know, but the work stops me thinking of what I am about to lose.'

'Tim, now listen to me,' said Mr Woodman growing ever more cross with him and his failure to stand up for himself, his voice growing louder as he continued, 'this is not like you. You are made of stronger stuff than this so stop moping about, ring her up and tell her you want to see her today. And while you are at it tell her you want to meet her mother. You need to get a grip on this, lad, or it's going to wither on the vine. She is an adult; she does not need to take orders from anyone, least of all her family. They need to learn that from now on it will be you and her. You must be as strong as they are. This is the rest of your life lad. For God's sake fight back,' he finished, by now almost shouting.

Tim felt himself becoming emotional again, he took a deep breath and said, 'Thank you for that, I needed it.'

'Ring her now,' commanded Mr Woodman.

'It's still very early,' he replied.

'TIM!' exploded Mr Woodman becoming exasperated. 'It starts now, lad. Draw a line in the sand and start again. There will be someone there.'

For a moment he couldn't remember her number, then he did and dialled it. A young pretty voice answered the phone.

'Can I speak to Sophie, please?' he asked her.

'I am sorry, sir, she is not in yet,' the girl replied. 'May I take a message?'

'Yes, please, can you tell her that it is vital that I meet with her today? My name is Cooper, Timothy Cooper. Will she ring me as soon as possible? Have you got that?'

'Yes, sir, I have,' she said hearing the anger in his voice.

He replaced the phone.

Mr Woodman was walking to the door to open the shop, silently clapping his hands over his head.

Sophie rang half an hour later. After the hallos she said, 'My secretary said you sounded really angry.'

'Sophie, I need to see you today. Can we have lunch?'

'Not today, Tim, I have a lunch meeting.'

A sudden gale of anger swept through him. He said goodbye and banged the phone down. The anger was a product of his loneliness and growing certainty that he had lost her. Harry had just come in and raised his eyes at Mr Woodman.

'Can you manage if I go out for a while and try and walk this off?'

He walked beside his beloved Thames for half an hour completely lost in thought. When he became aware of the time he turned around and banged into an old lady. He had to grab her before she fell over. 'I am so sorry,' he said. 'I have a lot on my mind, and I was not paying attention.'

'No harm done,' she said, insisting she was ok.

He had made up his mind to move on. He had learnt to cope with his mother's death when he was very young. He would learn to cope with the loss of Sophie.

When he got back to the shop, she was waiting for him just inside the door, obviously in a blazing temper.

He walked into the shop. As he approached her, she hissed at him under her breath, 'How dare you put the phone down on me.'

He felt his own temper rising. 'We can't have this conversation in here.' He strode out of the shop, across the road and stopped by the black wrought iron railings overlooking the river.

'Who the hell do you think you are?' Sophie shouted at him obviously beyond being reasoned with.

'I am the damn fool who hangs around for days on end waiting to see if you will have time to see me,' he fired back at her.

'I happen to be in a very difficult new job that is taking up all my time,' Sophie snapped at him. 'I have cancelled three appointments to come here.'

'It's obviously more important than our relationship,' he growled. His temper now a fire roaring out of control, burning away any caution or forethought.

'It looks as though it might be,' she said white faced and staring at him, displaying her own anger.

'If that's how you feel let's end it.' His voice now was all frost and ice.

Sophie looked at him and without another word turned on her heel and strode away without a backward glance.

He stood watching as she walked away. Feeling nothing, no sense of loss, his anger, now full grown, was blotting everything out. She was quickly lost to sight in the crowd. He stared at the ground for a minute, then he said out loud, 'If that's how she wants to play it then so be it.' He strode back into the shop, his heart as cold and hard as iron.

Harry said, 'Are you ok, Tim?'

'Never better,' he replied, turning to a customer he asked, 'Hallo, my love, what can we get you? The customers kept coming over the next hour. When questioned by his two partners he refused to answer, insisting he was ok.

Just after three o'clock the phone rang, Mr Woodman answered it and had a short conversation. He placed the phone on the varnished side table next to the cradle.

He crossed the shop and said quietly to Tim, 'It's Sophie's mother. She would like to talk to you.'

Tim shook his head and was about to refuse when Mr Woodman who had seen their blazing row through the shop window mouthed, 'Go on, Tim,' nodding his head at the phone.

Picking up the phone Tim said, 'Hallo,' his voice flat, and lacking any warmth, reflecting the hardening of his decision to end the relationship.

'Timothy, my daughter is in hysterics; I have never seen her this upset. It has taken a lot for me to make this phone call; would you come around and talk to her, please?'

Tim was silent while he thought it through.

'Hallo are you still there?' asked Mrs Vieri.

'Yes I am,' he decided if it was going to end it should not be like this. 'Where are you?'

'We are at my sister's, Sophia does not want to go back home because of her father.'

Confirming it was ok to leave his partners to manage without him and gaining the address from Mrs Vieri he stepped outside the shop and hailed a taxi.

Fifteen minutes later the taxi pulled into a pretty cobbled mews. The taxi driver allowed the vehicle to run down the slight slope while he looked for the number. The cobbles imparted a random wobble to the vehicle. Finally, the taxi came to a halt.

As Tim alighted from the cab the front door of the house was thrown open, Sophie came flying down the path and threw herself into his arms. Looking up at him trying to gauge his mood she said, through her tears, 'Tim, I am so, so sorry. I did not mean it. My temper got the better of me. Will you forgive me?' Her hair was in rat tails, her eyes red rimmed, and her makeup had run, she was holding a sodden hanky to her red nose.

'I am just as much to blame, my pride got in the way. Of course your job's the priority now, we just need to find ways of working round it.'

Sophie sensed a cool distance in him that she had not experienced before.

Tim found a nearly clean handkerchief to dry her eyes and blow her nose with, and then they kissed. His a little perfunctory.

There was an embarrassed cough from the front door and Mrs Vieri called saying, 'I think you should come indoors.'

Tim followed Sophie into the house. Now it was her turn to have a very firm grip on his hand.

It was as pretty inside as outside; the decor was a combination of pale duck egg blue and pastel pink plus lots of cut glass and expensive mirrors. There was another woman in the house who was introduced as Mrs Vieri's sister, Angela, the owner of the house. She looked a lot less forbidding than Sophie's mother. She was younger than her sister and very attractive. Sophie's good looks obviously run in the family, he thought. Angela clearly had a vibrant happy personality that was reflected in her behaviour and style of dress.

Mrs Vieri asked, 'May I call you Timothy?'

There was complete silence for a few moments while the two of them each took the measure of the other. Both held firm eye contact. Finally, he nodded agreement.

'Jolly good, now we can all breathe again,' said Sophie's aunt.

Tim realised she was not in awe of anyone.

'Tea anyone?' she asked, brightly.

The tea arrived. Tim, his mood softening a little said, 'I'm very sorry I lost my temper. I do apologise.'

'Tim, I was equally to blame; I have been so engrossed at work I had lost track of how long it has been since we were last together. We need to work out a plan, sort out when we can see each other. It is not just me working all hours is it, Tim? The shop is busy now so you must be doing long days as well?' Tim nodded.

Angela said, 'I am sure you will work it out, who would like cake?' They all said yes. Her aunt asked Sophie to help her with it.

After they had both left the room Mrs Vieri said, 'I am sorry, Timothy. Not very subtle I know but I think we need a brief chat. I have one very embarrassing request to get out of the way.'

CHAPTER 15

THE PROMISE

Tim noticed a blush starting on Mrs Vieri's face.

'Can you promise me that you will not sleep with Sophia? If she became pregnant out of wedlock her father would die of shame.'

Tim agreed immediately. 'I have friends,' he said, 'who had got the cart before the horse and it had jeopardised the rest of their lives. We will have children once we are married.' Tim hid a smile as he noticed her becoming even more embarrassed.

'How will you afford to keep her in the manner she is used to?' she asked.

'I won't be able to initially, but,' he continued, 'I have a plan.' He explained that he had a good team of experienced people around him. His bank manager was keeping a weather eye on the business. And he added, 'I intend to have Sophie's across London.'

'I beg your pardon?' said Mrs Vieri, visibly shocked.

Sophie and her aunt returned as she said this, and Sophie burst out laughing. She explained to her mother how the shop got its name and how very surprised and moved she had been when she saw it for the first time.

'Are you trying to tell me you spent what, three hours with my daughter and fell in love?' queried Sophia's mother clearly not believing him.

'I don't think it took that long but yes,' Tim replied smiling at Sophie.

'And what about you, Sophia, are you sure this is not an infatuation?'

'Mother, I know this sounds impossible, but I love Tim. I feel as though I have known I would meet him all my life,' stepping across the room and taking Tim's hand while she spoke. Sophie still felt the aftershock of the terror she experienced when she believed he was lost to her. 'And,' Sophie continued, 'we have discussed our immediate future. We thought we would have a private agreement for one year. At the end of the year we would become officially engaged and marry shortly after.'

Angela said, 'That all sounds very sensible does it not?'

Sophie mistook her mother's silence for acquiescence.

Angela continued, 'Olivia, you have only to look at them to know they are in love. Surely you can see that. Our task is to ensure that it comes to a proper conclusion. It is going to take some time for your husband to come to terms with the fact that his little girl is a grown woman with all that entails. Can I suggest that Sophia comes and lives here with me? I will be glad of the company and Tim can come and visit whenever. I will make sure there is no hanky-panky,' she said, wagging her finger at Tim.

'It will be nearer my job,' said Sophie, 'further for you Tim.'

'Not a problem,' he replied.

'When should I move?' asked Sophie.

'As soon as possible,' suggested her aunt, 'no point in dragging it out. Why not this weekend? I have a luncheon appointment, but I can cancel that. Then you will be all ready for work on Monday.'

'Is that alright, Mother?' asked Sophie.

'Well it is very generous of Angela, but it might well help to alleviate the terrible atmosphere at home. I shall miss you, Sophia, but I can come and see you here. You may have more visitors than you realise, Angela.'

'That sounds wonderful,' she replied.

'It is getting late,' said Mrs Vieri. 'I will treat us all to dinner.' Turning to Tim she asked, 'Is that alright, Timothy?'

Looking at his watch Tim said, 'Oh heck, the shop must be shut by now.'
Seeing his concern Angela said, 'Would you like to ring them, Tim?'

'May I?' he asked. 'I have left them in the lurch rather.'

'The phone is in the hall,' said Angela.

Tim left the room and Sophia's aunt said, 'He seems like a very nice young man, rather better than those stuffed shirts your father kept bothering you with, Sophia.'

'He was only doing what he thought was best for her,' responded Sophie's mother defensively.

'They were intellectual numb wits compared to Sophia. She would run rings around them. I think Tim is lovely.'

Tim entered the room obviously having overheard the last comment and looking very embarrassed said, 'Thank you very much.'

'Is the shop ok?' asked Sophie.

'Yes, Mr Woodman just took over as he does in a crisis. His only concern was that we were alright. He sends his love, Sophia.'

'He is such a lovely man,' she responded.

Angela went into the hall to ring for a taxi calling over her shoulder as she went, 'Shall we go to the usual?'

'That will be fine,' responded her sister.

The taxi deposited the four of them outside the same restaurant they had visited when Tim had discovered he had left his wallet behind.

The maître de recognised the three ladies and showed them to a nice table near the window. This time being less nervous Tim was better able to be more appreciative of the decor and ambience of the restaurant. He admired again the cut glass wine glasses, the china, the cutlery. All the cutlery with the same small mark. The deep maroon tablecloth with white linen napkins.

Once they were seated Sophie, with a wicked glint in her eye reminded Tim that this was where they came last time.

'Don't you dare,' said Tim obviously embarrassed.

'What's all this about?' asked Angela, intrigued by his confusion.

'Well…' said Sophie, drawing the word out to tease him even more.

Tim interrupted, 'If I am going to be made to look a fool, I will do it myself, if you don't mind.' He was looking pointedly at Sophie. He then related the whole story adding, 'I'm sure you can imagine how terrible I felt.'

Angela, laughing, scolded Sophie for being so cruel.

Her mother said nothing. The story endorsed all her worst fears. She was beginning to warm to him a little, now she was sure he was only after Sophia's money. Obviously, her daughter was blind to his faults. He was just as horrible as she had first thought. She remained very quiet through the rest of the evening.

During the meal, which was superb, Tim was able to quietly demonstrate his knowledge of Italian cuisine and explain his trips abroad to his food suppliers. He also disclosed to Sophie that the new range of special bread was going on sale this coming Saturday.

'Why special?' asked Angela.

Tim explained about the baker having been trained at a boulangerie in France and was now offering a range of wonderful new bread. He did add that they could not afford to take the whole range on straight away, but they would see how it goes.

'Mother, it is all so exciting is it not?'

Her mother agreed saying, 'It certainly sounds like it,' they could all hear the deep reservation in her voice.

Tim said, 'You are right to be wary; I don't know if it will work. Or to use one of Harry's expression's, we don't know if it will fly. I am going to try it for a month and then have a look at it.'

Sophie shared some details of her job with them, 'Mr Wells is allowing me to introduce some of the new accounting methods I learnt at Uni,' she said, 'hopefully it will allow us to speed up some of the administration.' It confirmed for Tim how clever she was and how much more demanding her job may become in the future.

After the meal Angela asked the waiter to ring for a taxi.

'Mother, do you mind if Tim and I walk a bit?'

Mrs Vieri shook her head.

'We can get a taxi at the station,' Tim suggested. 'I will make sure we are not too late.'

When all the goodbyes had been said and the taxi had swept the two women away Tim smiled to himself. Angela had said, 'Give me a proper hug, Tim.' There was rather more bodily contact than he had expected. She only let him go when Sophie complained, only half laughing, about her trying to steal her man.

It was a lot cooler when he had moved in to kiss Mrs Vieri goodnight. Drawing her face away slightly, she made sure that there was no contact, he half suspected that it was the story that had done the damage. He would talk to Sophie when they were alone

Tim and Sophie started to walk to the station strolling arm in arm along with other couples beside the river. The river as always was working its magic on them both. The multi-coloured reflections and the hard-black shine of the water as it slid downstream towards the sea.

Approaching a darker area under a tree where a streetlight was out Sophie asked him if he would kiss her properly. They stepped a little further into the dark and Tim pulled her into his arms. Sophie wound her arms around his neck, one hand in his hair at the back of his head. He was very aware of her breasts pressed firmly against his chest. Shortly her lips parted and just the very tips of their tongues touched. A few seconds of that and Tim growling involuntarily reached down and cupping her buttock with one hand pulled their bodies into full contact. For some minutes they were lost to the world.

When they finally came up for air there was a long pause while they both returned to the here and now.

Sophie, still standing in his arms and looking up at him, said, chuckling, 'It is nice to know everything works, but God knows how we are going to last a year.'

Tim, rather embarrassed at the effect the intimacy had triggered said, 'So Angela told you what the promise was that your mother was going to ask me to make?'

'Yes,' she replied, 'and because you are an old boy Scout you are going to keep it are you not?'

'I am but it'll be bloody difficult if you are going to do that to me too often.'

'We will have to see,' she giggled, pointing her toes as they began to walk on.

Tim saw her safely away on the train and turned for home himself.

As he walked homewards Tim gave thought to how fickle your fortunes could be, one moment in the deepest pit of despair, the next as happy as could be.

One thing that had begun to worry him was where he and Sophie would live once they were married. A brief look in estate agents' windows had scared him. There was no way he could afford the rent for even the most primitive of accommodation. He realised how generous his landlady was being to him and resolved to pay her a little more. She appeared hard as nails on the surface but was very generous if you obeyed her rules. She was a widow; she had brought up two daughters without any outside help, making a living from renting out rooms in her very large Victorian terrace to her male guests.

The rules were simple; the rent had to be paid every Friday night without fail. Should she not have the money by Sunday night the guest in question would find his belongings on the doorstep when he arrived home from work on Monday evening. Tim initially was not sure whether it was an idle threat or not until a new guest from Newcastle arrived.

On the second Friday he had not paid her his rent. The landlady, with his evening meal in her hand, leant over him at the dinner table.

'Have you got your rent money?'

'No, not tonight but I should have it next week.'

'Well you know the rules,' she said as she walked away, 'Sunday night at the latest.'

They could hear her scraping his dinner into the dustbin. The guest left the table and went out of the front door. Tim never saw him again. Nowadays Tim was her only lodger.

CHAPTER 16

LOAVES

The following morning arriving at work as usual he was surprised to see a table out the front of the shop with his father serving a customer. He suddenly remembered it was Saturday and the first lot of bread had arrived.

Tim stopped at the table and said good morning to the customer whom he recognised.

The man said, 'Your father has lost none of his skill, I only stopped to look, and he has sold me two loaves.'

'You won't be sorry,' said Mr Cooper. 'I've had a good chunk for my breakfast this morning, it's superb; far superior to that white putty you buy down the road.'

'I will tell you what I think next time,' said the man as he walked away.

Tim looked at the blue and white chequered cloth covering the plain deal table and saw a Sara touch in a tiny posy of flowers at the far end.

A smartly dressed lady asked how much one of the loaves was. Mr Cooper told her the price.

'I am not paying that! I might not like it,' she said a little indignantly.

'Please wait one moment,' said Tim 'and you can try it.' He rushed into the shop found a knife and a plate.

'Harry,' he called 'can I have a pat of butter please; we are going to do a

Sara with the bread.'

Mr Woodman stopped unpacking a box of supplies and took the items Tim had asked for from Harry who was serving a customer and went outside and set the table for a tasting.

Tim watched through the glass as the lady tried the small square of bread and butter. He saw her begin to nod and soon afterwards bought two loaves.

Tim kept an eye on the table as the morning wore on. The range of reactions from people was interesting. Some people liked it but would not buy.

One lady would have bought some, but her husband stopped her saying, 'You can't make proper toast with that fancy stuff,' and with that they walked on. Tim saw a pretty young mum who obviously really enjoyed the taster but shook her head when asked if she would buy.

Tim went out and asked her very politely why she would not buy it.

'It's too dear,' she replied, 'my husband is in work but since the baby has arrived things are a bit tight.'

'How about half a loaf at half the price?' asked Tim.

She thought for a moment and then said, 'You've talked me into it, I'll take it.'

The baby in the pram started to cry. Mr Cooper mimed giving the child a taster of buttered bread. The young mother nodded. Silence fell as the bread was consumed.

'Try half the loaf at half price if nothing else works, Dad,' said Tim, 'but add a penny to the price.'

Tim made a mental note to ask the bakers if they could make small loaves as well. All the loaves he had on sale were large except for the sandwich rolls.

The weather began to change. A cold wind slowly got stronger and a flurry of rain made umbrellas sprout up and down the street.

Sara arrived to take over during the lunch break. She started to help Mr

Cooper inside with the table. Mr Woodman spotted what she was doing and going outside insisted on taking over.

While retrieving her shopping bag from the end of the table. Sara said, 'I am stronger than I look, Mr Woodman,'

'I am just an old chauvinist,' he replied, 'I know that's all going out of style, but I was brought up to respect women and place them first. I doubt I shall change now.'

'Thank you, Mr Woodman,' she replied giving him a small curtsy.

'You are looking even prettier than usual today, Sara,' said Tim.

'I have bought myself a new dress,' she said, swivelling her hips to and fro to make the dress swirl. 'The confectionery is selling better, so I went mad and treated myself, not that Harry noticed,' she added.

'I always think you look stunning,' said Harry.

'Harry, when it goes dark stop digging,' jibed Tim, laughing.

CHAPTER 17

WORKING AT THE SHOP

Just after lunch Sophie walked in, stopping at the doorway to shake her umbrella. The men were so pleased to see her she became a little embarrassed. 'It has not been that long,' she said.

'No, lass, that's not it, we were worried we might never see you again,' said Mr Woodman.

'We have got very fond of you and this young man was in a shocking state,' added Harry, his Italian accent getting stronger with his emotion.

'I am so sorry,' she said becoming emotional herself.

Sara walked over to her and gently hugged her and kissed her cheek. 'Don't worry, shall we make these useless men a cup of tea?'

As Sophie passed Tim on the way to the stairs, she pecked his cheek. 'Hallo, you,' she said.

Tim kissed her back and smiled a huge ear-to-ear grin.

The afternoon got busier and busier. Sophie was everywhere at once, advising customers about what went with what and pointing people at Sara when they asked about cooking and preparing the various foodstuffs.

Tim watched Sophie from the back of the shop. She was glowing gently from her exertions. The ends of her golden hair were starting to stick to her forehead. She was wearing a cream silk blouse and a pleated navy skirt with flat navy shoes. Tim never tired of watching her. She moved as though every step had been choreographed. She was truly beautiful in every way. He was still amazed that she had chosen him. It went quiet a little later and she came and joined him at the back of the store and sat on some boxes next to him.

Running her forearm across her forehead. 'Phew,' she said puffing, 'I am hot.'

'You certainly are,' said Tim grinning.

'Please do not be rude,' then smiling, she wrinkled her nose at him.

'You don't have to do this; you could bring a book or something.'

'What!?' she said becoming indignant. 'Am I not helping?'

'Of course you are, but you work very hard the rest of the week, shouldn't you be having some time off on Saturdays?'

'Tim, I love being here helping you and the rest of your team. It's great fun.'

He shook his head perplexed.

'You do not understand, do you?'

'Understand what?' he asked.

Mr Woodman came to the back of the shop not realising he was interrupting and said, 'Tim, I don't know if you would agree, but I think that is our best day yet.'

'I reckon it must be. Dad why are you still here?' he asked noticing his father.

'I enjoy being here.'

'Told you so,' chirped Sophie.

'How many hours have you done today, Dad?'

'Twelve,' he said, looking at his watch.

'Dad, I must owe you thousands.'

'You owe me nothing, lad,' he responded very quietly. 'If you just let me keep coming in, I shall be very content.'

'Pleased to have you here,' said Tim, realising his father was saying a great deal in that short phrase.

He was slowly coming out of the terrible depression that the loss of Tim's mother had triggered in him.

Tim walked over to him and took his hand. Eventually the grip broke and Mr Cooper said again, very quietly, 'Thanks for everything, son.'

Tim could see his emotions were very near the surface. Having come so close to losing Sophie he understood for the first time what the death of his wife, Tim's mum, meant to him. His father's world had flown to pieces.

'You are very welcome, and by the way, I promise never to pay you a living wage,' Tim added, straight faced. Everybody laughed including his dad.

'Tim, Tim,' called Sophie, 'I am supposed to have invited you to dinner at Aunt Angela's this evening, is that ok?'

'Erm, yes,' he replied.

'Please say if you do not want to go, I can ring her.'

'No that's fine, it was just unexpected that's all.'

'What time?' he asked.

'In about an hour, but I would like a quick bath if you don't mind?'

'No problem,' was his response.

'I will clear up,' Mr Woodman said.

'I can help,' said Mr Cooper.

The late-night opening was now slightly curtailed. They had all agreed to help with the increasing workload on a rota basis provided they stopped at 7 pm.

Tim and Sophie went to the door and while he was holding the door open for her, he heard Mr Woodman invite his father for a fish and chip supper.

Perhaps now he could stop worrying about him.

Sophie said, 'A penny for your thoughts?'

Tim unknowingly had been silent for a few minutes. 'Oh, sorry, I was thinking about my father.'

'He has changed a lot since I first met him, you have given him a purpose, it is what I was trying to explain this afternoon; your vision has inspired these people around you; your belief that you can build something amazing; they believe you; I believe you.'

'And I haven't started talking about Poland yet,' he laughed.

'Tim,' she said in a reproving tone.

The walk beside the river to the station was as beautiful as ever. The rowing club were out again. The eight sliding along responding to the pull of the oars like something alive.

'Wait,' said Tim, 'he should be along any moment.' With that a rather rotund man on a very old bike came by. The bike rattling and wobbling only just under control. He was holding a megaphone in his hand into which he shouted instructions to the cox in the boat. The other hand gripping the handlebars. His trousers were tucked into his socks very untidily, his old gaberdine raincoat flapping out behind him. It appeared that catastrophe was only the next pothole away.

The boat was powered by a synchronicity between the oarsmen that could only have been achieved by countless hours of a dedicated desire to achieve perfection. The craft moved further away from the trainer and his bike with every meticulous stroke. Tim noticed the cox was a young lady who sounded very authoritative. He stood spellbound in awe of their precision, the perfect timing, the length and depth of the pull on the oars, so precise, the twist of the wrist at the end of the pull that allowed the oarsmen to feather the blade back flat across the water denying the wind any grip on the oar to disrupt the perfection. The progress of the boat marked by concentric rings laid out behind it that were made by the dip of the blades. Tim could imagine the joy of being able to do something that well. All the crew in perfect harmony with the boat.

Sophie was wiggling his hand; 'Can we move on please I am getting cold?'

'Oh, sorry, I was miles away.'

'Yes, watching the young lady in the boat,' she said.

'No, I wasn't, but I am fascinated by how amazing the rowing appears.'

Sophie quickly settled in with her aunt Angela. Whilst there was a disparity in years, they obviously had a lot in common. Tim was often invited to an evening meal or lunch at the weekend. On some occasions Mrs Vieri was there. Tim was not sure if she was thawing in her attitude to him. He realised that he was often the subject of discussion when he was not there from things the three women said. The various subjects that came up about him had obviously been a topic of conversation in the past. One or other of the women would say, yes Sophie told us that, or that's what Angela said. It appeared that Mrs Vieri was still reticent when any discussion was about him.

CHAPTER 18

MR VIERI'S DISTRUST

One night at Angela's, Tim asked Sophie if her father had softened in terms of his attitude towards him.

Sophie sobbed, 'I have never seen him so angry.' She became progressively more tearful as she explained that her father had again asked her to, 'shake that chap off'. He had gone on to say that if Sophie married Tim, he would disinherit her, and she would find out what that chap was really like once he realised that she was no longer wealthy. 'You will not see him for dust,' he added. He had concluded by saying, 'He is a gold digger and you are too infatuated to see it. The best thing he could do is to leave you now.'

They heard Angela's key in the lock, she entered the room and immediately saw that Sophie was in great distress. She crossed the room and pulled Sophie into her arms.

'Whatever is the matter?' she asked as she hugged Sophie tightly.

She looked over the distraught girl's shoulder and aimed a quizzical expression at Tim.

'Sophie, you must tell Angela while I make a cup of tea.'

Over the noise of the kettle he could hear Sophie become ever more hysterical and incoherent. He could stand it no longer; he strode across the kitchen and back into the lounge. Angela put her hand out to stop him and gently indicated he should go back in the kitchen. Tim took in a huge breath and did as she advised, his face showing his anger.

Tim made the tea and waited, he began to assemble the cups, saucers, milk and sugar whilst he did so. He could hear Sophie slowly becoming less distraught with low indistinguishable soothing words from Angela. Eventually she called him in. He placed the tea tray on the coffee table. Sophie reached for his hand. He knelt on the floor between the two women. He noticed Sophie looked a wreck. Once again caused by her parents. His heart went out to her and his anger began to build.

'How could anybody who purports to love you do this to you?' he asked leaping to his feet. He was visibly very angry.

'Tim, Tim,' repeated Angela, 'I know you are hurting but it will not help if you lose control. This situation must stop, or it will make Sophie ill.'

Whilst Angela poured the tea, Tim walking about the room said, 'I know what is wrong. I am not good enough for his daughter; he thinks I am only after his money. The money thing is easily solved; he can disinherit Sophie as he has threatened. I wish he would. I want us to be happy and successful in our own right; the last thing I want is for people to say we were only successful because of his money. I want us to look back in fifty years' time and be proud of what we have achieved, on our own, beholden to no one. In a nutshell, I want our family to be happy and comfortably off. I want Sophie to be everything she can be, and I need to be seen to have done well. I just need him to allow me the time to show him what I can do. I am twenty-six now, tell him to look at me again when I am thirty.'

'You really do mean that, Tim,' confirmed Angela, nodding. Aware that he meant every word.

'I do,' he replied.

CHAPTER 19

THE BUSINESS PLAN

'The team at the shop are all fully behind him,' added Sophie, 'and everybody is so excited by what Tim is doing. It is great fun. It is a super place to work. I enjoy working in the shop on Saturday enormously. There is a tremendous buzz about the place. The customers love it. They get tasters of new foods and recipes to help them with the different style of cooking.

'Sara, Harry's wife is a genius cook and comes up with different ways of preparing things every week. It is her that comes up with the recipes.'

'And she is the confectioner,' added Tim, 'she has been approached by a major confectionery company to sell her recipes on more than one occasion, but she will not.'

'Your father knows nothing of this you know,' said Angela. 'He will never respond to threats or aggression,' she continued, 'but he does understand a solid business plan. Would you two be prepared to put one together?'

'That seems to be a very strange thing to do,' Tim replied with a confused look on his face.

Angela broke in and said, 'You need to understand how his mind works. The most important thing in his life is Sophie, more important than his business, my sister or anything else. You are perceived as a threat to her. You are a jumped-up barrow boy on the make, condemning his daughter to a life of poverty. His words not mine. Tim you cannot prove that you will look after Sophie and any children to the end of life, but you can prove that your business is sound and growing. That he will understand.'

Tim and Sophie looked at each other. 'Can we do that, Tim?'

He realised there was far more behind the question than their ability to do so, the question also queried whether he could swallow his pride and make this gesture.

Tim looked at Sophie for a long time, recognising the rest of his life was bound up in this woman and that he would make any sacrifice to keep her.

It was obvious that aggression would only make things worse. He would need a subtler approach. Why not use his greatest strength, his sales skills, turn it into a sales campaign? Mr Vieri would almost certainly spot it but if it worked, so what. Better than floundering around ill-prepared.

'We are not going to write a business plan,' he announced.

Sophie jumped in and sounding rather desperate, saying, 'I can think of nothing else that will work.'

'We are going to put on a sales promotion. We'll write a business plan, we'll use all your skills with that, we can invite him to the shop on a Saturday when the place is full and give him the tour, the staff, the customers, the food, a glass of wine. I'll invite Mr Murdoch the bank manager, I think he will come, Sara can put plenty of tasters on show, and then present the books.

'It is becoming clear, to quote Harry, that this bird might fly. We need to show him that and we will present one of the best salesmen in the area.'

Sophie laughing now said, 'You are talking about yourself are you not?'

'Give that lady a prize. I am,' he admitted.

Angela joined in the laughter. 'I am off to my bed,' she added, 'do not be too late you two. You both look very tired,' saying goodnight as she left the room.

'Can you give me a cuddle, please?' asked Sophie, getting up from her armchair and indicating he should sit in it.

Once he was seated, she arranged herself on his lap, pulling his arms into place around her, she kissed him and snuggled closer. Tim started to talk quietly about the plan for her father and quickly recognised she was asleep. He sat for nearly an hour with her sleeping soundly on his lap. His left leg was now completely numb, he heard Angela tiptoeing downstairs.

She tapped quietly on the door and Tim whispered, 'Come in.'

When she saw Sophie sound asleep, she smiled and asked, 'Are you ok?'

'My legs are numb,' Tim replied. 'Sophie darling, it's bedtime,' he said softly into her ear.

She half woke, Angela helped her from the chair, 'Night, night Tim,' she mumbled as he made for the door.

'Goodnight both,' he responded as he walked out, closing the door carefully behind him.

Tim and Sophie, working at Angela's, put together a reasonable business plan. Sophie insisted that they both did it together.

'Father will question you, Tim, and if you cannot answer he will say it was only possible because of my input.'

'That may well be true,' mused Tim.

'Tim, do not be hard on yourself. Your sales skills and product knowledge are amazing, you know where the food is made and quite often the name of the family making it, how it should be cooked and so on. We make a very impressive team,' she continued, 'keep the faith, Tim.'

Tim explained what he had in mind for Mr Vieri and asked Mr Murdoch if he would be able to attend, the bank manager agreed, 'but,' he added, 'it will have to be Saturday afternoon after I have closed the bank, and Tim, do not let him intimidate you. I have every confidence in you, and I shall tell him so. You and your team have made a very good start, son.'

Tim told Mr Murdoch how very grateful he was for the kind words and how useful he found it having his support.

'You have no need to be grateful, Tim, it is the truth and I am happy to help.'

In the middle of that week a gentleman came into the shop and asked Harry if he could put a card up in the shop window. Three of the local traders that they all knew well had done the same thing. Tim was serving at the time but looked across and saw that Harry was in conversation with him.

CHAPTER 20

THE BOAT

Tim would have said the gentleman was an artist of some kind. Yellow trousers held up by a very loud tie, a creased, obviously expensive shirt with an open brown cord jacket and suede shoes. His hair was thick, curly and long. Tim also noticed he was a very handsome man.

Before leaving he walked around the shop and bought some sweets and bread off Sara. After he had gone Sara was wearing the biggest smile and a deep blush. Harry was muttering to her in the corner. She said something in response that looked like a rebuke and stalked back to her counter to serve another customer. It was a while before Tim could ask Harry what had happened.

'He is an actor and he wants to rent out his houseboat for a year. He has a part in a film in America,' Harry informed him.

'Have you upset Sara?' Tim asked, a half smile playing around his mouth.

Harry was still cross, 'I told her off for behaving like a silly teenager with that chap and she gave me the rough edge of her tongue.'

'Oh dear,' said Tim, 'we guys never learn, do we?'

Tim examined the postcard. The actor was putting his houseboat up for rent while he was away. The picture of it was very small and very white. Tim had an idea and put the advert in his pocket. He had noticed there was a note at the bottom that said it would not be available for about four months.

Tim spent considerable time putting together a letter to send to Mr Vieri. It read as follows.

Dear Mr Vieri

I deeply regret that our first meeting turned out as it did. I handled it very badly and I apologise for losing my temper and being so rude. Although I am not a father, I believe I can understand your need to protect Sophia from being hurt. However, I can assure you that I am not the fortune hunter you believe me to be. It would be easier for me if Sophia was penniless. Should you decide to disinherit her it would in fact make my position easier.

To enable you to make a fairer assessment of me and my intentions I would like to invite you to come and see what I and my partners are doing and hear what our plans are.

Mr Murdoch, our bank manager has agreed to be there provided it is after lunch on a Saturday when the bank has closed.

We are preparing a statement for you to look at. This will show our financial position after the first year's trading and will include a business plan. Mrs Vieri and Angela Brook are aware of what we are proposing. In closing I need to tell you that my feelings for your daughter are not infatuation or a passing fancy. I will always place her first in everything I plan both now, and in the years to come. I love her and always will. I would appreciate it if you could advise us of a date that is convenient for you. I very much hope you will take up our offer.

Yours sincerely

Timothy Cooper

Later that night as Tim was getting ready for bed, he remembered the advert for the boat rental the actor had given him. Searching his pockets, he finally found it. Although small the picture seemed to convey the impression that it was in good order. He thought it would be worth having a look before he put the advert in the window. He hoped that Sophie would be as taken with the idea as he was, but first he had to look himself. As he pulled the covers up and settled to sleep, he imagined he could feel the bed gently rocking and the quiet slap of the water against the hull. He fell asleep with a smile on his face.

The following morning, he awoke early and decided he would have a look at the boat before work. Pulling on last night's clothes a quick coffee and a shave and he was on his way. The boat was in a small boatyard about a mile away. Tim broke into a jog. He realised that he was a happy man. The business was finally moving into profit, Sophie had confirmed that she was not having any second thoughts about marrying him. Tim's dad was a new man and appeared happier than he had for years. Mr Vieri was the fly in the ointment. But there was no way he was going to stop him marrying Sophie. Sophie had shared with Angela and Tim that her boss had started to talk as though her directorship was a done deal.

He crossed the river bridge and found the boatyard tucked in beside it. There was an attractive long grey stone-built single-storey house flanking the entrance on the left and a tall laurel hedge on the right. The roadway down to the water was paved with old thin pale granite slabs making a series of shallow steps. As he walked down to the water, he heard a door in the house open behind him and a man's voice calling after him.

'Can I help you?' he asked.

Tim turned and took the few paces back to him. He explained why he was there.

'I doubt Rupert will be up yet,' the man said.

Tim replied he was not going to wake the actor, but he was hoping to get a look at the houseboat before he told his fiancée.

The man explained he was the owner of the boatyard and that he would walk Tim down. The man was not very tall and of medium build, he had a mane of white hair and was wearing a pair of well-worn overalls with an unlit pipe in his mouth. The pipe smoke had discoloured one side of his moustache. He gave the impression of being a very practical person, the screwdriver and tape measure peeking from one of his top pockets endorsed the impression.

Most of the houseboats were moored bow on to the bank. Some had a short ladder up to the deck. Others had a plank from boat to shore. One Tim recognised as a large ship's lifeboat was beam on to the bank. The actor's boat had a ramp that came down onto the concrete and made access easy.

'It's not that easy in the winter when the river floods, last year we had two planks to some boats.'

Tim shook his head saying, 'Sorry I don't understand.'

'When the river floods the bank gets covered but, because it is too shallow for the draught of the houseboats they have to stay where they are now, so it can be a lot further to dry land,' the owner explained. 'The idea is that you fill an old steel cold water tank with stones and put that out halfway to the boat, then there is one plank shore to tank then another tank to boat.'

'Isn't that a bit dangerous?'

Hoping to reassure him the man said, 'You do get used to it.'

The boat's name was Sea Maiden. It was mostly white with big windows. Tim noticed that none of the boats were still. They looked like live animals gently stirring in their sleep. The owner turned around and pointed to a row of sheds at the back of the yard. They all had the various boats' names on them.

'All your gear can go in there if you take on the rental,' he explained.

Tim could see two planks resting against some of the sheds. While their backs were turned a curtain on the Sea Maiden was twitched just far enough to reveal a very attractive young woman's face framed by auburn curls. As they made to turn back around the curtain was closed.

Walking back up the slope towards the road Tim explained he had to get back to work. 'Sorry, I don't know your name?' asked the man.

'Cooper, Tim Cooper,' he volunteered.

'Mine's Johnson,' was the response, 'but everyone calls me Tabby. Didn't your father have a stall in that little market up the way on the other side of the river? Don't tell me,' he put his head on one side and scratched the back of his neck with his right hand, his left arm across his chest repeating, 'Cooper, Cooper.' With his forefinger raised he said, 'Tom, Tom Cooper, he lost his wife if I remember. Oh, sorry, son, that was thoughtless of me, that must have been your mum.'

Tim reassured him saying, 'It was a long time ago now.'

'Ring after lunch, Rupert is usually up then.'

'Thank you for all your help, Mr Johnson.'

'Tabby, son, call me Tabby, as I said everybody does.'

At his doorway the two men shook hands and exchanged goodbyes.

Tim left the boatyard very hopeful that Sophie would like the idea and that Rupert would agree to their renting it. Tim rang Rupert later that day and spoke to a woman who had said that Rupert would be away for a few days, but she would ask him to ring Tim on his return. Tim gave her the necessary information and said goodbye.

It was late on the following Saturday afternoon and a growing band of regulars had congregated in the shop to taste the new foodstuffs and have a cup of tea. This had become a regular Saturday afternoon event now. Initially Tim was concerned as the numbers grew that it would be expensive to continue with, however, it was proving to be very worthwhile, not just financially which it was, but regular customers would bring friends who became regulars. The word was spreading amongst the catering trade and more restaurant owners were calling in.

Sophie was at home and some customers were concerned by her absence.

Tim explained that some relatives had come to visit.

Tim's dad revelled in the task of sharing his knowledge of continental cuisine and Sara would spend time with the customers patiently explaining how to cook the food. Her range of recipes on the wall had grown in number. Tim was amused that new customers would often stop just inside the door and take a long breath. The shop had now acquired a wonderful smell. It was a heady mixture of smoked ham that hung on hooks over the counter, wonderful cheeses on display in the glass-topped counters and all the different herbs and spices. His favourite was the smell of the still warm loaves delivered to the shop on Saturday morning. The different types of bread had become firm favourites with his early customers. His father informed Tim that there was usually a small queue waiting for him to open.

CHAPTER 21

THE ACCIDENT

The shop phone rang, and Mr Woodman went to answer it. He listened then placed the phone on the varnished shelf beside the instrument and walked quickly across to where Tim was serving a customer.

He interrupted their conversation and speaking to both Tim and the customer said,

'Sorry, sir, but Tim you must take this call.' Tim strode over to the phone glancing back at Mr Woodman to see if there was any more information, but he had his back to him.

Picking up the phone he said, 'Hallo.'

Angela answered him saying, 'Tim, I am so sorry. But Sophia has been knocked down,' he could hear the fear and panic in her voice.

'Oh God,' said Tim feeling dread spreading through his body. He seized the small phone table with his free hand for support as his legs threatened to buckle under him. 'How bad is it?' he asked, his breath coming short.

'Tim, she is unconscious', Angela explained.

'Is she going to be alright?' he asked.

'They will not tell us. I am very scared.'

'Which hospital is she in?'

'The Royal Free, Tim, please hurry.'

He could hear her voice breaking up. Tim said, 'Hold on, Angela, I am on my way.'

Mr Woodman had arranged a taxi for him. Before closing the taxi door, he said, 'Good luck, lad.'

Tim explained to the taxi driver where to go and what the problem was. The cabby said, 'Sit back, son, let's see how fast I can get you there.'

Tim thought he knew London, but the cabby knew it better. He shot down side streets, through a narrow alley barely wider than the taxi. Did a U-turn in the main road and pulled up outside the hospital.

Tim suddenly realised he had no money on him. Panicking he said to the taxi driver, 'My wallet is back at the shop. Can I give you my watch until I get back?'

'You don't need to do that, lad, I've known Mr Woodman all my life, I will call in at the shop. Go and see how your lady is. Good luck,' he called as Tim hastened towards the hospital entrance.

The receptionist spent a few moments checking where Sophie was then Tim corrected himself and said, 'Her full name is Sophia Vieri.' The woman told him that Sophie was in intensive care and explained how to find her.

Tim marched towards the lift searching the walls for the signs. In the lift he muttered, 'Come on, come on.' Finally, the lift arrived at the correct floor, and the doors opened releasing him. He pivoted around looking for directions, found them and hurried towards the intensive care department, trying to control the panic he could feel rising in his chest. Pushing open a door he found a corridor with a desk halfway down.

The nurse rose as he approached her and said, 'I am sorry, sir, but you are not allowed in here.'

Tim visibly worried said, 'They have just brought my fiancée in here; she was in a motor accident.' The nurse, her demeanour changing, asked for his fiancée's name.

'Her name is Sophie Vieri, no, I mean Sophia.'

She informed him that his fiancée was heavily sedated and was not having visitors. She did add that her mother and her aunt were in the waiting room.

'How is she?' asked Tim.

'We are still evaluating her injuries; we will know more soon. The doctor will talk to you in a while.'

The nurse indicated where the waiting room was. Tim thanked her and went to join the two women. As he walked in it was clear that Angela had been crying. Mrs Vieri sat stone faced on an upright chair eschewing the more comfortable pair of well-stuffed armchairs.

Angela stood up, saying as she did so, 'Tim, I am so glad you are here; nobody will tell us anything.'

Mrs Vieri, in a voice devoid of any trace of emotion said, 'I am sure they are doing everything they can, Angela. You will not achieve anything by getting in a flap.' She had still not said anything to Tim, she continued, 'They will tell us what we need to know when it is appropriate.'

'That is what the nurse has just told me,' confirmed Tim.

'You see,' said Mrs Vieri.

Tim continued, 'Apparently Sophia is heavily sedated and is not having visitors.'

Mrs Vieri just nodded.

Angela said, 'Thank you, Tim.'

Tim stood looking out of the window at the hospital car park. The weather had changed. Now there was a nasty fine cold rain that quickly soaked you. It was driven by a biting wind. His father called it a lazy wind. It went through you rather than around. Tim mused that even the weather seemed upset.

Tim's reverie was broken by the arrival of Mr Vieri deep in conversation with a doctor. He swept past the waiting room without so much as a glance. After a short delay he came back and entered the room. The space seemed to shrink with him in it. He seemed surprised to see Tim there but did at least nod in his direction.

That's one thing I have learnt about this strange family, thought Tim, they are good at nodding.

Mr Vieri announced to no one in particular, 'Sophia has a broken arm, that will mend they have told me without any complications, what they are worried about is the concussion. She is heavily sedated and will be for some hours otherwise she would be in a lot of pain. They will not know if there are any long-term problems until they remove the sedation. They will keep us informed.'

At that moment a nurse arrived, she was buxom with a wonderful Irish accent, clearly someone who would not brook any nonsense.

She said, 'Sophia has been given something to make her sleep, so everybody may as well go home.'

Tim made sure he was the last leaving the room. The rest went and stood by the lift. Tim said, 'I am going to use the stairs,' and then clattered noisily down the first flight. Hearing the lift start down he quietly made his way back up and stood peering through the round glass porthole in the door to the intensive care department. The nurse he had spoken to earlier was sitting with her back to him. A minute later she rose and went into the ladies' loo. Quiet as a mouse he slid through the door, controlling its closing he tiptoed to the waiting room. The room was in darkness. He sat in the light from the streetlamp and prepared for a long night. He was drowsing when the door came open and the light snapped on.

The same nurse said, 'What are you doing here? You must be Timothy. She keeps mumbling your name. Would you mind sitting with her? We can get you kitted up. She may rest more easily if she knows you are here. Are you ok with this?' He explained he had done the same thing for his mother when she was dying in this very hospital.

'She is not going to die, Tim,' said the nurse squeezing his arm. 'Let's get you sorted and then you can sit with her.'

Ten minutes later, dressed in a green hospital gown and a face mask, the nurse led him into Sophie's room, the sight of her wrenched at his heart, she appeared to be surrounded by equipment with lights, some flashing, and the cords coming from them were attached to different places around her body. She had a drip inserted in the back of one hand. Her other arm was encased in a large white plaster cast. He felt an acute physical pain twist his stomach. There was a large snake deep in his gut, writhing in agony, coiling and uncoiling. She looked so small and frail amongst all the machinery. He used the palms of his hand to roughly brush away the tears. The nurse pretended not to notice and explained that if Sophie started licking her lips, he could squeeze out the sponge and moisten them.

'Talk to her, Tim, she may be less frightened. We don't know if she will hear you, but you never know.'

'Can I hold her hand?' he asked.

'I don't see why not. I will bring you a cup of tea and a biscuit in a while.'

'Thank you,' replied Tim. He reached for Sophie's hand and started to talk to her. His tea and biscuits arrived, he tried to release his fingers but as his hand started to slide free Sophie's grip on it tightened.

He said to the nurse, 'She won't let me go.'

'That is a very good sign, but you have a long night ahead of you. When you need a break just call me and I will take over. She is certainly calmer now that you are here.'

Later that night just as Tim had decided he had to go to the toilet the doctor walked in with the nurse. Tim went to get up, but the doctor put his hand on his shoulder and restrained him.

'Stay there, I need to do some observations, unless you need to have a stretch.'

'I need the toilet,' said Tim.

'Carry on,' said the doctor, 'I will be ten minutes or more.'

He was returning to the room just as the doctor was coming out. 'The nurse tells me you have been through all of this before with your mother. The difference here, Tim, is that Sophia is not going to die. We cannot however know if the concussion will have any lasting effect, until we wake her up. I will keep you abreast of everything as we go along. She is resting well so that's a good sign. Are you able to carry on, you don't have to you know?'

'No, I am fine, I would not sleep at home anyway.'

The doctor said, 'I will ask the nurse to keep the tea coming. See you at dawn,' he said leaving the unit.

Tim resumed his vigil sitting beside her through the long night, talking to her when she became fretful, dozing when she did, and periodically moistening her lips.

Tim was not sure if he had a real faith, but he found himself praying in a whisper, 'Please, please God, let her get well.' He realised how bleak his life would be without her. What if she had brain damage, he knew a little boy who had fallen from a swing and hit his head. He was now considered slow. If that was the outcome for her, he would learn how to look after her. There was no way he was going to desert her, she gave purpose to his life, he loved her unconditionally, well or not, he made a solemn promise to himself he would always look after her.

He told her things he may not have told her if she could hear him. He found himself laughing out loud at the conclusion of one story.

The nurse poked her head around the door and asked him, 'Are we all ok in here?'

'Yes,' he replied, 'I was reminiscing, and the story made me laugh when I remembered it.'

'Tea, I think we need tea,' she said and went to prepare it.

He was very aware of having done the same for his mother all those years ago, but he reminded himself very firmly that Sophie was not going to die. As the dawn light began to creep into the room the nurse brought him another cup of tea and a sandwich.

An hour later the doctor came in accompanied by Mr Vieri. Looking at Tim dressed in the gown and face mask he was clearly shocked. 'Why is he here?' he asked beginning to grow angry.

The doctor replied in a manner that indicated whatever Mr Vieri thought, he was incorrect, he said, 'Tim has sat with Sophia all night long keeping her calm, talking to her when she became restless and keeping her lips moistened. Your daughter has had a much better night than she would have done if Tim had not been here with her.'

More nodding, thought Tim.

He was right, Sophie's father nodded at him and then, to Tim's complete surprise Mr Vieri said, 'Thank you, Tim.'

As the doctor and Mr Vieri were leaving the room the doctor looked over his shoulder saying, 'I will be back in a minute, Tim, if you can hang on.'

Tim nodded and smiled; this nodding business is catching, he thought.

The nurse returned with a colleague, 'Tim, there are things we need to do, it's best if you wait outside.'

'Sure,' he responded, 'I will get something to eat.' As he left the intensive care unit, he met the doctor coming in. Tim explained they were tending to Sophie, so was going to get something to eat.

'I could do with a coffee, mind if I join you?'

'No problem,' said Tim.

A little later sitting in the hospital café the doctor introduced himself. 'My name is Dr Richards.'

Relaxed for a minute, Tim realised the doctor was very young. Earlier he had only seen the white coat, as he suspected many of his patients did. The doctor went on to explain to him that they would be trying to lessen the amount of tranquiliser they were giving Sophie. They would continue with the pain relief because her broken arm would be painful but that would be as nothing compared to the headache she will have and if she is too uncomfortable, they would sedate her again.

'Can you tell if there will be any lasting problems because of her accident?' Tim asked.

'Not yet,' was the response. 'We will have to see what happens when she is fully awake. The good news is that she is very well otherwise, and her age is in her favour, so I have high hopes that she will come through ok.'

Tim was silent for a minute.

'What do you do for a living, Tim?' asked the doctor.

Tim said, 'I will tell you, but the rule is that when you get bored you put your hand up.'

The doctor smiled. Tim spent ten minutes enthusing about his partners and his business, occasionally interrupted by the doctor with a question.

'Sounds like hard work but great fun and you clearly get a real buzz from it. Oops,' he said looking at his watch, 'I must get on, will you be staying?' he asked.

'I would like to please,' Tim responded.

'Mary, the nurse, seems to think it's a good idea. Ok, let's see how the day goes,' said the doctor as he scraped his chair back. 'Thank you for last night,' he added before walking away.

Tim returned to find Mr Woodman sitting in the waiting area nursing a cup of tea. Even at this early hour, it was only just seven o'clock, he was immaculately dressed as always.

'Good morning,' said Tim.

Mr Woodman looked up seeing Tim for the first time, 'Hallo, how is she doing?'

Tim explained about the gradual withdrawal of the sedation and that Sophie would be monitored and medicated appropriately. He apologised for leaving everybody to it, but Mr Woodman waived it aside.

'What else could you do? Everybody sends their best wishes, even some of the customers are sending good wishes for a speedy recovery. Everybody is in, your dad, Harry and Sara. They all said not to worry we have got it all under control. Those two appointments you had have been postponed. When I explained the problem, they were very good and said for you to contact them when you return. Harry dealt with one chap who is going to open a restaurant just around the corner from us. Harry gave him some prices and he seemed quite pleased.'

'Well done all of you, thank you very much for everything you are doing,' said Tim anxious now to get back to Sophie.

Mr Woodman recognised Tim's concern and told him to give her all their love and best wishes, shook Tim's hand and said, 'I am sure she will be fine, lad.'

Tim nodded, said, 'Thanks again,' and walked away.

Mr Woodman took a few steps and looked around. 'Good luck to you both,' he said quietly.

Tim already was replacing the mask and making his way back into the unit. He sat through a long morning carrying on much as he had during the night. Leaving the room now and then when requested so they could carry out various tasks for Sophie. The nurse that had come on duty for the morning shift was very brusque and Tim felt, slightly military in her manner, but nice enough. There was one problem. The tea was less frequent.

At midday he was told to go and get some lunch in the cafeteria. They had to change her drips etc. As he exited the lift and walked across the main corridor near the main entrance, he heard a familiar voice calling his name.

'Hallo, lad, how's it going?' asked his father as he walked up to him.

'Hallo, Dad, she's still sedated but I think they are starting to reduce it as we speak, they will try to balance it so that she is not in too much pain.'

'Is that from the arm?' asked his dad.

'No, it's from the concussion.'

'Is she going to be alright, lad?'

'They can't tell yet, but Dr Reynolds seem to think she will be ok.'

Mr Cooper was concerned for Tim, he looked very tired and worried. 'How are you holding up, lad?' he asked.

'I must admit I was very scared last night, but it may be my imagination, but I think she has better colour this morning. I was terrified I was going to lose her, Dad.'

'Pain often comes with loving someone,' his father replied, his face clouding over.

Tim was reminded again how great was his father's loss with the death of his mother, 'I think we both need a strong cup of coffee,' he said leading his father towards the cafeteria.

When they had ordered and seated themselves his dad proffered a plastic bag full of envelopes at Tim. 'The word has gone around and lots of customers have been popping in with get well cards and of course some are from us. Sara is taking it badly. I think she had a relative in a car crash who died. Harry keeps reassuring her, but it does not seem to be having any effect. I notice she is often tearful.'

'Well hopefully later today we will be able to give her some good news,' responded Tim crossing his fingers.

Mr Cooper brought Tim up to date with the activities that were happening in the shop.

Tim suddenly remembered the boat details, ferreting in his back pocket and finally bringing out the rather crumpled advert he said, 'Dad, could you do me a favour, please? Will you ring this chap and explain who I am and tell him I am very interested in renting his boat?'

'What is this all about?' asked his dad, very surprised.

Tim explained what he had in mind.

'I hope Sophie is as keen as you are, lad.'

'I think she likes the river,' he replied.

'Maybe not as much as you do, son.'

'I must get back upstairs,' said Tim looking at his watch, 'thanks for coming in, Dad, and please give my thanks to everybody back there, see you later,' he said as he stood up.

'Give her our love when she wakes up,' said his father after he shook Tim's hand. He stood still for a few moments, his son turned and waved. While he waved back, he prayed that Sophie would be ok, realising that if she did not recover it would destroy the lad.

On his return to the unit Tim found Mary was back on duty.

'Hallo, Tim, what have you there?' pointing at the bag he was clutching.

Tim explained about the cards and all the customers' best wishes. Mary explained that he could not bring them into the unit but when she was transferred to a ward, she could have them then.

Tim got togged up again and went in to sit with Sophie. He followed the same drill, telling her stories, silly jokes he remembered from his childhood. He noticed she was becoming more restless.

Mary came and looking at the monitors said, 'She is starting to come too. I will sit with you Tim; I expect her to wake up soon.'

About an hour later Sophie moaned and opened one eye. The grip on his hand tightened and she tried to say something. The nurse stepped in and holding the small watch pinned to her uniform she took her pulse. Sophie closed her eyes.

'Tim,' she said, 'I am going to ring for the doctor, just hold her hand and reassure her please.' Leaving the room, she said, 'Call if you need me. I will only be outside.'

Tim was telling Sophie that she was going to be alright, that her arm would mend when suddenly, her right eye popped open, she saw Tim and started to cry.

She started to mumble through her tears. Tim could not hear what she was saying. Leaning closer, eventually he worked out that she was saying, 'My head, my head.' He rang the bell for the nurse who quickly reappeared. Sophie was no longer mumbling but had her eyes closed and was restless.

Tim explained what had just happened.

Tim continued to hold Sophie's hand and reassure her. The doctor arrived shortly after and began checking Sophie's pulse, lifted her eyelid briefly and then stood for some time watching her.

Eventually he turned to Tim and said, 'This is a very good sign, Tim. I think we can adjust the pain relief and the sedation and make her more comfortable. Are you alright to stay with her?'

'Certainly,' Tim replied.

'Ring the bell if you are worried, Tim,' said Dr Richards as he left the room with the nurse.

They both returned shortly afterwards, Mary the nurse changing the drip and Dr Richards giving Sophie an injection through the cannula. Turning to Tim he explained that he had slightly reduced the sedation and that the injection was a painkiller.

Another nurse popped her head around the door and said, 'There is someone to see you, doctor.'

After the doctor had left Tim said, 'I need the toilet.' He had not stirred from Sophie's side for quite some time.

'Ok, Tim, I will take over,' said Mary.

As he left the unit and made his way across the corridor to the toilet, he saw Mr Vieri talking to the doctor. Thankfully Sophie's father had his back to him. Tim sought refuge in the loo. Whilst in there he took the opportunity to rinse his face and had removed his mask to do so. On leaving the toilet he was face to face with Mr Vieri who had changed his position and was now staring straight at him.

Mr Vieri did not recognise Tim straight away. He saw a grey faced young man with deep shadows under his eyes, unshaven and looking terribly tired. Then recognition dawned. Tim nodded and began to turn away.

'Please wait,' said Mr Vieri.

Tim turned ready for an argument, too tired to care about diplomacy.

'Hallo,' he said.

'Have you been here all this time?' asked Mr Vieri.

'He has not left Sophia's side,' said Dr Reynolds.

'Can we talk?' Mr Vieri asked, very aware that Tim was more than ready to defend himself.

'You can use the counsellor's room,' said Dr Reynolds pointing at a door opposite.

'Sit down,' said Mr Vieri.

'I prefer to stand,' responded Tim, expecting another dressing down.

Mr Vieri, although used to getting his own way was not stupid and recognised that this young man was at the end of his tether and that for once he needed to tread carefully. 'How long have you sat with her?'

'Ever since she was brought in.'

'When did you last sleep?'

'I don't remember.'

'Please sit down before you fall down,' said Mr Vieri.

Tim did as he was asked, too tired to argue.

'I will ask the nurse to sit with her so that you can get some sleep.'

'No thank you, sir, I need to be with her. She is more comfortable when I am there.'

Mr Vieri looked at Tim for a long moment and said, 'I realise I have misjudged you and your intentions.'

'Yes, sir, you have, but I do understand why, but now I had better get back to Sophie.'

Mr Vieri did not correct him. As Tim left the room Mr Vieri said, 'I would like it if we could talk once Sophia is better.'

'Ok,' said Tim as he left.

Mr Vieri sat there thinking for a long time after Tim had left. Finally, nodding, he rose and left the room.

On Tim's return Mary the nurse said, 'She is sleeping now, Tim, and is much calmer. Would you like some tea and a sandwich?'

'Oh yes please,' he replied.

Later that evening he had fallen asleep and had indeed been asleep for some while.

Mary the nurse had looked in regularly and had smiled to see the young couple holding hands and sleeping peacefully. A while later Tim rose up from a very deep sleep hearing someone saying his name. Opening his eyes, he saw Sophie awake looking at him. It had been her.

'What has happened to me?' she whispered.

Tim explained she had been in a motor accident, but as yet he did not know how it had happened.

Still whispering Sophie said, 'You look terrible.'

'Thank you,' said Tim, smiling. He then realised that she had gone to sleep again.

Dr Richards called in later and said, 'The nurse tells me you have had a brief conversation with her.'

Tim nodded.

'Whilst we cannot know if there will be any long-term problems because of the concussion, these early signs are good.'

'Thank you,' said Tim.

Dr Richards patted Tim's shoulder as he left.

The two of them slept most of the night, Tim still holding her hand. At first light he was awakened by Sophie squeezing his hand. It was not a pleasant experience; his hand had gone to sleep and as the circulation returned, he had terrible pins and needles which for some reason Sophie found funny. Her recovery now speeded up. By mid-morning on the following day, she was fully awake, although understandably very sore. The nurse told the young couple that if the doctor agreed Sophie may be able to be transferred to the ward later today. At lunch time the doctor and two nurses came and told Tim and Sophie that she was being moved to a ward.

'Which one?' asked Tim. 'Wren,' was the reply.

The nurse who they had not seen before said, 'Sorry, sir, I am going to have to ask you to leave while we prepare your fiancée for the move to the ward. Go and have some lunch, we will be a while.'

'Tim,' said Sophie puckering her lips.

Tim kissed her very gently. 'See you later, darling.'

Outside Tim stripped off the gown and mask then used the bathroom to have a good wash. He was suddenly very tired and felt dirty. He decided that once he was sure that Sophie was safely installed on the ward he would go home and clean up.

Lunch in the hospital canteen was very welcome. He had existed on hastily grabbed snacks for two days and now his hunger made itself felt. A large baked potato with chicken curry helped. He polished the meal off with sticky toffee pudding and custard. This was all washed down with a glass of ginger beer. His mother had always had a tall glass container on the windowsill with what she called a ginger beer plant in it. As a child he spent a long time watching the gas bubbles struggle through the pale beige sediment that lay in the bottom of the jar. He was not sure what strange alchemy took place, but the love of the end result had stayed with him.

On his way to Wren ward he felt his tiredness begin to overtake him. Sophie was asleep when he walked into the ward. She still had lots of cables attached but she was looking better, her colour had improved.

CHAPTER 22

RECOVERY

Tim picked up a Country Life magazine from the rack and settled back to wait for Sophie to wake. Minutes later the magazine slipped from his fingers as he fell fast asleep.

One and a half hours later he was woken when a tin tray fell on the floor. As he came to he turned to check up on Sophie. Both her eyes were open, and she was smiling at him. Tim was rather taken aback and began to apologise.

In a quiet rather hoarse voice she said, 'The nurse made everybody be quiet whilst you slept. Mary had told the nurse that you never left my bedside. Thank you, Tim, I think I knew you were there. Did you tell me a very rude story, or did I dream it?'

'Umm, well,' said Tim, 'I don't really remember.'

'You did, you did,' she squeaked, immediately regretting it as her head let her know that getting excited was a bad idea.

The nurse appeared as if from nowhere. 'We aren't overdoing it in here, are we? You need to rest, young lady.'

'Tim, I think a bath and a rest would be a good idea for you, and maybe a change of clothes?' said Sophie.

'In other words, I stink,' he said.

Sophie nodded, gently.

'Ok, I give in,' he leaned across and kissed her forehead.

As Tim left the ward the two women smiled at each other.

The nurse introduced herself and said, 'My name is Ellen. Whatever you do, young lady, don't you let that one get away. He loves you like crazy. Not many young men would do what he has done over the last three days.'

Sophie said, 'I knew he was who I was looking for almost as soon as I met him. I feel I have always known him.'

Tim took a taxi home. He would normally have walked but he still felt completely drained. He resisted falling asleep in the bath and climbed into bed as God made him, one of his mother's expressions. He had set the alarm for three hours. Four hours later there was a gentle tapping on his door, and he could hear his landlady softly calling his name.

He climbed from his bed and said, 'Oops,' out loud. 'Hang on, Mrs Clarke, I need to put some clothes on.' Shortly afterwards he opened the door and invited her in.

'How's your fiancée?' she asked.

Tim replied that she was awake and had been moved to the ward.

'Oh, that's good news, I have been very worried about her because I know how much she means to you. One other thing, Tim, and I am sorry to bother you now, but the rent is overdue, and I've just had the electric bill in, and it's all gone up.'

Tim was mortified, 'I am so sorry,' he said reaching for his wallet, 'I tell you what I will give you another three pounds a week.'

'No, no, no,' said Mrs Clarke embarrassed. 'If you could spare half of that it would be a great help.'

'I tell you what,' said Tim, 'why don't we make it an extra two pounds, how's that?'

'Only if you are sure, Tim,' she replied.

'Don't tell anybody, Mrs Clarke, but we are starting to make a small profit so yes, I can afford it,' he said as he counted out her money.

'I am so pleased for you. You've worked so hard and what with your mum and everythin'. Is your dad any better? He misses your mum somethin' terrible, doesn't he?'

'He is a lot better lately, working in the shop has given him a new lease of life, he is really enjoying himself.'

'That's good news, he was lost without your mum.'

'I didn't realise how he felt, I was too young I suppose,' he said reflecting on the scare he had just had.

'Tim, I have cooked too much tea again, would you like some?'

'Yes please,' he said enthusiastically. He smiled inwardly knowing that Mrs Clarke had cooked for him in case he came home. Tim followed her downstairs. He noticed that she was taking the stairs slower than she once did and she appeared more stooped. She had always reminded Tim of a vigorous sparrow; always very busy, always doing something. Now she looked old and frail. He was worried. If he moved onto the boat in a month or two, she would lose his rent money. He decided to help her find another tenant if she would let him. She was a very independent lady.

On his return to the hospital he was stopped by Ellen the nurse. 'Sophie's mother and father are in there with her now. Sophie is sound asleep, we have given her a sedative, she will sleep until the morning. She had some pain which is to be expected.'

'She is ok though?' asked Tim, alarmed.

'She is doing very well. She is young, Tim, and very fit and well, all these things are in her favour. She will be fine.'

'Thank you,' he replied.

'There are only two visitors allowed by her beside so make yourself comfy on the sofa here and I will sort out some tea.'

He never did get his tea; he fell asleep soon after he sat down. The nurse brought him tea and seeing him asleep she decided the rest was more important than the tea. As she walked away, she said under her breath, 'Sleep on, lad, you deserve it.'

Tim woke around midnight and slowly became aware of how late it was. Struggling to focus on his watch he stood and asked the passing night nurse if his fiancée was ok.

The nurse confirmed she was and said that Sophie would not wake until the morning because of the sedative. 'Ellen said we should advise you to go home and see Sophie tomorrow.'

'Can I say goodnight?'

'You can, but please don't wake her,' the nurse replied.

Tim tiptoed into the small ward to find the only other occupant sound asleep and snoring her head off. Sophie appeared to be sleeping soundly. He kissed her gently on the top of her head, whispered 'goodnight' and tiptoed back out of the ward.

Tim was up very early the following morning and decided to go to the shop first before returning to the hospital. His concern for Sophie had lessened as she had slowly improved. He enjoyed his walk to work and even found himself whistling a favourite Sinatra number. The sun was shining out of a cloudless sky and the tree-lined walk was alive with bird song. A child aged about three rushed around a tree without looking and banged into his legs and sat down hard.

'Are you alright?' asked Tim.

The child did not answer him but peering up to see Tim's face asked, 'Are you a giant?'

His mother arrived and heard the child's question. She was a young mum, not very tall. She started to tell the child off, but Tim insisted that he was unhurt, and it wasn't a problem. The mother explained that her family were all short and young Sam was fascinated by tall people. Tim bent down to speak to the child, 'You are perfectly safe, I'm not a giant,' he assured him.

He arrived at the shop and discovered that it was already open. His dad and Mr Woodman were serving some early customers. Both men were pleased to see him and immediately enquired after Sophie. Tim confirmed that she was doing well and may be coming home soon.

He then asked, 'How come the shop is open so early?'

Both men looked at each other and then Mr Woodman explained that a couple of days ago they had admitted to each other that they both woke very early and then sat around and waited for the clock to tick round so they could open the shop.

'If you don't want us to do it, we will stop,' said his dad.

'No, it's not a problem,' replied Tim. 'I have been thinking it's time we started paying you for the hours you work. That will be influenced by how much business we do in the extended opening hours. What time did you open today?'

'Erm, just before seven,' replied his dad.

'It was half past six, Tim,' said Mr Woodman.

'How much business did you do?' asked Tim.

'Not a lot,' replied Mr Woodman.

'Tim, it's not all about money, I would rather be here than sitting at home staring at the walls,' added his dad.

At that moment a customer hurried into the shop. Mr Woodman moved away to serve him. Stopping, he said, 'Please excuse me for one moment, sir. Tim, Mr Strong rang, he said will you ring him this afternoon please about the boat?' Turning back to the customer he said, 'Sorry about that, now how can I help you?'

Tim asked his dad, 'What about Harry and Sara?'

'They are coming in at the usual time; it is not about the money, lad, this place keeps me busy; it's nice to have something to do each day. I love the work, I like the banter with the customers, and it gives me a chance to show my skills and, son,' he continued, 'I no longer sit and mope all day.'

Tim realised he had to back off but added, 'If it all becomes too much for you please promise that you will tell me.'

Mr Woodman finished serving the customer and re-joined them.

'That goes for both of you, I worry that you will overdo it,' continued Tim.

'Tim, we know what we are doing, to quote you, let's give it a go,' urged Mr Woodman.

'Well how about a 7 am start and we try it for a month?' responded Tim.

The two men looked at each other and nodded, 'Ok,' said his dad, 'but let's say three months.' He was still looking at Mr Woodman when he said it.

Mr Woodman said, 'That's fine by me, Mr Cooper.'

Tim shook his head.

When Harry arrived Tim filled him in regarding Sophie's condition. He was very pleased and asked Tim to pass on his and Sara's love.

Tim briefly explained about the new hours.

Harry raised no objection but said, 'I don't know what Sara will say.'

'We did not think you would be able to do it,' said Mr Woodman. 'We are not married so it is easier. Sorry Mr Cooper,' he added.

Tim's dad raised a hand palm out meaning there was not a problem.

'Sophie will not be too pleased if you work all the hours God sends when you are newly married' added his father.

'I think it might be her that's doing those hours when she gets this directorship,' replied Tim.

'Is that going alright?' asked Harry.

'The owner thinks it's a done deal.'

'Well done Sophie,' said Harry in a congratulatory tone with a big smile on his face.

'I will pass on all your good wishes, how are you getting on without me?' he asked.

'We are doing fine,' said his dad.

'That's a bit worrying,' responded Tim.

'You must do what you must do,' observed Mr Woodman. 'We will keep it ticking over.'

'We do need to talk about wages in the very near future,' added Tim. 'Ok, I must go. Thank you all very much,' said Tim as he prepared to leave.

'Don't forget Mr Strong rang about the boat,' Mr Woodman called to Tim's retreating back.

'Whoops,' said Tim. 'I had better do it now.'

Tim was about to hang up after a long wait when the phone was finally answered by a man saying, in what Tim considered to be a rather theatrical voice, 'Hallo, Strong here, sorry to keep you waiting. I am painting the other end of the old girl. The boat that is, not the girl friend you understand. She doesn't need painting. Anyway, enough of that, what can I do for you my dear fellow?'

Tim explained he was the shop keeper and he was interested in renting the boat.

'Ah yes, got it now. A chap phoned me and said you were interested. Your wife was in hospital. Is she ok?'

Tim explained that it was his fiancée, and that she had been knocked down.

'Everybody has been very worried about her, but she is on the mend now and should be home soon. About the boat, I am very interested in renting it. Obviously, I wanted my fiancée to see it before I said yes. We would have looked at it before now, but she couldn't get there.'

'Quite understand old chap, trouble is I have to go abroad at the end of the week.

It's earlier than they said but you know what film people are like, though I don't suppose you do. Why would you, in fact almost certainly you would not. Sorry, rambling again. I only make any sense when I have a script don't you know. When could you come?'

Tim found himself smiling, amused at Mr Strong's wonderful plummy theatrical manner of speech. 'I could call in now if that's ok? It will be a brief visit; I need to be at the hospital as soon as possible.'

'That's fine,' replied Rupert Strong. 'I have not had any other calls, see you in a few minutes.' He hung up.

Tim felt a pang of guilt. There had been no calls because he had not displayed the advert. A short taxi ride later he was deposited at the entrance to the boatyard. He spotted Tabby the boatyard owner and then recognised the man talking to him as Rupert Strong. He looked a little smarter than the last time Tim had seen him.

Tabby recognised Tim as he walked down the slope towards them, the pipe was well

alight in the corner of his mouth. The wind was blowing the smoke into his eyes making him grimace.

'Hallo, young man, how is your fiancée?' he asked, 'Rupert here was just telling me.'

'She's on the mend thank you,' Tim replied. 'I'm off there after this.'

'Well let's get it done then,' said Rupert.

Rupert showed Tim around pointing out where the gas bottles were and the cold-water tank and how it was filled. A solid fuel stove heated the water and warmed the cabin. The back cabin was the bedroom. The whole space was filled with light. The reflections off the wavelets on the river threw dancing diamonds of light onto the cabin ceiling.

'Oh crikey,' said Tim, 'that's amazing.'

'You're not wrong,' said Rupert. 'Let's get down to the nitty gritty,' he continued. 'I was hoping to get a fair bit for the rental.'

'What were you thinking?'

Rupert named a figure that was considerably more than Tim could afford. He had to tell Rupert he was sorry; the boat was just what he hoped it would be, but he could not afford it.

At that moment the phone rang. Rupert said, 'Please excuse me, I must take this.'

Tim stepped out onto the deck to allow Rupert some privacy. Looking around at the boat traffic, the water, the people working on the river, he realised that this was where he would really like to live, to wake up to these sights and sounds every morning. But he could not afford it.

The phone call took about five minutes and then Rupert joined Tim on deck. 'Tim, I have had an idea, how are your DIY skills?'

'Not too bad, I used to help my dad at home.'

'How much could you afford to pay me say, monthly, old thing?'

'Not very much really, we are only just going into profit.' He told Rupert how much he was paying in rent now.

'Well how about this then m'dear; you live on the boat for the rent amount you just mentioned, and you paint her stem to stern and the interior. Any colour as long as it's white. Any major expenses you consult me first. You buy all the paint, et cetera. Tabby is a mine of the old info, so he will guide you if you ask him and he will report your progress to me. What do you think? I would rather have someone I trust rather than the money and to be honest what they are paying me for this film is mind boggling.'

Tim said, 'Just one question, the major repairs other than those that are our fault will not be our responsibility?'

Rupert thought for a moment and then said, 'That seems fair.'

'We will have to draw up something covering the basics, my wife will insist, she is an accountant.'

'Agreed,' responded Rupert.

The two men shook hands on the deal.

'I must fly,' said Rupert already stepping off the ramp. 'Ring me when you have got something worked out. I am sure there will not be a problem.' With that he pulled an old grubby tarpaulin off a Norton ES2 motorcycle and stepped astride. Starting the bike with an easy familiarity and shouting above the noise of the engine he called, 'Cheery pip old thing,' as he roared away, his long hair waving in the wind.

Checking his watch Tim realised it was later than he thought. He hailed a taxi the other side of the bridge and was soon standing outside the hospital. Making his way to Wren ward a nurse he had not seen before asked him who he was looking for. She informed him that the doctor was with her now so would he wait please. He plonked himself down on the chair he had previously decided was the most comfortable and waited. He began a series of mind games that he had used when his mother was in this same hospital. He had struggled with maths when he was at school, so he would practice his times tables. Using mental arithmetic he extended the tables beyond twelve times as far as he could.

He had been shown up in the maths lesson when they were doing percentages because, initially, he could not grasp the concept. His teacher had kept him behind after class one day and got him started by showing him some simple tricks. Now as an adult he was very quick and both skills had proven to be essential in his business.

The doctor came through the door from the ward talking over his shoulder to the nurse following him. Spotting Tim sitting there he finished his conversation with the nurse then turned to Tim, who stood up.

'Good morning, Tim,' he paused for a moment then said, 'Sophie has had a little set back in the night. She had a bout of quite intense pain and we had to step up the medication again. I think it is just a blip, but I want to keep her in for one more day just to make sure. All these head traumas are different. We will watch her and respond accordingly. You can go in, she has been asking for you, but don't be surprised or worried if she falls asleep. If you are concerned call the nurse.'

Tim noticed the nurse was standing behind Dr Reynolds listening. Tim mouthed a good morning at her. She nodded.

'I must press on,' said Dr Richards, 'there has been a motor accident, nothing very serious, thank God, but a couple of broken bones. I will see you later if you are staying?'

'I am,' Tim replied entering the ward. He could see Sophie was drowsy but otherwise looked reasonably comfortable. He pulled the curtains around to give them a little privacy.

'The doctor tells me you had a difficult night?' said Tim.

'I thought my head was going to burst,' she replied.

'Can I kiss it better?' he asked.

'Yes, please,' she replied.

He kissed her very gently. Tim thought he ought to tell her about the boat but as he began Sophie drifted off to sleep. Shortly afterwards the nurse arrived with tea, biscuits and the paper.

The morning drifted by. After lunch Sophie had another visitor. Tim was engrossed in a book he had found in the rack by the door. Sophie was sound asleep. The newcomer standing at the end of the bed looked very prosperous. He was dressed in a well-cut grey pinstripe suit and black Italian shoes, the only anomaly in his attire was the red socks.

Tim took a moment to understand what the gentleman was saying. He was still with his hero on page forty-seven. Tim apologised and said, 'Sorry, I didn't get your name.' Both men were speaking just above a whisper.

The stranger said, 'Wells, Terry Wells, Sophie's boss.' He appeared younger than Tim had believed him to be and looked very fit. 'I am sorry I have not been before, but I had not realised how much Sophie had taken on.' He finished by saying, 'She is very good at what she does you know.'

'So she tells me,' laughed Tim quietly.

Mr Wells smiled and said, 'Seriously though, the new systems she is piloting are amazing. If it will help her to get better, you can tell her she has got the Finance Director's job.'

'Thank you very much, she will be so pleased, but would you not prefer to tell her yourself?'

'No that's fine,' he replied. 'I have left some flowers outside for her. I understand you have just opened a shop; Sophie is very excited about it. We must get together some time. I am sorry I must dash, nice to have met you, bye for now.' With that he left the ward.

Twenty minutes later Sophie awoke although she was still drowsy from the medication. 'Sorry,' she said, 'I keep drifting off. At least my head has stopped hurting.'

CHAPTER 23

SOPHIE'S JOB

'You've had a visitor,' Tim told her.

'Who was that?'

'Your boss.'

'Oh crikey, what did he want?'

'He came to see how you were and he asked me to give you a message.'

'What was it about?'

Smiling, Tim said, 'He was very impressed with the new systems you are trialling.'

'Was that all?' asked Sophie sounding puzzled.

'Not quite,' said Tim, 'you have got the director's job.'

'Oh my goodness,' she said very quietly, her hand went to her mouth and the tears welled up in her eyes, 'you are not kidding me, are you?' she asked.

'I wouldn't do that to you,' he said.

'Oh, Tim, it is what I have always wanted,' she said with the tears running down her face and a widening smile. 'It would never have happened had I not met you.'

'How do you arrive at that conclusion?' he asked.

At that moment Ellen the nurse popped her head around the curtain and seeing Sophie's condition asked, 'Whatever is the matter with you, my dear? Are you in pain?'

'No, she's not,' said Tim. 'Her boss has offered her the finance director's post.'

'I am so pleased for you,' she said. 'I think a cup of tea is in order,' she added leaving the ward.

Tim was about to tell her about the boat when Mrs Vieri and Angela arrived.

'I will leave you to catch up,' he said to the women, 'Sophie has some amazing news.'

He kissed Sophie on the forehead and left the ward waving as he went. As Tim started down the stairs, he heard Mr Vieri's voice talking to the doctor as they exited the lift.

That was a lucky escape, he said to himself as he continued down. It was not that he was frightened of any of Sophie's family it was just that he was becoming tired of the tension and constantly walking on eggshells. He hoped this would get better, but he suspected there would always be a certain level of discomfort between him and the family.

He took a taxi back to the shop. I can't keep spending money like this, he thought. He then remembered he'd had a bike when he was younger. I wonder if it's still at Dad's house, he thought to himself.

When he arrived back at the shop it was to find the shop full of customers and his whole team working flat out. Shrugging out of his jacket he called out, 'Who's next?' and at the same time waving hallo at everyone.

They all worked hard for nearly two hours before the shop became less frantic.

'Tea, anyone?' called Mr Woodman. They all put their hands up including one of the regular customers. 'Milk and sugar?' asked Mr Woodman.

'I was only joking,' the customer replied.

'Would you like a cup of tea?' Mr Woodman repeated slowly and rather forthrightly.

'Well, yes please then,' the customer replied, 'milk and two sugars please.'

'Right you are,' said Mr Woodman making for the stairs. A faint note of censure in his voice.

Tim walked over to talk to Sara and make himself a sandwich. He was suddenly aware he had not eaten since breakfast and it was now late afternoon and he was hungry.

He began to carve a slice of smoked ham and at the same time enquiring after Sara's health.

'I am very well, thank you Mr Tim, would you like me to make the sandwich?'

Tim handed her the knife and holding her arm gently he asked Sara if she would please stop calling him Mr Tim. 'It makes me feel uncomfortable,' he said. She went very red and began to stammer an apology.

Tim stopped her and saying, 'Sara, you are a major contributor to the success of this shop and are equal in every way to the rest of us. Your confectionery has been the only thing that has kept us afloat a couple of times so as I say we are all equal in this establishment.'

'Thank you... Tim,' she had paused before using his name. She busied herself making his sandwich.

Tim told everyone the latest news about Sophie and explained that she might be going home soon.

'That's good news,' said Mr Woodman, this was echoed by the rest of the team.

Sara approached him and asked, 'When are you going back to the hospital Mr, I, um, Tim?' she went red again, 'I have a little box of some of her favourite food.' She handed Tim a good-sized Tupperware box that given the weight was obviously full.

'Thank you, she will be delighted.'

When Tim arrived back at the hospital he was greeted by a very bonny Sophie.

'Tim, Dr Reynolds has said I can go home later today. Angela has agreed to watch out for me. I am so, so, pleased.'

'That's great news,' he replied. 'In the meantime I have a little treat for you.' He passed her the box.

Lifting the lid and seeing all her special favourites she said, 'Sara.'

'Of course,' said Tim. He went to help himself to some of the food.

'You cannot have that,' she squeaked, 'it's my favourite, have some of that smoked sausage.'

Ellen came in and said, 'Hallo, Tim.' Lifting her nose and sniffing she asked, 'What is that wonderful smell?'

'It is some food from Tim's shop,' Sophie replied offering her the box.

'Try the smoked sausage,' suggested Tim.

She took his advice and rather tentatively sniffed the slice of sausage and then put it in her mouth. 'Oh my, that's very nice.' She was about to ask for another slice when Mr Vieri walked in. She disappeared.

Tim rose from his seat and started to say that he would leave the two of them alone when Mr Vieri interrupted him.

'I would like you to stay please,' he said.

Tim thought for a moment and then sat back down. Surely Mr Vieri would not start an argument in here. Tim recognised there was not the usual level of tension that seemed to exist when he and Mr Vieri were in the same room.

Addressing Sophie her father asked, 'How are you, my dear?'

'I am much better now, Father, they are sending me home this afternoon.'

'What is that smell?' asked her father.

'It's food from Tim's shop,' she replied, 'please have some.'

'It was put together by one of our team. She is a fabulous Italian cook,' added Tim.

Mr Vieri took a slice of tomato and basil bruschetta. After a moment he started nodding, 'That is very good.'

Tim thanked him.

Sophie chimed in, 'Tim has a shop full of food like this. Try the smoked sausage,' she suggested.

He did as she requested. After a long pause while he chewed, he looked up and said, 'I would like to see this shop.'

'You have had an invitation,' said Sophie softly.

He was silent for a while, his arms crossed, one hand grasping his chin. Tim and Sophie exchanged a quick look of enquiry. Neither of them understanding the long silence. Finally, he said, as though speaking to himself, 'So I have, so I have.' The second phrase quieter and more introspective. Another pause, then, with more vigour, 'Let us get you better and then we shall see.'

'Thank you, Father,' said Sophie reaching for his hand and squeezing it.

Mr Vieri, rising, said, 'I will leave you young people together. I will come and see you at Angela's. Goodbye to you both,' he said as he swept from the room.

After he had gone Tim and Sophie stared at each other wide-eyed. Both in shock. Sophie had her hand to her mouth again.

'Well I am damned,' said Tim frowning.

'Tim, you have just witnessed the biggest climb down my father has ever made,' said Sophie, visibly moved. 'He must have finally recognised how much we mean to each other.'

'Do you think he will come to the shop?' asked Tim.

'I think he will,' she replied drying her eyes as she spoke.

'Oh, Tim, a nice policewoman called in to tell me that I was knocked down on a zebra crossing by a motorcyclist, I told her that I have no recollection of the accident at all. I remember nothing before I woke up in here. Apparently, Father is handling it, is that ok? I can get him to let you do it if you would rather?'

'Oh! No,' he said firmly shaking his head and putting his hands out as though to fend the idea off. 'I think we both have enough on our plate without that, and anyway your father won't do it, the company solicitor will.'

'Yes, you are right.'

*

Ellen bustled in. 'Sorry to interrupt, Tim, we must ask you to leave now please. Getting Sophie ready to go home will take a while. We will give her some painkillers to take with her. Sometimes the move can set things back a little. I would suggest if you don't mind that you see her tomorrow.'

'Ok, if you think it best,' kissing Sophie gently on the forehead as he spoke.

'I will be glad when you can kiss me properly,' said Sophie with a wicked grin on her face.

'Well I never did,' said Ellen, 'it's a good job my dear mother cannot hear this, so it is.'

'I will see you tomorrow,' promised Tim smiling, and with a goodbye to Ellen he left the room. He could hear them both laughing as he walked away.

Outside in the corridor he met Dr Richards. Shaking the doctor's hand he said, 'Can you say thank you to everyone for looking after Sophie so well, please?'

'I will. I am sure she will be fine now.'

Repeating his thanks Tim walked away.

He phoned later that evening to see how Sophie was. Angela told him that she was asleep but doing well. Tim thanked her for looking after her and said goodnight. Although it was a long way, he decided to walk home from the shop, so he had a chance to think. There were a lot of loose ends, he had still not told Sophie about the boat for a start. Then there was the matter of organising proper wages for everyone.

He had woken up the other morning thinking about the second shop. He realised he could not do anything about it straight away, but he could start a discussion amongst the partners and with Mr Murdoch. On reflection he decided to ask the bank manager about what increase he might reasonably pay the team. There was also the matter of getting his father to take a wage. The next three days passed quietly with Tim making frequent but short visits to Angela's. Sophie slept a lot. The family doctor called regularly and was pleased with her progress. The headaches were coming less often and with less severity.

On Sunday morning Angela rang and invited Tim around for an evening meal. She told him that her sister was also coming, and did he mind.

Tim replied he did not mind in the slightest. 'What time would you like me there?' he asked.

'I thought we would eat earlier than usual so that Sophie does not get too tired.'

'Good idea,' he agreed. 'Do you want me to bring anything?'

'No thank you, just yourself,' she replied laughing.

Tim thought he would take some wine, but then remembered the very good bottle of Blandy's Madeira he had been given as repayment of a favour to a friend.

He decided to dress smartly for the meal. They had all seen him in his everyday clothes, so it would not hurt to put on a bit of a show. Although his wardrobe was small, he had always bought well. He chose his dark navy lightweight jacket, pale blue chinos, a white shirt having a thin pale blue check, double cuffs and tan leather casuals. The cufflinks were expensive, mother of pearl, a present from his great aunt Victoria on his twenty-first birthday. He took a taxi to Angela's mews house. He could have walked but did not want to arrive sweating and out of breath. He was there in good time.

CHAPTER 24

FAMILY CHATS

The front door was opened very promptly by Angela who looked very agitated. Stepping out onto the street and pulling the door to behind her she whispered, 'Sophie's father is here.'

Tim laughing, asked, 'Is that why you are looking so agitated? Please don't worry, it will be fine.'

'Well if you say so,' she said, still looking perturbed.

Tim gave her the bottle and followed her indoors. Mrs Vieri remained sitting. Mr Vieri was standing by the fireplace. Sophie was on the couch looking as worried as Angela was.

He smiled as he went across to her mother and said hallo. He felt her tense as their cheeks barely touched.

Straightening up he took the two strides to the fireplace and offered his hand as he said, 'Good evening, sir.'

The two men's eyes met and held for a moment. Tim sensed a hidden smile. A silent recognition that Tim was not overawed.

Mr Vieri said, 'Good evening, Timothy,' and released Tim's hand.

Angela in the meantime had taken the wrapping off the bottle and said, 'Oh, thank you Tim, that's one of my favourites.'

'And mine,' said Mrs Vieri. Her comment surprised herself and the others.

'I thought we might have a glass after dinner,' added Tim. As he was speaking, he had settled himself on the couch next to Sophie. She reached for his hand, he squeezed hers and smiled at her. She slid down the couch to be closer to him. He could see she was better than she had been, but he sensed a certain fragility in her.

He was glad that he had tried with his clothing, the women were in long dresses and Mr Vieri was very smartly dressed, a pale cream silk shirt, black trousers, finished off with a smart silk cravat. Mrs Vieri's dress, a dark grey, was tightly buttoned around her neck. Angela's in contrast was a deep red with a very attractive décolletage that Tim worked hard to ignore, given that he could sense Sophie's eyes on him. She looked stunning in a modest cream dress, again wearing her single strand of pearls with tiny matching earrings.

'We have all got a drink, Tim, what would you like?' Angela asked.

'Do you have a sweet sherry, please? I have a terrible sweet tooth.'

'I can do that,' she said leaving the room.

'How are you, Sophia?' Tim enquired, remembering to use her given name.

Mr Vieri interrupted them. 'Can we do away with this farce about Sophia's name? I know everybody else calls her Sophie behind our backs so let us stop the charade and call her what you will.'

Mrs Vieri became very angry. 'I do not agree, Victor, I want her called Sophia,' she scolded.

'Can I interrupt?' said Tim looking across at Sophie who had her hand in front of her mouth again signalling her growing distress. 'I am more than happy to call her Sophia in or out of your company. I think it is a beautiful and magical name and it fits your daughter perfectly.'

Both the Vieris looked shocked. Mrs Vieri, after a pause said, 'Thank you, Timothy.'

Mr Vieri gave a bark of laughter and said, 'Well I'll be damned,' and lapsed into silence.

Angela hastened away to check on the meal.

Tim turned to Sophie and asked again, 'How are you?'

'I am getting better every day and the headaches have all but gone. Apparently if I keep on like this, I may not need any further tests.'

'That is good news, Sophia,' said her mother.

Both men nodded.

Angela reappeared saying dinner was ready.

Tim asked Sophie if she needed a hand.

'No, I am fine, thank you,' she replied.

It was not until she got up to proceed into the dining room, he discovered that there was not much back to her dress. From behind she was effectively naked to just below her waist

As he slid the chair under her, he bent down and whispered in her ear, 'I wish we were alone.' She blushed, looked down at the table and smiled a woman's smile. Angela, sitting opposite Sophie, saw the exchange and shot Tim a look as he stood up; she had one eyebrow raised in query and an almost hidden smile. He ignored her.

The table laid out in the dining room was beautiful, there was elegant silverware, cut glass and the white porcelain dinner service had a fine blue line around the edge. The first course was delicious, a selection of crostini. The first Tim tried was prosciutto, figs and mint; next, he had buffalo mozzarella and chilli.

The second course was an Italian stew. It had pork chops, potatoes, prosciutto, pancetta. Tim could not recognise any other flavours. Angela divulged it had dried apricots and lots of other ingredients.

Mr Vieri, who was now under the influence of a good quantity of a fine merlot and was beginning to visibly relax said, 'At home, I mean in Italy, it was called *costolette di maiale con salvia*.'

The last course was Italian vanilla ice cream. Sophie later disclosed to Tim that she had told Angela that it was his favourite dessert. They finished the meal with Tim's offering of the port. It was much appreciated.

Mr Vieri drew a cigar from his top pocket and raising a hand to halt Angela's complaint mid-sentence said, 'I will go outside.' Rising from his chair he asked, 'Do you smoke, Timothy?'

'No sir, I don't,' he answered.

'Perhaps you will join me outside anyway?'

'Ok,' said Tim.

Sophie and Angela both gave him worried looks. Tim smiled and shook his head briefly, trying to tell them not to worry.

Once outside Mr Vieri turned to Tim and said, 'I recognise you have not had the best of introductions to this family. I feel I need to explain a few things to you, but first I want to thank you very much for the way you looked after my daughter recently.' There was a short silence while he lit his cigar. Waving the smoke away, he continued, 'The doctor was very clear that your care made a considerable improvement in Sophia's recovery and future wellbeing,' he said between clouds of aromatic smoke. 'So, we will always be grateful to you for that. Not many men would have been able to do that.'

'I have had some practice,' he replied.

'Practice, what practice?' asked Mr Vieri, rather abruptly.

Tim explained that he had sat for many hours in the same hospital when his mother was dying of the flu.

'Good God,' said Mr Vieri, 'how old were you?'

'Thirteen! My father had to run the stall all day, so I just sat with her and looked after her until she passed away.'

'Well I am damned,' said Mr Vieri. 'What I wanted to say, Tim, may I call you Tim by the way?'

Tim could see the humour in his eyes, 'Yes sir,' he replied. He noted there was no suggestion that Tim should call him anything else but 'sir'.

'You need to understand why we are so protective of Sophia. Mrs Vieri nearly died in childbirth, she was very ill for some time afterwards and we were warned that it would be very dangerous for her to have any more children. We wanted a big family like most Italians. I just assumed when we were married that that would happen. But Sophia is our one and only so is extremely precious to us. So, I need to know what you intend?'

Tim was silent and very still for some time. His gaze fixed on the ground at his feet.

'Well?' asked Mr Vieri, becoming impatient.

'I was trying to decide if I told you the truth whether you would believe me,' responded Tim thoughtfully. 'There is no other way of putting it, but the truth is that I fell in love with your daughter that day on the train.'

'I am sorry, but I find that hard to believe.' The two men were holding firm eye contact.

'That's why I tried to find another, perhaps cleverer way of saying the same thing. The truth is simply what I have just told you.' Pausing, he then continued, 'I put her first in all my thoughts and every decision all the time, every day. I cannot match your income or hers come to that but give me time. I intend to have a chain of Sophie's across London.'

'Do you believe you can do that?'

'It's not just me,' Tim replied, 'we have a great team. People who have been in the retail industry all their lives and very successfully, given where they started from.'

Tim realised he was fighting for his future with Sophie. 'We did give you an invite to come and see for yourself. It would be best if it was a Saturday afternoon, Mr Murdoch has said he will come if you come.'

'Really?' said Mr Vieri, clearly surprised.

At that moment Angela popped her head around the back door and said. 'I have come to rescue you, Tim, and Victor we miss your company.'

As the two men followed Angela indoors Mr Vieri looked over his shoulder and said,

'Ring my secretary and fix a date.' The rest of the evening passed reasonably amicably. Eventually Tim said he had to say goodnight.

On the doorstep Sophie kissed him and said, 'Did my father grill you?'

'No, not really, I think we have a better understanding of each other. I hope so anyway. I told him that I fell in love with you at first sight that day on the train. I don't know if he believed me this time, but I know it is true.'

'So do I, you lovely man,' she said and kissed him properly. Tim, feeling very unsteady on his feet, and not because of the drink, finally insisted he had to go.

She bit him gently on the chin, laughed and released him.

Tim walked away into the night with a mix of emotions. Delight that Sophie loved him as much as he loved her, but still concerned about her family's ambivalence towards him.

The following morning Tim woke remembering Mr Vieri had agreed to come and see the shop and meet his team. He also remembered he had not told Sophie about the proposed visit. He rang her as soon as he got to the shop to be told by Angela that she had left for work.

He rang Sophie's office. The girl on reception with the pretty voice said she was sorry, but Miss Vieri was in a directors' meeting and she had been told they were not to be disturbed.

'Please tell her I rang,' said Tim.

'I will do that,' she promised. She remembered the mixture of fire and ice in his voice last time they had spoken.

Sophie rang back an hour later. Answering Tim's concern about the meeting she said that far from a problem it was to welcome her officially as a director and to discuss the future now she was in post. 'I am so excited, Tim.'

'Well done, darling. You deserve it, we must go out for a meal or something to celebrate.'

'That would be very nice,' she replied, 'thank you.'

'Love you loads,' said Tim, 'see you later.'

'Love you too,' she replied and hung up.

A few days later Tim looked up from his reading to see Sophie standing by the sunlit window lost in reverie. Angela's beautiful cut glass ornaments standing on the windowsill reflecting a thousand diamonds of light around her. The image stopped Tim's heart in his chest. He was stunned once again by her beauty. He was reminded of something his art master had said at school. The task for the lesson, a still life, was to draw a Venetian pot he had brought in. He was describing how proportion was everything. He then said that all the most beautiful shapes in the world could be found by observing the female form. All the boys burst out laughing and the smut and innuendo began. Tim saw the look of disappointment and embarrassment on his face. The master shook his head, turned and went to his desk. Tim, for the first time, fully understood what he meant. He realised that far from being crude he was trying to give them a gift. To open their eyes to the beauty in the world. Tim, scrolling back through the memories of his classmates knew that some of them would go to their graves thinking the art master was a mucky old man.

Tim and Sophie's relationship had grown ever more intimate. On more than one occasion having to exercise great control not to give in to what their bodies craved. Some few weeks later Sophie's tearful revelation one Wednesday evening was a bombshell.

'I am very scared that I may be pregnant, I have missed two months' periods.' Tim reached for her hand. He was too stunned to do more.

'I cannot be pregnant, can I?' she asked beginning to cry harder. At that moment they heard the key in the lock announcing Angela's return. The drawing room door came open, Angela's cheerful voice saying good morning. There was a swift change in her demeanour when she saw Sophie's tears and their worried expressions.

'Whatever is wrong?' she asked.

Sophie looked at Tim. She looked like a rabbit caught in the headlights.

'We must tell her, Sophie.'

Turning to Angela he said, 'Sophie thinks she may be pregnant.'

Angela's face went white. 'How, no I mean, when? No, I do not mean that either. Tim you promised.'

'I have not broken that promise,' he replied.

'You must have done,' Angela was now clearly very angry. 'You have broken that promise and now you are lying about it. My sister's warnings about you appear to be bearing fruit.'

'He is not lying, he is not, I promise you, Aunty. I am so scared.'

Tim said, 'Can I talk to you alone in the other room please, Angela?'

They both went next door. Still standing they faced each other across the carpet. 'How could you let this happen?' asked Angela, a growing desperation in her voice.

'Do you really believe I am a liar? This is as big a shock to me as it is to you. I swear that as far as I am concerned Sophie is still a virgin.'

Angela stared at Tim for a long time. Eventually she said, 'I consider myself a good judge of character. I am inclined to trust you, but God help you if I find out you are lying to me.'

'I promise you I am not.'

'We should re-join Sophie,' said Angela moving towards the door.

When they returned to the other room Sophie was mopping her tears and blowing her nose.

'Sophie, Tim has promised me that you cannot be pregnant, sorry but I need the same promise from you.'

'Aunty, I cannot believe that you could think I am lying,' the tears were starting again. 'I promise you Tim and I have done nothing wrong.'

'Right, we need to sort this out. I will arrange an appointment with my doctor tomorrow, and we will find out for sure. In the meantime we shall keep this between ourselves. Your mother and father do not need to know. I will ring the doctor now and arrange an appointment.' She left the room. The young couple could hear her speaking on the telephone in the hall. When Angela returned Tim and Sophie were sitting on the sofa's edge holding hands in a bleak silence.

'Ten am tomorrow morning,' Angela informed them, 'at the local hospital.'

The following morning found them perched on some very hard chairs in the Ginny Department waiting for Sophie to be called in. Eventually her name was called, and she rose, gave Tim's hand a squeeze and followed the nurse.

His heart went out to her. She looked as though she were going to the scaffold. He realised that if she was pregnant, life for them was going to get very unpleasant. A tiny maggot of doubt crept into his mind while he sat waiting. Supposing she was pregnant, he knew it would not be his child. He knew that she was very friendly with some of the men at work and there were those drunken office parties. He realised that her beauty was always going to attract other men's attention. He had seen them look at her with hungry eyes. He knew he loved her more than he could ever quantify in words. He would marry her whatever the outcome. Life without her was unimaginable. With that he swept those thoughts aside and told himself she was not pregnant. Some while later the nurse returned and asked him to follow her. He could not tell from her demeanour what the outcome was. His heart fell when he entered the examination room. Sophie was crying again.

The doctor said, 'Please sit down, Mr Cooper.'

'It's Tim, my name is Tim,' he said in a very small voice.

'Well Tim,' said the doctor, 'your fiancée is not pregnant.'

Tim slumped back in his chair, his eyes closed, the air rushed out of him and his body appeared to collapse in on itself. When he opened his eyes again the doctor and Sophie could see he was welling up. He dried his eyes with the palms of his hands. He felt a great weight lift from his shoulders. He reached for Sophie's hand. He was then aware that her tears were tears of relief.

'Why did her periods stop then?' asked Tim.

The doctor continued, 'When couples are as close as you two, the woman's body is awash with hormones and it almost expects to become pregnant. Quite a lot of women have phantom pregnancies. Whilst it is not my place to say so I suggest you go away and get married. Then everything will fall into place.'

They both said goodbye to the doctor. Tim found himself shaking the doctor's hand rather too vigorously. The doctor smiled.

Outside in the corridor Sophie said, 'Will you hug me, please? I was so scared Tim. Can we get married very soon, please?'

Walking on, he replied, 'We need to talk to Angela, and yes, I will marry you tomorrow if you like.'

She stopped and tugged his arm and turning him to face her offered him her lips. He swept her into his arms and for a few moments they were lost to the world.

They came to when a hospital porter pushing a trolley said impatiently, 'Alright, alright, can I get by, please?'

Arriving back at Angela's house, she had obviously been watching for them. As Tim held the front gate open for Sophie, Angela opened the front door. The worry on her face quickly cleared when she saw their smiles.

Later, sat in her beautiful front room having heard all that had happened that morning she said, 'We need to get you two married.'

'That is what the doctor said,' replied Sophie.

'Did he though?' responded Angela with one eyebrow raised. 'I am not sure that is within his remit, but he is right. I need to talk to your mother, Sophie.'

'I am very worried that she may refuse to agree,' said Tim.

Sophie, becoming annoyed jumped in and said, 'I am a grown woman and I will decide who I am going to marry and when. They both still treat me as though I am five years old.'

Tim and Angela both asked her to calm down.

Looking no less angry she leapt to her feet saying, 'I am going to make some tea,' and swept out of the room. They could hear her banging the teapot and kettle about in the kitchen.

Angela stood saying, 'I had better try and stop her breaking all my bone china.'

Tim could hear a low murmur of conversation with occasionally Sophie's voice raised in anger. Tim was very worried, he remembered Angela's comments the day before implying that Mrs Vieri still did not trust him.

The two women returned. Sophie looked less angry but very determined.

'Tim, can I tell my sister what occurred today?' asked Angela. 'I think it may force her to face the fact that you two will marry one way or another and that it will be a lot better if it is done with her and Victor's consent.'

'Better to tell her rather than have it come to light later,' agreed Tim. 'My concern, Sophie, is that your mother still does not trust me. She thinks I am just after your money.'

'Tim, she will just have to learn. She wants me to marry one of those chinless wonders she keeps inviting to dinner who went to the right school and whose parents are filthy rich. She is just a ferocious snob.'

Angela jumped in to protect her sister saying, 'Some of what you say may be true but deep down she is just trying to protect you. You need to bear in mind you are her only child. She loves you very much. We did have a very strange mother, looking back now I realise she was very hidebound, everything had to be just so. You had to be seen in the right places with the right people. There was the social round, the balls, getting invited to the right parties. Cowes Week, Ladies' Day at the races, Cannes in the summer. Your mother was expected to attend them all. The biggest problem of all was that your mother was a total disappointment to your grandmama. She wanted boys to carry the family name forward not silly girls as she called us. Nothing your mother did was ever good enough for her, Sophie. I think she had a very hard time of it.'

'Angela, at the risk of putting my foot in it, how come you two are so different?' asked Tim.

'We had very separate lives, Tim. Firstly I think our mother was embarrassed by becoming pregnant relatively late in life with me, and also, I believe she was very fed up with children. She did not in my opinion have a single maternal bone in her body.'

Tim was still shaking his head, not understanding why there was such a distinct difference between the two women.

'I was sent away, Tim, at a very young age to the villa in Puglia with my nanny, who, by the way, I loved dearly. She passed away a few years ago, I was very upset, she was the woman who mothered me.' Angela became quiet while her memory scrolled back to her childhood.

Eventually she came back to the now and whispered, 'I called her Mumsy.' Another pause, 'So you see, Olivia and I had very different childhoods. Hers was in grey old England, very strict, joyless, mine in the early years, running barefoot in the sunlit fields in Italy, then later, schooling in the local convent; the nuns were very kind. Mother could not be bothered with me, I was always 'Silly Angela', so I was sent away to Italy. Mother was a grim stranger, so I never missed her. Then of course with the threat of war we came home to England.'

Sophie lent across and hugged her.

CHAPTER 25

BREAD AND BOATS

The two women were talking about Sophie's job when Tim remembered the boat.

'Sophie, I do have one piece of good news; well I hope you think it is. I have found somewhere to live after we are married,' standing now so he could find the boat photo in his back pocket.

Sophie's mood changed immediately. 'Where is it, is it a house, a flat, or what?' she asked excitedly.

'No, it's neither of those so I hope you won't be too disappointed.'

'Stop prevaricating, tell me, tell me,' she insisted.

'It's a houseboat,' replied Tim.

'Oh crikey, how marvellous,' she said stepping across to him and throwing her arms around him. Craning her neck to look up at his face she asked him, 'Where is it? what sort of boat is it? What colour is it?'

Angela interrupted Sophie saying, 'How wonderful. I will pour the tea and then Tim can tell us all about it.'

A little later he explained the details in full to both woman and finished by saying, 'Mr Strong, Rupert, and I have agreed a low rent. I just have to keep it in good condition, repaint it, et cetera. That will cost money, but it won't cost what rent he could ask for it and it also gives me some flexibility as to when I have to spend the money.'

'Gives us flexibility, Tim. I am now part of this team,' Sophie reminded him.

'Thank God you are,' said Tim fervently, leaning over and kissing her firmly on the lips whilst cupping her head in his hands.

'Steady the buffs,' said Angela. 'Goodness knows what that means,' she laughed. 'My father always said it when he was embarrassed.'

Tim explained, 'It was what the officers used to say as the redcoats marched towards the Russian guns. The idea was to keep the line of men steady as they came under fire.'

'Oh, how awful,' said Angela thoughtfully, 'I do not think I shall say it again.'

'Sorry if we embarrassed you,' said Tim.

'Please do not worry,' said Angela with a smile. 'It is wonderful to see two young people so much in love. But we must get you married. Now Tim has found such wonderful accommodation there is nothing to stop you.'

'When can we see it?' enquired Sophie.

'I will see if Rupert is available on Sunday,' replied Tim.

'Ooh, can I come?' asked Angela. 'It sounds awfully romantic,' she added.

'Yes, if you like,' agreed Sophie.

'No, I am only kidding; it should be just you two first. I will look forward to seeing it later.'

Tim was both excited and nervous about Sophie seeing the boat. He hoped that if she didn't like it, she would be honest with him.

*

The shop was getting much busier, there was now a regular queue of people waiting outside the shop early in the morning. Regular customers were asking for the special bread on weekdays as well as Saturday. Early on

Saturday morning Tim arrived at 8 am to find his father had virtually sold out of the bread already.

'Morning Tim,' called his father as Tim approached the table. It was set up outside the shop as usual.

A regular customer turned to Tim and rather disgruntled asked, 'Why can't I place an order for my bread? My usual has sold out already.'

'Please choose a loaf on us. I am sorry you have been disappointed.'

'Well, thank you,' said the man slightly less put out.

'Can I ask you, sir, what bread you usually buy from us and how many loaves?' enquired Tim.

The man described his usual purchase. Tim was surprised by the amount. And the man added, 'It would be nice to be able to buy more on say, Wednesday.'

'Can you tell my father what your requirements would be for the two days and we will see what we can do?' He left the customer talking to his father and went inside to serve another early regular.

After the lunch time crowd had gone Tim's father approached him and started to talk about the bread situation. He made it clear to him that this morning was not a one off.

'Customers want to be able to place an order,' he said. 'We should remember that our supplier's shop is only a good walk away.'

Harry had come across to listen to the discussion.

Mr Woodman was pushing a broom around the shop, stopping he placed both hands on the top of the handle, rested his chin on them and said, 'You need to do a survey, Mr Cooper.'

'I think you are right,' was his father's response.

'We need a sign,' opined Mr Woodman.

'Harry and I can talk to our suppliers and see what they can do,' said his father.

'Are you going to open early on Wednesdays?' perfectly aware that his father and Mr Woodman were opening early all week.

'I suppose we will have to,' said his father. Mr Woodman's face was inscrutable.

'Shall the three of us do some numbers and talk to the suppliers and then talk to you?' asked Harry.

Tim replied, 'I don't think you need me anymore,' he observed. They were all pulling his leg when the arrival of a small group of customers sent them back to work.

Tim phoned Rupert Strong on Friday morning enquiring when he could show Sophie the boat.

'Sunday's out, I'm in rehearsal. I could show you around on Saturday evening if that would be ok?'

'That'll be fine, I will ring Sophie to tell her.'

The phone call confirmed that she would be able to look at the boat on Saturday, but she was not able to see him later.

Ok, Are you at the store tonight?'

'No, you will never guess. My father's climb down is continuing. He has asked me to do some meeting and greeting for him tonight. He was very surprised when I told him what it was going to cost him. He laughed, until I asked him when was the last time he did anything for nothing.'

'What did he say?' asked Tim, 'was he angry?'

'No, he thought for a moment and then he laughed again saying, "I have taught you too well", then he agreed.'

Saturday dawned cold and wet. Tim was soaked through by the time he reached the shop. Just for a change there was no table outside. However, there was a large sign in the front window asking if customers would like to place orders for their bread. Please talk to any staff member. Tim was pleased to see that so far the weather had not made any noticeable reduction in business. He hoped that it indicated that most of the customers were regulars.

Sophie arrived after lunch and all the team and the customers were so pleased to see her looking so well. He saw she was very moved by the attention she was receiving. Mr Woodman rescued her by suggesting she made herself a cup of tea. She beat a hasty retreat upstairs.

The normal Saturday buzz persisted in the shop despite the horrid weather. Tim was very concerned about how the boat would look in the rain. Supposing it was leaking, or if it was cold inside. Oh well, better to find out now rather than later. That evening having had a snack in the shop they called a taxi to take them out to the boatyard. The weather if anything was even worse. The wind was strengthening, and the rain was hammering down.

Halfway there Tim suggested it might be a good idea to ring Rupert and cancel the visit.

Sophie disagreed. 'If we are going to live on it this is a very good test.'

Arriving at the boatyard and running down the path towards the river the rain, if anything, was even harder. Sophie ran ahead, Tim watching discovered that she even ran beautifully, there was a carefree gaiety about her movements; her short black coat with the collar turned up, the umbrella held akimbo, her pretty legs and ankle-length high-heeled boots dancing through the rain; her body in silhouette against the bright lights beyond her. He was reminded again how all-consuming was his love for this woman and how overwhelmed he was by her beauty.

They were both soaked by the time they reached the boat and climbed the ramp. Rupert had felt them arrive, the boat moving gently as they stepped on board.

'Oh, I say,' said Rupert, 'the weather is a little inclement what? Come in and get warm.'

Entering the cabin, they were entranced. The boat was wonderfully warm. Small candles in attractive glass jars were lit on the table throwing dancing shapes of soft yellow light on the walls and ceiling. The two of them realised that Rupert had company, a stunningly attractive redhead who Rupert introduced as Arabella, his girlfriend. Dressed in a dark wine-red dress, she was nursing a mug of hot cocoa.

Rupert, comfortable in a pair of much washed brown cords and an Arran cardigan retrieved a large glass of what Tim guessed was whiskey, put to one side temporarily whilst answering the door. The firelight was intensified in the amber liquid.

Both were toasting crumpets in front of an ideal boiler with the front down. The fire was a bright red glow. And clearly very hot. Arabella became very concerned that they were so wet and encouraged both to give her their coats and she would get them dry.

Rupert asked, 'Do you want a drink or a mug of cocoa?' They both chose cocoa. 'Do you want to sit at the table or in front of the fire.' The fireside was unanimous.

Their hosts insisted that they had the first toasted crumpets.

Arabella left for the table to butter them. She asked, 'Would you like to try them peppered?'

Tim, always keen to try something new, said, 'Yes please.'

Sophie said, 'Could I try a bite of Tim's and then say?'

'That's a clever trick,' laughed Tim handing her his crumpet.

After taking a mouthful and a short pause she said, 'That is very nice, so yes please, may I have pepper?'

After the second round of crumpets Tim realised they had not yet looked around the boat and the time was slipping away.

Rupert had noticed Tim looking at his watch and said, 'We had better show you around.'

'Oh yes please,' said Sophie, 'I am already in love with it.'

'It is a lovely lifestyle,' agreed Arabella, 'however I think we should warn you about one thing. You will have a constant stream of visitors.'

'That sounds like fun,' Sophie responded.

Arabella led them through the boat with Rupert bringing up the rear.

Tim was working hard to remember everything he was told and shown, Sophie was just in awe of the whole thing and was in raptures over everything she saw.

The final cabin at the stern was the master bedroom. There were large windows on three sides looking out over the river. Arabella had not switched on the light. The river, by now in darkness, was a black canvas with myriad coloured lights, some moving. A disembodied navigation light floated downstream apparently not attached to anything. As the boat moved away to their right it was silhouetted against a brightly lit building on the other shore. It was a tug towing a string of barges. A man's face was highlighted by a soft glow in the small cabin as the helmsmen lit his pipe.

Sophie stepped closer to Tim, slid her arm through his, leant against him and said, 'Please say we can live here.'

Tim looked down at her and realised she had become emotional. Her spare hand was up to her mouth and when she looked up at him her eyes were swimming.

'That's rather up to Rupert,' said Tim.

'I think Sophie just clinched it,' responded Rupert. 'She obviously feels the same about the old lady as we do. All I want is to have someone living here who feels the same as us. You obviously both do so it's a deal.'

There were further explanations about the toilet arrangements.

Arabella coaxed Sophie back towards the bow saying, 'This is men's work, Sophie, nothing to do with us.'

Sophie laughed.

As they were saying goodbye Rupert said, 'Sophie, are you Sophie or Sophia?'

Sophie looked at Tim and said, 'I was christened Sophia but everybody except my parents call me Sophie.'

'Oh no, my darling, if anybody was ever a Sophia,' pausing, he then continued, 'you are, if I may be so bold, a very beautiful young woman. Did you know that you are named after a Greek goddess renowned for her great beauty and her wisdom? You are aptly named Sophia. Would it upset you if

I called you that in future?'

Sophie now very red in the face said, 'Well, no, thank you.'

Arabella gently slapped Rupert on the arm and said, 'Stop now, the poor girl is very embarrassed.'

'Very sorry, Sophia,' said Rupert, bowing to her. After their hosts had done the goodnight kisses and the handshakes and seen them off the boat the young couple walked back towards the exit. The rain had stopped, and a full moon could be seen behind the clouds.

After a few paces Sophie stopped him and turned back towards the river. Leaning her head on his shoulder, she said, 'We are going to be so happy here.' The moon appeared from behind a cloud and lit the scene with a silver glow. 'Oh, Tim, it is beautiful.'

'It is, very,' he agreed.

After a few minutes they walked on. As they passed a dark corner a voice close at hand said, 'It's always magical.'

Sophie jumped. Tim said, 'Hallo Tabby, how are you?'

'I'm good ta. I always come out for a last look before I go to bed.'

Tim introduced Sophie. Then like the captain on the barge Tabby's face was lit by a ruddy glow as he drew on his pipe. 'Safe home, you two,' he said, as they made their goodbyes and walked away.

'It's like a fairy story,' said Sophie in a little girl voice.

They took a taxi back to Angela's, and as Tim walked Sophie to the door it came open and Angela was standing there. 'Have you time to come in, Tim? I would love to hear all about it.'

Sophie looked up at Tim, he nodded and followed the two women into the house.

Before Tim left it was agreed that Angela would talk to her sister and her husband about the boat and the couple's marriage.

Tim pointed out that it still had to be him who asked Mr Vieri for permission to marry Sophie.

'Why is that?' asked Angela.

'Because he is an old boy Scout and has a sense of what is correct,' laughed Sophie.

'I knew I was right about you, Tim,' observed Angela giving him a hug as she kissed him goodnight.

Standing in the darkness hugging each other tight Sophie repeated between kisses how much she had loved the boat and Rupert and Arabella. 'It was a magical evening Tim, thank you.'

Sophie shivered, Tim realised how cold it was and that Sophie had no coat. 'I think you should go in. I don't want you becoming ill.'

'I am cold,' she agreed. She kissed him quickly once more and slipped through the door closing it quietly behind her.

Tim was latching the gate behind him when he heard a knocking on the glass in the bay window. Looking back, Sophie had partially drawn the curtains aside and was waving at him backlit by the soft glow from the candles. They exchanged blown kisses and Tim set off homeward still looking over his shoulder. After he had gone a few yards he said out loud, 'By God I am a lucky bugger.' He strode on at an even faster pace.

*

Tim arrived at the shop the next morning full of vim and vigour. There had been a sharp frost the night before and the roofs and roads were gilded by a white mantle that sparkled in the morning sunlight.

Mr Woodman watched him for a few minutes as he raced through one job and moved onto the next. Then he said, 'By golly, lad, by your manner I assume everything in your world is pretty good?'

'It's better than that, Mr Woodman, everything in my world is great. Sophie loved the boat. Rupert and his girlfriend made us very welcome and fed us. The river worked its magic as usual.' Right, he thought, that's the accommodation sorted, now I've only got her mother and father plus the wedding to manage.

CHAPTER 26

RESISTANCE

Angela and her sister Olivia had agreed to go shopping together for some clothes that morning. Angela decided to seize the moment. She had described the visit to the boat the evening before and how much Sophia had loved it. 'Therefore,' said Angela, 'there seems to be very little reason not to start the arrangements for the marriage.'

Steeling herself and taking a deep breath, knowing her sister would react badly, she appraised her of the scare that the young couple had experienced, fearing that Sophia may be pregnant.

Mrs Vieri was horrified, she stumbled to a bench and sat down. 'Angela, how on earth can you suggest they should marry? You have just confirmed all my suspicion, my worst fears. He has lied to all of us, broken his promise to me. God knows what Victor will say. Clearly, he has you under his spell. You apparently can see no wrong in him.'

'Olivia Vieri! You always get the wrong end of the stick.' Now very cross with her sister and allowing it to be apparent in her tone of voice continued, 'The young people have done nothing wrong. Sophia is still as God made her and will remain so until they are married, and have no doubt about it, married they will be with or without your blessing. Tim is one of the nicest men I have ever met. If I were twenty years younger, I would give Sophia a run for her money.'

'Now you are just being crude, Angela, you do on occasion appear a little common.'

Angela, becoming angrier still, her face bright red, now almost shouting responded 'No, Olivia! I am not common, I am pragmatic. I see a couple very much in love. Timothy adores your daughter and she him. Would you rather she married someone who was of the right type and social class or someone who will make her happy for all of the rest of her days? Timothy is a good man and with the support he has from his team at the shop who knows how high he will fly. You need to make up your mind quickly, if you and Victor make the wrong decision you will lose your daughter and your grandchildren; they plan a large family.'

Angela noticed her sister had begun to cry. She took her hand and with her temper cooling said, 'I am sorry I have had to be tough, but you must face the facts. Sophia will marry Tim whatever anybody else says or does. She takes after Victor. Like him, when she has made up her mind nothing will change it. You do not see them together as often as I, but when Tim arrives at the cottage in the evening Sophia lights up. Her feelings for him are almost tangible. So, the question is simple, do you want to be part of her and Tim's life and have the pleasure of grandchildren or never see her again? Her course is set; she will not be moved.'

'Angela, I had envisaged a wonderful life for her,' explained Mrs Vieri still sniffing and dabbing her nose with her hankie, 'first class all the way, now she is throwing it all away.'

'Have you spoken to Sophia about all this?'

'Only once,' replied Mrs Vieri, 'she was adamant that is not what she wanted. I assumed she would come around.'

'What she does want, Olivia, and one of the things that drives her is she wants to be more successful than her father. I think she may well achieve that. The other thing she really wants is to marry Tim, and she will, with or without you two.'

'Tim insists he will ask Victor's permission to marry your daughter so that it is done properly. He is an old boy Scout, as Sophia calls him. I lost any doubts about whether he loved her or not when she was in hospital. He sat at her bedside for three days and nights sleepless. In the same hospital that he had helped nurse his mother until she died. He was thirteen. How many of your eligible bachelors would have done that? None of them that I have met.'

'Did he do that?' asked Olivia in a small voice.

'He did, and he has been a prop for his father who had never, until recently, got over the loss of his wife. Sophia tells me that after his mother died his father was rendered incapable of doing anything for a while. Tim left school and ran the stall with his good friend on the stall next door keeping an eye on things.

'The shop has worked miracles for his father, he is a new man apparently. Tim's doing. Do not underestimate him, Olivia.'

'But Angela, what will people say, we will be ridiculed. Sophia married to a barrow boy. We will lose our standing in society; I will never be able to show my face anywhere.'

Shaking her head in disbelief Angela said, 'I cannot believe that you would put what your so-called friends will say above the happiness of your daughter. I can tell you what I think Olivia, in a few years' time, Tim, working with Sophia and his business partners will be able to buy and sell these people.' Angela had no idea how prophetic her words would turn out to be.

Later that evening Angela repeated all that had occurred that morning. Sophie was quite upset. 'She does not understand me. I do not want what she wants. I am not bothered about being seen in the right social circles. I have done that, it is boring. I enjoy the pressures of work. The Saturday afternoons spent in the shop. The sense of achievement when I succeed at something, and whatever they say, Tim and I will be married.'

'Well I have started the ball rolling. We must see what happens,' said

Angela. 'Is Tim coming around tonight?' she asked.

'No, apparently not, they are fitting another display unit and Tim expects it to take a while. He is helping Charlie; he is the man who did all Mr Woodman's repairs and modifications. He did all the work in the shop. His son Tommy normally works with him, but he is at Scouts tonight, so Tim is assisting. He was pleased to help. He thinks Charlie and Tommy will be a useful contact for the work on the boat.'

'I think that is so exciting,' enthused Angela.

'Sorry?' said Sophie, 'what, making a display unit?'

'Living on the boat, silly,' she replied.

'Oh, yes it will be superb. I am looking forward to it. I hope it will not be too cold in the winter.'

'You are both young, just put on another jumper.'

'Is that more fun than cuddling?' asked Sophie with a big grin on her face.

'It is a lot less dangerous, and I did spot the euphemism. As you have brought the subject up what are you going to do about contraception?'

'Aunty! What are you saying?' said a shocked Sophie loudly, mouth agape, having rocked back in her chair and drawn her legs up to her bottom, now very wide eyed and bright red in the face.

'I believe you when you tell me you two have not slept together but can you guarantee you will not?'

'I am stunned that you have raised the subject,' replied Sophie, by now she was deeply embarrassed.

'Someone must, my darling, your mother will not, so I guess it is down to me. Think how hurt and embarrassed your mother and father will be if you are pregnant before you're married. Also, I would not think you want children straight away. You have your career.'

'And the shop is just coming into profit,' added Sophie. 'Tim is already thinking about another one.'

'How exciting is that?' responded Angela. She paused for a moment then said, 'Also people still frown on pregnancy before wedlock in spite of our so-called permissive society.'

Sophie went to interrupt her, but Angela hushed her saying, 'I know you will say you do not care what people think but it is a stigma that will stay with you all your life. I am quite sure you do not want your children to be labelled as illegitimate or worse. There is no need to get pregnant today because we have the pill.'

Sophie was silent for a long time. Angela let her think it through.

Eventually Sophie said, 'Why does it have to be so sensible and practical? What Tim and I have is so special and wonderful why can we not just love one another with all that it entails?' Sophie was becoming upset.

'Sophie, my darling,' responded Angela reaching out to hold her hand, 'it can and will be all of that but there is a simple measure you must put in place to protect not just yourselves but all of us who love you.

'I suggest that you make an appointment to see our doctor and sort it out. I see no point in telling your mother or father. You do of course have to discuss it with Tim.'

'Oh God, I shall die of embarrassment.'

'Sophie,' said Angela, smiling, 'once you are married the embarrassment will quickly fade. Shall I make an appointment for you at the end of the week? That will give you time to tell Tim.'

Sophie was biting her thumbnail, 'I suppose it is the sensible thing to do. I will not have to be examined or anything shall I?' she asked with sudden concern.

'No, my darling, all that may happen is he may take your blood pressure.'

'Will you come with me, please?' she asked sounding like a little girl again.

'Of course,' replied Angela wrapping her arms around her and hugging her tight.

*

Tim realised that Angela's conversation with her sister was going to alter everything. He wanted to strike first and invite the Vieris to come and see the shop and look at the business plan before they discussed the wedding.

Fearing that he may have mislaid Mr Vieri's secretary's phone number he finally found it in his back pocket along with several other names and numbers of varying importance all written on odd scraps of paper. He made a mental note to get himself better organised. The phone had only rung twice before it was answered by a very well-spoken woman. Tim visualised an attractive woman of medium height, well-groomed and very well dressed in a formal dark business suit, black high heels and red hair. At a later meeting when he met her face to face, the only detail he had got wrong was the colour of her hair, it was black and plentiful. He explained that Mr Vieri had asked him to phone to make an appointment to visit the shop. She revealed that he had checked with her earlier on that week to see if Tim had called.

'He has left a message; he can come this Saturday at about two pm if that is ok?'

Tim confirmed that it was. After replacing the telephone, he realised that the next few days were crucial to the rest of his life. Tim didn't know if he was excited or a little afraid. He decided it was a mixture of both.

He rang his great aunt Victoria and apologising for the very short notice asked her if she could come on Saturday afternoon and bring some of the Hampstead set?

'What is afoot, Timothy?' she asked.

He explained to her about the wedding plans and a broad outline of the problems he and Sophie had faced.

'You want to make a good impression, Tim. We can certainly help. Beatrice's husband Hubert has a wonderful vintage Daimler. He can bring us in that. What time did you say, dear?'

'About two pm this Saturday, Aunty.'

'It's a date, Timothy, we will be there.'

Tim thanked her profusely and hung up. Next, he rang Mr Murdoch the bank manager and advised him of the situation.

'Umm,' said Mr Murdoch, 'Tim I know I am supposed to be doing something this Saturday afternoon. Just let me check.' Tim could hear him leafing through his diary 'Oh, I have promised to accompany my wife on a shopping trip.'

'Never mind, I do understand,' said Tim. His heart falling.

'This is important is it not, lad?' asked Mr Murdoch.

'It almost certainly affects the rest of my life with Sophie.'

Mr Murdoch could hear the concern in Tim's voice. 'Alright, Tim, but it is going to cost you the biggest bunch of flowers you have ever bought,' said Mr Murdoch.

'How about a hamper with a selection of our produce instead?' he offered.

Mr Murdoch burst out laughing, still chuckling he said, 'Very clever. Keeps the costs down and acts as advertising for your products. You are learning fast, lad. Lots of Sara's confectionery though, ok? See you then,' said Mr Murdoch. Still laughing, he rang off.

Tim recognised the hamper idea very likely had wings and might well fly, to quote Harry. For now, though, one each for the Vieris and Mr Murdoch. He would ask Sara to put them together.

Tim awoke on the following Saturday morning to the sound of wind and rain beating against the windowpane. His heart fell, he knew that in the past bad weather made quite a difference to the numbers of customers through the front door. His sleep had been broken by regular checks on the time. At 6 am he had given up on sleep and had made himself a coffee. He switched on the radio, very quietly so as not to wake his landlady. The forecast said the rain would stop in the early afternoon and that it would be bright later. 'Please let it be accurate,' he pleaded, speaking out loud.

Tim spent the morning in the shop willing himself not to keep looking at the clock, usually unsuccessfully. The shop ticked over during the morning and as Tim feared trade was quiet and well down on the numbers on a normal Saturday. At one-thirty the rain stopped and a few minutes later the sun broke through the cloud. Shortly afterwards the sky had cleared, and the pavements were steaming in the warmth of the sun.

Tim's father, who had been looking outside, came back in and said to Tim, 'You have the luck of the devil, Tim lad. Help me, we can get the table outside and set up before he arrives.'

At that moment Sophie appeared folding her umbrella as she came through the door. She passed Tim carrying one end of the table with his father smiling at her on the other end. The young couple kissed as they passed each other.

One of their regular customers called out, 'Don't look, Mother.'

His wife slapped his sleeve and said, 'Henry,' in a loud cross voice. She apologised to Sophie who laughed.

Sophie followed Tim and the table out of the shop and confided in Tim that her mother was coming. Sara had followed them and was busy preparing the produce on the tablecloth. Lots of small white plastic containers displaying all sorts of delicacies under their clear tops.

Sophie had gone back into the store when Tim had an idea.

'Sara, my love, I would like you to man your counter inside as usual please.' Tim noticed her disappointment and then explained that Sophie's mother has a very sweet tooth and he wanted Sara to explain all the various confectionery, 'And make sure she has whatever she wants,' he added. 'Also, Sara, make sure you tell her that they are all your recipes.'

'Most are my mama's.'

'That's fine,' he said, 'and stress the Italian connection please, if you don't mind.'

Sara laughed, 'You are setting traps for these people, Tim.'

'You are very wise, Sara,' he agreed smiling. 'Let's hope they work.'

The first of their special guests to arrive was Tim's great Aunt Victoria and her friends. Tim thanked them all profusely, especially his aunt. The old Daimler they had all arrived in was enormous with two-tone paintwork. The bulk of the bodywork was a pale caramel and the huge sweeping wings were a warm coffee colour. The car sat in the sun and gleamed. Tim asked Hubert what it did to the gallon.

'Best not to ask, old chap,' was Hubert's response.

His aunt and the other ladies greeted the rest of the staff and made a special fuss of Sophie.

His aunt pulled Tim by the wrist to a quiet corner and said, 'Timothy, Sophia is beautiful, inside and out. You must do whatever it takes to keep her. You are clearly made for each other. You will have a wonderful life together. Now I must sit down.'

Tim apologised profusely. His aunt waived it away. 'Please do not worry, Tim, I just cannot stand for long nowadays.'

Mr Woodman was already offering chairs and cups of tea to the ladies.

The shop was packed and noisy when Mr and Mrs Vieri arrived. Tim, now quite nervous, noticed the chauffeured car had pulled away as soon as they entered the shop. He must have been told to come back after a certain time. I wonder how long we have been given. Well whatever, here we go, win or bust, he thought to himself as he walked towards them.

He was a very good salesman, no bluster, no false bonhomie. He had learnt to be himself, do what he was good at. He got a smile from Mr Vieri, recognising that Tim was at work as they shook hands. Mrs Vieri was, if anything, even more cool towards him than before. Angela has spoken to them he realised. Oh well, whatever, he thought.

Sophie had still not noticed her mother and father and was laughing and joking with one of the customers. She was then asked a question and was in the middle of a comprehensive answer when she noticed her parents. The smile disappeared, she waved and mouthed 'see you in a moment' and then turned back to the customer. Mr Vieri had noticed the smile's demise and frowned.

Tim took the opportunity to introduce Mr Woodman to them and explained it had been his shop and that he had run it for almost fifty years and was now a partner.

Tim's father was hovering. Tim introduced him explaining to the Vieris that his father had run a stall across the road for many years and was the person who had found the foods in Italy and had begun to import them. The shop used his knowledge to do the buying. His father explained they usually bought direct from the producers in Italy and France. Also, a little from one or two other countries.

Tim walked the couple over to meet Harry, the third partner. Harry, in his wonderful Italian accent explained that he and Mr Cooper had had stalls across the road, side by side for many years. Tim recognised that Harry was playing up the accent, but never mind.

He noticed that Mr Murdoch had arrived with his wife. Brilliant, thought Tim.

Mr Murdoch made straight for the Vieris. 'Hallo, Victor, Olivia. May I introduce my wife, Daphne?' They shook hands all round. 'So, what do you think then, Victor? I can tell you now, this lad and his team are going a long way with this enterprise. I do not often say this but if ever a business was a sure-fire thing, this is it. As Tim told me when we first met, this business is of its time. The world was black and white, now it's filled with excitement and colour. There is new music, new clothes, why not new foods. That's about what you said to me is it not, Tim?' Tim nodded. Mr Murdoch continued, 'If everybody keeps working like they are now, well you just wait and see.'

Sophie arrived and passed Tim a folder. She kissed her mother and father and said to her mother, 'Would you like to meet the finest confectioner on the planet?'

'Really, here?' asked her mother, disparagingly.

'Yes, Mother,' said Sophie a little sternly. They were deep in conversation as they approached Sara's counter.

Mr Murdoch and his wife had moved away and were chatting to some of the customers.

'How can you afford to give everyone tasters, Tim?' asked Mr Vieri.

'Initially, it was to encourage people whose tastes were very conservative. They would not buy something they had not tried or tasted. Also, they had no idea how to cook it. Sara our confectioner puts together the recipes you see around the walls. I have been thinking about a cookbook, perhaps.' Tim was lying. The idea had just come to him new-born.

He saw Harry raise his eyebrows out of sight of the Vieris. 'But now we find that the tasters pay for themselves in increased sales,' he added.

'Hmm,' said Mr Vieri, sounding unsure.

Sophie returned bearing one of the hampers and offered it to Mrs Murdoch. 'I have just given Mother one and this is for you. Just to thank you for coming. I know you put off other commitments.'

'Very kind of you, Sophia,' said Mr Murdoch, keeping a straight face, 'very kind indeed.'

Tim's great aunt came to join the group, Tim introduced her, then turning to Mr Vieri she asked, 'May I speak with you for a moment, please?'

Having drawn him to one side she said, 'I am too old to waste time beating about the bush so I will come straight to the point. I understand that you have serious reservations about your daughter marrying my great nephew. I have two things to say; firstly, I have known Timothy ever since he was a baby. He is thoroughly sound in every way. He describes himself as an old boy Scout. That is in my opinion a very accurate description of his character.

'The second thing is that he is my sole beneficiary in the event of my demise. He knows this. What he does not know is the size of his inheritance.

By any measure it is considerable. He will be more than able to give your daughter the lifestyle she is accustomed to for the rest of their lives. I do hope you do not think me rude, but I felt you should know. I would appreciate it if you did not tell Timothy. I do not want him to know until a time when he cannot argue with me. He will one day be a very wealthy young man. However, I, like Mr Murdoch, think as Harry has a habit of saying, that this business has wings, it will fly. Finally, I think it obvious to anybody who takes the trouble to look that they are very much in love, each with the other and they should be together. That is all I have to say, thank you for listening.'

'Thank you for confiding in me. I have come to believe that he is as you put it, a very sound young man. I will give him the opportunity to ask for her hand today. We need to get this done.'

'Thank you,' she said. 'My greatest hope is to see him settled and happy. He deserves it.'

CHAPTER 27

ENGAGED

Mr Vieri strode across the store and said quietly to Tim. 'Is there somewhere we can speak privately?'

'Err, yes, upstairs,' said Tim, a little nervously. 'I must just check with Mr Woodman.'

A minute later Mr Vieri was following Tim upstairs. Once they were seated Mr Vieri looked quickly through the figures in the folder that Tim had given him.

Closing it Mr Vieri said, 'Timothy, I must admit I was very worried when you and Sophia got together but, having seen you at the hospital and since then people whose opinion I respect have spoken well of you and seeing what you have put together here, I must say I am very impressed. Therefore, if you would like to ask me the question?'

Tim sat opposite him, too stunned to do anything for a moment. What on earth had triggered this reversal. Mr Vieri was about to speak when Tim said, 'Please sir, may I marry your daughter?'

'I am placing great trust in you, Timothy, but yes, you may.'

He did not know what to say. He could feel himself welling up. He cuffed the tears away, thrust out his hand and grasped Mr Vieri's. 'You've made me very happy. Thank you, sir. I will take great care of her.'

'I believe you will, Timothy. You had better announce it. Get it done, lad.'

'I will do it now,' said Tim, jumping up from his seat and making for the stairs almost at the run.

As he appeared at the top of the stairs Sophie, who had been watching for him, read his face and saw how excited he was. His arm, beckoning her towards the stairs drew her to him.

She joined him halfway up the stairs and he grasped her hand. Very quietly he asked her, 'Will you marry me?'

Sophie looked at her father who had joined them. He nodded at her. She answered Tim with a simple, 'Yes!'

Mr Woodman, who as always was one jump ahead of everyone, in a very commanding tone said, 'Can we have some quiet, please?'

The shop went silent as people saw the young couple on the stair top holding hands. One or two people who were slow in recognising what was happening were nudged and hushed.

When he had everyone's attention Tim said, 'I have enormous pleasure in telling you that Sophia has just agreed to marry me, so we are now formally engaged.'

'Well kiss her then,' said someone.

Tim did as he was told and then said to her, 'I have a public apology to make. This has happened so fast I do not have a ring for your finger.'

'Yes you do, lad, if Sophie will accept it,' said his father. 'It's your mother's engagement ring that I put on her finger nearly forty years ago. I have been carrying it around until you had the sense to get the job done. I will understand, Sophie love, if it's not to your taste but perhaps it will do for now.' He handed the ring up for Tim to take.

'Are you ok with this?' whispered Tim.

Sophie, catching sight of it, said, 'Tim, it is beautiful.' Looking down at Mr Cooper she said, 'Thank you so much.'

'Are you sure?' repeated Tim.

'Oh yes, it is very special, Tim.'

The ring itself was dark antique gold. There was a blood red ruby in the middle of the setting with a surround of sparkling diamonds. Tim slipped the ring on her finger to loud applause.

Sophie took two steps down the stairs, reaching out to Tim's father who stepped up to meet her. Wrapping both arms round his neck she kissed his cheek and said very quietly, so that only he could hear, 'It is a wonderful gift, I will never take it off. I am very moved that you feel able to entrust me with it. I know how much it means to you.'

'You're welcome, lass,' was his quiet response.

Mr Woodman and Harry had already started opening bottles of wine. When everyone had a drink in their hand Mr Vieri proposed the toast. 'The toast is to the happy couple. May they be this happy for the rest of their lives.'

The clapping and shouting as people wished them good luck was deafening. Sophie avoided looking at her mother. The two of them descended the stairs to be hugged and in Tim's case, back slapped.

Tim turned and shook Mr Vieri's hand saying, 'Thank you, sir.'

'You are very welcome, Timothy. I am sure you will both be very happy.'

Mrs Vieri was seething, all her plans for her daughter had been brushed aside, the embarrassment she would face with her so-called friends sniggering behind her back. She could hear the sneering voices in her head. 'Did you know Olivia's daughter has married a barrow boy, he has not a penny to his name,' they would be saying. 'Apparently, he has her working in the shop all hours and does not pay her a penny. I do not know how Olivia will be able to show her face in public again for the shame of it.' Her anger continued to grow. On top of it all her husband, who could have snuffed out all this terrible business with a simple refusal to agree to the marriage had condoned it without even asking her. How could he do this. She found herself fighting to stop herself screaming out loud.

Sophie, unaware of her mother's rage had made her way over to speak to her.

Before Sophie could utter a word, her mother, her face screwed into a fierce scowl said in a hard, cruel voice, 'You may wipe that smile off your face, madam,' then continuing, spat out, 'you have made your bed, now you must lie in it.'

Sophie uttered no response but made out that she needed the toilet upstairs. Once in there she burst into tears. How could Mother say that? she thought. Why does she hate me? Why does she despise Tim when father has accepted him? Her line of thought was interrupted when Sara knocked on the door.

Sara had seen her distress when she had spoken to her mother and had followed her upstairs. She called out to Sophie saying, 'Can I come in?'

'I am alright,' said Sophie.

'No, you are not, I saw you.'

Sophie came out of the toilet crying and threw her arms around Sara. 'My mother was horrible,' she sobbed. 'She said I had made my bed and now I must lie in it. She was so angry and spiteful.'

'I am sure she will regret saying that. She wanted you to marry a prince and live in a castle. She cannot see that you will marry a prince and that he is building you a castle as we speak.

'But whatever, we must get you presentable before people start wondering where you are. Here, this cold wet flannel will help. Hold it on your eyes.' A few minutes later Sophie would just about pass muster.

'Are you ready?' asked Sara.

After a long breath in, 'Yes,' was the response.

Standing at the foot of the stairs was her father. He read her distress immediately. He had seen the interaction between her and her mother.

Hugging her to him he whispered in her ear. 'I am very happy for you and I am sure he will make a terrific husband. Please do not worry about your mother, she will regret her behaviour tonight.' Looking beyond his smile she saw in his eyes the towering rage he was holding in check. Giving her one more hug and saying, 'I love you very much,' he strode across to her mother. He plucked the glass of wine from her fingers and placed it down, then taking her elbow in what was a very firm grip propelled her towards the door. Their car had just drawn up.

As the car drew away Mrs Vieri turned on her husband, she was obviously very angry. 'How dare you treat me like that in front of everybody, and I will have a bruised arm in the morning.'

There was a long silence in the car and then Mrs Vieri spoke again saying, 'I demand an explanation and apology.'

There was another, but shorter silence broken by Mr Vieri in a near whisper that was ice cold. 'We will talk about this when we arrive home. Until then I would like to travel in silence.'

Mrs Vieri went to say something.

In a voice grown quieter and even colder he spat out, 'Damn it, be silent woman.'

*

Tim sensed a change in Sophie and asked, 'Are you ok?'

'I am fine,' fibbed Sophie. 'I would like to ring Angela and see if she will come. It is important that she is here.'

'I agree,' said Tim.

Sophie made her way through the happy crowd and rang Angela. Sophie explained that her father had given his blessing to their wedding and they had just announced their engagement. 'Can you come to the shop, please?' she asked, 'I want you to be here.'

'What is wrong? You sound very upset.'

'Can I tell you when you get here?' she replied trying hard to hold back the tears.

'Oh Sophie, my darling, I am on my way.'

Tim noticed Sophie dabbing at her eyes from across the room but as he started towards her another good customer came up to shake his hand and congratulate him. For the next few minutes he was trapped in a corner. Frequent glances at Sophie seemed to indicate that she was ok. Perhaps he had imagined her tears. Angela entered the shop, smiled and waved at Tim over everyone's head and headed towards Sophie. Mr Murdoch and his wife also decided to leave. Tim thanked them both for coming and said how important their presence had been. When he next looked, Angela and Sophie had disappeared.

Tim's great aunt rose from her chair and hugged him hard. 'I am so happy for you both. You must come to tea in the near future.' Looking around she said, 'I think we are about to leave. Please tell Sophia how happy I am for you both.'

Standing in the middle of the room upstairs Angela was hugging Sophie while she cried. Angela held her until Sophie became calmer.

She said, 'I will make us some tea, then you can tell me what on earth is wrong. This is supposed to be one of the happiest days of your life.'

Minutes later Sophie, now sitting and nursing a cup of tea, was explaining how happy she had been when her father had given them his blessing to their marriage. 'It was him who had told Tim to announce it. Everyone was so pleased for us. Afterwards I went over to talk to Mother. She said spitefully, "well now you have made your bed and you must lie in it". Aunty, she was horrible.'

'Where are they now?' asked Angela.

'Father saw how upset I was and marched her out of the shop and into the car.'

'She has gone too far this time. Your father when he really loses his temper is very frightening.'

'I do not understand her reaction,' said Sophie, shaking her head. 'Father has obviously come to like and trust Tim and there is no better judge of character than him.'

'I expect your mother is frightened of losing you,' replied Angela, thinking to herself, if she keeps this up, she will achieve exactly what she is frightened of, and Tim will not put up with her nonsense. Angela also realised this was about her sister's snobbery and bigotry. 'But I still love you, Olivia,' she said to herself.

The crowd in the shop was slowly thinning. Tim had lost all track of time. To his complete surprise, he saw it was almost nine o'clock. Mr Woodman, aware as always, spotted Tim's glance at the clock and wagging his head as a query was asking Tim what he wanted to do.

Tim nodded and then indicated that it was time by pointing his head at the door.

Mr Woodman called, 'Time please, ladies and gentlemen, thank you all for coming.' With outspread arms he began shepherding everyone towards the door.

Some wag called out, 'What about last orders then?'

Mr Woodman gave him an old-fashioned look and wished everyone safely home. Finally, he was able to shut the door, flip the closed sign over and slide the latch.

Harry called across the shop, 'It's a good job you will only get engaged once, Tim. I am too old for all this partying.'

Mr Woodman saw Tim looking for his bride-to-be, 'She is upstairs with her aunt,' he said, pointing at the ceiling.

Tim swung around the newel post at the foot of the stairs and then galloped up them two at a time. He heard his father say, 'It makes me tired just watching him.'

The two women were sitting holding hands on Mr Woodman's sofa.

He saw immediately how upset Sophie was. Kneeling beside her he grasped her hand and asked, 'Whatever is wrong?'

Angela said, 'Obviously we will tell you, Tim, but you must promise not to overreact.'

'Please, Tim, promise me you will not do anything,' pleaded Sophie.

'I don't know what I am promising but ok then. Now tell me, please.'

Sophie, in a very quiet voice began to explain but her words were drowned out by raucous laughter from the shop below.

'Sorry, sweetheart, I didn't hear what you said.'

Sophie looked at Angela saying, 'Will you tell him, please?'

Angela explained how angry, rude and spiteful Mrs Vieri had been to Sophie, 'Saying, "well you have made your bed, now you must sleep in it".'

Tim exploded. 'God damn it! I cannot believe it, one of the most important days of your life and she behaves like this. I know she thinks I am not good enough for you. Have I got two heads or the plague? That's how I feel when we are with her, and I have just agreed not to say anything. Even your father trusts me to look after you now.' Tim was striding about the room throwing his arms around.

'Tim,' said Angela, 'what you are saying may be true, but they can hear everything you are saying downstairs.'

'Oh, yes, sorry, but I am so damn angry.'

Reaching out her hand Sophie said, 'Tim, will you just hold me, please.'

'Sit here, Tim,' said Angela rising from the couch, 'I will make some tea.'

Tim and Sophie sat holding hands in silence, lost in thought. They were both all too aware of the problems Mrs Vieri's reaction presaged for the future of their marriage.

As the kettle started to sing Mr Woodman made his way quietly up the stairs. 'I hope I am not intruding,' he said. 'We heard Tim shouting.'

'You are not intruding, Mr Woodman, this is your home.' Turning to Sophie, Tim continued, 'Can I tell him?'

Mr Woodman spoke before Tim did, 'I am sorry, but we heard what Tim said from downstairs.'

'Sorry, Sophie love,' said Tim.

'It would be difficult to keep it quiet; I know at least three people heard her,' added Mr Woodman.

'I will always defend my sister,' declared Angela, 'but this time I do not know what to say.'

'What the devil do we do now?' asked Tim.

'My father was as angry as I have ever seen him. I almost feel sorry for Mother,' said Sophie. 'He will make it very clear to her that she has behaved badly and to answer your question, Tim, I really do not know.'

'Can I suggest that we leave this be for tonight and discuss it in the morning?' said Angela. 'I expect that she will ring later this evening and we can discuss what to do next.'

'Tim, I know we should be out celebrating but I just want to go home to bed, do you mind?'

'No,' responded Tim, 'I do understand. But I do need to make this clear now, I will not put up with a repeat performance of tonight and remain silent. No way.'

'Please do not get so angry, Tim, I am sure Mother will come around in time.'

'Hmm, I hope so,' he responded. His tone of voice clearly indicating he did not think she would.

'The tea is made if anybody would like one,' said Mr Woodman.

'That's very kind,' said the two women, 'but we would like to go home.'

'Will you be coming, Tim?' asked Angela.

'No, I don't think so,' he said, 'I expect you would be better getting some sleep, Sophie, if you can. I will have a cup of tea with Mr Woodman if that's ok?' said Tim glancing at him.

'Of course, lad,' he responded.

Tim saw both the women off the premises, giving them both a hug, adding, 'There must be a way of sorting this out.'

'I am sure there will be,' Angela said, trying to sound upbeat.

Tim stood in the shop window watching while Angela hailed a cab. Neither of them looked round or waved.

He went upstairs to have his tea. Both men discussed the situation for some time. On this occasion Mr Woodman was unable to come up with a plan.

It was a very sad and worried young man who made his way home that night.

Early the following morning Tim had only just started his breakfast when he heard the phone ringing downstairs. His landlady called up to tell him the call was for him.

It was Angela. 'Tim, it was as I expected, Mr Vieri was in a furious temper, tore my sister to pieces verbally. She admitted that she was frightened because he was so angry. Apparently, he has moved into one of the spare rooms. He told her that she was a snob and a bigot, then he went on to say you were the ideal partner for their daughter and how dare she criticise a decision he had made. Especially in public. My sister is in a terrible state. As he walked down the landing towards a guest bedroom he had apparently shouted "if you do something like that again I will not be responsible for my actions". Where that leaves us, I have no idea,' she finished.

'How is Sophie this morning?' Tim asked.

'Very subdued. She has gone to her office for a couple of hours, she will ring you later.'

CHAPTER 28

MOVING ONBOARD

Tim had no sooner put the phone down than Rupert called. 'Tim, I am off to America tonight, so can I drop the keys in to you?'

'I did not realise you were leaving so soon.'

'This is the film business, Tim; nothing happens for ages old chap and then it all happens in the most fearful rush. Are you alright with our agreement?'

'Yes, it's great, we are both really happy with it.'

'Good, good,' replied Rupert. 'I will call in at the shop today.'

'No, you can't do that we are not open today.'

'Why is that?' asked Rupert.

'It's Sunday,' replied Tim. 'I am more than happy to call on you at the boat. I could do with a trip out.'

'I sometimes tell myself, "Mr Strong, you are losing your marbles my dear old thing." That's only true of course if I had any to lose in the first place. Whoops I am rambling again, bad habit of mine. I will be gone at ten am. Can you get here by then?'

'Yes, I may walk, I could do with the exercise.'

'See you soon, old bean,' said Rupert and hung up.

Tim strode through the London streets towards the river. As always, the sights and sounds of the river, its vibrancy and the various smells improved his mood. The sun was playing tag with the clouds, their shadows racing across the river. The night had been a long one, trying to find a solution to the problem, namely Mrs Vieri. He had not succeeded. He remembered his mother told him that he should never be cowed by people who were better off than him or considered themselves superior. She truly believed that if you worked hard and persevered anything was possible. This was clearly part of his credo, and his desire to prove his mother right.

Arriving at the boatyard Tim was just in time to see the arrival of what turned out to be Rupert's Taxi. He stepped aside to let it pass him.

By the time he had walked along the bank to the Sea Maiden Tabby was helping Rupert carry some large cases off the boat and into the taxi.

Rupert shook Tim's hand enthusiastically; he was clearly very excited. 'Big day, Tim. Get this right and who knows where it could lead.' Tim wasn't quite sure whether Rupert meant a big day for him or for Rupert.

The actor saw his puzzlement and said, 'Big day for me, Tim, my dear old thing. If this is a hit, I will not be playing bit parts anymore.'

Rupert climbed into the taxi and Tim suddenly realised he still did not have the keys. The taxi had started to move so Tim banged loudly on the roof, the driver looked at him and saw that he was telling him to stop.

Rupert wound down his window and asked brusquely, 'What's wrong, Tim? I cannot afford to miss the plane.'

'I still don't have any keys,' said Tim, patting his pockets in case he had forgotten being given them.

'Whoops,' said Rupert. 'Tim, look on the work surface just inside the door.'

Tim half ran up the ramp onto the boat opened the door and saw the keys. Turning back towards Rupert he gave him the thumbs up. Rupert gave Tim both thumbs up and shouted, 'Tally ho, driver.' The cab swept him away and out of sight.

Tabby, who had watched the mayhem, shook Tim's hand. 'Welcome aboard, young man. If you need anything at all just ask.'

'Thank you, I expect there will be plenty of questions.'

'That will never be a problem, Tim, just ask.'

He spent the next hour exploring the boat. He had a couple of queries, but Rupert had assured him that Tabby knew everything there was to know. Rupert had been very kind. He had left a bottle of very good wine, bread and butter and half a cake and all the makings for a cup of tea. Tim was not to know but the boat would, over the next few years, become a magnet for his work colleagues, Sophie's friends and boss and especially his father who would fall in love with the boat on sight. Tim found a note from Rupert: 'Keep the fire ticking over, it keeps the boat dry.' It was signed, 'Have fun, Rupert.'

Tim saw the phone on the side, picked it up. There was a tone. He rang Sophie's work number, there was no response. He tried Angela's; he was just about to hang up when she answered.

'Hi, it's me, I am at the boat, I have the keys. I wondered if Sophie would like to come over. It may cheer her up. I have tried ringing her but there is no answer.'

'I will try, she may respond to my number, what is your number there, Tim?'

He read the number from the centre of the handset.

'I will ring you if I can contact her, bye for now.' She hung up.

Tim decided that he would start at the back of the boat and look in all the cupboards and lockers. In the main bedroom he found spare sheets and pillows in one locker and blankets in another. In the drawer under the wardrobe there were two hot water bottles. A low cupboard on the other side of the cabin appeared empty until he got down and lay on the floor. At the back of the cupboard against the hull of the boat were three horizontal copper pipes. Two with large brass knurled taps. They were painted bright red between the knuckles of the knurls. There was no indication of what their purpose was. I hope Tabby does know all about this boat, thought Tim.

Half an hour later Tim had worked his way forward, looked in the small side cabin and had the kettle singing on the top of the stove in the kitchen when there was a slight movement of the boat followed by a tap-tapping on the front door. Sophie and Angela were standing there.

'I went and got her,' said Angela, giving Tim a hug and a kiss.

'Hallo,' said Sophie, winding her arms around his neck and moving her body as close as she could and giving him what later they would come to call a bedroom kiss.

After a few moments Angela was becoming very embarrassed. 'Shall I make the tea?' she asked.

'Oops, sorry,' said Tim. 'No, I will make the tea. Sophie, can you show Angela around the boat, please?'

'Shall we start at the back?' Sophie suggested.

'Stern,' muttered Tim.

'Pardon?' said Angela.

'Ignore him,' laughed Sophie. 'He has gone all nautical.'

Whilst making the tea he could hear the two women talking, and occasionally laughing. The tea was brewing, and Tim had the bread ready to toast when they returned. A few minutes later they were sitting around the stove with the front open using long-handled forks to toast the bread. Much later with the dusk falling they were still sat around the fire talking quietly. The remains of a fish and chip meal sat on the side. Sophie had lit some candles. With the candles and the glow of the fire reflecting off the glass and the mirrors and the soft warm colour of the varnish, the cabin was magical.

'This is a very special place,' said Angela. 'A place of love.'

Nobody said anything, Sophie reached across and squeezed Tim's hand.

Tim realised that they were all avoiding discussing yesterday so as not to spoil the evening.

*

Tim decided he would move onto the boat as soon as possible. He worried about telling his landlady. She would miss the money and he suspected his company. He would pay her the rent until she found someone. Perhaps he could help find his replacement. Tim walked through the boat checking it was all safe to leave. Then he and the two women made for home.

The following Sunday was the first opportunity for the young couple to clean the boat before Tim moved in.

Later that evening, both of them tired and dusty, Sophie asked, 'Have you tried the bath?'

'No, not yet,' he replied moving towards the bathroom and spinning the hot tap open. The stove had been on all day on tick-over. Soon piping hot water started to fill the bath, steam misting the small mirror over the hand basin. The bathroom had varnished wooden panelling, a small mid green bath and a white basin and toilet. There was a porthole in the wall with frosted glass.

I will have to bath with my knees up, thought Tim. He called To Sophie, 'Ladies first. Leave the water, I will get in after you, not sure how much hot water there will be.'

Sophie appeared beside him and kissed him in the ear, gently pushed him out of the bathroom and closed the door. Later he could hear her singing to herself over the splashing of water. Tim felt his love for her fill him up. He realised how lucky he was to find her. He suddenly remembered that he had a spare clean jumper in his rucksack. He found it and tapped on the door.

Sophie Squeaked, 'You cannot come in, I have no clothes on.'

Tim laughed, 'You're safe, I have a clean jumper out here if you want it. I will leave it on the doorknob.'

A short while later she called out, 'Please do not look, I am coming out.'

Tim being the gentleman he was walked into the galley and turned his back, then called, 'You're safe now.' He heard the patter of her feet as she made her way to the bedroom. He smiled.

Stripping his clothes off in the bathroom he lowered himself into the bath.

The knees up idea didn't work. He found that if he crossed his ankles and then pulled his feet towards him, he could lower his buttocks into the water. The room was scented with Sophie's perfume. A little later he was dressing when there was a tap on the door.

'Can I have my bra please, Tim?'

He opened the door just enough to pass it to Sophie.

She slowly pushed it fully open and stepped into the bathroom wearing his jumper. She saw Tim dressed only in his jeans, chest still damp from the bath, his black hair still wet and tousled. She stepped up to him and into his arms. They were both lost in time, the tips of their tongues touched, and Sophie was aware of his arousal. The kiss got deeper. She took his hand and backing out of the bathroom, their lips still locked together they shuffled towards the bedroom that was lit by the full moon. His hands exploring her body discovered that apart from her knickers she was naked under his borrowed jumper. He thumbed her nipple erect; she bit his lip. Hauling on his belt she had undone his jeans and he kicked them across the bedroom together with his underpants.

She stripped off the borrowed jumper along with her knickers.

Sophie threw herself backwards on the bed and reached out her hand towards him.

'Oh God, you are beautiful,' he whispered, placing his left knee on the bed he moved forward and covered her body. Their lips met again. Her hand reached down, grasped him and spreading her legs lifted herself towards him.

Tim groaned out loud, 'Sophie, I can't do this,' he said, raising his body up and away from her.

Sophie, not believing what was happening said, 'What do you mean? You cannot leave me like this. Tim, please. I have not told you I am on the pill, please come back.'

Tim already had his jeans back on and was making for the door.

'Tim, please, please, come back.'

He continued towards the door.

'You bastard!' she shouted throwing a shoe at his retreating back. It bounced off the back of his neck.

He collected his clothes from the bathroom and putting them on and went outside and stood on the front deck. It had grown dark and the sky was alive with stars.

*

A long time later Sophie joined him; he could see that she had been crying. He carefully wrapped an arm round her checking that it was ok to do so.

'I am sorry I swore at you,' she said. 'I do know that in the future if you make a promise you will keep it. God knows how you kept this one.' They were both silent looking up at the stellar display. Eventually Sophie said very quietly, 'I hate the bloody Boy Scouts.'

Later at home with Angela, Sophie gave her a very brief resume of what had happened. Sophie admitted that Tim keeping his promise was driving her crazy.

Angela, though a little embarrassed listened to her, finally saying, 'We need to give your parents an ultimatum. They arrange a proper wedding soon or you go to the registry office. There may be a few problems there though. I understand from your mother that your father is still sleeping separately.'

Sophie getting cross said, 'I am fed up tiptoeing around my parents. I can afford a nice wedding. They can choose whether to come or not. Tim and I have plenty of friends. It will be fine.'

'I know and understand your anger, Sophie darling, but we need to be a little more tactful,' advised Angela.

'No, I will not do this anymore. I am an adult with a high-powered job. I have a wonderful man who loves me. It is time I started exercising some self-determination. Can I ask them to come here one evening, please?' she continued. 'I will tell them it is to talk about our wedding.'

Angela shrugged and shook her head. 'Your mother will make a terrible fuss.'

'She will never agree to my marrying Tim. So, we just do it, I am beginning to sound like my father,' she smiled.

'You are your father's daughter that's for sure,' Angela agreed.

Sophie rang Tim the following day and explained what she wanted to do.

Tim replied, 'Yes, that's fine with me. Only one change, we ask to go to their house. We need to do this through the front door. Your father will think more of us this way. Also, we have nothing to apologise for.'

'If they, or rather my mother, makes it too difficult I will get married in a registry office. Would you be ok with that Tim?'

'I would rather have a small wedding that we have arranged, you and I, and everybody is invited and then it's up to them who comes. One thing we must consider is that your father will insist on walking you down the aisle, quite rightly in my opinion.'

'When should we ring them?' asked Sophie.

'Now,' said Tim, 'I can't go through last night again.'

'Nor me,' she replied. She had lain awake most of the night, torn between a deep embarrassment knowing that she had thrown herself at him and been rejected and that he had seen her completely naked. Her hormones ran amok when she remembered him naked and aroused.

'I will ring your father now if you want me to.'

'No. I think it is better if I do it. It's a father-daughter thing. When can I ring you?'

'I have a restaurant owner coming in to discuss a contract about ten, after that I am clear.'

'I will ring you later?' she said as she rang-off.

Sophie advised her secretary that she would not be taking calls until she told her otherwise. Ringing her father's office, a voice she did not recognise said, 'Can I help?'

'May I speak to Mr Vieri, please?'

The girl using a very officious tone said, 'Mr Vieri is not taking calls now, will you ring back later please,' and then rang off.

Sophie jerked back upright in her seat, frowned, looked at the phone and shook her head in surprise. She redialled the number. Before the girl could start her usual script, Sophie said, 'This is Sophia Vieri here, will you put me through to my father please, and can I give you a piece of advice? Before you are rude to people it would pay you to ascertain who they are. I will consider whether I shall tell my father or not. Now will you put me through, please.'

'I am so sorry, Miss Vieri, please, please accept my apology.'

'Let me advise you, if he had got to know of it you would be out of a job. He does not give second chances. I will not mention it this time. My father, please.'

Oh God, thought Sophie, I am beginning to sound like my mother.

CHAPTER 29

WEDDING PLANS

'Thank you, Miss Vieri, I am putting you through.'

'Hallo, Sophia darling,' said her father, 'what can I do for you?'

'Hallo, Father, are you well?'

'Yes, I am very well thanking you, and I can guess from this preamble that the subject matter in this conversation is difficult. Is it your mother you want to talk about?'

'Not directly, you remember Tim's and my wedding plan, well, to talk in language you will understand we want to action the final part, the wedding, and sooner rather than later.'

'It's not a subject I want to discuss over the phone,' said her father.

'Of course not, Father, Tim is asking if we can come to the house and discuss it properly?'

'Did he though? He is one of the very few people who is not afraid of me.'

'No, he is not but he does hold you in very high regard and always listens carefully to what you have to say. He will not admit it, but I think you are his yardstick. He measures himself against you. Please do not ever mention that I told you this. But he did say he wanted to outdo you.'

'Cheeky beggar,' laughed her father. 'He must catch me first, good luck to him.'

'Can we make it tomorrow or is the day after better for you?' asked Sophie.

'Sophia, I do still recognise an assumptive close when I hear one. Hold on a moment.

Sally,' called her father, addressing his secretary, 'can you bring my diary in, please?'

Sophie could hear them talking in the background. She heard her father say, 'What about tomorrow night.' Sally pointed out that the new pool maintenance company was calling that evening.

'Can you put them off, please?' he asked. There was a brief quiet discussion that Sophie could not hear.

'Sophia,' said her father, 'can you two make tomorrow night at home? Come for dinner.'

'I would prefer supper, please, Tim works late, and it will be less formal. We could have it in the lounge.'

'That's fine,' said her father, 'what time could you be there?'

'About eight thirty,' she replied.

'Would you mind if Sally came?' he asked, 'she is an organisational wizard. Bearing in mind how busy you and Timothy are she can take some of the load.'

'It will be nice to see her. One thing up front, Father, we have waited the year as promised. So, we would like to be married in one month's time.'

'Sophia, Sally is shaking her head. Remember, I know this will make you frown but this is a major Vieri family occasion. Therefore, it must be done properly. Senior family members will come from Italy and they will soon tell me if they think it is not fitting.

'Sally thinks two months.'

'Six weeks,' responded Sophie.

There was more quiet conversation between her father and Sally. Her father said, 'Sophia, darling, talk to Sally. She has just pointed out I must make some phone calls. Sally will ring you back from the conference room, I assume you are at work. You do not need to worry; this will happen, and Sally can use whatever resources she requires.'

'Thank you, Father.'

'You are very welcome, my darling, bye for now.'

Sally rang Sophie back a few minutes later saying, 'Hallo, Miss Vieri, thank you for allowing me to help,'

'Sophie, please call me Sophie.'

'Can I call you Sophia in case your father overhears?' asked Sally.

'Yes, ok then,' she agreed, pulling a face.

Sally confided in her that she loved organising weddings, she had done three now and loved it. 'Oh, and by the way,' she added, 'there is no financial limit on this event.'

Later, Sophie rang Tim and Mr Woodman answered the phone. After they had exchanged the normal pleasantries she asked, 'Is Tim there, please?'

'He is with a supplier now; shall I interrupt him?' asked Mr Woodman.

'No, not if he is busy, can you ask him to ring me as soon as possible, please?'

Tim rang about twenty minutes later; Sophie shared the news. Tim was stunned.

'You have made a big impression on him,' said Sophie. 'He would not be doing this in so lavish a style if he had any doubts about you.

'Do you mind Sally being involved?' she asked.

'Not at all,' he replied, 'if this is going to happen in the way your father has described we will need lots of help. How has your mother taken it?' queried Tim.

'I do not think she knows yet,' she replied, 'wait for the fireworks.'

'Would it be useful to have Angela there? She seems to have the measure of your mother. It might help.'

'That is a good idea, Tim. I will ask her and then contact Sally. It will save bothering Father. Sorry, Tim, I have a call I must answer. See you later. Love you.'

The following evening the taxi dropped the two of them outside the Vieri home. A black cat ran across in front of them, he could not remember if that was a good thing or not. Tim remembered the last time he was here and his angry rapid departure.

Sophie looked up at him, 'Are you ready?' she asked, as they walked up the path.

He realised she was quite nervous. 'Don't worry, my darling. Remember we have royal approval.'

Sophie laughed, 'For God's sake do not tell him that, he will become even more impossible.'

Reaching the heavy ornate dark wood door. Tim said, 'Here we go,' knocking on the door as he said it. There was a long pause, Tim asked, 'Shall I knock again?' Sophie shook her head in denial.

It was Mr Vieri who finally opened the door. 'Sophia, darling,' said her father pulling her into a bear hug. Turning to Tim, 'You are very welcome, Tim,' he said offering his hand and gently guiding him across the doorstep into the house.

I must learn how you do that, thought Tim. 'Good evening, sir,' he replied.

Tim had little memory of his last visit in terms of what the house was like. Now he saw that the hallway was long with honey coloured parquet flooring. As they followed Mr Vieri he noticed Tim's glance at the study door that was firmly closed but made no comment. Most of the doors off the long hallway were varnished wood with small squares of bevelled glass set in them. The lighting was supplied by glass chandeliers set in a row down the length of the hall.

Angela was standing at the entrance to what turned out to be the lounge.

'Hallo, you two,' she said hugging them in turn.

Sophie moved over to her mother and hugged her. Mrs Vieri kissed her cheek. Tim moved in and offered his hand. She was clearly relieved that he was not going to get any closer. In a voice that came from the Arctic she said, 'Good evening, Timothy.'

He responded with a big smile and said in a jolly voice that indicated he was not going to allow her to put a damper on the evening, 'Good evening, Mrs Vieri, how nice to see you. I hope you are well.'

'I am,' she replied in the same cold tone as before.

Sophie was looking at him with one eyebrow raised and a very quizzical look on her face. He would explain later that this was his new strategy with her mother.

Sophie called him over to be introduced to Sally. She was older than her voice, but still a very attractive woman. Dark brunette and a wonderful complexion. She was wearing the traditional two-piece pin-striped navy suit and black high heels. She remained seated. Her pretty legs crossed at the ankles. She, shaking Tim's hand said, 'It's nice to meet you, Timothy.'

'Tim, please call me Tim. Thank you for your offer of help. I don't know what we would have done without you, I know that's what everyone says, but in this case it's true.'

'I am sure we will manage, Tim.' As Sally was speaking to him, she leant forward and retrieved a notebook and pen from her handbag. Turning to Sophie she said, 'After tonight I will type up my notes and let you have a copy.'

'And me, please,' said Mr Vieri. 'Are you two hungry?' he asked, starting to rise from his chair. 'I will call Martha.'

Sophie said, 'We have not eaten, we have come straight from work. I will go if you like.'

'No, you are fine,' said her father.

Sophie was talking to Angela; the rest were silent. It gave Tim a chance to look around. The deep red heavily patterned Axminster fitted carpet was obviously expensive. The furniture was dark and heavy. A brightly lit all-glass display cabinet contained some beautiful cut glass. Tim guessed most of it was antique. While Tim's family had never been able to afford fine glass or art, he seemed to have an instinct for the better pieces.

Tim, facing Mrs Vieri, asked, 'May I look?'

She was clearly surprised and said, 'Yes, but please do not touch anything, it is all very expensive and irreplaceable.'

Stepping over to the cabinet he kept his hands behind his back, so she could see them. He looked up from the cabinet and said, 'I would guess that a lot of it is antique.'

Mrs Vieri replied, 'Yes, you are correct.'

Sally came to join him beside the glass display cabinet and said very quietly and with wonder in her voice, 'It is so beautiful.'

Tim did not let on that his great aunt Victoria collected antique glass and had often told him about the provenance of some of the collection when he was very young. He realised how much she had trusted him not to break it. 'Is that vase Venetian?' he asked Mrs Vieri, pointing to an exquisitely shaped small vase in a very soft feminine pink that got deeper towards the bottom of the vessel.

She was clearly stunned that he knew anything about any of it. 'Err, yes,' was her surprised response.

Tim did not disclose it was the only thing in there that he knew anything about. 'It's all very beautiful,' he said and meant it. As he turned, he saw Sophie with the same surprised look on her face. Angela, making sure no one could see gave Tim the thumbs up. He gave her a surreptitious wink. Maybe over time Mrs Vieri would realise he was not the common lout she thought he was.

Mr Vieri followed Martha into the room both carrying plates of food.

Sophie jumped up, 'Can I help? Hallo, Martha, how are you?'

'Hallo, Miss Vieri, I am very well, thank you. Are you very excited?'

'I am,' Sophie replied, 'Tim come and say hallo to Martha. She has been in this house ever since I was a child.'

Tim rose from the couch and stepped across to her. 'Nice to meet you, the food looks great,' he added. She was short and homely in appearance and flushed from the kitchen.

Martha smiled a little embarrassed smile. 'Thank you, Mr...?' she became even more embarrassed not knowing what to call him.

'Please don't worry, call me Tim.' He could see the food looked superb. A range of Italian dishes adorning each plate.

She said, 'Thank you, Mr Tim.'

He was reminded of Sara.

The family were soon seated, feasting on the wonderful food and drinking fine wine. Mr Vieri said, 'Can we get some broad outlines down for this wedding. White?' he asked.

'Yes, Father!' said Sophie, indignantly.

Only just, thought Tim.

Mrs Vieri said, 'Victor, please.'

Ignoring them both he said, 'Catholic church?'

'Yes,' said Tim, 'if your church will marry us.'

'You must agree to bring the children up as Catholics,' confirmed Angela.

Tim looked at Sophie and nodded.

'There will be a nuptial mass,' said Mrs Vieri.

'Will that be in Latin?' asked Tim. 'I went to a funeral some years ago, that was in Latin. I found it very impressive. Mystical and theatrical at the same time.'

'No,' snapped Mrs Vieri, correcting him. 'It must be so that ordinary people can understand it.'

'I agree with Tim,' said Angela. 'It has lost some of its magic I think.'

Mrs Vieri tutted.

'Moving on,' said Mr Vieri, 'you will get married from this house I hope, Sophia?'

'Yes please, Father.'

'Timothy, I hope you do not mind but it must be the full regalia for us menfolk. I can suggest a very respectable men's outfitter that will hire us what we need.'

'Sophia,' said her mother, 'you can use my couturier for your wedding dress.'

'Thank you, Mother, but I have seen the dress I want already.' She mentioned the name of the shop.

Angela raised her eyebrows. 'Have you seen the prices? They are astronomical.'

'I have already told Sophia that she is to have what she wants,' said Mr Vieri. 'I have only one daughter and this will be done properly. Anyway, we must remember that the Italians are coming.'

Rising from her chair Mrs Vieri said, 'I think I will retire. All this talk has tired me out. Please keep me informed, Sophia?'

'I will,' said Sophie. 'Goodnight, Mother.' Everyone wished her a good night as she departed the room.

Tim felt the atmosphere in the room improve as the door closed quietly behind her.

'I suggest we use Claridge's for the reception.' It was more of an instruction than a question. 'Is that ok, Sophia?' asked her father.

'That assumes that they can fit us in at short notice,' said Sally.

'Do we need to go to that level, Father?'

'Remember the Italians,' he responded.

She laughed. 'You make them sound like the mafia.'

'I have never been sure,' he said with no hint of a smile.

Tim raised an eyebrow. What am I marrying into? he thought.

'Sally, I think you should take over from here, Tim I think we can leave the ladies to it,' said Mr Vieri as he stood up.

'Father, I said six weeks remember,' said Sophie.

'Sally?' asked Mr Vieri.

Sally thought for a moment. 'Not with my present workload at the office.'

'Right,' said her boss, 'is there a girl in the main office who could be moved up to cover the basic stuff? Under your instruction, of course.'

'Yes, Emily is new but thorough. She worked for an author before he died.'

'I will need you to do the interpersonal stuff as usual,' he continued, 'the rest of the time you can work on this wedding. If there is overtime or anything charge it to the company. You can keep me in the loop with the daily briefing.

'Ok, Tim, let us leave them to it.'

As the two men were leaving the room Sophie reached out and squeezed his hand. Tim smiled at her.

Mr Vieri led Tim to a room opposite his office. It was furnished as a small viewing room with buttoned dark red leather armchairs and a big screen set on the far wall. Beside Mr Vieri's chair stood a large wood cabinet that glowed in the subdued lighting. He pressed a button on the back and the door on the front came slowly open carrying the shelves with it. The interior was brightly lit. The cabinet was stocked with a range of bottles. Tim noticed a bottle of Jura single malt, a drink he had become very partial to.

'What do you fancy, Tim?'

'If I may I would like a glass of Jura, please.'

'Good choice, I think I will join you.'

After the drinks were poured, sampled and the appreciative noises made, Mr Vieri said, 'Tim, I want to do two things this evening. I need to apologise for the way my wife and I treated you in the beginning; it was rude and unnecessary; I hope you can forgive us.' Tim went to say something, Mr Vieri raised a hand, 'Please let me finish. I also want to welcome you to the family. I have watched how you behave around my daughter and I recognise that you two are made for each other. I think if she lost you now it would break her heart.'

'I do recognise how lucky I am, sir, and I am not going anywhere.'

'Do you drive, Tim?'

'No, I don't. My father has a little old van, but I have always used the buses and the tube.'

'You told me your mother died suddenly when you were young, and that you nursed her.'

'Well the neighbours helped but father was running the stall. So, there was not much choice and after my mother died my father fell apart. I have been running the business ever since I was fifteen, I worked evenings and weekends before that.'

'How did you know what to do?'

'I had been helping my father ever since I was very young, six or seven I think I was. I received a lot of help from Harry, you met him, he used to have the stall next door, and now he is a partner in the business.'

Mr Vieri, shaking his head, poured himself another whiskey and waved the bottle at Tim.

'No, thank you, sir.'

'Before we go back to the ladies, Tim, I know you will not accept money from me, you made that very clear, but I you ever want another opinion please come and talk to me. I know Mr Murdoch is watching the financial side for you but please, I would be happy to help.'

'Thank you, sir. I expect that will be very useful.'

Mr Vieri drank the rest of his drink in one long swallow. Rising from his chair he said, 'We had better not leave the ladies alone any longer.' When the two men were standing Mr Vieri thrust out his hand to Tim and said, 'At the risk of repeating myself I am very happy that you are marrying my daughter, welcome aboard.' Ushering Tim towards the door he said, 'The ladies!'

As they joined the women, Sophie said, 'I hope you have not been lecturing him, Father.'

'I have given him a thorough wire brushing.' Both men laughed.

A little later Sophie started to yawn.

'Time for bed young lady,' said her father. 'Excuse me one moment.' He went to the kitchen where he could hear Martha still clearing up. He returned to the lounge and said, 'Martha has gone to get Thomas and the car.'

'Father,' said Sophie, very concerned, 'look at the time, he may be in bed.'

'No!' he replied, 'Martha said he will still be up, and, young lady,' he continued lowering his voice, 'they are very well paid.'

CHAPTER 30

MRS VIERI

The following evening Sophie, Angela and Tim were sitting in Angela's lounge discussing the previous evening's meeting. As usual the discussion had swung around to Sophie's mother.

Sophie asked, 'Angela, why does she behave so badly?'

'She is our mother's daughter,' said Angela. 'Mother was hard. I never saw her cry. Olivia was brought up to be just like her.'

'But you are not like that?' observed Sophie.

'The truth is mother found me an embarrassment. She had been caught out doing something naughty. Ladies of her age and social position did not do that anymore.'

'How terribly sad,' said Sophie.

'You were married though,' said Tim.

'Yes, for just over a year, although I worked out we only spent a few months together. His Spitfire was shot down over Dover. He was a beautiful man.'

'You never remarried?' queried Tim.

She sighed, 'When I was younger, I always felt it would dishonour him in some way, silly really.'

Sophie changed seats and took her hand, rubbing the back of it. 'There is still time, Aunty,' she said.

'Maybe,' she was silent for a few seconds, her mind was back in 1942.

'The difficulty with Olivia,' continued Angela, 'is she does not know how to give comfort. She immediately steps in with questions about how it happened, why did you do it? What were you thinking? You should be doing this and this. All the recipient wants of course is to be held while they cry. To be comforted. She does not withhold comfort on purpose. She simply does not understand the concept, and then of course when the responses are vague and illogical, she gets cross. But I do love her very much.'

'Why, though, is she behaving so badly over our wedding?' asked Sophie.

'I am sorry to say this but, her group of friends are terrible snobs and very narrow-minded bigots and she has become like them.'

'The truth is,' said Tim, becoming angry, 'she must tell her friends that her only daughter is marrying a barrow boy who does not have two pennies to rub together and didn't go to the right school.'

'Tim, please do not get so angry,' begged Sophie. 'It is not your fault.'

'Well,' snorted Tim, 'this sort of thing makes me damn cross.'

'Use that anger to build your future, Tim. You are worth ten of them,' said Angela.

'Thank you,' said Tim, still simmering.

'Tim, darling, I have always valued my father's judgment above all others, and he has blessed our marriage. He would not do that unless he had the very highest opinion of you. He has entrusted you with what he holds most dear in the whole world. Me. You need not worry about what anyone else says, including my mother.'

'Sophie, my darling, your mother is never going to change so we must just work around her,' confirmed Angela. 'By the way,' she continued, reaching for some magazines on the shelf under the coffee table, 'I have bought some wedding magazines.'

An hour later Tim could stifle a yawn no longer. The two women broke off their discussion about place settings and both laughed. 'Poor Tim,' said

Sophie 'this must be terribly boring for you?'

'No, I am really interested.'

'Tim, you are a terrible liar, shall we call it a night?'

'No, please don't on my behalf. We have been very busy at the shop and it has finally caught up with me. I am off to my bed.' He said goodnight to Angela, and Sophie walked him to the door.

Pulling the front door shut behind her Sophie moved into his arms saying, 'I cannot wait until we are married.'

'Me neither,' the kissing became more intense. Tim pushed Sophie's bottom hard against the front door with his hips, she became aware of his growing excitement.

Minutes later a soft tapping was heard on the door from the inside. They broke apart with faces flushed and Sophie's hair in disarray.

Tim whispered, 'Give me a head start,' as he gave her a quick kiss. He heard Sophie giggle as he walked away into the dark.

CHAPTER 31

MOVING OUT

The following morning Tim broke the news of his imminent departure to his landlady. He was dreading doing it but there was no alternative.

She was crestfallen, 'I realise you will need to move now, Tim m'dear, but I shall miss you.'

Taking both of her hands in his and looking her in the eye he said, 'I'll miss you too, you gave me a home when I was very down and could not see any way forward. I dread to think what I may have become if it were not for you taking me in.'

She was visibly upset, on the edge of tears and appeared to shrink in size. He stepped up to her side and put his arms round her. Something he had never done before.

She was crying silently against his chest. Eventually he could feel her searching in the sleeve of her old grey cardigan for her hankie. After she had sniffed a bit and soundly blown her nose she apologised to Tim for her silly behaviour.

'It's not silly at all,' he replied. 'I could have a good bawl myself,' he said, as he wiped his eyes with the palm of his hands. It was only now that he realised how much he was going to miss seeing her every day.

'I don't know what's come over me lately,' she said, 'everything is so hard.

I am getting old.'

'I shan't disappear, I promise. I would like to call in and see you and if you want help with anything, please call me.'

'No. I won't do that,' she said, 'you're too busy.'

'It is just repayment for everything you have done for me. I won't desert you; I have always thought of you as family.'

Appearing to brighten a little she said, 'Do you really feel like that? That's lovely Tim, thank you.'

He gave her another little hug.

Tim explained what he planned with regard to his moving out. 'I cannot move everything at once,' he explained, 'so if it's ok with you, I will keep on paying the rent until I've got it all sorted. So, I will be in and out. Also, and this of course is up to you. Would you like me to help you look for another lodger?'

She started to shake her head, thinking to refuse his help. Then Tim watched her change her mind.

Looking up at him and wiping her eyes she said, 'Do you mind? I find everything such a fuss nowadays.'

'We will sort something out; don't you worry about it. You can come to the boat for tea,' he added.

'No, I don't like boats.'

'Have you ever been on one?'

'No, but I know I won't like it.'

'It is firmly tied to the bank and the water is only about two feet deep,' he said with a smile in his voice.

'We'll see,' she said.

We will, thought Tim.

A few weeks later Mr Cooper received a phone call from Joseph Gold. He explained that his wife's cousin had just died. 'She has left a son who is not coping very well,' explained Joseph. 'I was wondering whether Tim had moved out of his digs yet?'

'Doesn't he like living on his own?' asked Tom Cooper.

'The lad is a little slow, always has been. He is nice enough though, just not capable of looking after himself.'

'It could solve several problems,' said Mr Cooper. 'I know Tim is worried about Mrs Clarke being on her own and having no income. How old is he?'

'Mid-thirties I think,' replied Joseph. 'As I say, he is a nice boy, just needs a bit of looking after.'

'What's his name?'

'Nigel.'

'Joseph, Tim's not here now, I will tell him as soon as he gets back. He will ring you.'

'Thanks, Tom, I'll wait for his call. Bye for now.'

On the following Sunday Tim and Nigel were sitting in Mrs Clarke's front room enjoying tea and biscuits. One of Tim's first impressions of Nigel was how polite he was. Mrs Clarke was obviously taken with him. He was slightly overweight and soft looking. His dark green jumper was pulled down low over his brown cords emphasising his tummy. He was wearing sandals with no socks. He looked much younger than his years. She established that he had a job; he filled shelves in a local supermarket. He volunteered the information about his wages. They were sufficient to cover his keep and rent.

'I can do you bed and breakfast plus an evening meal and lunch on Saturday and Sunday if you want.' She named a figure.

Nigel agreed.

'Mother always said I should keep doing my trainspotting and stamp collecting when she was gone.'

Tim thought he was going to cry but Nigel took a deep breath and asked, 'Do you do trainspotting, Mr Cooper?'

'Not now, I don't have time. We would stand by the railway line and shout "why don't you scrap it". Now of course they have done exactly that.

When I was younger, I was a little worried that it was my fault.'

'It's not your fault, Mr Cooper, it's progress. That's what the government say. Diesels are the future.'

'Hmm,' said Tim.

On his way out, he took his last few belongings from his old room, stood for a while realising that his life was moving on and up, then closing his bedroom door quietly behind him he went downstairs. He wished Nigel well, hugged Mrs Clarke and walked on into the future.

The wedding arrangements took over all of Sophie's and Angela's time. Sally was a frequent visitor. It appeared to Tim that it was growing like an insatiable beast with a voracious appetite for money. There was a constant stream of hairdressers, florists, makeup artists and numerous others. There was a long discussion with the priest who talked Tim, Sophie and Angela through the nuptial mass. Tim was disappointed that it would be in English. He did not voice his opinion on this occasion. There was a lot of haggling over the cars, how many, whether they should be new or veteran vehicles, and who should ride with who.

The seating for the wedding breakfast took hours to arrange. Angela's dining room table was rimmed with place names. These were apparently reshuffled most evenings. The two women had long discussions about who would not sit next to who. One couple had to sit at the far end of the table from another couple. One husband and the other's wife had an affair. Apparently over now. The gay couple messed up the one-woman one-man arrangement by insisting on sitting together. Julian and Frederick had been an item for years, although it was rumoured that Frederick occasionally strayed. He was always forgiven after a suitable period of being sent to Coventry. On one occasion, he was away for a week. On his return, he discovered the locks had been changed and Julian refused to talk to him or let him in. But as always, he relented in the end.

Tim began to wish that they had eloped, he saw little of Sophie. When he did, she invariably had a pad and pencil and was jotting down more details or sitting with the pencil behind her ear while she, Angela and Sally wrestled with another problem.

As the wedding day approached the organising reached fever pitch. To Tim it appeared that even more people were coming and going. Nerves were becoming frayed and there was the occasional outburst when something did not work or was wrong.

CHAPTER 32

BEST MAN

Two weeks before the wedding Sophie had asked him what his best man's name was. He had given it no thought at all.

Late one evening sharing a cup of tea with Mr Woodman he asked his advice.

'What about a school friend?'

'I lost contact with all my school friends. Mum's death, and not going to school much after she died because I had to work, meant I lost track of them.'

Mr Woodman said, 'There is one person who has always been there for you.'

Tim shook his head while he tried to think who Mr Woodman was referring to. Realising that Tim was not going to come up with an answer he said, 'Harry!'

'Harry?' echoed Tim in surprise.

'He has been looking after you for years. Could you have taken over from your father if Harry had not been there for you? We would not be sitting here now if it was not for his input.'

The more Tim thought about it the more right it felt.

'But your input has been huge as well,' argued Tim.

'Thank you for saying so, Tim, but it's not the same at all. Our families have always been so close helping you was the natural thing to do, and I know that you would do the same for me if needed.'

'Of course,' replied Tim, 'that goes without saying.'

'You need to bear in mind that when you stepped up to take over from your father Harry was a virtual stranger. Think of the countless number of hours he has provided help, advice and support, he did not have to do any of that.'

Tim was silent for a while, he realised that he'd been very remiss. He was ashamed of himself; his behaviour was totally selfish with no real appreciation of Harry's selfless contribution at all. Both men remained silent for quite a while. Mr Woodman allowed Tim the time to think it through.

Eventually Tim spoke, 'I am not very proud of myself, Mr Woodman, I have been totally selfish, and I have taken Harry for granted, haven't I?'

'Yes, Tim, you have, but don't be too hard on yourself. You were very young and on your own really what with one thing and another, your mum and all. And there are not many boys, which was all you were then, Tim, who would take on the stall like you did.'

'You helped a lot as well though.'

'Kind of you to say so but Harry is the right choice.'

Again the two men sat in silence for a while, then Tim started to nod. 'You are right, Mr Woodman.'

'I am,' he confirmed.

The following morning, Tim arrived at the shop early. The two early birds were already at work. He could hear the banter and the laughter. As he walked in his father and Mr Woodman were laughing their heads off. Not something he had heard his father do in years.

A customer said, 'Tim, your father is a proper caution.'

Mr Woodman turned to Tim and said, 'Harry will be in very soon, would you like to take him upstairs?'

'Thank you, Mr Woodman, that's a good idea.'

Harry and Sara walked in a few minutes later. After they had said good morning to everyone Tim asked Harry if they could have a chat upstairs.

Harry, obviously concerned, said, 'Is there a problem?'

'No,' laughed Tim, 'far from it,' as he followed him up the stairs. Looking back, he saw Sara obviously worried staring after them. 'Don't worry,' he mouthed.

'What's this about, Tim?' asked Harry, his Italian accent getting stronger.

'Please sit,' replied Tim. 'I want to ask you a very big favour.'

'What favour?' asked Harry looking nonplussed.

'I would like you to be my best man, please?'

'Oh no, no, no,' said Harry, waving his big hands and shaking his head in denial. 'Thanks for asking me, Tim, but I could not do that. I am no good at speeches and things, and why me?' He was clearly becoming more concerned every minute.

'Why you, Harry? I will tell you why you. It has been pointed out to me that my treatment of you has been wrong, I owe you a debt I can never repay. All those years you looked after me working on the stall. Giving your advice. Now, supporting me in this venture. I know you gave up your independence to become a partner and that it was a big step for you. As I said, I owe you a very great deal and I have been very selfish and just taken your and Sara's help for granted. I apologise for that. I am asking you to do this as a way of saying thank you. I would be very pleased if you would do it for me. I know Sophie will be delighted if you agree. We can keep the speeches down to just a few words if you like. We would both be very pleased if you would do this for us.' Tim felt a little guilty because he had not discussed it with Sophie, but he knew if she asked Harry a favour, he would walk through fire for her.

Harry thought for a while and then taking a deep breath in said, 'You must help me if I get tongue tied. Who said you have done me wrong?'

'Mr Woodman said I should ask you because I owe you so much and that I have been very selfish, and he is right. You are the obvious choice.'

'I will have a word with him,' said Harry with a wry smile. 'Yes, I'll do it, Tim.'

Tim shook his hand vigorously and with a big smile on his face said, 'I am delighted, thank you.' Both men went downstairs.

Tim saw Harry explaining to Sara. She kissed Harry and then came across the shop and said to Tim, 'You have made us very proud; he is very moved that you asked him. Thank you, Tim.' Standing on tiptoe she kissed him on the cheek, went bright red and walked away.

Mr Woodman, aware as usual, gave Tim the thumbs up. Tim smiled and nodded.

Later he told his father who congratulated him on making an excellent choice.

To Tim's surprise, two days before the wedding he arrived at Angela's to discover Mrs Vieri sitting amongst the apparent chaos. She appeared very calm and was at least civil to him. After a while he excused himself and went back to work. His father had collected Tim's wedding attire from the shop and suggested to Tim that he try it on. Checking with Mr Woodman he went upstairs. A short while later he stood at the top of the stairs and said, 'So, what do you think?'

A little old lady, a regular customer, said, 'Ee, you look right lovely.'

A man said, 'You scrub up well, mate, don't he, Glad?' turning to his wife. She nodded.

Top hat and tails looked good on Tim. Surprisingly he felt comfortable wearing the formal attire. He had been concerned that he would be embarrassed, but he was not, indeed he realised there would not be a problem converting to the lifestyle that he hoped lay ahead. He could read loud and clear the pride showing on his father's face. He approached Tim and said, 'I am very proud of you, son, and your mother, God bless her, would be as well.'

Tim's only real concern was trying to remember the order of service and what he had to say and when. At the rehearsal the priest had promised him he would guide them both through it, but he was still anxious. He had not gone to church regularly since his mother had died. They used to attend the 11 am Sunday service together. He had sung in the choir, descant, until his voice broke. He was paid one shilling and six pence on Sundays.

Regrettably his voice never returned and one day the choirmaster took him aside and explained his time as a chorister was over. Tim missed the money and the singing. He had still met some of the other boys when he used to go to Sunday school.

CHAPTER 33

THE WEDDING

Tim and Sophie found a few moments to be alone the afternoon before the wedding.

'Are you still sure you want to marry me?' she asked him.

She watched as in an instant his face became ashen, his mouth fell open, his features first displayed a terrible shock, this was immediately replaced by an awful fear.

For Tim this was all his worst nightmares come at once. He became terribly cold. All those people who had warned him that Sophie was marrying beneath herself. She had changed her mind! He was destroyed, he could feel his life flying apart.

Struggling to breathe he asked her, almost in a whisper, 'Have you changed your mind?'

Sophie was distraught at the obvious pain she had unknowingly caused him. Taking both his hands in hers and noticing the unshed tears in the corner of his eyes she said,

'Tim, I am so sorry, I love you and want to marry you, I have never been more certain of anything in my life. I am so, so sorry that I have hurt you. I did not think.'

Tim said still in a whisper, 'I could not carry on without you, you are my reason for living, my life only makes sense with you in it.'

Putting both her hands either side of his face and feeling the passage of her own tears she looked deep into his eyes and said with a catch in her voice, 'I have always loved you; I have waited all my life to meet you.'

With both of them very emotional she pulled him into a close embrace saying, 'Tim, I am so sorry. I did not mean to upset you.' They used their kisses to banish their tears.

*

Tim stayed with Harry and Sara that night. They made him very welcome. Sara had cooked a meal for him.

She said, 'I didn't know if you would be hungry, Tim, so I have done *spiedini di salsiccia e manzo,* with a large bowl of white polenta. So, you may eat as much as you like.'

'Tim, that's Italian sausage, beef and pancetta cooked with sage leaves, lemon and garlic on sticks of rosemary to give even more flavour,' said Harry.

Tim restricted himself to one good glass of Italian red. He realised he would need his wits about him the following day. There was some discussion about Sophie and how lucky Tim was to have found her.

Harry, sitting beside Sara on the couch, reached for her hand and cupping it in both of his, said, 'Tim, I think like me you have found your soul mate. I know you will be as happy with Sophie as I am with Sara. We are lucky men.'

Sara said nothing, she leaned towards Harry and kissed him.

'Are you nervous, Tim?' asked Harry.

'No, not about getting married. I knew from the day I met her that we would be married. I just want to get the responses right.'

At ten o'clock Harry said, 'Tim, as your best man I think you should go to bed.'

Tim thanked them both for their hospitality then went upstairs. He lay thinking, his mind roaming back over the last few months. The lead up to the wedding had been chaotic. The shop had been busier than ever, and Sophie had made sure he agreed with the choices that were being made for the wedding. Everything was on such a grand scale he had found little to disagree with. Mrs Vieri had become fully engaged in the wedding plans. It was clear from her input that she had been planning this wedding for a very long time.

He knew Sophie and Angela often found themselves in heated discussion with her,

Sophie especially; she worked hard to simplify and modernise some of her mother's ideas.

He had noticed a growing strength and determination in Sophie. It was clear that she was growing in confidence, she was more likely to defend her decisions. Especially in discussion with her mother. She would never be rude but now would explain to her mother why she was uncomfortable with some of her mother's diktats, previously she would have agreed just to keep the peace, now it was different, she was more than capable of defending her corner. He thought it was a number of events that had conspired to effect this change in her. She had confided in him that the accident had made her stop and think about her life and what she wanted from it. Also leaving her father's employ and landing a top-flight job and finding, as she put it, 'that I am damn good at it!'

Angela had shared a confidence with him, saying that in her opinion Sophie had changed from a girl into a woman since meeting Tim. She was no longer a wind-blown leaf on a pond going wherever others blew her.

Surprisingly he slept well.

*

The church was all white lilies and tall candles.

The first rousing notes of the Trumpet Voluntary rang out. Tim's heart leapt in his chest and he experienced a great feeling of relief knowing she had arrived.

'Here we go, lad,' said Harry looking over his shoulder towards the doorway.

Tim turned and saw her walking through the door on her father's arm. It was as if the sun shone for her alone. Her golden hair, the beautiful pure white of the dress and the lace, the pearls, and her simple jewellery all reflected the sunlight. The stunning, simple form of her dress, hugging her upper body to her hips and then falling away in a cascade of white satin to the floor. It set off her natural beauty perfectly. There was an extended audible sigh as people caught sight of her. His thoughts flew back to the day when she walked back into his life through the shop doorway after he thought he had lost her. She was giving off light on that day as well.

Tim remembered little of the service, the priest was very kind and shepherded him and Sophie through the protocol. His emotions nearly got the better of him on two occasions. The first was as they were making their vows to each other and the second was when the priest said, I pronounce you man and wife. Sophie noticed how moved he was and squeezed his hand.

The reception was a happy boisterous affair. Harry delivered his speech perfectly, but with a heavy Italian accent because Tim realised, he was very emotional. When he finished speaking, he received a loud ovation.

Tim surprised Sophie when it came to the opening waltz. He had never mentioned it, but he used to dance in the kitchen with his mother when he was very young.

When they walked off the dance floor, she said, 'Crikey.' He surprised her again when, after thanking yet more guests for coming, the band started playing Cliff Richard's Move It.

As he led her onto the floor, she looked at him enquiringly. 'Just follow my lead,' he whispered into her ear.

Seconds later they were flying around the dance floor, their movements completely uninhibited, driven by the joy of now being one. The deed was done, now no one could separate them or keep them apart.

Many of the guests had risen to gain a better view and were clapping to the music.

Returning to their seats, and looking up at him, her face glowing as a result of the dancing and wearing a happy smile she said, 'What else do I not know about you?'

Looking very smug and smiling back, he said, 'Who knows?'

Tim realised that the Italians loved family parties, especially weddings. It felt as though an endless stream of new relatives came to congratulate him and give advice, some of it best forgotten. One of the grandfathers was rather scary. He was not very tall and quite thin with a stern face, his black suit, white silk shirt, black stick and sunglasses that he kept on made his appearance very similar to a member of the mafia whose picture he had seen in the paper years before. He could no longer recall the details.

He and Sophie toured the room trying hard to speak to everybody and thank them for coming. He was pleased to see that the doctor and Mary the nurse had made it. Sophie hugged them both. Then they found Mrs Clarke, his old landlady, and her lodger Nigel. They had been befriended by a section of the Italian contingent.

'We have learnt a thing or two about you, Timothy,' one said.

Mrs Clarke becoming embarrassed said, 'I haven't told 'em nothin', Tim.'

They all laughed.

CHAPTER 34

THE HONEYMOON

Late that night Tim and Sophie said goodnight to everybody and went upstairs to their hotel suite.

On reaching the room Sophie kissed Tim and looking up into his eyes said, 'Could we go to the boat tonight, please? This is a beautiful room, but it is very impersonal. I would like to spend our first night together on the boat, can we, please? I love the boat and it is far more romantic.'

'Are you sure? This suite is very grand.'

'Tim, it is not special to me. Working for my father I have stayed in dozens of hotels all around the world. It is the boat that is special, on your river. Please can we?'

Tim corrected her, 'Now it's our river and yes, if that is what you want. I don't know how we are going to fix it, though.'

'We need to get changed quickly and then we can sneak away,' she added.

Tim said, 'I suppose we can get a taxi. I will need a change of clothes and my washing gear.'

'Get changed first and then we can sort all that out. Do you mind changing in the lounge, I am a little shy?'

Tim laughed, grabbed his travel clothes and left her to it. As he was pulling his jumper over his head there was a knock on the door.

Tim called out, 'One minute please.' Tidying himself he walked to the door and opened it.

Mr Woodman was standing there smiling. 'Your car awaits, sir,' he said.

Tim suddenly realised he had been set up. 'Sophie,' he called, 'I don't suppose you know anything about this do you?'

Sophie came out from the bedroom and said, 'Hallo, Mr Woodman, what are you doing here?'

'Oh ha, ha,' said Tim, 'who else is in on this charade?'

'Just me and your father, oh, and Sophie of course,' replied Mr Woodman.

'Please say you are not cross; it will be beautiful on the boat.'

'How can I refuse? We will need a little time to pack, et cetera.'

'No need,' said Sophie, 'it's all done and whatever we leave here will all be sorted out tomorrow by Martha.'

'I thought you just said the only people involved were Mr Woodman and—' Tim broke off. 'Never mind, if this is what you want, we will do it. Are you ready, Sophie?'

'Yes, Tim, and thank you.'

'Lead on, Mr Woodman,' said Tim.

'We are going down the back stairs,' Mr Woodman explained, leading the way.

Mr Vieri and Angela, peering through a door held just ajar further down the corridor, watched them go.

'Tim will have a tough job controlling her,' said Mr Vieri.

'I think he will manage,' replied Angela.

Outside the rear of the hotel Mr Woodman's vintage Rover stood gleaming in the light from the streetlamps. The exterior was black with bottle green door panels. The running board sat just under the doors and then ran forward to meet the elegant front wings that in a beautiful curve swept up and over the front wheels. A large round chromed headlamp sat on the highest part of each black wing.

Sophie stopped for a moment and said with wonder in her voice, 'Mr Woodman, it is beautiful.' Sophie stepped onto the running board and ducked her head to enter, she was amazed when she saw the interior. The inside was furnished with mahogany woodwork, green leather seating and brass and chrome fittings.

'Thank you so much, this is just perfect,' she said as she dabbed her eyes with her hanky.

Mr Woodman drove carefully through the near-deserted streets. Tim and Mr Woodman discussed the various attributes of the car, the rod brakes, the hinged windscreen and the freewheel device that removed the engine braking.

Sophie just sat back, holding Tim's hand and enjoying the ride. She found it quite magical, sitting in this amazing car being quietly transported through dark, empty lamp lit streets with the man of her dreams sitting beside her. Each streetlamp casting its own perfect circle of golden light on the pavement below. Finally, they had succeeded despite all the problems.

Reaching the boatyard Mr Woodman parked near the entrance. He and Tim carried the bags down the shallow marble steps towards the river. As they passed the boatyard owner's house a voice from the porch said, 'Congratulations, you two. I am sure you will be very happy together.'

Sophie jumped in the air as usual but then said, 'Thank you, Tabby, you are very kind.' Tabby came out from under the porch, kissed Sophie on the cheek and shook Tim's and Mr Woodman's hand.

'I won't keep you out here in the cold. See you in the morning.' With a last puff on his pipe, lighting the four of them in a warm glow, he turned and went into the house.

As they approached the Sea Maiden Tim noticed a spiral of smoke from the chimney and the low lighting within the boat. As they stepped aboard and walked towards the door it was opened by Mr Cooper. 'Hello, come on in,' he said, stepping aside.

Sophie stepped in first and immediately her hand went to her mouth. The interior of the boat was a mass of flowers and presents set off by candles burning in pretty glass holders.

'I am speechless,' she said. 'How has this happened?'

'They are from everybody in the shop and lots of customers gave cards and presents,' explained Mr Cooper.

'Can you thank everybody for me, please? And thanks you two for arranging this for us,' she added. Stepping forward she kissed both men on the cheek.

'You are very welcome, lass, right, we will be off then.' With a last look round the two men went ashore.

Tim walked their bags through to the back cabin, stopping as he stepped in and turned on the light. There were more flowers and the bed was strewn with red rose petals.

Sophie called, 'Can I use the bathroom first?'

'Of course, you should see what they have done in here.'

'Is this a trick?' Sophie giggled.

'No,' he laughed.

Sophie walked in, put both hands to her face, and burst into tears again.

'Oh, Tim, it is wonderful. People have been so kind and generous,' she said wiping her eyes.

Tim was very moved. He realised how hard people had worked to make the boat so special. 'We are very lucky people,' he said kissing Sophie.

The kiss deepened until she said, 'No, no, I want to do this properly. I will have a shower.'

Twenty minutes later Sophie called out, 'Are you decent? I am on my way.'

Tim was sitting on the bed in his dressing gown as she walked into the cabin.

She was wearing white silk stockings, white pearled slippers and lace edged white lingerie. She stopped just inside the door.

Tim was stunned, he was immobile, for once he had no words. His heart was banging in his chest. Breathing was difficult.

'Do you not like it?' she asked looking down at herself.

'Oh my God,' he said, his voice filled with wonder, speaking barely louder than a whisper, 'You are the most beautiful woman I have ever seen.' He walked over to her and kissed her very gently, shutting his eyes as he did so.

With that he scooped her up in his arms, laid her down on the bed and kissed her again, his passion in full riot.

*

Fifteen minutes later he was holding her while she cried. She kept repeating, 'I am so sorry. What are we going to do, it is so painful?'

Tim replied, 'I think we've had a very emotional and tiring day. Let's go to bed and worry about it in the morning.'

Sophie cried herself to sleep lying on his shoulder.

Tim lay awake for a while eventually deciding that they cannot have been the first couple to have had this problem and therefore they must be able to sort it. He fell asleep shortly after.

In the small hours of the morning he was woken up not knowing for a moment where he was. He quickly became aware that Sophie's hand was gently encouraging his arousal.

'What's the time?' he asked.

'Do not worry about that, I want to try again,' she whispered, 'and this time you must not stop, just take me.'

Minutes later he felt her start to tense up again. As he began to lift off her, she barked at him angrily, 'Do not stop, damn you.'

Shocked by her anger he thought, ok, and with that thrust into her. He felt the resistance break as their bodies met.

'Please do not move for a minute,' said Sophie in a tight thin little voice waiting for the pain to abate. She had a fierce grip on his arms.

Tim, exercising a massive amount of self-control did as he was asked. There was a long pause, eventually Sophie moved against him and their lovemaking carried them away. Later they were both lying on their backs trying to get their breath back.

Sophie, staring at the ceiling still short of breath gasped, 'I knew it would be wonderful between us.'

A few minutes later she turned to him and said, 'Can we do that again, please, but much more slowly?'

'Good God, woman, I'm not superhuman, I will need a while.'

'Let me see if I can help.' She wound her arms around his neck, pressed the full length of her body against him, tangled her legs with his and began kissing him.

The following morning, he was propped on one elbow watching her come awake.

She stretched like a cat and grinned at him.

Tim noticed Sophie was wearing an almost invisible smile emanating from deep inside her. He was also aware of a subtle change in her eyes. When he investigated them, they displayed a new knowledge, a warm darkness that had not been there before. Tim could only guess but he supposed that the step into womanhood was far more significant for women than the act itself was for men.

'Would you like some breakfast?' Tim asked her.

'Is that a euphemism?' she giggled.

'No,' he said a little sharply, 'I need food, how about bacon sandwiches?'

'Well, if you do not want me, I suppose I will have to settle for breakfast,' she said pretending to be upset.

Tim had the kettle singing and was frying the bacon dressed in his pyjama bottoms when Sophie, naked but warm from the bed, pressed herself up against his bare back. He could feel her breasts moulded against his skin triggering all kinds of erotic sensations, she placed her hand on his tummy and allowed it to slowly slide south. Tim switched off the kettle and the gas. Turning around he leant down and kissed her. Lifting her off the floor to lie across his arms, still locked in the kiss he made his way back to the bedroom. Breakfast became brunch.

The afternoon sunlight was streaming in through the back-cabin windows. Brunch had been taken in bed.

'Can we go for a walk? The river is beautiful.'

'Yes indeed. I can show you some of the quiet places that the public don't know.'

Locking the door as they left, Tim suddenly spun round and unlocked it. Stepping inside he walked back through the boat and picked his wallet off the sideboard. Back outside and relocking the door he saw that Sophie was talking to Tabby further along the bank. After saying hallo to Tabby and walking up the shallow slope out towards the road, Sophie asked him what he had forgotten.

'Do not tell me,' she said, 'it was your wallet, was it not?' Poking him in the ribs and laughing she said, 'You, boy, I am going to have to keep an eye on you.'

'At least I did remember it this time,' he responded still feeling rather embarrassed about the previous incident.

'I am only pulling your leg; I will not mention it again. I know it was not on purpose.' She tightened her arm around his waist and lifted her face to be kissed.

They spent a magical afternoon wandering the banks of the Thames with him guiding her to some of the out-of-the-way cafes and little pubs that were starting to do specialist beers. One he took her to, called the Boat, was one of his favourites. They sat on rustic three-legged stools near the open fire. The ceiling was blackened by decades of wood smoke and the draught beer was drawn straight from the barrels ranged along a large strong rough-sawn wooden shelf behind the bar. The landlord knew Tim and his father and when Tim called in for a drink he always asked after his father.

'Is this your girlfriend?' asked the landlord.

'No, this is my very new wife. Sophie Cooper. Her proper name is Sophia.'

'Please call me Sophie,' she said quickly. 'Only my parents call me Sophia.'

'I'm Chick, Chick Evans, I have to say you look like a Sophia to me,' he added.

'Tim, lad, whatever did you say to this young lady to get her to agree to marry you?' asked Chick. Turning to Sophie he said, 'You do know he is penniless, and all but a vagrant, don't you?'

Sophie, going slightly pink, said, 'Yes, but he does have other skills.'

Chick guffawed and said, 'I think this conversation should end here. What would you like to drink?'

Tim had his usual pint of draught from the barrel and Sophie a small lager. When Tim raised an eyebrow, she explained that the girls in university were not very well off and drank lager because it was cheap. 'I did not want to stand out, so I got used to it. I do still enjoy a glass of Châteauneuf-du-Pape, though.'

'Oh, good, I will order a case as soon as we get back,' he said with a smile on his face.

'You will be able to one day.'

'Thank you for believing in me,' he said, squeezing her hand.

Chick came over to them and said, 'Would you like to eat here? The wife tells me the food and drink are on us this evening. I have put a reserve sign on that little round table by the window, the chairs are comfy, and you can watch the sun go down over the river.'

They both chose the steak and kidney pie with mash potato, carrots and a warming red wine gravy. They washed it down with a glass of Cabernet Sauvignon each. Pudding was spotted dick. As the sunset deepened it set the river alight with a shifting red fire. The sun was finally extinguished beyond the buildings and the river clothed itself in its night garb of black sliding water and myriad dancing lights. Sophie yawned, and Tim realised it was getting late. He went to the bar and asked Chick for the bill.

'Nothing to pay, lad, as the misses said, this was on us, a belated wedding present. I will call the wife down, she wanted to wish you well before you go.' Stepping across to the wrought iron circular staircase behind the bar he called up, 'Molly, Tim and Sophie are going.' Turning back, he said, 'She will be right down. Say hallo to your father for me, lad.'

'Will do,' said Tim.

Molly appeared, a jolly buxom lady with a ready smile. Her twinkling green eyes were set off by her ruddy cheeks and mass of red hair. Her musical Irish brogue revealed her ancestry; she told them she was from County Cork. She noticed Sophie trying to stifle a yawn. Sophie apologised profusely, very embarrassed.

Molly smiled and turning to Chick said, 'And you can keep a still tongue in your head or I will soften your cough for you.'

'I was not going to say anything,' replied Chick, talking through his laughter, 'only that it is a long walk to here.'

'Ignore him, my dear, and sure isn't he just a rude old man,' said Molly slapping Chick.

Shortly after, the young couple left to walk home, waving goodbye as they went.

The bedroom was lit by a low light that was on in the galley. Tim was lying on top of Sophie. He was taking most of his weight on his elbows. Teasing her with quick little kisses. After a while she gently guided his lips to her breast. She slowly became more excited. Tim felt her part her legs further and then there was pressure on the top of his head. He obliged with feathery kisses down her body until he reached the destination she intended. There was the sound of growing mewing and suddenly she climaxed pushing his head away from her. Then he was making his way back up from under the covers. As he surfaced Sophie wiped the moisture from his face with the corner of the sheet and with her other hand guided him into her. Their growing passion carried them away to another place. Eventually they both fell asleep in a tangle of limbs.

Sometime later Tim was lying naked on their bed, hands behind his head. Sophie, similarly unclothed, was still sleeping after their lovemaking. Her leg thrown across his thigh, her arm across his chest, her head nestled into his neck, her soft breath warm against his skin. He was marvelling at the fact that he and Sophie were so well matched in their needs and desires. He treasured the fact that there was so much joyful laughter in their lovemaking. He sometimes had a silly worry that perhaps he was dreaming. He knew this beautiful woman lying beside him loved him.

She could have chosen yachts in the Med, a second house in the South of France, a Rolls-Royce at the door. These were the things her mother had planned for her.

Tim whispered, 'Thank you for loving me, you wonderful woman.'

Sophie mumbled something unintelligible. Tim was more determined than ever to succeed and to give her the lifestyle she deserved.

*

Sophie was sitting on the floor sorting through some photos from their wedding one evening. One photo held her attention. Tim could not see the picture from where he stood.

She asked, 'Did you go camping with the Scouts?'

'No.'

'Is that because of your mother?'

'Partly, but more importantly because of my father. I couldn't leave him.'

'Oh dear,' she said.

'Why do you ask?'

'I do not know if you met this lady at the wedding, she was our patrol leader. We camped all the time, I loved it. Waking up in the morning somewhere beautiful and quite often you have it all to yourselves. We could try it perhaps.'

'I thought holidays would all be very expensive hotels in Nice or Cannes,' said Tim.

'That's my mother's idea of a holiday, it is not mine. I have done it, Tim, and it is so boring. I am sounding like one of those debutantes,' laughed Sophie, 'but, Tim, it really is boring. Living on board Sea Maiden and having camping holidays is my idea of heaven.'

*

Tim saw Sally and Mr Vieri through the slightly open office door. He realised they had been working together. He was sitting at his desk with her standing beside him gathering up the papers.

She said, 'I will have these figures ready for you this afternoon,' and then leaned in and kissed him. He placed his hand gently on the back of her head to prolong the kiss. Tim was stunned, for a moment he froze then he realised if he stayed where he was, they would know he had seen them. He tiptoed back to the front door that he had left ajar, seized the large iron knocker and knocked loudly, calling out as he did so. He then stood waiting.

Martha appeared from the kitchen drying her hands on a small towel. Her face broke into a smile and she said, 'Hallo, Mr Tim, how are you?'

'I am good, Martha, thank you, you are looking well,' he continued. Martha smiled and said, 'Thank you, Mr Tim, I think Mr Vieri is in his study, I will knock for you.' She walked across to the door Tim had just looked through and tapped gently. Mr Vieri called out, 'I will be with you in one moment, Martha.' One minute later Mr Vieri followed Sally from the room asking her, 'Is that all clear, Sally?' She replied that it was.

CHAPTER 35

THE SECOND SHOP

Six months after the wedding Tim called a formal meeting with his partners to discuss the second shop. The business was now very busy with a high consistent turnover.

Tim had spoken to Mr Murdoch about a loan. The amount he offered was not a great sum, but it might buy a very small shop. Tim was resolute in his determination not to rent. His father always said it just made others rich. Tim had another plan up his sleeve that he hoped the others would agree to.

Once Mr Woodman, Harry and Tim were seated, Tim started the meeting off by advising his partners of their financial position which was in his opinion very good for two years' trading.

He distributed papers for both men that laid everything out. There were one or two questions, but they both agreed things were going along nicely. Tim then moved onto the next item. This was the second shop. Tim laid out the figures. These included Mr Murdoch's loan offer and a small lump sum from Tim. He was going for broke again.

Mr Woodman said, 'Tim, shop and house prices are going up all the time. I still don't think that will be enough. You could get a tiny place, but we could not carry enough stock to make it viable.'

'There is another option, gentlemen. As you know, Sophie has been working as our unpaid accountant for some time. She would like to come on board properly, as a partner. She is prepared to buy her way in. Before I throw this open, I want to tell you if you say no neither of us will hold it against you. I am going downstairs to let you think it over. Please call me when you have decided.'

His father was busy stacking shelves at the far end of the shop.

Sophie raised her eyes in a query. 'Not yet,' he mouthed, shaking his head.

Initially Tim had a mild objection to accepting Sophie's money. He wanted in the future to be able to say he did this all alone. Then he realised it was his ego that was getting in the way. He was helped by a lot of selfless people working very hard on his behalf for very little money. No way was it only his efforts. With Sophie's offer he could improve everybody's income and together with the bank loan buy the right shop. Sophie was adamant that she wanted to be part of the adventure not just an unpaid member of staff.

In anticipation of being called upstairs he closed the shop and dimmed the lights.

His father said, 'It's only ten to, Tim.'

Tim nodded and pointed upstairs. His father was aware of the discussion about the second shop but only Tim and Sophie knew about her offer.

After a further fifteen minutes Mr Woodman looked over the stair rail and said, 'We are ready.'

Tim could not tell from his countenance what the decision was. Sophie whispered as she climbed the stairs behind him, 'I am rather nervous, what if they say no?'

'We will have to look for another accountant.'

'That is silly, Tim, I will do it anyway.'

Arriving in the sitting room Mr Woodman and Harry were pouring more tea. Tim did notice each man had a glass of whiskey in front of him. He hoped this was a good sign.

'Over to you, Harry,' said Mr Woodman.

Looking surprised, Harry said, 'Oh, ok then. We are quite happy to have Sophie on board, thank you for your generous offer, my love.'

Sophie jumped from her chair and hugged both men in turn thanking them profusely.

'But,' said Harry interrupting Sophie's continuing expression of gratitude, 'there is something we think needs doing to make it feel right. Obviously, this company is going to fly, and in our opinion, fly high,' he was looking at Mr Woodman as he said this who responded by nodding.

'We need a designated leader.'

'Tim, we are small now, but we will be big in the future. We would like you to take on the post of chairman. You cannot be the owner, we all own a bit, some more than others,' again, looking at Mr Woodman, who this time made no comment. 'Senior partner sounds naff, so it has to be chairman. What do you say?'

'Well, I'm blowed. Sophie and I thought we would surprise you, now you have turned the tables on us.'

As he finished speaking his father called up the stairs, 'Goodnight folks, I am off to my bed.'

Tim, thinking quickly, asked quietly, 'Can he join us?'

They all nodded. Leaping from his chair Tim bounded to the stair-head calling, 'Can you come up please, Dad, if you don't mind?'

'Oh! Ok, lad, I'm on my way.'

Once his father was seated and had tea placed in front of him, Tim asked Harry if he would please recap. Harry explained that Tim had proposed that Sophie become a partner in the business. 'She is prepared to buy her way in,' he added.

'Do we need to vote on that?' asked Tim.

Mr Woodman said, 'We have agreed so we could say it has been carried unanimously.'

'Thank you, gentlemen,' said Sophie. 'I am very excited to be part of this team. I am prepared to invest enough to top up the bank loan for the next shop and maybe a little more. I do not want to become the major investor.'

'Also, Mr Cooper,' continued Harry, 'we have proposed that Tim becomes chairman, but he has not accepted yet.'

'Oh, yes, thank you. I am very flattered, yes, I will accept,' he was smiling inwardly. This is all getting very formal, he thought to himself, well I suppose as we get bigger it will have to be done correctly.

'Oh, well done, lad,' said his father.

'Thank you all,' said Tim. 'There is one more thing I would like you to consider. I want the business to pay us better from now on. I would like you to discuss it with all the team and Sophie and come up with a figure. However it is arrived at I will leave up to you. But pay you more we must. I watch everybody, and you are all working your socks off. It simply must be rewarded. I know what you are going to say, Dad, but we need to sort this out.'

To conclude the meeting and seal the deal, as Harry put it, Mr Woodman poured them all a whiskey, including Sophie.

The toast was, 'The Company.' Sophie surprised all of them, Tim included, by taking a good swig and obviously enjoying it.

Laughing at their surprise she said, 'You learn a lot at finishing school. Not all of it is on the curriculum.'

They talked of the future for another half an hour then the increasing number of yawns forced them to call a halt.

'We will need to talk to the solicitor,' said Tim. He and Sophie wished everybody goodnight and they all went their separate ways.

Walking to the river arm in arm, Sophie said, 'Tim, darling, can we have a taxi, I am shattered and exhausted?' They both laughed as Tim flagged down a cab. It was one of the few nights since their marriage they didn't make love. Sophie, sleeping on her tummy, fell fast asleep as her head hit the pillow.

Tim said, 'Goodnight, Sophie darling.' There was no response.

CHAPTER 36

No 2

Finding another shop was no easy task. Tim decided it needed a wealthy area nearby, but this put the price up. Any property on a high street became unaffordable.

Mr Gold rang Tom Cooper early one morning. After the usual pleasantries had been exchanged Joseph Gold said, 'I understand you are looking for another shop?'

'How do you know that, Joseph, I am not aware that we have told anyone?'

'I bumped into Mr Woodman and he asked me if I knew of anywhere. I didn't at the time, but I have just been asked to clear a little shop. It's a small side road, a very trendy part of town; nowadays the haunt of the new young middle classes who apparently are very well off. The owner died recently, and his wife is not well enough to run it. If you are interested, I think you will have to move fast.'

'Thank you for that, Joseph, Tim is out at the moment, but I will let him know as soon as he returns.'

One evening two days later Tim and his father were standing outside the premises waiting for the estate agent to arrive. The shop was in a very attractive location. It was at the top of a steep narrow cobbled street leading down to the river. The shops looked as though they were marching downhill. Many of the premises, little pubs and bistros, were entered by stone steps, some leading up, some down. All provided with black wrought iron handrails.

Pots of flowers and large, coloured umbrellas flanked the roadway. It was clear that the owners of the businesses were from a wide spectrum of nationalities. There was a real continental feeling to the area. Tim was quite sure that Sophie's would fit right in.

His concern was that the shop looked too small. The front of the shop had a door and a wood-framed bow window to the left. It was very attractive, but…! He voiced his concern to his father.

'Tim, lad, let's not jump to conclusions before we have seen it,' admonished his father.

The estate agent turned up shortly afterwards. Tim smiled to himself. The agent was exactly as he had envisioned him, very sharp pale grey suit, crisp blue shirt, pointed black Italian shoes and he was very young. His clipboard was the final touch.

He and his father exchanged a look, Tim with one eyebrow raised.

He introduced himself as Jonathan Wainwright, 'Everybody calls me Jono,' he added. He spoke with a strong upper-class accent.

Entering the shop Tim realised that it had not been modernised for a long time. Where the old fittings in Mr Woodman's premises had lent it real appeal this was just uncared for and shabby and it was very dark, even with the light on. He was fast losing interest. Even without all the clutter it would still be too small.

His father, who had always been able to read him like a book held his hand up, frowned, and silently motioned him to be patient.

'As you know,' said Jono, 'there is an upper floor,' moving to an even darker area he led the way upstairs.

Tim was last up and his heart fell. This upper floor had obviously been used as a rubbish dump. Unable to see the floor for the rubbish he stood on something that moved under his foot and he turned his ankle over, not seriously but still painful.

At that moment Jono committed a major blunder, turning to Tim's father he said, 'So, Mr Cooper, what do you think?'

'You need to ask my son, he is the company chairman,' said his father pointing at Tim.

Evidently surprised, and with a hint of disbelief in his voice Jono said, 'Really, I say, I am sorry, silly old me, you do not look old enough.'

Tim turned on his heels and walked towards the stairs.

'You just blew it, young man,' Mr Cooper said to Jono as he made to follow Tim.

Tim was waiting for them outside. 'How much are they asking?' he enquired in a voice that betrayed how angry he was.

Jono, now crestfallen, told him and started to apologise again.

Tim cut him short. 'That's far too much. We will be paying cash. Who's your manager?'

'My father,' Jono replied, appearing to get smaller by the moment.

'Tell your father that we are still prepared to think about it, but tell him the deal is off if you are involved. You need to get some training, young man, before you wreck your father's business. Do you have my phone number?'

'Yes, sir,' said Jono nodding.

'I will wait to hear from your father. That is if he still wants to do business with us. Good afternoon,' he said as he walked away.

'Blimey,' said his father after walking a few yards, 'I've never heard you give anybody a wire brushing like that before.'

'Dad, I am sick and tired of the so-called upper classes treating me as some kind of inferior being. Mrs Vieri does it all the time. I have decided I'm not going to put up with it anymore.'

'Good for you, lad, your mother would have been proud of you.'

'She always said they were no better than us didn't she, Dad?'

'I, lad, she did, bless her.'

'Why are you hobbling?' asked his father.

'I turned my ankle over on the rubbish. So, what do you think then, Dad, about the shop?'

His father thought for a moment and then said, 'Well, Joseph has been asked to clear the shop so that is one cost you won't have. The cleaning and decorating plus the fittings and the lighting will be expensive. You've set a very high standard at the first shop. It has to be at least as good as that. Having said all that it does have appeal, and the area is ideal.'

'Should we worry that it is on two floors?'

'No, I don't think so, many large stores have more than one floor. Provided the stairs are safe it should be ok.'

Later that afternoon Mr Woodman answered the phone, listened for a moment and then waved the phone at Tim.

Tim said, 'Hallo, Tim Cooper here, how can I help you?'

'Mr Cooper, George Wainwright here, I am ringing you to apologise for the behaviour of my idiot son. I am really sorry things have gone so badly today. If you are still interested, I am prepared to cut my commission and I will handle the sale myself should you wish to continue.'

'That's very generous of you and I do appreciate the apology. What I would like to do is wait until Joseph Gold has emptied the shop and then ask my partners to have a look. Between them they have decades of experience in the retail trade.'

'That's not a problem. Joseph tells me you are married to Mr Vieri's daughter.'

'That's right,' said Tim. 'Can you let me know when Joseph has cleared it and we can get everyone together for a proper viewing?'

'No problem, Mr Cooper, and thanks again for being so understanding. We will talk soon,' he said as he hung up the phone.

It was Saturday afternoon before they had the phone call from George

Wainwright. He said, 'It has taken Joseph four days, there was so much rubbish, it is clear now, when would you like to view it?'

'How about tomorrow?' Tim asked.

There was a short pause on the other end of the phone and then Mr Wainwright agreed. 'Can we make it about ten am?' he asked.

'Erm, can I ring you back in a minute?' asked Tim. 'I want to make sure all the team who want to come can.'

'Of course,' agreed Mr Wainwright.

Because it was Saturday afternoon everybody was in and working hard. Tim never got tired of the buzz in the shop on these afternoons. He made his way around the counters getting everyone's agreement.

All except Sara who said, 'I will be making confectionery.'

'Can't you leave it for one day?'

'We will have empty shelves on Monday if I do,' she replied, waving her hand to indicate the rapidly disappearing display of confectionery.

'We need to talk about your hours,' said Tim.

'No. please don't, I love my work on a Sunday. I go to mass early; Harry will not come with me, he is a heathen, and then I go home to create my chocolates. It is one of the best days of the week for me. I do not want to change anything. I love all of this. It reminds me of the markets at home in Italy. Busy, busy, all the time. Thank you, I do not want to change anything at all, Mr Tim.' Her Italian accent had got stronger the longer she talked, and she was very adamant.

'Ok, Sara, and thank you,' he replied.

Sophie, who had been working near Sara, walked back across the shop with him.

'What is it that you do not understand? The team are just as determined to have this place succeed as you are.'

'I do know that really, just sometimes it surprises me,' he said.

*

Sunday morning was grey and dismal with a cold easterly wind. The boat had an action they had not experienced before. It was moving back and forth on the mooring ropes and giving a nasty jerk as the rope tightened.

Sophie asked, 'Is there anything we can do about that?'

'I will ask Tabby later,' Tim replied as he left the bed. Looking at his watch he said, 'Whoops! We had better get a move on, it's just gone nine.'

Sophie, naked, swung her pretty legs out of the bed and went to walk past him to the bathroom. Tim caught her in his arms and pulled her to him, growling as he did so. She began struggling to free herself. His hands were all over her body.

'You just said we were going to be late, let me go,' she said in a voice that was growing crosser by the moment. Putting both hands on her bottom he pulled her up against him. She was immediately aware of his arousal. Tim was still growling, his face in the corner of her neck.

Sophie placed both hands on his chest, kissed him hard and said, 'Later, Tim, I promise you, when we get back.'

Reluctantly he let her go. He went to follow her into the bathroom. She pushed him away and while he was stumbling backwards, closed and locked the door.

A little later as they were walking up the slope to the road from the boat she said,

'What was all that growling?'

'Your fault. You drive me mad.'

'Oh good,' she replied giggling as they arrived at the waiting taxi.

They reached the shop a little early. Nobody else was there yet. Sophie suggested they take a walk down the street to have a look at the other shops. They were as Tim remembered. Next door was a small florist with some pretty flowers in the window, some in small metal cans. The next shop down was a tobacconist with a range of pipes, tobacco pouches and lighters in the window.

'I have often thought I might smoke a pipe,' mused Tim stopping to look in the window.

They walked a little further down, past a pub and a religious bookshop. Tim, glancing at his watch said, 'We had better go back.' It was as they started back that they realised how steep the street was. After one hundred yards they were both puffing. When they arrived back everyone was there. His father chided Tim for being so unfit.

Tim just nodded and then said, 'Can I introduce everyone?'

'We have done that, Tim,' said Mr Woodman.

'Mr Wainwright, this is my wife Sophie.'

After the pleasantries were over the estate agent opened the shop and ushered them in. Thanks to Joseph Gold's efforts there was a considerable difference in the appearance and indeed the apparent size of the premises.

Mr Wainwright said, 'As you can see, like many of these properties it is narrow, but it goes back a long way.'

'With all the rubbish in here it looked a lot smaller than it really is,' said Tim.

'There is a small toilet with a hand basin through that door at the back,' continued Mr Wainwright.

The stairs were on the left-hand side of the shop against the wall running from front to back. There was a row of small, attractive old windows running along just under the ceiling on the right-hand wall. The heavy black oak beams gave the clue to just how old the shop was. There was an infill of faded red bricks between the timbers.

Harry called out from the back of the shop, 'This will not take long, we will be up in a moment.' He and Mr Woodman were measuring the floor area.

Reaching the top of the stairs, Tim noticed there was an even bigger difference in the appearance. The space was twice the length from when Tim first saw it. Up here the bricks that occupied the spaces between the wall beams had been painted cream or white, but he was not sure which.

'This is a nice big space,' observed Mr Woodman as he reached the top of the stairs.

Harry, looking around, said, 'This is wider than downstairs.'

'Yes, it extends out over the small sideway that connects with the back yard,' explained the estate agent.

'It is called a flying freehold,' volunteered Sophie.

'One thing to point out is that above this part of the ceiling is a roof light. It was sealed up. I don't know why.'

Quite soon everybody except Tim, Sophie and the estate agent were crawling all over the building.

Mr Woodman started down the stairs. Waiving his hand at the walls, he said, 'When this is painted white and with the dark beams it will look lovely.'

'I am getting the right vibes from them all and now we can see what space we have it looks viable. The price is too high, though. I know Harry and my father have been doing some research and they say it is about a thousand pounds too high. We are going to have to spend a lot of money to put it right. Is it listed, by the way?' asked Tim.

Mr Wainwright shook his head.

Sophie, standing close enough to overhear the conversation between the two men, said, 'Make it one and a half thousand less and any deal depends on the results of a full survey.'

'I realise that, and I will let the owner know,' confirmed Mr Wainwright.

'Right, what do we think?' asked Tim.

They all looked at each other and the nodding started.

His father spoke first, 'I think it is a very attractive building, but it is going to need a lot of work,' he gave emphasis to the words, 'a lot'. He was clearly undecided.

'It will require some clever design, but I do think it's viable,' added Mr Woodman.

'Harry?' said Tim.

'I think it has appeal, but, and this is a big but, we must do something about that damn hill.'

Everybody laughed.

'Sophie, what do you think?'

'To be honest I am unsure. The truth is this building has been sadly neglected over recent years. I have very real concerns over what we may find when we start work. It is essential in my opinion that the building is subjected to a thorough structural survey, this will be expensive. We are going to have to keep a tight hold on the expenditure. It may be that we do some things now and others in the future.'

'Such as?' Tim asked.

'This roof light,' she said pointing above her head. 'It could be very costly once you disturb it.'

'You are right, Sophie, the bathroom also needs redoing completely. It will just have to have a good clean for now and be refitted in the future,' said Mr Cooper.

'The staircase seems ok, but we need to be very sure of that and we need handrails on each side,' added Mr Woodman. 'Can I suggest that we get Charlie in to give us some ideas?'

They all agreed that this was the correct next move.

'So, what do we offer?' Tim asked.

'According to my research it is a thousand too dear,' said his father.

'I want to take off another five hundred contingency money. Who knows what we might uncover,' said Sophie.

A general discussion broke out. Under the cover of the talking Mr Wainwright said quietly to Tim, 'You have good people here and your wife is very clever.'

'You're not wrong,' confirmed Tim, 'Sophie is the financial director of a large company and a partner in Sophie's.'

'I envy you your team Mr Cooper.'

'Thank you. Can you call me Tim, please? As you can see, my father is still alive.'

'Only if you call me George. By the way, do you anticipate buying any more shops?'

'Yes, we aim to have a chain of shops across London and maybe further afield. That will not be for some time. We must get this into profit first.'

'Of course,' George Wainwright replied.

'Ok, our offer is as discussed subject to survey.'

'That's fine, Tim, I expect to come back to you tomorrow.'

Everybody shook hands with the estate agent and departed for their homes.

Shortly after they arrived back at the boat Sophie kept her promise.

Waking before her the next day Tim buried his head in her hair near her ear and took a long slow breath in. There was a subtle hint of last night's ecstasy. Her perfume had faded, and by some primal alchemy blended into something that was much bigger. It now encompassed her body's scents to produce a warm aroma that was essentially Sophie and intoxicatingly female.

Sophie, more asleep than awake, mumbled, 'Stop sniffing me.'

'I don't think I can. I am hooked on you.'

Giving a little giggle she wiggled her bare bottom into his lap, pulled his free arm around her and went back to sleep.

The following morning George Wainwright rang just after nine. Tim was first to the phone. 'Hallo, Tim, George Wainwright here, I have spoken to the vendor and surprisingly she still wants more money for it. She says that she is prepared to come down a little but not as much as you have said.'

'Has she been to the shop lately? I think she would change her mind. I have arranged a survey, who knows what that may find. Do you have any other property of a similar nature?'

'I have one modern shop that has been on the books for some time. To be honest it has no character compared to the one you have seen in Fish

Hill. It is ready to move into; clean, light and bigger than her one. It is also considerably cheaper.'

'How come it hasn't sold?'

'It is down a very quiet street, there are no other shops there. It will only be the local residents that pass the door.'

'Will you show her the details of the modern one that we are going to look at and tell her the price, I cannot see anyone offering how much she wants considering how shabby it is, and I don't know why, but I am becoming increasingly worried what the survey may show. Can you also inform her that as far as she is concerned ours is a cash offer?'

'I will do that, Tim. I will call you as soon as I have her response. Goodbye for now.'

It was late the next afternoon when George Wainwright rang the shop. 'Hallo, Tim. The last time she went there it was all clean and bright, apparently. Her husband had never told her how run-down it had become. She is quite unwell and has not been there for some years.'

'The survey is being done as we speak so we shall soon know the worst,' Tim informed him.

The survey turned up two days later. As Tim read through the first page, he became more and more disappointed. Rotten floorboards, rewiring required and a faint smell of gas. As he went to serve a customer, he handed the letter to Mr Woodman. After he had finished Tim returned to where Mr Woodman was topping up a display.

Tim was clearly upset. 'I think we are going to have to look elsewhere. What a shame, I had begun to plan it all out.'

'Now hold hard there, Tim, let's find out what this survey really means?'

'Sorry, I don't understand?' he replied.

'Why don't I give Charlie a ring and he can explain in real terms what this means and what it will cost?' suggested Mr Woodman. Ten minutes later he returned saying, 'Charlie is having a day off, but he said that because it was us, he would go and get a key and have a look.'

'Can you thank him for me when you see him.'

Walking over to where Harry was working, he said, 'Do we have any of the hampers left, I thought I may give one to the hotelier I have to see today?'

'There may be one or two, would you like me to go and look?'

'No don't worry, I can do it.' Tim found two left and chose one at random. Taking both out of the storeroom with him he said, 'Can you two work out a price for this please?' plonking the other hamper on the counter. 'Whatever it comes to for the contents could you then put twenty percent on it and put it on sale.'

'Do you ever switch off, Tim?' Harry asked, as Tim made to leave.

'Not often, Harry, not often, also could you float the idea to Sara about her putting a recipe book together, please?'

'I will ask her, but I am not sure what she will say,' responded Harry in a doubtful voice. I don't know how she will find time to do that, he thought to himself.

'She will get help,' said Tim, sounding as though he had read Harry's mind. 'I would just like to know what she thinks of the idea at this stage.' He left the shop with a drawn out, 'Bye.'

Both men were shaking their heads as the door closed behind him.

When Tim returned to the shop two hours later Charlie was nursing a mug of tea sitting on a tall stool in the corner.

'Hi, Tim,' said Charlie as he climbed down from the stool, his right leg clanking against the metal leg of the chair. 'How are you?'

'Yes, I am fine thanks and you, Charlie?'

'Yes. Good thanks, now about number two.'

'Sorry what do you mean, what is number two?'

'The second shop. This shop is one, the new shop number two.'

'Erm, ok,' said Tim, a little unsure.

'Do you want the good news or the bad?'

'I am surprised there is any good news,' said Tim sounding depressed.

'Let's talk about what you can leave for now. The window in the roof can be left. It has been tiled over outside so it should be ok. The smell of gas, I don't think that it is a leak. It is turned off at the main stop cock. I expect when you clean and decorate the smell will disappear. The rotten floorboards are in the back upstairs. I don't know what has caused it, but we will find out when I lift the boards. If the customers are kept away that could be put off. What you cannot put off is the rewiring. As it is, the place is a fire trap. The fire brigade would condemn it. The whole lot needs ripping out and renewing. Are you happy for me to put a quote together? I will use the same electrician as did the wiring here if that is ok?'

'You must tell him, Charlie, it is just a quote.'

'He will understand, I have worked with him for years,' Charlie replied.

When Tim told Sophie about the wiring later that night her immediate response was, 'We need to drop our offer.'

'I feel really bad about doing that I was hoping we could increase the amount we offered.'

'Tim, this is a very old building, I know you have fallen in love with it, but my best advice would be to forget it and move on.' Just for a moment he could hear her father talking.

'I assume we are going to hold a meeting to discuss and vote on this?' Sophie asked, 'I will be advising that we pull out of this deal.'

Tim grunted.

'Alright, at best I would want the offer to be reduced by the amount of the rewire,' argued Sophie. 'Tim, you cannot go through life rescuing old ladies. We cannot afford it.'

Tim called them all together on Saturday evening after closing, in Mr Woodman's flat. Copies of the quote were handed round together with cups of tea and sandwiches, thanks to Sara. It was a bit of a squash, but Tim and his partners had decided that everyone should have a say.

Tim told them how much had been offered and briefly explained the quotes.

'Tim, this rewire seems to be an awful lot of money?' queried his father.

'That is because it is a big job. Charlie warned me that it was a serious problem. He said that if the fire brigade saw it, they would condemn the building.'

Mr Woodman broke in, 'I have dealt with Charlie or his father for at least thirty years. I trust him completely.'

'Does anybody else have a question?' asked Tim. 'No? Sophie has something she wants to say.'

'I know I am the new girl on the block, but hopefully you took me on because of my skills and my knowledge. Tim and I have had a vigorous discussion about this.' She gave her husband a hard look, 'Given all the information,' she continued, 'my first recommendation is that the board look elsewhere for a property. This is a very old building and I suspect we will have to spend a fair amount of money over the years to keep it in good repair.'

Suddenly everyone wanted to have their say.

Tim said, 'Hold on please, can we let Sophie finish what she is saying?'

Sophie continued, 'The only other option I believe is to reduce our offer by the amount of the rewire, i.e. three hundred pounds. Now you are going to think this is my father speaking, but we simply cannot afford to nursemaid every little old lady. Part of my job is to tell you the hard financial facts as I see them and until you tell me to stop, I shall continue to do so.'

There was a long silence after she stopped talking. Tim let the facts hang there while people thought them through.

After what he thought was a reasonable period he said, 'Ok, now I am going around the table and I would like you to tell me what your decision is, but briefly.

'Dad, would you like to start?'

'Son, it is very attractive, but I would not touch it with a barge pole.'

There was another silence. Some shaking their heads in disagreement.

'Mr Woodman?'

'Well, Mr Chairman, I think it is a very memorable building. People will say you can't miss it. It's the little shop with a bay window at the top of Fish Hill. I choose Sophie's second option.'

'Sara?'

'You may laugh at me all of you and I know I have only looked in through the window, but I can feel that the little shop has a warm heart just waiting to be revived. I choose Sophie's second option.'

Tim, adding her decision to his notes, asked, 'Harry?'

'I know I am just an old softy,' he said, 'but I would increase our offer a little.'

'Harry,' said Tim gently, 'that has not been made an option. I need you to choose between the two please.'

Harry, getting annoyed, said, 'Then I choose neither.'

'So, you abstain then Harry? Something you are fully entitled to do.'

'Yes,' he said. With that he swivelled in his chair, turning away from them he crossed his legs, folded his arms and fixed his gaze on the carpet obviously deeply upset.

Tim noted his decision.

'Sophie?'

'I choose option one.'

Tim noted it down then sat with his chin on his hands very aware that now, once again, it was all down to him. He held the decisive vote. Nobody spoke. Eventually he said, 'As you are all aware, I have the casting vote. I am torn. The first option is the sensible one. But I have a vision for this little shop, we carry the same décor, et cetera. from here to there. The same ethos as here, the same feel. People don't just come here to buy things. They come for the experience. This shop is different to others. We are different to others. Sara is right, number two, as Charlie calls it, just needs reawakening.

That is what we are going to do. You are a great team.'

The last part of his impromptu speech was nearly drowned out as people started clapping.

Mr Woodman started serving drinks.

As Sophie walked past him, she whispered, 'These people would follow you into the gates of Hell itself. I still think you are wrong.'

'As long as you still love me,' he said.

Sophie turned and kissed him.

Mr Cooper, who was trying to squeeze by, said, 'Careful, you're frightening the children.'

As Sophie moved away Tim muttered, 'Tell me I am wrong when I've finished.'

'I heard that,' she said, looking back over her shoulder.

Harry was still sitting, clearly distressed. Tim walked over, put his hand on Harry's shoulder and said, 'Can we have a chat downstairs, please?'

It looked for a moment as though he was going to ignore Tim, then, obviously thinking better of it he rose and followed him downstairs.

Harry was the first to speak, his Italian accent very strong, indicating how upset and angry he was. 'I do not like this, Tim! This lady is very poorly, her husband has died, she is all on her own and we are going to take even more money away from her. I think this is a terrible thing we do.' By now he was pacing up and down and throwing his arms around.

Both men heard light footsteps coming down the stairs and turned to see Sara coming to join them.

She had overheard his last words. 'Harry, my love, let us hear what Tim wants to say.'

'Harry, first of all can I say how sorry I am that you are so upset. Can I be honest with you?'

Harry nodded.

'I still believe the price we have offered is too high, but please don't tell

Sophie I have said that.'

Harry went to walk away.

'Please, Harry, let him finish,' Sara took his arm as she spoke.

Harry gave a long sigh and faced Tim again, shaking his head, his hands locked behind him and looking at the floor between his feet.

'The truth is that this property needs a lot of work and over time that means a lot of money. Hard-nosed businesspeople like my father, Mr Vieri and Sophie, if they bought it at all would offer a great deal less. I believe our offer is still better than she could get elsewhere, and it gives her the money now, not in a year's time or whenever.'

Mr Woodman appeared at the top of the stairs and called out, 'The tea is poured,' then disappeared again.

'Please go on up, Tim, Harry and I will talk.'

Halfway up the stairs Tim looked back; Sara was talking, Harry was listening and stroking his beard.

At the top he met Mr Woodman who was holding three teas on a tray, he raised an eyebrow.

Tim took one and said quietly in response to his query. 'I think he's ok. Sara is talking to him.'

'I will take this to them anyway,' continued Mr Woodman.

Harry was still awake when he heard the old grandfather clock in the hall chime midnight. Lying very still trying not to wake Sara, who was lost in dreamless sleep, her breathing a steady rhythm. As often happened when he could look at her without her knowing, his love for her flowed through him. It was not the conflagration of their early years but was now a steady constant heat lodged in the deepest part of his being. Harry silently thanked the forces that had thrown them together all those years before.

Unlike her he was very upset over the decision to reduce the offer for the new shop. Although he had never met the lady owner, he had a vision of her, recently widowed, elderly, unwell and unable to cope. He felt sure the company could afford to pay the extra £300. Sara had tried to placate him while they were downstairs. He had made out that he had come to terms with the decision but the sideways look she had given him told him, as they went to join the others, that she didn't believe him.

As they walked home hand in hand as usual, Sara had explained to him this was just business. It didn't help, he felt it was wrong, sometimes like now he wished he was back on his stall. Then there were no really difficult decisions to make and he was in charge. He had given away his independence, his right to do it his way. He had never shared these thoughts with Sara. She often said he was an old softy, but she loved him anyway. Surprisingly she thought they were better off in a bigger organisation, and, she had pointed out he was no longer outside all day, in the wind and rain. He lay awake for another hour but still came to no real conclusion. He knew the decision made would cause him anguish when he recalled it in the future.

On Monday morning Tim phoned the estate agent and told him what the team had decided. When he explained about the wiring Mr Wainwright was shocked, 'Is it really that dangerous?' he asked.

'Charlie and his electrician think it is.'

'Charlie is sound, if he says that's the case then that's that,' observed Mr Wainwright.

'The bad news is that we are going to have to reduce our offer by three hundred pounds, the cost of the rewire.'

'Oh, dear. That is going to upset her,' said the estate agent.

'Our accountant, my wife, is telling us to drop this deal and go elsewhere.'

'Right.' There was a long pause. 'I will get back to you when I have a decision, Tim.'

'Ok, George, I will wait to hear from you but please tell her I cannot wait much longer.'

The next phone call was to Charlie. 'Hi, Charlie, I am ringing to keep you up to speed.' He explained about the lower offer, 'Hopefully she will play ball otherwise we will have to look elsewhere. There is another reason for my ringing you. I want you to do something for me. Assuming we get to buy it, I would like you to look at the window in the roof. Opened up that should make a huge difference to the shop in terms of the light.'

'You won't recognise the place, Tim.'

'When you get the go ahead can you work out a quote for me separately, please?'

'Sure thing, for your eyes only, eh?' Charlie started humming the James Bond theme.

'Ok, ok, thank you Charlie,' said Tim brusquely. As he went to hang up, he could hear Charlie was still humming.

Mid-morning George Wainwright rang back. 'Hi, Tim, you have a deal. Her brother was visiting this morning. He was the one who asked Joseph Gold round to empty the shop in the first place. He told his sister that if anybody offered anything for it to snatch their hand off. Apparently he explained what it would cost to put it right. She has agreed to your latest offer. I spoke to her brother briefly and he was just pleased to unload it at any price. I will start the ball rolling today.'

As he replaced the phone it rang again. It was Charlie. 'Hallo, Tim, I wanted to let you know I have completely disabled the electrics because I was so worried about them, if you go there you will need a torch.'

'Ok, Charlie. Oh! and by the way, I have just agreed to purchase Fish Hill, so it's full steam ahead.'

'That's great, Tim, can I ask for some money up front? This isn't gonna be cheap.'

'How much do you need, Charlie?'

'Can we say three hundred, Tim?'

'Is a cheque alright? Can you call in the shop for it? I will do it today.'

'That will be fine, Tim, thank you.'

Tim was busy writing the cheque when the phone rang again. This time, much to his surprise, it was Mr Vieri.

'Hi, Tim, Victor here, I have a free afternoon and wonder if you felt like showing me the new shop? Sophie has told me a lot about it.'

Tim, unsure what Sophie had told her father said, 'Ok, where are you now?'

'I am in a little bistro a hundred yards from the shop.'

'I'll get a taxi; I will be with you in about fifteen minutes.' It took a little longer, he had to find a torch. Arriving at the shop he saw Mr Vieri striding up the hill towards him.

Tim called out, 'Hallo, sir.'

When Mr Vieri reached him, he shook Tim's hand. Still holding it he said, 'I think you should start calling me Victor. Family should use Christian names.' He sounded unusually Italian as he said it.

'Thank you, sir, Victor, I do appreciate your trust in me.'

He let go of Tim's hand having given it a final squeeze. 'Right then,' he said, all business again, 'let's look at this shop.'

Tim spent the next half hour showing Victor Vieri around the premises and discussing their plan for the refurbishment. Back at the front of the shop he said, 'So what do you think?'

'My head says Sophia is right. This wants knocking down and rebuilding.' He saw Tim pull a face. 'But I can see why you would want to restore it. Too many lovely old buildings have been torn down and ghastly blocks of Russian Brutalist concrete have replaced them. My heart agrees with you. However, I think you will need a restoration fund, not just for now but also for the future upkeep. Thank you for showing me round, Tim, I would like to watch the progress if I may?'

'Of course you can, I would be grateful for any input.'

'Right, I must be off, Tim. I will see you soon.'

'Goodbye,' an almost imperceptible pause then, 'Victor.' They shook hands as Mr Vieri departed. Tim had still not told anyone except Charlie about his plans for the skylight.

When Tim told Sophie about her father's visit she was not surprised. He had apparently quizzed her at some length about the new premises.

'He has asked me to call him Victor, because, he said, family should use their first names,'

Sophie was visibly moved. 'Father has often said how much he wanted a son; I think he feels he has found one. I am so proud of you Tim. I know the family forced you to jump through lots of hoops, but you did it.'

'I had a great incentive to succeed. To have you for my wife.'

Sophie was now on the edge of tears. Tim pulled her into an embrace and kissed her.

George Wainwright and Tom Cooper's solicitor worked hard to get them access to the shop as soon as possible. Working through the lady owner's brother some basic paperwork was signed and a large deposit paid. The work, once started, proceeded apace. Charlie, working with Larry, worked hard the first week ripping out the old wiring and installing some temporary lighting, so they could see to work. In the middle of that week Tim's father, Mr Woodman and Harry stayed behind to discuss with Tim the fittings for the shop. They revealed that they had been working together to design the interior, counters, lighting etc. It was apparent that they had gone into considerable detail. Tim was very impressed and said so.

'Can I take this away?' he asked. The others agreed.

Later that evening after dinner the plan was spread out on the table with Tim pushing dirty plates around to make room.

'Tim,' complained Sophie, 'if you give me a moment I will clear away. You are the very end.'

Only half listening, he apologised, already concentrating hard on the detail in the drawing. A little later he asked her to join him. She stood bent over the drawing on his right-hand side; her lower arms flat on the table taking in his explanation of the detail. He had a wonderful view of her cleavage.

As always when she was close to him her scent and proximity started his heart beating faster. He slid his hand up her arm and stroked her armpit under her short-sleeved blouse with the back of his hand.

'Tim!' she shouted at him as she slapped his hand away, 'Stop it.' Pushing his chair back he threw an arm around her waist and pulled her onto his lap, easily overcoming her resistance. She had her back to him, and he kissed the nape of her neck where it joined her shoulder, knowing that he had previously found it to be a very sensitive place for her. His lips and tongue went to work on her neck and her protest faded away, cupping her breast with his hand he gently played with her nipple. Turning towards him she kissed him with a bedroom kiss and their tongues started a well-rehearsed dance.

Later, much later, they returned to the drawing in their dressing gowns.

'What is this in the bay window?' she asked, this time sitting on his lap by choice.

'I think it is a series of shelves,' he replied.

'That will not work, the shop needs all the light it can get.'

He thought for a moment and then agreed. He started to say something else when she interrupted saying, 'I have got it. A broad flat shelf with a blue and white cotton cover the same as number one. Then you could vary the things on display over time.'

'Do you know what, you're right?'

'Please do not sound so surprised,' she responded a little tersely.

He kissed her in the ear. Pulling away and standing up she frowned at him, he was smiling up at her. She realised he was teasing.

'Coffee?' she asked, forgiving him.

'Yes please,' he replied, already once more immersed in the drawing.

Over the next few weeks the second shop, number two, as everybody called it, consumed all his waking hours. Even when he was out socially it was always in the front of his mind.

Sophie began to recognise when his mind was elsewhere and would ask rhetorically,

'What are you thinking about, as if I did not know?'

Early one evening Tim was standing across the road from number one, his hands on the black wrought iron railings watching the traffic on the river. He watched the ferryman row two people across to the far side. Mr Woodman had told him previously that the youngster rowing the ferry was the third generation of his family to do the job. Coincidently, a few minutes later Mr Woodman walked up and stood beside him looking out over the river.

'Penny for them, Tim?'

'I am not sure if they are worth it,' he replied.

'It doesn't take much intelligence to know what you are worrying about, lad.'

'The first shop was fun, this seems to be just hard work,' said Tim.

'The reasons are simple, Tim, there is a great deal of money involved this time and just as importantly you are trying to do it all yourself. The first shop was a team effort. We are starting to feel excluded from this one.'

Tim turned to face him, 'It is because of the money and the risk we are taking. It could all come crashing down round our heads.'

'Tim, lad, you have not made any mistakes so far, and if I felt this second shop was wrong, I would have made a hell of a fuss. The money we have borrowed will not exceed the resale of the shop if that becomes necessary. Which it won't. The only other thing you must do is let us help. Everybody without exception wants to get stuck in and frankly, son, you are stopping us. Now that is a mistake.' Mr Woodman put his hand on Tim's shoulder. 'You have built a great team here, use it, step back half a stride, let us take some of the load. Shall we hold a meeting, then we can define what needs to be done and who by?'

Sunday found everybody in the second shop just after ten. Charlie, when he heard, had volunteered to come with Tommy. There was a further surprise when Larry the electrician turned up. People were up and downstairs reacquainting themselves with the layout.

Charlie turned to Tim and said, 'Can I tell you where we are with the work. There is one surprise that I will tell you about at the end. Can we go upstairs?' They all trooped up after him. 'This is where the wood rot is. As you can see, I have taken up the floorboards. The good news, the joists are still sound. I think there is a leak in the roof that has made this wall damp. That is not a big task.'

Tommy piped up, 'We can do that while we are doing the window.'

'I thought we were going to leave that?' questioned Mr Cooper.

'I was going to do it as a surprise,' said Tim.

'I think that is a decision for the board,' said Sophie.

'Sophie is right, Tim,' said Mr Woodman.

'We can talk about it later,' added Sophie.

Tim pulled a face and nodded, knowing he was in trouble.

'You must let me know what you decide,' said Charlie. 'Now, the surprise is downstairs.'

They gathered on the ground floor. 'Can you step aside, Mr Woodman?'

'Look,' said Charlie, pointing at a heavy ring set into a stone floor slab.

'I know what that is, can you show us, Charlie?' asked Mr Cooper.

Tommy handed his father an iron bar and watched as Charlie started to lever up the flagstone. Larry the electrician stepped in to help.

'A well,' said Harry, 'well I'm blowed.' Everyone laughed at the pun.

'There are lots of these in buildings across London. What some places have done is to put a glass cover over instead of the flagstone and light the interior,' suggested Larry.

'I knew this shop was special,' whispered Sara.

'A job for the future perhaps,' said Sophie looking at Tim.

'I found a key that fits the back door,' said Charlie. 'Shall we look?'

After a short struggle with a sticky lock the door came open and they followed him into a small yard. There was an outside toilet. Tim poked his head in. It was not as bad as he had feared, old but reasonably clean. Looking at the back wall of the shop he wondered if it would be possible to build it in to the building. When he looked round everyone had disappeared. He could hear the voices coming from a narrow opening at the side of the building. Opening a rickety old gate he followed the rest of the team out into the street.

Mr Woodman, turning around and looking at the beams and brickwork above the alleyway, said, 'That's why the upstairs is wider than downstairs.'

'Yes,' added Sophie, 'the section over the top is called a flying freehold. I think I mentioned that before.'

Re-entering the shop, Tim, with an apologetic smile on his face, said, 'At the risk of getting my wrists slapped again can we ask Charlie for a quote for the window, please?'

Sophie shaking her head said nothing.

'Just a quote then, Charlie,' said Mr Cooper, looking around to ensure everyone agreed.

Tommy reached into his father's bag and handed Charlie an envelope. He offered it to Tim who indicated he should give it to Sophie. She opened it then passed it around.

'While you are looking at it,' said Tim, walking to the bottom of the stairs, 'this is why I would like us to do it. Imagine the stairs and this area bathed in sunlight,' he said, turning around with his arms outstretched. 'Then, when you look up you will see the sky.'

'It will be wonderful,' whispered Sara enthralled by his description.

Harry said, 'I think it is a great idea. It will bring the outdoors indoors. It will feel as though I am working in the street again.'

'Timothy, you are incorrigible,' said Sophie, still cross with him.

'Shall we let Sophie do the numbers and then we can see?' recommended

Mr Cooper.

'Before I go can I just mention, it will be more expensive as two jobs rather than one. I will have to rehire the ladders, et cetera,' said Charlie.

'Understood,' said Tim.

'Will we be looking to Joseph Gold to supply the counters as before?' asked Mr Woodman.

'I have had some thought about that,' said Mr Cooper. 'New ones are, as we found out last time, very expensive. I think we should make them.'

'How?' asked Tim, surprised that his father would even suggest it.

'Do you remember the counter with the broken glass?' everyone nodded. 'Well to fix that I virtually took it to pieces. All we need made are the wooden frames. I know a man who can do the woodwork. The assembly I have done once. That is straightforward. The doors are sliding, so the glass work is fairly simple. Shall I get a quote?' he asked, looking at Sophie and the others.

They all nodded. Tim said nothing.

Charlie and Larry replaced the flagstone and said their goodbyes. Tim watched as the three of them walked away. Charlie gave Tommy a thick ear and was still telling him off as they disappeared.

Later that evening back at the boat, Sophie, obviously furious with him, threw her coat across the cabin and kicked off her heels. 'If you are going to ignore my professional advice and my role within the company,' she shouted, her face aflame, 'I will step down from the board. I am really too busy to do it anyway, and while you are at it you can look for another accountant.'

Tim heard her out and then apologised. He remembered his mother's advice in these circumstances; least said soonest mended. Sophie slept on the far side of the bed that night.

Tim lay awake. He realised that he need not carry the whole burden himself as he had after his mother died. Still unable to sleep at 1 am he got quietly out of bed and started to list the jobs that needed doing. He crept back to bed an hour later, clearer in his own mind about what was ahead of them.

Sophie was up first the following morning and found his notes. When he finally came to, she asked him how long the notes had taken him. His answer of 'not long' did not satisfy her.

'You are still trying to do it all yourself,' she said becoming cross again.

Tim felt that he was now being accused unfairly. Controlling his growing anger he said, 'You are wrong. The reason I did that work last night was so that I could present it to the team. And as for doing it all myself, what do you think I have had to do ever since I was thirteen. My father, bless him, was useless. I sat with my mother while she died. I ran the stall afterwards. I provided for both of us. Harry was all the help I have ever had. I find it very hard to accept help. I realise I have to change but it is not easy.' His anger now had free rein.

Grabbing the notes he had made and waving them at her, he shouted, 'This is my way of trying to change. Hopefully we can distribute the work between the team and take the load off you and me.'

'I am sorry,' said Sophie, 'I did not realise. Can I make you some breakfast?'

'No don't worry, I need to walk.'

'I really am sorry, Tim.'

'So am I. It was my fault in the first place, I apologise for losing my temper.' He gave her a peck on the cheek and walked out closing the front door quietly behind him.

Sophie felt the boat rock as he went ashore, this happened when he sprang from the deck and started running. She sat for a while over a cup of coffee. Her mind went back to when he had faced down her father. She could not remember anyone having done that before. She recognised there was a point past which you could not push him. She would ring him from work and make it up.

Tim felt bad about shouting at Sophie. Later that morning he rang and said how sorry he was.

*

Tim arrived at shop number one the following day to find his dad and a stranger measuring up the glass counters. He walked over to introduce himself. His father groaned and held his back as he straitened up.

Tim, concerned, said, 'Are you alright, Dad?'

'It's just the march of time and before you say anything about taking it easy, I love what we are doing here, and I have no intention of stopping. Thank you for your concern but I am fine.' He introduced the man he was assisting. 'This is Gerry Cornfield. Gerry, meet my son and the chairman of the company.' They both shook hands.

'Is this a difficult job, Gerry?' Tim asked.

'No, I don't think so. The glass is simple so that makes it a great deal easier.'

'Gerry has an extensive workshop just across the river,' broke in his father.

'We can do most things,' Gerry confirmed. 'These wooden parts won't be that dear especially as your father is going to do the assembly. We do them on the router, they come out all the same that way. I can organise the glass as well if you want?'

'Can you source all the parts as well please, that seems to make more sense than us doing it?'

'Yes, I can do that.'

'That's great,' said Tim, 'can we have the quotes first though, please?'

'Certainly, I won't start till you say.'

'Can I help, Dad? I always fancied doing some woodwork.'

'By all means, lad. Mr Woodman said he would lend a hand.'

'Ok, I have all I need for now. I will ring as soon as I have the quote for you.'

'That's great, Gerry, can you work with Dad please. Is that ok, Dad?'

'Yep that's fine, lad.' They shook hands all round and Gerry left.

The following Sunday found them all once again at the new shop, except Sara who was making her confectionery.

Sophie had worked out the numbers and had handed round a sheet for all of them. 'Can I explain the details? The amount at the top is the total of the monies we have to spend on the shop. What follows are the quotes we have received for all the work. I have added fifteen percent for overspend. As you can see something has to wait. We need to decide what.'

There was a long pause, finally Mr Woodman said, 'I think the decorating, the counters and the lighting are essential. That then leaves the blind, the well and the roof light. The numbers indicate that we can only afford one of the three.'

'Thank you for laying it out so clearly,' said Sophie.

'The well is an option for the future,' said Tim.

They all agreed.

Sophie was looking around the shop and saw how dark the stairs were even though it was a sunny day. She walked across to stand under the hidden skylight and realised that to open it up was the right decision.

Turning to the rest of the team she said, 'Tim is right. We have to do the skylight now.' The rest all looked at her in disbelief. 'Not for the reason Tim said, sorry darling, but because we will have to pay for the extra lighting that is required to make the stairs safe.'

CHAPTER 37

SHOP PROGRESS

The work in the shop continued apace. The plan for the counters that Harry and Mr Woodman had drawn up required very little modification. Larry the electrician had made a couple of suggestions and Charlie wanted to change some of the shelving to make it more adaptable in the future. He also confirmed the need for a bannister on the blank wall of the stairs. 'Otherwise,' he said, 'if two people are passing on the stairs one will have no support if they slip.'

Tim asked Charlie to give some thought to enclosing the outside toilet, so the girls especially didn't have to go out in the rain and the cold.

A few days later his father asked if he could have some manpower to help install the counters.

Tim was very embarrassed, 'I do apologise, Dad, I said I would help with that. I am really, really, sorry.'

'Don't you worry, Tim lad. Sophie has said that you have been working all hours. Harry, Mr Woodman and I have done them in our spare time. Gerry let us use a corner of his workshop, but he can't help us move them, he is very busy at the moment.'

'It will mean a number of trips in my little van. Can we hire a bigger one?' He gave Tim the list of prices he had found.

'Will we get all the counters in in one go?'

'Yes,' was the reply. Tim could not see Mr Cooper's crossed fingers. His father knew the last one would be a snug fit.

'Sunday?' asked Tim.

'Aye, Sunday it is, lad.'

The counters did fit, just. Mr Cooper drove the van because he was the smallest. His knees in the driver's seat were hard up against the dashboard. The rest of the team followed in Mr Woodman's Rover. There were some aching backs by the time everything was in the right place.

Harry said, 'If we ever sell this shop, they will have to buy the counters as well. We will all be too old to bring them down again.' There was a lot of rueful laughter.

'I think I am too old now,' observed Mr Woodman, holding his back.

The men stood back in silence to look at the counters in place. Tim had paid close attention to the workmanship while he had been installing them. He was very impressed by the quality.

Very moved, he said, 'Gentlemen, I would like to say something and please don't take this the wrong way. You have done a totally professional job on these counters. God knows what we would have had to pay to buy new counters to this standard; I am blown away, thank you so much.' He shook hands all round.

The following week saw all the work they had agreed to almost completed. Tim popped in that Friday afternoon. The day had been bright sun and cloud free. Entering the shop the sight that greeted him took his breath away. The counters, the lighting, the bright scrubbed flagstones downstairs and the sanded and waxed honey coloured wood flooring upstairs that he had seen previously were perfect. The cream walls and white ceiling made an impressive feature of the heavy variously shaped black oak beams but the sunlight coming through the roof light was truly stunning. He felt he had to go and stand under it. His eyes were closed but he could see a red light through them. Looking up, his face was warmed by the sun's rays. With arms outstretched, just for a moment he was transfixed, it felt as though they had trapped the sun itself. When he finally came to, he noticed Charlie and Tommy were finishing off a little bit of painting in a far corner.

Charlie turned and seeing him standing in the light said, 'You were right, Tim, thank goodness you could see what it would look like, it's amazing. I reckon people might come just to see it.'

'Let's hope so, Charlie. Is the phone working?'

'Yes, it's on the counter by the door.'

'Is there one upstairs?' asked Tim as he made his way to the phone

'Erm, not yet, I'm sorry I didn't know you wanted one.'

'It's best I think, otherwise people will be rushing downstairs to answer it,' he said starting to dial. 'Hallo, Tim Cooper here, can I speak to Sophie, please?' there was a short pause then, 'Hallo, Sophie, can you get an hour off? I am at the second shop. I will tell you why when you get here. Bye.'

Tim became concerned whilst he was waiting as the sky became cloudier. When Sophie walked into the shop clouds were covering the sun. Tim made the pretext that he wanted her to see the shop finished before anyone else. He noticed that the clouds were moving and engineered it so that her back was to the stairs until the light was streaming in. It was the sun that made her turn round.

'Oh, Tim, that is magical,' she said as the light got brighter still. It drew her to the foot of the stairs, putting her hand over her eyes to shade them, she looked up at the window.

That momentary picture of her standing in the light was another vision of her he would hold in his heart forever.

Reaching for Tim's hand she said, 'Thank God I did not veto it.' He realised she was quite moved.

Charlie and Tommy joined them. Charlie said, 'It looks great, but I think you'll need a sunshade up there in the summer like.'

Sophie looked at Tim who nodded. 'Can you put that on the list please, Charlie?' asked Sophie, 'and can I choose the blind, please?' looking at both men for agreement and receiving it.

'That leak was a couple of missing tiles. I've fixed 'em.'

'Thank you, Charlie,' said Tim. 'Do you have a completion date yet?'

'There is little bit of painting to finish off, the shade and phone.' He was stroking the top of his head as he spoke. 'Two days should do it. Tim, I am going to have to add somethin' for all the extra work that we found once we started moving things, though.'

'Hopefully we have allowed for that,' said Sophie. 'I must get back to work,' she added. 'It is beautiful, Charlie, and you Tommy, thank you.' Kissing Tim, she strode away.

'She is proper beautiful isn't she, Dad?' said Tommy, clearly in awe of Sophie as he watched her walk away.

'Tommy, you can't say that kind of thing,' said his father, 'it isn't polite.'

'Don't worry, Tommy,' said Tim, 'she still has that effect on me.'

CHAPTER 38

THE PARTY AT No 2

The party at the second shop was well underway. Tim had invited everyone who had contributed to the refit. Mr Murdoch was deep in conversation with Victor Vieri. Sally and Angela were in fits of laughter over something Sally had said. His aunt and two of her friends had arrived but had said they would not stay long. They had complimented him on the décor.

Mrs Vieri had not attended. She was slowly retiring from social occasions, not just this one. Some of their regular customers had been invited including hoteliers, Tim's suppliers and their partners. Mr Cooper and Harry were running the bar which was well attended.

Tim was talking to one of the regulars when out of the corner of his eye he saw Kate wobbling towards him on incredibly high heels, trying not to spill her glass of champagne. She was clearly very drunk. The emerald green sheath dress was skin-tight and left little to the imagination. It set off her bright copper hair to perfection. When she arrived in front of him, she slid a knee between his legs, pressed her thighs and breasts against him and whispered something he could not hear in his ear.

Sophie recognised her as Kate, the woman she had questioned at Tim's stall the day she had gone to contact him after his return from abroad. Her lies had almost wrecked their lives. Sophie's Italian temper exploded inside her, arriving full grown.

Sophie crossed the room in two long strides. Seizing the arm that was now around Tim's neck she swung Kate around and slammed her back against the wall, the champagne from the drunken woman's glass flew in a perfect arc, becoming diamond droplets of light as they fell. It looked to Tim as though it was happening in slow motion.

With her face very close to Kate's, spitting with anger, she warned her in a whisper that promised terrible retribution, 'If you come anywhere near my husband again, I will hurt you so badly.' Sophie was a wild cat, primeval in her ferocity, marking her boundaries. Saying quite clearly, this man is mine.

Tim noticed Sophie's grip on Kate's arm had left white finger marks and there were indents where her nails had dug in.

Mr Woodman, aware as always, came and took the arm of the now crying Kate and led her away. He found her coat and sorted a taxi for her.

Sophie watched her leave, turned to Tim, kissed him full on the lips in view of everyone and walked away.

'Blimey,' said a customer who Tim had been talking to. 'By golly, Tim. In future it will always be "good afternoon, Mrs Cooper, ma'am".'

'Never cross an Italian,' said Tim.

'You're not wrong,' was the response, 'she frightened the whatsits out of me.'

Mr Vieri, who had seen the whole thing, turned away and smiled to himself. Sophia had put down another marker. She had made it abundantly clear to everybody that she would not tolerate any attack on her husband or their happiness. This apple had not fallen far from the tree. He was very proud of her.

CHAPTER 39

THE FIRST DAY'S TRADING

The first day of trading in the new shop was very quiet. The rain hammered down all day driven by strong gusts of wind. Very few people walked by and if they did, they were in a hurry. Mr Woodman had made a sign to stand outside but the second time the wind blew it down Tim retrieved it. He was concerned it might harm someone.

'I don't think you are going to be lucky this time,' said his father.

Tim realised he was referring to the opening of the first shop when after the early rain the sun had blazed down all afternoon.

'This is like the old days, son, you and me working together.'

Tim smiled. 'Would you be prepared to work here most of the time?' he asked.

His father thought for a while and then said, 'Can I let you know, lad? I do love working at the old shop.'

'That's the trouble, Dad, we all do. Perhaps we need to employ someone who would work here permanently.'

'A girl, lad, she would be cheaper to employ and hopefully Sara could train her up on the confectionery.'

'We will have to ask her,' said Tim. 'You know how she defends her recipes. That is a good idea though, I do feel that customers are happier with a familiar face whenever they come in.'

'And, she could end up managing the shop if she proves herself,' said his father.

Tim nodded thoughtfully in agreement.

'Returning to your question about me working here full time. Why don't we all do say, two days each here? I don't think you should be part of that, Tim, you were busy before, now I think you will find there are no spare hours in your day.'

'I expect you are right,' he agreed. 'I will ask the rest of the team and see what they say. Sophie first, she will tell us if we can afford it.'

Two weeks later having gained agreement from everyone, Tim asked Sophie if she would help with the interviews.

'Yes,' was her response, 'but I want someone with me.'

'Who?'

She thought for a short while then said, 'Sara, yes Sara. Two reasons. Firstly no one else knows anything about the confectionery. Secondly, she will be less intimidating than all you big hairy males.'

'I'm not intimidating,' complained Tim.

'Oh, really,' said Sophie laughing.

The three girls who had answered the newspaper advert were interviewed in Sophie's office at work.

Her boss, Mr Wells, had suggested it when she had asked, 'Did he know of an office she could rent?'

The three girls sat on a row of chairs across the corridor.

They were all very different. The first girl to be interviewed was big, blonde and very loud with a scary laugh that seemed to erupt from her at quite inappropriate moments. It was possible to hear most of what she said through the closed office door.

One comment was, 'Nah, you can't tell me nothing about sweets, luv. They've been me downfall sweets have.' She was not in there for long.

The second girl was obviously very shy and short-sighted. She spoke barely above a whisper. When Sophie asked what her present job was, she explained that she had just started working in a library.

She then said, 'But my mother thinks I need to get out more. To be honest I don't want to get out more. I love my job in the library.'

Sophie told her to go back to her job in the library, 'I expect you are very good at it she added.' The girl was smiling as she left.

Sophie ushered Daisy into the interview room. Sophie could see that she was clearly bright but poor. Her shoes were worn but clean. Her dress was covered in a print of small flowers, also clean, but it had frayed cuffs and hem.

When questioned she said, 'Me name is Daisy.'

She told them that she had been helping her mum with her cleaning job for three years since she had left school, but she wanted to make more of herself.

Her answers were clear and quick, and she admitted when she didn't know an answer when appropriate. It did not hurt that she thought the confectionery was beautiful and that it looked too good to eat. Sara promptly offered her one.

The two women looked at each other and nodded.

Sophie said, 'We would like to offer you the job if you want it?'

Daisy's heart stopped in her chest, 'Do you mean that?'

Both women nodded at her, she was completely overwhelmed, then she was crying, hands up to her face, tears spilling between her fingers.

Sara was beside her in an instant offering her a hanky and putting an arm round her.

Gaining some control she said, 'I'll work real 'ard I promise.' She was now smiling through the tears.

Sophie added a small cautionary note saying, 'The wages would not be much to start with but, if you work hard who knows where you might end up. When can you start?'

'Now, if that's ok?'

'Welcome aboard, Daisy, Sara will take you to the shop, I must get back to work.'

A short bus ride took them to the second shop. That afternoon, between serving customers it became apparent that Daisy was a quick learner, especially with regard to the confectionery that she was entranced by.

CHAPTER 40

DAISY

Sophie spoke to Tim one evening after dinner on the boat three months after the second shop had opened. 'Tim, I am concerned about the turnover on the second shop. It is reasonably steady all week but on Friday it is lower than the rest of the week.'

'Is that intermittent or regular?'

'It appears to be regular; the actual amount varies slightly but it is always less.'

'I can't believe Daisy is a thief,' said Tim.

'I do not either, but something does not add up.'

'Mind you, Daisy is on her own for an hour or so in the early afternoon whilst whichever of us is helping her goes to lunch,' mused Tim.

'I will ask her tomorrow if she can shed any light on it.'

'Tim, please let me do it, I may get more out of her?'

The following Friday morning Sophie stopped by the second shop mid-morning, and flipping the sign to closed, said to Daisy, 'Can we have a quick chat?'

Daisy immediately burst into tears and said, 'I told him you would find out and I would lose 'me job. He said you toffs are too stupid to notice.' She was sobbing hard now. 'When I've tried to stop 'im, he shoves me out the way.'

'Who is doing this, Daisy?'

'Me dad. He drinks most of his wages on a Friday lunch time and he calls in for what he calls a top up. I've told me mum, but she's terrified of 'im. If she says anything, he hits her.'

'Does he though. You have not lost your job, Daisy, but we will put a stop to this. Dry your eyes and open up again. When your father calls today behave as you have in the past. Please leave the back door unlocked.'

Later, Tim was in the shop with Daisy keeping watch for her father. Mr Cooper and Mr Woodman were chatting across the road.

'This is 'im,' said Daisy pointing down the road.

Tim, looking over Daisy's shoulder, saw this fat drunken lout weaving his way up the hill.

'Right, Daisy,' said Tim, 'when he gets here open up. I will be just outside the back door.'

Shortly afterwards Tim heard hammering and her father shouting. The front door was unbolted, and he heard Daisy say, 'Dad, you can't do this no more.'

Tim heard a blow land and then something soft hit the floor followed by heavy footsteps across the shop.

When he stepped through the back door into the shop, he saw Daisy lying on the floor holding her face and her father at the open till with a bundle of notes in his hand. At the same time Mr Woodman arrived through the front door closely followed by his father.

Mr Woodman stepped into the gap in the counter trapping the drunken man.

Daisy's father said, 'Get out of my way, you silly old bugger,' and took a swing at Mr Woodman.

Tim didn't see what happened, it was all too fast. He heard three distinct blows and the sound of Daisy's father hitting the floor. Mr Cooper was helping Daisy to sit up. Tim noticed she had a deepening red mark on her face.

'I will get you a glass of water, lass,' said Tim's father, first ensuring she would not fall over again.

At that moment a customer tried to enter the shop. 'Sorry,' said Tim, 'we've had an attempted burglary, but it is all under control. Can you call back later, please?'

The woman looking very worried scurried away.

Tim walked over and changed the sign to closed. As he returned, he said to Mr Woodman, 'Can you wake him up, please?' As he walked back, he heard some very heavy slapping taking place, then the groaning began.

The drunkard was lying on his back staring at the ceiling. Tim placed his right foot on the man's chest and leant on it.

'I can't breathe,' he croaked.

'I don't care,' said Tim. 'Now it may surprise you to know we are not going to call the police. But we will watch you and if you come anywhere near Daisy, or I hear you have hit your wife again we will come for you. Do you understand?' The man was choking and could not answer.

Tim removed his foot and said to Mr Woodman, 'Can you get him to answer me, please?'

'No, don't let 'im hit me again. I ain't gonna do nothing. I'm gonna go up norf I am. You won't see me again.'

Tim leant very close to the man and whispered something in his ear. Tim saw real fear in his eyes.

Tim and Mr Woodman hauled him to his feet and walked him to the front door and released him. Unable to keep his feet he measured his full length on the pavement. Unseen by Tim or the others the local bobby was crossing the road.

'Are you having trouble, gentlemen?' he asked.

'No, thank you, officer, it's all under control.'

'Is he still breathing?' he enquired. Lifting the man's face and finally recognising him he said, 'Oh! He's a Green, they are all thieves and liars.

Next time I see you, Mr Green, I will arrest you. I am sure this young man can give me enough information to do so. Is that right, sir?'

'I dare say so,' Tim replied.

'Who is this young lady?' he asked.

'I'm Daisy Green,' she replied, obviously deeply ashamed of the reputation her family had. The bruise on her cheek rapidly darkening.

'She tried to stop her father robbing the till,' said Tim.

'And he hit her,' said the policeman finishing the sentence. 'Do you want to press charges, young lady?'

'No thank you,' said Daisy. 'He gets so drunk he don't know what he's doing.'

'Well, it's a night in the cells for you Green, pending possible charges. Up you come, man,' said the policeman hauling Green to his feet none too carefully. 'Good day to you all,' he said over his shoulder as he marched away, dragging the shambling man along beside him.

'We can't allow Daisy to go home,' said his father, 'who knows what mood he'll be in when they let him out.'

'You're right, Dad, but what do we do with her? Sorry, Daisy, we are talking about you as though you aren't here.'

'I don't wanna be no trouble,' she replied. 'I could move away. Mum always said we could go to her sister in Southend.'

'We don't want you to move away,' said Tim. 'You are a great asset to the company.'

Later she was overheard asking Mr Woodman what an asset was. Mr Woodman replied, 'It is something or someone that is of real value to the company.'

'Who me?' she asked wide eyed.

'Yes, you,' he replied.

'I've had a thought,' said Mr Cooper, 'let me make a phone call.'

'Right,' he said as he returned, 'I've fixed up a couple of nights at Harry and Sara's. I was going to offer but it didn't seem appropriate somehow. Sara says she will love to have you. How does that sound, Daisy?'

'Are they real posh, Mr Cooper?' she asked very quietly.

'No, lass, they are just ordinary decent folk like the rest of us. It'll give us time to sort out something permanent for you. I'll come and help you with your clothes and so on, or should I fetch the van?'

'I don't have many clothes or stuff. It'll fit in a couple of bags and I can manage them.'

'Where do you live, Daisy?' asked Mr Woodman.

'Just ten minutes' walk away,' she said.

'If you give me the shop keys, Daisy,' said Tim, 'I will take over and you can get your stuff and tell your mother what's happening.'

'Mr Cooper and I will come for a walk,' said Mr Woodman.

Later that evening Tim's father rang him.

'How did it go, Dad?'

'It was enough to make you weep, lad. We told her mum what had happened, and she said this was the final straw. She was going to her sister's. She said hitting her was one thing, hitting Daisy was another. Daisy came down with two shopping bags of clothes.

I said we can come back tomorrow for the rest with the van. She burst into tears and said this was everything. Her mother told her to wait a minute, then disappeared into another room and came back with a beautiful brooch. Apparently, it was her mother's and she had managed to keep it hidden. We waited outside while they said goodbye.

'After we had walked a few paces she took my hand and looked up at me, silent tears streaming down her face. You know Mr Woodman never misses anything. He said, "this is the start of a new life, Daisy. A better life." I nearly cried myself, lad. How can anyone do that to their own child? She is at Harry's now with Sara fussing over her like a mother hen. By the way, what did you say to Green that made him look so scared?'

'Oh, that,' said Tim chuckling. 'I told him he should have been more careful because I was a member of the Vieri family. I know that the mafia stories are rubbish, but on this occasion, it was quite useful.'

'I am not so sure, Tim, a lot of the old timers would disagree with you, me included.'

'Whatever,' he replied, 'it worked this time, I don't think we will have any more trouble from him.'

CHAPTER 41

THE WILL

Three months later, Tim had just arrived at the shop when the phone started ringing. Mr Woodman answered it, spoke for a moment or two and turning towards Tim pointed at the phone and mouthed, 'This is for you.'

Tim walked towards the phone completely unaware of how this phone call would change the rest of his life. Taking the phone from Mr Woodman and thanking him he said, 'Hallo, Tim here.'

A very cultured voice asked, 'Is that Mr Cooper, Mr Timothy Cooper?'

'Yes,' said Tim, his attention taken with a delivery that was just arriving that he had not been expecting. 'Sorry, can I ask you to hold for just a moment, please?' covering the mouthpiece with his hand he called out to the delivery man saying, 'Sorry, mate, that's not for us, try two doors further down the hill, we keep getting their stuff.'

Returning to the phone call he said, 'Sorry about that. How can I help you?'

'I am Robert Carstairs of Carstairs and Carstairs Solicitors. I have some sad news I am afraid, your great aunt Victoria Longstaff passed away in her sleep yesterday.'

Tim felt as though he had been punched in the chest, all the air had been driven from his body. He lowered his head fighting back the tears. He realised in that instant how much he loved her and how important she was, had been, to him.

A few seconds passed, and Mr Carstairs said, 'Hallo, are you there? Hallo, hallo.'

Struggling to draw breath, Tim said in a small voice, 'Can you give me a minute, please? No forget that, can I take your phone number and I will ring you back.' Tim stood with his head bowed, his left hand covering his eyes and his shoulders shaking, the phone forgotten in his right hand.

Mr Woodman had noticed Tim's distress. Putting his hand on Tim's shoulder he said quietly, 'Can I do it, Tim?'

Tim handed him the phone.

Mr Woodman could read the terrible pain in Tim's eyes. Putting the phone to his ear and saying, 'Hallo,' he listened for a moment, then told Mr Carstairs his name and explained that he was one of the company's partners. He jotted down the number, ascertained that the solicitor would be there all day and said, 'Mr Cooper will ring you back.'

'Tim, the solicitor didn't realise how close you were. He wanted me to pass on his apology. Do you want to ring him now?'

Shaking his head, he asked, 'Can I go for a walk, please?' It was clear he was struggling to control his tears.

'Of course, Tim, we're not that busy. Would you like me to ring Sophie?'

Tim nodded his agreement.

'No problem,' Mr Woodman replied.

'My father should know. Do you know where he is?'

'Yes, he's at the dentist. He said he might be a while. Do you want me to tell him?' 'Yes please.'

As he left the shop a regular customer paused to chat to him. 'Hallo, Tim, how are you?'

Tim replied, 'I am ok, thank you,' as he continued to walk away.

Entering the shop, the customer asked Mr Woodman why Tim was so abrupt with him.

'He's just lost a family member.'

'Oh, I am so sorry, please give him my condolences.'

Tim sat for a while on a bench not far from the shop, watching the river. He recalled how his aunt had mothered him through the worst of the time after his mum had died. She had always been there for him. He already missed her terribly. The world was somehow colder. Thank God he had Sophie.

She was waiting for him when he returned. She took his hand and scanned his face recognising how much he was hurting.

'Go upstairs,' said Mr Woodman.

Once there, Tim broke down. Sophie held him as the silent tears fell unchecked. When the worst of the storm was over Sophie sat him in a chair and made a cup of tea.

Passing him a cup she said, quietly, 'I am going to take one to Mr Woodman.' As she was returning upstairs, she met Tim coming down wiping his eyes.

'I'd best get this phone call out of the way.'

*

The following afternoon, Tim, his father and Sophie sat in Mr Carstairs' office. He went through all the formal stuff, disclosing which bank Mrs Longstaff used, who managed her property etc. She had been very clear about the detail for her funeral.

'I can give you a copy of all this before you leave,' he said. 'Now for the main body of the will, Mr Cooper.'

Tim interrupted him, 'Can you call me Tim, please, otherwise this is going to become very confusing with my father here, if you were talking to me that is?'

'I was, Mr, err, sorry, Tim,' replied Mr Carstairs, continuing, 'your aunt left some money to those charities she had always supported. Mrs Cooper, or is it, Sophia?' he asked.

'Sophie, please,' she replied.

'Mrs Longstaff has left you two thousand pounds.'

Sophie was dumbstruck, 'But I only met her three times.'

'You obviously made a good impression,' Mr Carstairs replied. 'Mr Cooper Senior, you have been left ten thousand pounds.'

'My goodness,' Tim's father said, shaking his head, 'who would have thought it.'

'Tim, Timothy, the bulk of the estate has been settled on you. I understand that your great aunt informed you of that. There will be taxes, charges, et cetera but the present value is as follows; there are five houses, excluding your aunt's house. Four are let, the fifth house is let rent free. The occupants are an elderly couple who have worked for your aunt as housekeeper and general handyman. They are the Grahams. You will need to decide what you want to do about them. I will furnish you with the details of the letting agents.

The remainder of the estate includes a wide range of investments. The estate has an estimated gross value of four hundred and ninety-seven thousand pounds. As I say, there will be monies to pay out of that, but it is still a very considerable sum. You are a very wealthy young man.'

'How much?' asked his father in disbelief, his mouth open and a shocked look on his face.

Mr Carstairs repeated the amount.

'Good God,' said his father, shaking his head.

There was a long silence. Tim had said nothing, sitting very still with his chin in his hands, his eyes everywhere. Sophie reached across and took his hand and squeezed it. She knew that he would give the money away if he could have his aunt back.

'As I promised, here are your aunt's requirements for her funeral. Most of the people she has named for certain functions are already aware of what she requires. It should be quite straightforward. I always found her to be extremely efficient and well organised.'

Everybody was very quiet in the taxi going home, especially Tim. They dropped Sophie back at work and then returned to the shop.

On the way, his father observed, 'You are very quiet, lad.'

'I wish I could refuse the money and have my aunt back.'

'I knew you would say that, son.'

'It changes everything, Dad. People will say I have succeeded because of the money. I wanted to be seen to be successful in my own right, by dint of hard work and expertise, not because I am extraordinarily wealthy.'

'Well, you can always point towards the fact that you had two shops already and more planned prior to this money.'

'Hmm,' said Tim. 'Can we keep the amount quiet please, Dad?'

There was another long silence. Tim was staring out of the window, his eyes blurred by unshed tears transported back in time to when his mother had died, he was very young, and his aunt was so caring of him.

Finally he said, 'I haven't a clue what to do, Dad.'

'Of course not, son, may I suggest you go and see Mr Vieri, he is used to financial success. He may be able to help.'

Later that evening, Sophie and Tim were sitting in Angela's lounge and were discussing the funeral.

'We need to make it special,' said Tim. 'She was a very remarkable old lady.'

'We do have a problem,' said Sophie. 'We are both working flat out. I do not see how we can organise a big funeral.'

'Big is not required. I want the church full of flowers and filled with wonderful music. We need to put something in the Times newspaper. She had friends and interests all over the world. There are all the charities she supported for a start. They will have to know. I expect they will want to attend. I have seen Mr Carstairs' list of the charities and I will continue to support them.'

'Can you afford that, Tim?' queried Angela, clearly surprised. She immediately apologised and said, 'I am sorry, it is no business of mine.'

The subject of the settlement of the estate had not come up during the evening, Tim was still in shock. Nothing was said for some while. Tim and Sophie looked at each other. Finally, Sophie nodded at him.

Angela very worried by the continuing silence said, 'I am so sorry, I should not have said anything. I do apologise, it was very rude of me.'

'You're not being rude,' he reassured her. 'It is just that we are both still in shock, as is my father. I think the family need to know; do you agree Sophie?'

'Yes,' she replied, 'keeping secrets just causes trouble.'

'Well, Sophie was left two thousand pounds. My father, a lot more, and the rest to me.' He paused.

Angela sat wide eyed.

'Tell her' Tim,' prompted Sophie.

Taking a deep breath, he continued, 'I am absolutely stunned by the whole thing. The final figure will be something over four hundred thousand pounds.'

'Good God,' said Angela, clearly shocked.

'That is what Tim's dad kept saying,' remarked Sophie.

'I am having problems coming to terms with it,' said Tim.

'You are a very wealthy young man,' observed Angela. Privately she thought, I wonder what my sister will make of that.

'Tim's dad suggested he talked to my father,' said Sophie.

'That is a good idea,' agreed Angela.

'Coming back to the funeral,' said Tim, wishing to change the subject, 'do you think your father would agree to us borrowing Sally again?'

Both women agreed that it would certainly make things easier.

'I will ask him,' replied Sophie.

Her father agreed.

The funeral took place two weeks later. Tim wondered if there would be an autopsy, but it was not required. His great aunt had been seen very regularly by her doctor who had informed her, at her insistence, that he tell her the truth, that her heart was, in his words, worn out.

The church was full of flowers and tall white candles. A boys' choir sang. The music was wonderful and uplifting, all chosen by Victoria herself. Sophie had a very firm grip on Tim's hand knowing how difficult the service was going to be for him, and how great his loss. There were a lot more people there than he thought there would be. The vicar spoke well of her, highlighting all the work she had done for the church and others, both at home and abroad.

The vicar continued, saying, 'I know she will be greatly missed. In closing, can I say I will miss her as a personal friend, she was a truly good woman.'

The journey to the cemetery was led by a black hearse drawn by two black horses dressed in black feathers. Tim, Sophie and those who could, walked behind. The rest followed in black limousines. The weather had become fitful with ill-tempered flurries of rain and wind. The ladies held on to their hats while the gusts pulled at their clothing.

The vicar kept the prayers at the graveside short.

At the wake afterwards, Tim thanked everyone for coming, pointed out how important his aunt had been in his life, and he knew in a lot of other people's lives as well. He had a brief word about his aunt's charitable giving, which by any standards could be considered generous. He announced his intention to meet with the charity leaders as soon as possible.

Turning to Mrs Vieri as she was leaving, he said, 'Good afternoon, how are you?'

'I am very well, thank you,' she replied, in a voice that was even more Arctic than usual. Her husband had disclosed not the amount of Tim's windfall, but he had indicated the sum was large. This lout, this barrow boy, this nobody, would end up with everything. She knew her husband had left the bulk of his estate to Sophia. She was seething, he would end up with all the family's money and now this inheritance, and on top of everything he had stolen her daughter away. Mrs Vieri, grinding her teeth with rage, also realised her friends would be laughing at her behind her back.

'I understand congratulations are in order regarding your recent inheritance. Such a shame your aunt had to die so you could benefit.'

Tim's anger flared, it was a writhing python coiling and uncoiling in his guts. He fixed her with a look of hatred and scorn. He knew she was fully aware of how much he loved his great aunt. Her words were carefully chosen to wound him. He held her gaze until she became red in the face and could not meet his eyes anymore. He said goodbye and turned away to speak to one of his great aunt's close friends. What Mrs Vieri could not have known was how profound the goodbye was. For Tim, it meant the end of any attempt to placate her, accede to her wishes or make any allowance for her behaviour. Any decisions he made in the future would not take her needs into account at any level. In future, it would be hallo and goodbye and only so that he would not upset Sophie.

Mr Vieri agreed to meet Tim for a chat five days after the funeral. 'Can you tell me what it is about?' he asked.

'My inheritance,' he replied.

'Would you like me to come to the boat?'

'That would be good,' said Tim, 'I will ask Sara to make us a supper hamper.'

'That will be nice, I will bring the wine,' said Mr Vieri, 'and Sally if that is ok? She is very good at all this.'

As arranged, five days later the four of them were sat around the stove as usual, all bathed in the light and warmth from the hot coals. The wine had been poured and they were picking wonderful Italian delicacies from the hamper.

Tim mused on how things had changed. In recent memory, he and Mr Vieri had almost come to blows. Now, Tim believed, the four of them were comfortable together.

Eventually, when the food had nearly all been eaten Mr Vieri interrupted the chatting and asked, 'What was it that you wanted to discuss, Tim?'

'My aunt has left a very large estate.

Sophie has been left some money, as have my father and I. Sorry I meant Sophia.'

Mr Vieri interrupted him saying, 'Tim, please do not worry, if it is what Sophia wants that is fine. Just do not call her that in front of her mother, please.'

'Fair enough. Sophie, do you want to say how much?' Tim asked.

'It is two thousand pounds, Father.'

'Goodness me,' exclaimed Sally, 'that is very generous.'

'My aunt left my father a considerable amount, but I think that is up to him if he wants to disclose how much. The real problem is how much she has left me.'

'Do you want to tell me?' asked Mr Vieri.

Tim paused and then said, 'Something in excess of four hundred thousand pounds.'

With an explosion of breath, Sally said, 'Good God,' evidently very surprised.

There was a long silence. Mr Vieri had sat back in his chair, crossed his arms and was gently nodding. Clearly, he was giving the information a lot of thought. No one else spoke.

Finally, he said, 'You are right, Tim, you do have a problem, but firstly can I congratulate you. Given your history you deserve this, but this amount of money needs to be husbanded very carefully. If you want, I can put you in touch with my people who look after my investments. They can advise you of the tax implications, et cetera, and advise on its management. I think I would suggest a separate company is set up to handle this money. I think you may need to find yourselves a Sally and no, this one is not available.'

Later that night sitting up in bed nursing a mug of cocoa each, Sophie said, 'I think my father's idea of a separate company is a good one.'

There was a prolonged discussion about the name, some hilarious and some were just silly

Eventually, Sophie said, 'Can I suggest Cooper and Cooper Holdings Limited? Then you can have other businesses under one parent company if you want.'

'Brilliant, Sophie, you are a very clever woman, brains and beauty all in the one package.' He continued, 'I need to do something useful with this money. I am not sure what yet, but I will come up with something.'

Sophie put her cup down, took Tim's cup away from him, ignoring his protest that he had not finished, placing it beside hers, she rolled towards him. Eventually they fell asleep.

Tim woke very early the following morning with a full-blown idea in his mind as to what to do with the money. 'Soph, Soph, are you awake?'

'No, I am not, and I hate being called Soph so please do not call me that if you do not mind. Why have you woken me up at this hour? What is the time?' she asked grumpily as she rolled away from him towards the bedside table to look at the clock. 'Tim,' she complained, becoming strident, 'it is only five thirty.'

'Sorry, my darling, but I just want to run something past you, but it can wait till later,' he said apologetically.

'No, tell me now you have woken me.'

Tim said, 'Mental note to self, do not wake your wife early in the morning.'

'I am sorry, Tim, but I was *soundos*,' said Sophie sounding less angry. 'What have you come up with?.'

'I will make you a cup of tea in a moment by way of an apology. What I was thinking was that money invested carefully should show quite a good return.'

Sophie agreed.

'You remember I explained how rough my secondary school was? Well, nobody went to university except one guy. He had been just as wild and unruly as the rest of us. One day he got us all together and said he wanted us to leave him alone. He was going to be a doctor. He changed overnight, got himself a job out of school and started saving for university. He succeeded.'

Sophie, interrupting the story said, 'Ok, he did well but what has that got to do with your money?'

'Amongst all the boys from my school, and in fact the grammar school as well, he was the only one who went to university and I bet you the situation is similar today. You must go to the right school and be of the right class to go to university.'

Sophie said, 'I am sorry, but I still do not understand.'

'Right, well supposing we set up a scholarship for boys from poor backgrounds, a bursary or whatever you call it?'

'Why would you do that? The state funds most of the costs these days.'

'Yes, but many of these families are only just managing, they expect the youngster to get a job and contribute to the family's standard of living. That stopped the boys I grew up with going on to higher education. They were told it was time for them to get a job. Sophie, a tiny percentage of young men from working class families go to university. For most it is out of school straight into the factory. The ones I knew had so much more to give if only they had the chance. University is still the preserve of the well-to-do.'

'How would it work? How would you find the young people? How would you establish what they needed? How would you pay them?'

'The simple answer at the moment is I don't know. All this would have to be thought through. We could meet with headmasters and make them aware of what we proposed. They would suggest the candidate. There could be an exam and a face-to-face meeting with us and others. This is all off the top of my head at the moment, one thing in our favour is that most factory and menial jobs are poorly paid for young people so the outgoing per student would not be very high. I anticipate the money would be paid to the parent to make up for the fact their child is not contributing to the family purse. We could assist them through university.'

'You are keen on this, are you not?' she asked him.

Tim was nodding.

'Your aunt would be very pleased.'

'I think so,' he responded. 'We would need your skills if you don't mind.'

'As my father suggested, we are going to need a Sally,' mused Sophie. 'We will never handle all this without help.'

Tim agreed. 'Sorry I woke you. Tea madam?'

'Yes please, and toast and marmalade.'

'Certainly, madam,' he said, knuckling his forehead.

'Finally, proper respect,' she said, chuckling.

Minutes later he was sitting on a low stool carefully encouraging the remains of the fire they had banked up overnight to light a stick of kindling, while his mind ran through the bones of his idea. The kindling flared into life. He started to prepare breakfast as the flames gathered strength throwing a warm glow on the galley walls.

Later that day after work, Sophie joined Tim in the shop, doing what Tim termed the late-night vigil. The arrival of customers was sporadic, so they could talk.

Sophie revealed that Tim's idea had really grown on her. 'Also,' she confided, 'it is useful with regards to tax.' Tim went to interrupt; holding up her hand she stopped him. 'I know that is not why you are doing it, but we must be hard-headed about this if it is to work. This is my area of expertise,' she continued. 'This is the kind of thinking I can bring to the table.'

'You're an amazing woman, Mrs Cooper, but we need to take the weight off somehow, for both our sakes.'

'I have been thinking about that as well,' she responded. 'An old girlfriend of mine lives not far from here. I had visited her when I saw the shop that day. Jessica fell pregnant on her honeymoon a few years ago, I think Polly, her daughter, is about six. Jessica mentioned that she would like a little job now Polly is at school. She is an incredible organiser. We always asked her to arrange things at uni. Shall I ring her?'

'If she is as good as you say, she may be the answer.'

'I will ring her now, what is the time?' asked Sophie.

'Err, seven,' responded Tim looking at the large old round clock at the back of the shop.

CHAPTER 42

JESSICA

'I always forget that clock,' said Sophie, responding to the quizzical look on his face.

She went to the phone. Ten minutes later the conversation was still in full flow. Tim could never understand what women found to talk about for so long; unless his calls were business in nature two minutes was a long call. He walked to the front door to flip the sign to closed just as a customer made to come in.

Shortly afterwards, putting down the phone Sophie gave Tim a thumbs up. He was busy serving the customer. He changed the sign to closed as the customer left.

Sophie asked, 'When would you like to meet her? She says she is free any evening after her husband gets home.'

'Is she free tomorrow?' he queried.

Sophie, her brow creased in thought, finally said, 'As far as I know.'

'Can you arrange that then, or would you prefer me to do it?' he asked. 'It would be good if she could come to the boat,' he added.

Mr Woodman, knowing somehow that Tim had closed the shop, called down from upstairs, 'Anyone for tea and biscuits?'

They both took him up on his offer.

The following evening both Tim and Sophie had been detained at work. As they walked past Tabby's house, he called out to them from his open window, 'I have a guest of yours in here.'

After profuse apologies and thanking Tabby they guided Jessica to the boat. She reacted the same as everybody did and was bowled over by the boat, the river and the lights.

Tim looked on as Sophie showed their guest around the boat. Jessica was, he guessed, early thirties, not very tall, but as his father would have said, small but perfectly formed. A quietly attractive woman with dark hair and a good complexion. Tim would have described her as neat and tidy; this would later prove correct in her work as well as her appearance. They shared their supper with her and in a relaxed manner asked her the relevant questions. This was very much Sophie's area of expertise; using her skills she gently extracted the information they needed.

Sophie asked, 'Am I right in remembering that your father is a doctor?'

'Yes, he is, but mother would like him to retire. His practice is very successful, but it is getting too much for him, although he will not admit it. Before I was married, I helped him with quite a lot of the admin.'

'What did you read at university?' asked Tim.

'I read Business Studies and Politics.'

Tim nodded, 'When I was younger and first running the stall, one of my regular customers, a well-dressed Jewish gentleman who owned a large fashion business in Mayfair, told me that if ever I found myself in a position of authority, I should surround myself with clever people. It would appear I am taking his advice, and of course it doesn't hurt that you are not hard to look at.'

Jessica blushed bright red and Sophie went mad, reached across and slapped him across the arm, 'How dare you say that to her,' she shrieked. 'I would not be surprised if she turned the job down. Now apologise you rude, rude, man.'

Tim, with a barely hidden smile and laughter playing in his eyes, said, 'I am very sorry, Jessica, I shall try not to do it again.'

Jessica, already having the measure of him, just smiled.

Sophie explained the requirements of the job to her which did not seem to cause Jessica any great concern.

'Jessica, do you have any questions?' enquired Sophie.

Jessica thought for a moment and then said, 'I understand about the shops, I think. You will want me to take the day-to-day admin off your shoulders? Sophie also mentioned something about a charity of some kind. I am unclear what that entails.'

Sophie said, 'This is very much Tim's vision so over to you, Tim.'

Jessica saw Tim suddenly become very focused. He was silent for a moment, holding his chin in his hand. Sophie now recognised that this signalled that he was thinking hard.

'Until recently it was reasonably simple. I intend to have a chain of Sophie's across London and maybe in the long-term further afield. This is still the intention, but things have become more complex. Very recently I inherited a large sum of money. Whilst it is good, it also brings its own set of problems with it. I need to do something beneficial with it. We have been discussing assisting clever young men from poor backgrounds through university. Only in a small way to begin with, a pilot,' looking at Sophie who nodded, 'but hopefully it will grow.'

'Only young men?' asked Jessica.

'Good point,' said Sophie. 'Tim?' she said requesting an answer.

Tim's hand went to his chin again, this time accompanied with a slight nodding.

After the usual pause he said, 'I admit I was only thinking in terms of boys, but if you two want to give me some numbers of how many girls would like to go to university, we can look at it.'

He thought to himself, This lady is no pussy cat. 'What do you prefer to be called?' he asked, 'Jess, Jessie, Jessica?'

'Jessica is good,' she responded.

She again confirmed his recent thoughts about her.

Tim continued, 'We are talking about setting up a holding company, Sophie's suggestion. It will allow us to do different things in the future under the same umbrella. This is new territory for me, but Sophie knows a lot about it.'

'It all sounds very exciting,' Jessica responded.

'It really is,' confirmed Sophie.

'We will need you to meet the other partners,' he said, 'but hopefully that will not cause any problems. Sophie has told me you have a child. When would you be available to work?'

'I can do school hours, less the taking her to and fro.'

Sophie, turning to face him, said, 'Tim, we cannot really say how many hours now can we?'

Tim was silent for a moment, looking at Sophie and resting his chin on his fists. After a long pause, he tilted his head to look at Jessica and said whilst rubbing his brow, 'We cannot know what lies ahead. Obviously, I have given it a lot of thought lately, there are so many things happening all at once. If you think in terms of a breaking wave roaring up the beach we are standing right in the way. Bearing that in mind you must tell us if the workload gets too much.'

Sophie, realising it was getting late asked, 'Jessica, do you have any more questions for us?'

'I do,' she replied, 'where would I work from, please, is there an office?'

'Is there an office, Tim?' asked Sophie, smiling at him, thinking there was not.

'Well, smarty pants, trying to catch me out, yes there is.'

'Where?' demanded Sophie, very surprised.

'My aunt's house,' he countered. 'It will become the company office. And we can live there while the boat is repainted. That reminds me, we must talk to Charlie about that.'

Jessica went to ask another question.

'Sorry Jessica,' said Sophie, 'can you hold that thought just for a minute. So are we keeping the houses?'

'Yes,' he said.

'Houses?' queried Jessica.

Sophie put her hand up saying, 'Sorry Jessica. Why keep them, Tim?'

'They are in my opinion the safest investment we can make,' he replied. 'Barring world war or terrorism if they are properly insured, they return a steady income. If all the rest goes pear shaped, we will not be penniless.'

'But they will need managing,' Sophie continued.

'They are managed now, Sophie, and it would appear very well. I see no reason not to continue,' he replied in a manner that implied the subject was not up for discussion.

Sophie wagged her head from side to side, frowning as she did so, unsure of the decision, she then turned to Jessica and apologised for their rudeness. 'We have both learnt something, as you can tell. We had not discussed any of that before tonight,' she said giving him a hard look. 'There are six houses, four are rented, one has Mrs Longstaff's housekeeper and driver handyman in it, Mr and Mrs Graham. The sixth one, is now the company office,' explained Sophie snapping a look in Tim's direction with what was a silent rebuke.

'Do you have any more questions, Jessica?' asked Sophie.

'I do,' she replied, 'but I am a little embarrassed to ask it. How will I be paid? Sorry, but it will be my husband's first question.'

'Sophie has some figures,' said Tim.

'Jessica, as we said earlier, we have no real idea of what will be required, but obviously there are some things that will have to happen immediately. Firstly, you will have to meet the other partners in Sophie's and gain their approval for your employment. Secondly, we need to set up the company office. Then you will need to meet people like the bank manager and so on. Now the money, will you be comfortable with a three-month probationary period?'

'It is what I expected,' Jessica replied.

'Good,' continued Sophie, 'I suggest initially that we pay you on an hourly basis and then review it in three months. Is that ok?' asked Sophie, telling her an amount.

'That is more than my husband said you would offer me. I am really excited about this job. I had a lot of responsibility when I worked for my father, but he only paid me pocket money.'

'I would like to get this rolling as soon as we can,' said Tim. 'When can you meet the team?'

'Tomorrow if that is not too soon?' she replied.

'Yep, that's good, tomorrow is usually a bit quieter. I think that just about wraps it up for tonight. How did you get here?' asked Tim.

'By taxi,' she said.

Sophie rang the local taxi company. They were very prompt and soon collected Jessica and whisked her away. Tim paid.

Before the two of them went to sleep, they both agreed she was the right person for the job.

Tim and Sophie arrived early at the shop the next morning to find Jessica already there talking to Mr Woodman and Tim's father.

'Good morning, Jessica, you're nice and early,' said Tim looking at his watch.

'My husband offered to take Grace to school. He did add he would not do it every day.'

Tim noticed she was very smartly dressed in a dark navy jacket, a matching straight knee-length skirt, high heels, a cream blouse and a thin gold necklace. Looks efficient, he thought approvingly.

'Have you all introduced yourselves?' asked Tim.

Mr Woodman said, 'Yes, we have, haven't we, Jessica?'

'They have both been perfect gentlemen,' agreed Jessica, looking at Tim. Sophie poked him in the ribs.

While they were still chatting Harry and Sara arrived, as did a small group of customers.

'Can I ask you and Sara, Dad, to see to the customers while we have what I think should be a short meeting?'

'No problem,' replied his father, moving towards the counter. Sara walked over to the confectionery counter where two people were looking at the selection.

'Jessica, can you wait just a few minutes while we fill in the detail with Mr Woodman and Harry. Then I will give you a call, are you ok with that?'

'Of course, Tim,' she replied turning towards a customer looking at the cheeses.

As Tim followed Sophie up the stairs, he heard Jessica say. 'I know nothing about any of this, but one must start somewhere. What would you like?'

'Sounds like you,' whispered Tim into Sophie's ear.

'Good schooling,' she replied.

Tim and Sophie spent the next twenty minutes filling the two men in about Jessica. Her salary and hours of work. Her previous experience and her university degree. Tim did diverge a little explaining about using his aunt's house as the company office. Both men thought that was a good idea. When the questions stopped, Sophie volunteered to go and get Jessica.

She was gone a little longer than Tim expected. When she reappeared leading Jessica, she said, 'All ok, just helping a customer.'

The questions the two men asked were predictable; where she had worked, what her responsibilities were. They were very impressed that her father was a doctor and with the work she had done for him.

Mr Woodman asked, 'How will you travel around between the shop, the office and home.'

'I thought that during the day I would use the tube and at night I would get a taxi. I do have a bicycle,' she added. 'My only real concern is the cost of travel if there is to be a lot.'

Harry said, 'There won't be a lot of your wages left if you have to pay to get around.'

Mr Woodman added, 'Tubes during the day will not be too bad and at other times I could give you a lift if that helps.'

Sophie broke in saying, 'Tim, if Jessica has to pay for her travel the job may not be worth having.'

Tim's hand went to his chin as usual and after a pause, said, 'Jessica, one of your first jobs is to devise a document to record your journeys.'

'Sophie, would you mind auditing it and agreeing payment?'

'No problem,' she replied, 'but it needs to include a record of her hours as well.'

'Is that alright with everybody?'

There was general agreement.

Jessica said, 'Thank you.'

'Are there any more questions?' asked Tim. This was met with a general shaking of heads.

'Right, Jessica, if you can step out for a moment, we can hold a vote.'

'Hold up, Tim,' said Mr Woodman, 'is there any need for that? I am quite sure she is right for the job. You two are obviously content. Harry, do you want a vote?'

'No, I am very happy that she is joining our team.'

'Well there you are, Jessica. Now it is down to you, will you accept the job?'

'Yes, I will, thank you everybody. It is all most exciting.'

'We normally have a small scotch to seal these deals. Now it will have to be a cup of tea or coffee,' offered Mr Woodman.

'Right,' said Tim, 'while you are doing that, I will have a word with Dad so he knows what is going on. Jessica, are you alright for a few hours' work today?'

'Yes,' she replied.

'In at the deep end, Jessica,' said Sophie, as she made to follow her husband downstairs. Jessica smiled.

Kissing Tim goodbye and waving at Mr Cooper, Harry and Sara, she went off to work. Mr Woodman accompanied her. He was working with Daisy at the second shop, number two as it was now known.

His dad said, 'Welcome aboard, lass.'

A customer overheard Tim telling his dad that Jessica had accepted the job offer.

'Blimey mate, how come you only employ beautiful women?' he asked.

'Because they are also very clever, sir,' Tim responded. Turning to his father he said, 'We need to have a chat soon to bring you up to date.'

'Ok, lad,' he responded.

'Will you all manage without me today?' asked Tim as he was leaving.

'We will do our very best,' answered Harry, smiling.

As an aside, Mr Cooper said to Harry, 'Tim will find that he will be spending less and less time in the shops.'

As the two of them walked to the station Tim started to explain the itinerary for the day. 'I am hoping to be able to introduce you to Mr Murdoch, the bank manager. Then we will go to my aunt's house. It should be nearly clear by now; an old friend of my father's is doing the house clearance. After that we will try and meet your opposite number, Sally, she is Sophie's father's PA.'

'I met him once, he is a very scary man,' she said.

'Not everyone fears him.'

'Meaning you do not?' said Jessica. Tim simply shook his head.

There was a brief silence as they approached the station. As they descended the station steps, Jessica asked, 'Am I a PA, I thought I was a secretary?'

At the foot of the steps he turned away from the moving crowd, stopped and called Jessica back. She had not realised Tim was not following her. She returned to where he was standing in a corner out of the way of the stream of commuters.

'This job can turn into whatever you want it to, I intend to have a string of shops across London and maybe beyond. The housing side may expand. I like the security I feel it offers. Also, there is the charitable trust we have spoken about. Who knows what the future may hold? I need someone by my side to keep me on track. You will make me look good. As you know Sophie is incredible, but she has her own career and I can see her running that business in the future, and if not that then her father's. Your job will be a vital element in the future of the company if you want it. It is up to you. By the way, I did mean what I said. You must let us know if the workload becomes unsustainable.'

They rode in silence on the train, Tim was reading through a sheaf of papers.

Jessica took the time to recap on all she had heard in the last two hours. Did he mean what he said? Sophie was good at reading people and she was full of praise for what he was attempting. Should half of what he planned come to fruition hers would be a very exciting job. It would be an end to the dreadful boredom that was her life at present. She loved her daughter and her husband but the hours on her own while they were at work and school was mind numbing and was a terrible waste of her first-class degree. Gerald, her husband, was always tired when he came in and only wanted to sit and watch football. It was not of any interest to her. She loved having her daughter in the evenings, but her bedtime soon arrived and then the boredom returned. The future suddenly looked bright and exciting.

She wanted to hug him, but she thought better of it.

Arriving at the bank, Mr Murdoch's secretary advised Tim that he had someone with him.

Tim, looking at his watch said, 'This is our new PA, Jessica.' The two women shook hands. Mr Murdoch's assistant introduced herself as Moira.

'I was hoping to introduce her to Mr Murdoch so that he knows who she is.'

'Let me find out if he can see you this morning, Mr Cooper.'

'Tim, it's Tim,' he reminded her.

'Sorry Tim,' she replied looking back at him and smiling as she tapped on the bank manager's door and then entered his office.

She reappeared some moments later saying, 'Mr Murdoch would like to meet Jessica. Can you wait ten minutes or so? I can make you a coffee if you would like one.'

Tim looked at Jessica enquiringly. She nodded and said, 'Yes please.'

'Take a seat and I will arrange it,' said Moira, walking away.

The tray of coffee arrived as Mr Murdoch was ushering his customer out of the door.

The bank manager turned towards Tim and smiled, saying, 'How nice to see you Tim, and this is?'

'Jessica,' replied Tim.

'Good morning, Jessica, please come in,' he said holding the door open for her and Tim.

The meeting was brief and informal. Mr Murdoch and Tim between them furnishing Jessica with all the information needed to get her started. When the coffee had been drunk Tim used it as the moment to take their leave.

As he got to the door Tim turned, saying, 'We are working through a new idea. When the detail is more certain I would like to come and discuss it with you.'

'That all sounds very interesting,' responded Mr Murdoch. 'I think this young man will be keeping you extremely busy, Jessica.'

'I am looking forward to it,' she replied.

*

His great aunt's house was in an attractive street of semi-detached houses. London red brick and slate roofs were universal all down the road. Each house apart from his aunts had a single bay window. Her house was double fronted and detached. The street was lined both sides by plain trees. All of the houses were well kept, it was clearly an affluent area.

The visit to his great aunt's house was the first he had made since her death. He was not looking forward to it. It was useful having Jessica with him. Her presence would help him to maintain his self-control. As Tim was trying to find the right key for the front door Mr Graham walked up the path behind them. He was short and thin, slightly stooped and pale grey, both his hair and clothing were a similar grey. He spoke very quietly.

'Good afternoon, Tim,' he said, not much above a whisper.

As Tim turned to face him Mr Graham said, 'Can I offer my sincerest condolences for the loss of your great aunt. Mrs Graham and I are devastated. I keep finding her weeping silently in a corner. It's not just the loss of your aunt. That has upset her terribly. She thinks we will also lose our jobs and be thrown out of our house. I am sorry to dump this on you like this, but we are both worried sick.'

Tim reassured him saying, 'We are still deciding what we will do regarding the estate, but I can assure you I have no intention of selling off the houses and you have no need to worry for the immediate future.'

'Thank you very much,' said Mr Graham retreating up the path to the gate.

Tim finally found the right key and the front door swung inwards. Ushering Jessica through the door ahead of him he followed her in. He was immediately assailed by a faint trace of his aunt's scent. He found himself struggling to retain his self-control. Jessica did not notice as she proceeded him further into the house. Taking a deep breath he cuffed his eyes and stiffened his resolve. The property was virtually devoid of furniture. Obviously, Joseph Gold had finished. There were a few pieces left. Even Tim could see with his limited knowledge of antiques that these were rather special. Jessica found a note on the dining room table and handed it to Tim. It was from Mr Gold. He said that he had not taken the furniture that was left because it had, in his opinion, a very high value. He assumed Tim would want to keep it. He also offered his condolences.

Tim passed the letter to Jessica. 'Here, your first bit of filing. We need to sort out which room you think should be the office, Jessica.'

They walked through the downstairs. The two front rooms were a good size and light. At the back of the house there was a small study and a nice kitchen.

'Jessica, I suggest you choose one of the front rooms to work in. I am going to use the study as my office. The other front room could be a meeting room. What do you think?'

'Could I have the left-hand room with the tree outside, please? It is very pretty.'

Tim nodded. 'The only phone appears to be in the hall,' he continued. 'We need two, one in the main office and one in mine, we need it so that you can switch calls through to me as required.' He saw the notepad and pencil were out and in use. 'Erm… I hope Sophie will be able to help you set the office up. She will be able to guide you as to what you need if you want some help. As you know, invoices for everything. It is all tax deductible. We don't want the stuff with bells and whistles. Solid and functional, oh, and always ask for a discount.'

They were interrupted by a gentle tapping on the front door. Jessica walked down the hall and opened it. A little grey-haired lady stood there and said hallo to Jessica and started to explain who she was.

Tim walked forward saying, 'Hallo, Mrs Graham, please come in.'

She matched her husband in that she was also short and grey in both appearance and dress.

She walked towards him as tears appeared in her eyes. 'Oh, Tim, I am so sorry for you. It's a dreadful loss.'

'It is, but, let me take that tray from you.'

Through her sniffing, she said, 'I thought you might like a cup of tea and a piece of cake, it's still warm. Thank you so much for talking to my husband. He has been in a terrible flap over the house and his job and everything.'

'Not a problem,' responded Tim. 'Will you still be able to clean in here. I assume that is what you were doing for my great aunt?'

'It was, Mrs Longstaff has been very kind to Mr Graham and me,' she sniffed, as the tears started again.

Tim nodded at Jessica who took over and started to placate Mrs Graham by asking about the kitchen. As the two women made their way there Mrs Graham explained that Mr Gold had left some crockery etc. Jessica soon had Mrs Graham dry eyed, sitting on a kitchen stool with a cup of tea in her hand.

*

Their next stop was Mr Vieri's store. Walking in through the large glass revolving door, Tim, as always, was impressed with the size of the building. The wide curving white marble staircase, the very high ceiling and chandeliers all helped to emphasise the grandeur of the place. The staff, he noticed, were all dressed in black with a white shirt. Tim approached a man in a black suit who was giving instructions to another member of staff. He had a very military looking posture and even from a distance it was apparent the staff held him in high regard.

The man caught sight of the two of them as they approached. Turning towards them, he said, 'Good morning, Mr Cooper, how can I help you, sir?'

Tim was stunned, 'How do you know who I am?' he asked.

'I try and keep abreast of things, how is your wife, sir?'

'She is very well, thank you. Can you call me Tim, please?'

'Certainly, sir, are you shopping, sir, or did you want to see Mr Vieri?'

'I expect he is busy; I was hoping Sally may be able to give us a few moments. I wanted to introduce Jessica, our new PA.'

'Good morning, Jessica, may I call you that?'

'Of course,' she replied smiling, a little beguiled by his old-world charm.

'Sorry,' said Tim as they walked towards a counter with a telephone, 'I don't know your name?'

'Rodgers, sir.'

'Well it's nice to meet you, Mr Rodgers.'

'Rodgers will do, sir.'

Lifting the telephone to his ear and spinning the dial around three times with his finger he waited. Tim heard a muffled voice on the other end of the phone then Rodgers said, 'I have Mr Cooper here to see Sally if possible, please?'

More muffled conversation then Rodgers said, 'Sally is in with Mr Vieri. She should not be long, apparently. Would you like to go on up? The lift is in the corner over there. It's the top floor, sir.'

'Thank you,' said Tim. Looking at the staircase and then at Jessica. 'The stairs?' he asked. She nodded.

Rodgers allowed himself a small smile as they set off with youthful vigour.

Tim was to learn later that Rodgers was ex-army, a regimental sergeant major, who received complete obedience from the shop floor staff and demanded a very high level of performance both from himself and those under him.

Jessica was soon in the lead and stood waiting for him at the top.

He arrived puffing and blowing. 'I need to get fitter,' he gasped.

He took the next flight at a slower pace. Jessica climbed the stairs beside him. It was not sensible, she thought, to make your new boss look silly.

His breathing was not a lot better when they reached the top floor. Up here the floors were carpeted, the offices he could see into were well furnished with solid oak desks and executive leather swivel chairs, and it was warm and quiet.

Sally's secretary was very polite and explained, saying, 'Sally knows you are here, and she will be out as soon as possible.'

At that moment, a door opposite came open and Sally was standing there and inviting them in. Mr Vieri's office was vast, situated on the corner of the building with floor to ceiling windows taking up the two external walls. The views over London were stunning. The oak floor gleamed in the sunlight, a large dark red Indian carpet with an intricate design sat in one corner of the room, placed centrally on it was a huge antique dark wood desk that dominated the space. To the right was a large cabinet that was clearly a partner to the desk. Tim noticed the cut glass ships tantalus placed on it. The crystal reflecting the sun in a myriad of patterns, enhanced by the colours of the contents of the three decanters.

Mr Vieri rose from a large buttoned conker brown leather chair and walked round the desk to shake Tim's hand. Sally hugged him and kissed his cheek.

He introduced Jessica. Both Sally and Mr Vieri made her welcome.

'How are you finding it so far?' asked Mr Vieri.

'This is my first day,' she admitted, 'so it is all a bit of a blur, but it is very exciting.'

Nodding, Mr Vieri said, 'Tim, while I remember, that hamper you were kind enough to give me, could we discuss some time what it might retail at and how many you could supply? It would work in our gift department.'

'Funnily enough, we are in the middle of sorting all that out. As soon as we have some prices and the packaging worked out, I will give you a call. How do you feel about having our name on it?' he asked.

'You mean Sophie's?' he queried.

'Yes,' confirmed Tim.

'Not a problem, I would like to see the final design though, please.'

Sally, laughing said, 'Jessica, you will learn these two men are never off duty.'

Mr Vieri winked at Tim who jerked his head and smiled.

Jessica and Sally were making notes. When they both saw what they were doing they laughed together.

'I know this is a bit of a cheek, Victor,' said Tim, 'but I had hoped that Jessica might be able to pick Sally's brain occasionally.'

Sally looked at her boss who said, 'I do not see why not. She may not always be able to do it straight away though.'

'Thank you, I am sure that will be a great help, at least until Jessica gets into gear.'

'I am not throwing you out, but there are things we must get done. Very nice to see you both. Perhaps we can come to the boat soon?' he said.

'I will have a word with Sophia,' said Sally.

As they were going down in the lift Jessica said, 'Goodness, I did not realise I would be working at this level. It is a bit scary but very exciting.'

'Can I share something with you, Jessica? That is exactly how I feel, that's why I do it. We are all on a steep learning curve.'

CHAPTER 43

SALLY AND VICTOR AT THE BOAT

One evening after dinner someone tapped on the door of the boat. Sophie and Tim were lying naked on their bed getting their breath back.

'Oh hell,' said Tim, 'who is that?'

Sophie peered through a crack in the curtains and said laughing, 'It is Father's Jaguar, Tim, we must open the door, all the cabin lights are on. I will jump in the shower, you put on some clothes and let them in.'

'Do what?' said Tim. 'Oh heck,' he grumbled, pulling on some clothes. Tim strode to the door and trying to smother a laugh he pulled the door open, as he did so he heard the shower start.

Mr Vieri was holding the door open to allow Sally to re-enter the car.

'Hallo,' Tim called, 'I didn't hear you; I am sorry; please come in. Sophie will be so upset if she missed you.'

'Are you sure?' asked Sally stepping out of the car. He had the opportunity to admire her legs once more.

Holding the door wide open in invitation he said, 'She is in the shower, she won't be long.'

Sally secretly nudged him in the ribs as she kissed his cheek and said hallo. He could see the laughter in her eyes. Mr Vieri entered with a, 'Hallo, Tim,' and shook hands and followed Sally through the door.

Sophie emerged from the shower cloaked in a large fluffy white towel looking fantastic.

Sally said, 'You are a very lucky man, Mr Cooper.'

'I know that alright,' he replied.

Sophie blushed, and said, 'I will be out in a minute.'

Mr Vieri coughed. Sally, Sophie and Tim all laughed.

Tim put the kettle on, Mr Vieri followed him into the galley asking, 'Have you had those numbers from the vineyard yet?'

'They arrived today,'

Sally stepped in and asked, 'Are you gentlemen talking shop? I think we ought to make it illegal on the boat.'

'Sorry,' both men replied.

Sophie reappeared in fluffy red and white striped pyjamas. She kissed Sally and her father.

This was the third time Sally and Mr Vieri had visited the boat. They both seemed very relaxed on board. The evening passed very pleasantly. They observed the ritual of toasting the crumpets and drinking a fine wine curtesy of Mr Vieri and good coffee from the shop.

Sally and Sophie were talking together, and Tim overheard Sally say, 'I love your boat.'

Mr Vieri said at the same time, 'I am going out for a cigar, Tim, will you join me?'

'Yeah sure,' he replied.

There was silence as Mr Vieri lit his cigar enveloping them in a cloud of aromatic smoke, both men watching the night-lit river as it slid by. Then he asked, 'Tim, can you keep a secret?'

'I can.'

Mr Vieri, pausing before he spoke, eventually said, 'Sally and I are lovers. Mrs Vieri has not let me near her for the last five years. She has, I regret to say, grown into a cold hard woman, and I know she is very rude to you on occasion, for which I apologise. I am telling you this in the strictest confidence. I still love my wife in a strange way, and I am Catholic and Italian, so I cannot divorce her, but I cannot live like a monk. I am very fond of Sally and she says she understands how things must be, so, can you promise to keep this a secret?'

'Yes, I can, I have known for almost a year.'

'I beg your pardon!' exclaimed Mr Vieri with steel in his voice, jerking his head back and fixing Tim with a hard look, 'How can you know?'

'I saw you kissing in your office months back and it was not a peck on the cheek.'

'Have you told anyone?' asked Mr Vieri obviously concerned.

'No.'

'Sophia?'

'No.'

'You continue to surprise me, Tim. Thank you. The reason I am telling you is that this boat would appear to be the only place we can be ourselves, somewhere we do not have to be on our guard all the time. Will you tell Sophia for me, please? I hope she will be alright about it.'

After Sally and her father had left, Tim and Sophie were getting ready for bed. Sophie was saying how good it was to see her father so relaxed. 'Sally is very nice, is she not?'

'It's strange that you brought this up. Your father asked me to tell you something.'

'What, to tell me they are having an affair?'

'Yes, but he put it differently. He said they were lovers.'

'Oh, I have known for ages,' laughed Sophie. 'You only have to watch them together to know they love each other.'

'Apparently, your father is not considering divorce?'

'No, he will not do that; too proud, too Italian and too Catholic.

'Anyway,' she said pushing him backwards onto the bed, 'enough of what my father wants, let us concentrate on what I want.'

'Certainly, madam,' he responded as she draped herself across him and started with the bedroom kissing. Then there was only the sounds of pleasure and laughter.

CHAPTER 44

AN UNLUCKY CUT

Tim arrived home late one evening to find Sophie washing a nasty looking cut under a running tap at the sink.

'That looks painful, how did it happen?'

'I went to the shed in the dark for some firewood and tripped up. I think I fell on a broken bottle, anyway, I have washed it well, so it will be ok.'

'It'll need a dressing and a bandage,' he stated. 'Do you think it needs stiches?'

Giving a shudder Sophie replied, 'I am sure it will be fine; I have seen enough of hospitals of late.'

'We will have a look in the morning,' promised Tim, his tone of voice inferring that hospital may be an option anyway.

The following morning Tim was woken early by the sound of running water. Rising from the bed and walking quietly up behind her he discovered her swallowing painkillers. 'Is that for your hand?'

'Yes, but it is not too bad.'

'Can you let me have a look, please,' he asked in a firm voice.

'Tim, it is not too bad, honestly. I do not want to go to hospital,' she stated sounding adamant.

'Just let me look, please, I am worried about you.'

The wound was lying open and whilst there was not much blood the skin around the injury was red and puffy and when he put his mouth to the area to test the temperature it was very hot.

'OK, we need to get dressed, I am taking you to the hospital, I'll ring for a taxi.'

'Please, Tim, I do not want to go,' her distress was becoming obvious.

'I'm sorry, Sophie darling, but that wound is infected and needs treatment.'

The taxi arrived and shortly afterwards they were sitting in a small side bay in A&E with the curtain drawn across waiting for the doctor. An hour later they were in another taxi on their way home.

The cabby said, 'You look as though you've been in the wars, darlin.'

Tim explained that the wound had been cleaned, stitched, and an anti-tetanus injection had been administered and antibiotics prescribed.

'Gordon Bennett,' was his reply.

Sophie was very dejected, sitting with her heavily bandaged hand on her lap having been advised not to use it.

'I suggest,' said Tim, 'that you have a day off and get some sleep, I'll ring Angela and tell her what's happened.'

'No, please do not disturb her, I will be fine.'

'And what will she say if we don't ring her?'

The prescription was filled on the way home. On arrival Sophie was installed in bed, Angela telephoned, and Sophie's boss informed. He sent his best wishes. Angela arrived shortly after and took over. When Tim left for work the kettle was singing and scrambled eggs were being prepared.

A week later, shortly after they had gone to bed Sophie propped herself up on one elbow and looking down at him asked, 'Have you gone off me?'

Tim, looking puzzled, said, 'What do you mean?'

'Well all this week you have been turning over and going to sleep as soon as we get into bed.'

'I didn't want to hurt your hand.'

'Let me worry about my hand,' she said as she slowly slid the sheet down below her breasts.

Growling, he rolled towards her; giggling, she spread herself for him and welcomed him in, purring as she did so.

The injury soon healed leaving a thin scar.

CHAPTER 45

THE MISCARRIAGE

A few weeks later she confided in him that had she not known better she would think she was pregnant because she had missed two periods.

'I might just have a check-up,' she said.

Two nights later, arriving home, he found her sitting staring out of the window.

'Are you ok?' he asked.

Tim, about to fill the kettle was stopped when Sophie asked him to come and sit down. Sensing the seriousness of her tone he did as she asked.

When he was sitting, she reached for his hand, and watching his face closely to gauge his reaction said, 'I am pregnant!'

He was momentarily stunned, he still held her gaze, then a growing sense of wonder overcame him. I am going to be a dad, he thought. Wearing the biggest smile he had ever smiled he left the chair and dropped to his knees in front of her. Putting one arm round her waist he placed the other hand very gently on her tummy and looked up.

She could see the joy and amazement in his eyes. 'I am going to be a dad,' he whispered.

She placed her hands over his on her tummy. 'I was not sure what your reaction was going to be, it sets all our plans awry.'

'No problem, we will just change the plans.'

'I asked the doctor how I could be pregnant, he asked me some questions and said it was almost certainly the antibiotics.'

They spent the evening planning their new future.

*

Two months later in the early hours of the morning the toilet light went on. Tim could hear Sophie crying. Rolling over in the bed towards the sound he saw her framed in the toilet doorway. She was naked apart from a blood-stained bath towel clutched to her tummy.

'Tim, I am bleeding,' she sobbed, 'I think I am losing the baby.'

Tim moved forward and wrapped her in his arms, 'We need to get you to hospital, they can do all sorts of clever things nowadays.'

'I am so scared,' said Sophie still crying.

'I will be with you. Where are your nighties?'

'In the bottom drawer,' she responded, pointing.

Pulling out the first one he came across in the tall boy he helped pull it over her head, she was still crying. She reached behind the bathroom door for her dressing gown.

Tim was already on the phone.

He sat opposite Sophie in the ambulance, holding her hand as they made their way to the hospital. He could see she was terrified. He was soon following her into A&E. She was being pushed by one of the ambulance crew in a wheelchair. Tim watched as she disappeared through another set of doors. He was guided to reception. His brain had become a complete blank. His only concern was Sophie's wellbeing. He found himself praying silently, 'Please, God, make her alright,' repeating this over and over like a mantra.

The receptionist was very patient with him, gently repeating the questions when he looked at her blankly.

Eventually she said, 'That will do for now, please take a seat over there. The doctor will come and talk to you soon.'

Tim was not aware of the passing of time. It was a long time later when a tired looking doctor in a white coat approached him and asked his name. He explained to Tim what they had done for Sophie and that she was now heavily sedated and resting well.

Tim, very concerned for Sophie, asked if she was going to be alright. The doctor was very reassuring and said that he felt sure she would be fine.

'There is one thing I want to make very clear. If there is any risk to her, she must come first,' Tim insisted.

'I understand what you are saying, Mr Cooper, I do not believe it will come to that. Now, I suggest that you go home and try and rest. You can come in first thing in the morning. If anything changes, we will ring you.'

'Thank you, doctor.'

When he got back to the boat, he debated whether to ring Angela. He decided he would. Angela answered the phone sounding very sleepy but also concerned at the call at 3 am.

Tim explained what had happened and that he had been reassured that Sophie would be ok.

'Oh, Timothy,' she exclaimed, he could hear the fear in her voice. 'Have you rung my sister?'

Tim explained he had only just got in.

'Would you like me to ring?' she asked.

'Yes please,' he replied.

'I will do it now,' she said and rang off.

Ten minutes later his phone rang again. Frightened, he leapt to answer it. It was Victor Vieri. He had rung the hospital and had the same advice as Tim, that Sophie was sleeping peacefully, and she was comfortable.

'Did you know she was pregnant, Timothy?' he asked. Tim realised that Mrs Vieri was listening in, otherwise it would have been Tim.

'We found out a few days ago. We discussed telling people, but we decided to wait until things were further along.'

'As it happens that was for the best. We can keep the problem contained,' said Mr Vieri.

Tim didn't answer, what a strange thing to worry about, he thought. The image was all important.

'Timothy, I will ring you in the morning,' he said as he rang off.

Tim dozed in an armchair, fully dressed, the rest of the night. At about six o'clock he finally fell asleep. Waking with a start at eight and wondering where Sophie was, he suddenly remembered what had happened last night. Fear like a great weight descended on him. He rushed around. Kettle on, teeth brushed. Extra milk in his tea so he could drink it quickly. The taxi arrived as he was drinking the last of it and whisked him off to the hospital. Stopping at reception to ask which ward she was in he made his way down the corridor.

'Are you Mr Cooper?' asked a tall thin dark-haired lady doctor, stopping him halfway down the corridor.

Tim confirmed that he was.

'You have just lost your baby boy,' she said. Then without another word turned and walked away.

Tim stepped across the corridor into a corner and held the wall for support. Trying to hide his tears with his spare hand he struggled to regain control.

He felt someone put their hand gently on his shoulder. He turned to find an elderly vicar standing beside him.

'Shall we find somewhere quiet for you to sit down, son?' Tim could only nod. The vicar led him a few steps away to an empty room. He guided Tim to a seat and then left.

Tim was torn by the fiercest pain he had experienced since his mother died. He had not realised how passionately he had been looking forward to the birth of their first child.

There was a soft tapping on the door. Tim was unsure how much time had passed since he entered the room, scrubbing his eyes with the back of his hands he tried to say come in, but it was just a croak. Clearing his throat, he tried again, successfully this time.

The vicar entered carrying a tray of tea, 'I thought this may help,' he said.

Tim, who by now was regaining some self-control, thanked him.

'Do you want to talk about it?' asked the vicar.

'My wife has just miscarried,' he said fighting once again to keep control. 'The doctor just told me out in the corridor, and then she walked away.'

'Good God,' said the vicar as he started to pour the tea.

'Would you like me to visit your wife later?' he asked.

'Yes please, I will drink this then I will go on up.'

'You can come and find me whenever,' said the vicar. 'I do not know your name,' he continued.

'Sophia Cooper,' said Tim, unsure why he had answered the question as he did. 'No, sorry, my name's Tim Cooper.'

'Please do not worry. I have known people forget their own name in these circumstances.'

Tim swallowed the last of his tea and stood up. The vicar took his hand and shook it, 'I mean what I said, if you would like to talk please come and find me.'

'Thank you very much,' said Tim as he left. Making his way upstairs he knew how upset Sophie would be.

As he entered the ward a staff nurse asked him his name, then she ushered him into a small side room saying, 'Please take a seat.' Once he was sitting, she asked, 'Do you know what has happened to your wife?'

'Yes, a lady doctor told me as she passed me in the corridor.'

'She did what!' exclaimed the nurse, he could hear the disbelief in her voice.

'She just asked me my name and said, "you have just lost your baby boy". Then she walked away.'

The nurse closed her eyes and shook her head. 'Are you sure that is all she said?'

'I am very sure,' he replied, 'the vicar took me into his room and made me a cup of tea.'

'I will follow this up if you agree. You should not have been told like that; I am very sorry.'

Tim made no reply.

'Now let's talk about your beautiful wife. She was very distressed during the miscarriage, so she has been given a mild sedative.'

'Is she ok in herself?' he asked, 'she is not in any danger?'

'No, she will be fine, but she will be in for a few days. We need to tidy her up internally. Three days or so at the most.'

'I don't know if she has told you, but her birth was very difficult and her mother could not have any more children, I know that will be on her mind. Will it be the same for Sophia?' A little voice in his mind queried why he was calling her Sophia, he brushed it aside.

'The doctor has said there is no reason why she cannot have more babies once you are both ready,' replied the nurse. 'You can go through and see her now. She may be asleep.'

He tiptoed into the ward. Two mums breast feeding their new-born's gave him sympathetic looks as he passed. The sight of the babies had him again fighting back the tears. He sat quietly down in the chair by Sophie's bed.

She awoke as he crossed his legs. Seizing his shirt front, she pulled him towards her, buried her face in his neck and holding him very tightly began a silent sobbing that wracked her body. She was whispering repeatedly, 'I am so sorry. I am so sorry.'

'It was not your fault,' he whispered back. He was now in floods of tears. They held each other while they cried themselves out. When the tears had subsided, she mopped his face with her hankie and then her own.

'Tim, will we still be able to have babies?'

'The nurse told me the doctor said he sees no reason why not when we are both ready.'

'When can I go home?'

'In about three days, the nurse said.'

'Oh no! Why can I not go home now?'

'They want to keep an eye on you.'

She slumped back in her bed.

Tim was sitting in the hospital corridor while Sophie had a shower and the other women tidied themselves ready for the day. Suddenly the pain of losing his son began to overwhelm him. Using a great deal of self-control, he managed to avoid crying. Then he remembered a discussion he'd had with his mother when he was quite young. He had noticed that a little old lady who lived over the road was often dabbing her eyes with a little handkerchief she kept up the sleeve of her multicoloured jumper.

He'd asked his mother why the old lady cried a lot. 'Timmy, when people get old, they remember the people they have loved and lost, the disappointments in their lives, they remember when they could run and laugh and dance. Can you imagine a pool of tears inside them because of the sad things that have happened to them? My Gran used to call it a pool of sorrow. Sometimes something reminds them of a sad time and then they find themselves walking beside the pool of sorrow and it makes them very unhappy, so they cry.'

Tim realised the loss of his son had added to his own pool of sorrow.

CHAPTER 46

BABY

When Sophie came home, she began to recover physically very quickly as the doctor had promised, but Tim saw a change in her personality. There was a shadow inside her, a diminishing of her sparkle. She worked harder and longer, laughed less often and appeared more reflective. Six months later she returned from work and asked Tim to sit down so they could talk. He realised from her demeanour that it was serious.

'I have been to the doctor, Tim, and he has examined me and said there is no reason why we cannot have another baby. I want to try again, I want a baby please, Tim, I know I have been down but now I am just broody. I see the mothers in the park, and I am so jealous of them, Tim, I want a baby of my own to hold, I have never wanted anything so badly, apart from you of course, but that was just lust,' she said smiling. 'Please say yes, Tim, please.'

'Are you sure you are fully recovered?'

'The doctor says I am, but he did warn me it may take some while for the effects of the pill to wear off. It can take six months.'

'I would love us to have a baby, but you will have to reduce your workload.'

'If it is going to take a while, I can taper my hours and train up a girl in the office to take over the mundane stuff.' Sophie was becoming more and more excited.

Tim went to interrupt her, but she would not let him. 'And, and, I can put more work Jessica's way.' She was jigging about in her chair in her excitement. 'She eats up her current workload.'

'Do you still want to live on the boat?'

'Of course,' she replied. 'I can start working out how to turn the single cabin into a nursery. Also, Tim darling, I promise you I will be super cautious. No more lifting heavy boxes or running for buses.'

'Will you stop work when the baby comes?' hoping as he said it that he was not tempting fate.

'Would you mind if I found a nanny? I had a nanny and I loved her. I will go back to work part time.'

'I don't approve of latch-key kids,' he replied. 'Society blames the children rather than the absent parents when the children get into trouble.'

'They will not be latch-key children,' she responded indignantly. 'In the early years the children will be with me, or you or the nanny.'

'You said children, how many is children?'

'Two to start with then we can see how it goes.'

'Will the nanny be expensive?'

'Very,' she said, 'but I can easily afford it.'

Tim frowned, 'I feel I should be paying for this.'

Sophie rose from her seat and rearranged his limbs so that she could sit on his lap. Then she wound his arms around her.

She kissed him gently and said, 'I know you are a very proud man, Tim, but please let me do this. I really want to be a mother. We could start practising for having babies tonight, but, Tim, you will need a bath.'

'Am I that bad?'

'You are,' she said, pulling a face. 'I will get in first.'

'And I will bath you.'

'That sounds wonderful,' she said kissing him again and making for the bathroom.

Ten minutes later Sophie was standing in the bath surrounded by steam, while Tim gently soaped every inch of her body, his hands lingering occasionally. Finally, he let her sit down and helped wash the soap off.

She kissed him with softened lips as she climbed from the bath. 'For goodness sake do not be too long please, Tim.'

'Of course, madam,' was his response. He broke his best time ever for bathing; twelve minutes from stepping into the bath and then stepping out again, hair washed, shaved and bathed top to toe. Drying was brief.

He did not know what to expect in the bedroom. Their love life since the miscarriage had become occasional and perfunctory.

Pulling the bath plug and switching off the light he left the bathroom. As he entered the back cabin all the curtains were drawn, and the candles were alight. Sophie was lying on her back waiting for him on top of the duvet.

Tim, damp and naked, lay down beside her and went to roll towards her. As always, his proximity to her when she was nude immediately excited him. She pushed him onto his back and sat astride him. Grasping him she rose onto her knees and guiding him into her slid down onto him. He reached up to hold her breasts. She seized his hands and used them to steady herself as she began to ride him. The rhythm increased, faster and faster until finally her back arched, her head went back, and she shouted out his name as she climaxed.

She carefully lifted herself off him then collapsed onto his chest. Breathing hard she said, 'Oh my God, Tim, that was amazing.'

'It certainly was,' he replied, astonished at the storm that had erupted above him.

A few minutes later, lying on top of him she asked, 'Can we do it again gently when you are ready?'

Guiding her hand, he proved he was ready.

'That was quick,' she said, wide eyed. 'How did you do that?'

He just shook his head and shrugged, what he didn't say was that he was completely taken by surprise with the intensity of her passion, it was not something he had experienced since the miscarriage.

He rolled on top of her and this time it was gentle. Sleep claimed them both soon after.

The following morning, she kissed him softly, 'Thank you for last night, it was wonderful. This morning I feel as if a great dark cloud has been lifted from me, and we are going to make beautiful babies together, you lovely man.'

Tim was reading late one evening. Sophie had just gone to bed. He was aware of her turning the bedroom light out. A few minutes later he saw movement from the corner of his eye. When he looked properly, he saw Sophie in a white silk negligée dancing in the bedroom in the moonlight. She had clearly not forgotten her ballet training. It was the most beautiful thing he had ever seen. He kept perfectly still so as not to disturb her. Shortly after she must have sensed his gaze. Snapping her head around she saw him watching and obviously very embarrassed stopped dancing and leapt out of sight onto the bed. Tim rose from his chair and walked into the bedroom. She had buried herself under the covers.

He could hear the tears in her voice as she said, 'Please do not say anything, I am very upset. It was childish of me.'

Tim began gently rubbing her back and then saying very quietly, 'It was not childish. It was one of the most beautiful things I have ever seen. It was magical. You are very gifted.'

'Are you laughing at me?'

Tim denied it, speaking very softly, and clearly in awe of what he had just seen, he asked, 'Why do you no longer dance?'

There was a long silence, then a little damp face appeared with red rimmed eyes and lots of sniffing. In a little girl voice, she said, 'I was told I was too tall, then Mother found me practicing one day and said I should stop. Then she added, "I know they said you were too tall, but I think they were just being kind. I expect really you were just not good enough, dear."'

Tim looked at her for a moment shaking his head and thinking, 'It's not me, her mother really is a nasty spiteful cow.' He buried his anger so that Sophie would not notice then, taking both her hands in his, after a long pause he said, 'You must dance again for me, you are amazing, it was very special. At the risk of repeating myself it really was one of the most beautiful things I have ever seen, I will remember it for ever.'

'Thank you, Tim,' she said, and slid under the covers.

He tucked the eiderdown around her, kissed the top of her head and said, 'Night, night, I will be in soon.'

*

Early one morning three months later Sophie shook him awake.

Rising through the layers of a very deep sleep Tim was unable to make sense of what she was saying. One thing he did understand was that whatever it was she was extremely excited about it.

In a rather grumpy voice he said, 'I haven't a clue what you are talking about.'

'I think I am pregnant,' she said with a huge smile on her face.

'How can you know?' he grumbled, 'And the doctor said six months, not, how long is it now, five months?'

'He said up to six months. I feel as though a switch has been thrown inside me. Something has changed.'

He just looked at her with one eyebrow raised.

'Ok, you cynic. Just you wait and see,' she said as she bounced out of bed and made her way towards the galley. 'I am making tea; would you like one?'

'Yes, please,' he replied, worrying that she might be wrong.

A month later the doctor confirmed that Sophie was pregnant.

Sophie rang her father from work and asked, 'Can we call round later?'

'Is there a purpose behind this?' queried her father.

'Tim needs to talk to you.'

'Bring Angela,' he said, 'we will make an evening of it.'

In the taxi on the way to the Vieri', Angela and Sophie were sitting in the back, Angela was studying Sophie closely. A few minutes later she took Sophie's hand and whispered in her ear, 'I know why we are going to your parents, congratulations, my darling.'

Sophie whispered back, 'You are right, but please do not say anything yet.'

Angela kissed her and hugged her close all the rest of the journey.

There was not the usual delay after they had rung the bell, Mr Vieri pulled the door open, kissed Angela and Sophie and shook Tim's hand and once again guided him through the doorway.

'Come in,' he said, 'the tea is on its way.' Coats were removed and then they followed him into the lounge. Mrs Vieri was sitting in her usual chair. As they were seating themselves the tea arrived, the three of them greeted Martha as she put the tray down.

'We can pour,' said Mr Vieri, 'Angela, do you mind?'

'No,' she said, jumping up.

Mr Vieri noticed her obvious excitement. 'What can we do for you, Timothy, nothing serious I hope?'

'It is serious... Sophie,' he said handing the conversation over to her.

'I am pregnant,' she said.

'Bravo,' her father said in a heavy Italian accent. Springing from his chair he strode across the room, rising to meet his advance she was quickly enveloped in a huge bear hug with her father kissing her hair.

Finally, he released her, looked into her eyes, kissed her again and said, 'I have never been happier.' Timothy was also hugged and had his back slapped. 'Congratulations, you two, you have made us very happy, have they not, Olivia?' he said as he turned towards his wife.

It was then they all noticed she was crying. 'Will you excuse me?' she said through her tears as she stood and walked towards the door. It so surprised everybody that nobody moved while she left the room.

'I will go to her,' said Angela.

'No, you will not,' growled Mr Vieri, 'I will,' and with that he marched out of the room.

Mrs Vieri did eventually return to the room and was polite. She even congratulated Sophie; she did not however say anything to Tim. Champagne replaced the tea.

The following afternoon Mrs Vieri was having afternoon tea at her sister's. The events of the previous evening were being discussed.

'Why did you leave the room in tears?' Angela asked.

'Angela, I am so upset that she has married this… this "barrow boy", this lout, and now she is going to have his child. I am sure he will dump her and clear off when he has had enough of her. He could not be more-lower class if he tried, I am so angry.' The last words were spat out.

'Olivia, you need to listen to me now, you are a damn fool!' Angela's voice was level and measured, stopping her sister's indignant response by saying angrily, 'Just listen to me.'

'Victor and Timothy have one thing in common, they would both put themselves in harm's way to protect your daughter, she is the centre of their universe. They both place her first in everything.

'You are on the edge of losing your husband, your daughter and your grandchildren if you continue on your present course. You have been listening to your narrow-minded bigoted friends again, have you not?'

Mrs Vieri, crying now, said, 'I never thought you would be so rude to me, Angela.'

'I am trying to get you to see sense before there is no way back and you find yourself living all alone somewhere. I warned you before about underestimating Timothy, his life experiences have made him tough, look how he stood up to Victor that evening. None of your chinless wonders would have managed that. Do not take him on, Olivia, you will lose, and I promise you, Sophia will never give him up.'

'Victor was horrible to me last night and now you are copying him.'

Angela went to take her sister's hand, but it was snatched away. 'He said that if I kept on causing Sophia all this pain he would walk out and never return.'

'Olivia, surely this is a big enough sign. Victor never makes idle threats. Can you not just be polite to Timothy as you would be to anyone else?'

Watching her sister being driven away, Angela shook her head not knowing how things would turn out.

The next day Tim made sure that one of the first people he told was his father who pulled him into a bear hug and pounded his back.

Mr Woodman, always aware of what was going on, came over and with a questioning look said, 'Obviously good news, Tim.'

'Sophie is pregnant, Mr Woodman,' said his father, wiping his eyes. He immediately apologised to Tim, 'Sorry, lad, it was not my place to have said that.'

'Don't worry, Dad, yes Sophie is pregnant, Mr Woodman.'

'That's marvellous, Tim,' Mr Woodman replied, crushing Tim's fingers in a handshake whilst pounding his upper arm.

The announcement of Sophie's pregnancy triggered an incredible explosion of excitement. There were phone calls and cards arrived from people Tim had never heard of.

The Italians were beside themselves. Flowers arrived until there was no more room to put them in the boat, so some were moved to the office.

✳

Tim and Sophie were sitting on their favourite bench watching the boats go by. Tim was lost to her for the moment, the river had captured him again. She was used to this now. Looking around her immediate surroundings she was aware again of how pretty this spot was. The footpath wound between the small trees. A soft warm breeze rustled the bright green leaves. The golden sunlight filtered through the branches and sprinkled dancing patterns of light on the pathway.

Sophie realised she was the happiest she had ever been. Overcome by the moment she rested her head on Tim's shoulder. This broke his reverie. He turned his face towards her and smiled. She lifted her lips to be kissed.

As she rose from the bench to walk home there was an almost imperceptible movement in her tummy, it made her start. Was that the baby?

Tim had felt her reaction, turning his head on one side to look at her he asked, 'Are you ok?'

Unsure of what she had felt, she replied, 'Yes I am fine,' then it happened again, the faintest movement. She opened her mouth to tell Tim but then stifled the urge to do so. Overcome by the miracle that was happening inside her she wanted to enjoy it in private for a while before making it public. Her mood on the way home was euphoric, internally there were bands playing, people singing and wild dancing.

All that appeared externally was a tiny smile.

[The End]

Bill Carmen was born on a boat on the River Thames in post-war Surrey. This gave him his lifelong love of all things water based. He now lives in Worcestershire with his second wife. He has two daughters and two grandsons. Now retired, he spends time developing his three passions: creative writing, martial arts and growing orchids. Love in Store is his debut novel.